LIVING
VICARIOUSLY

The Unpublished and Best Stories
of
JOHN PATRICK

Edited by
John Butler

STARbooks Press
Sarasota, FL

CONTENTS

INTRODUCTION
by John Butler

Few people in Sarasota, Florida who spotted the very tall man riding around in his white 1989 Toyota convertible, with the top down and a tam on his head, would have suspected he was one of the world's leading writers and publishers of gay male erotica. Yet, that's who he was—Patrick John Powers, known to the world of gay pornographic literature and the gay world generally as John Patrick. He was known as "Patrick" to his friends, and "John" to others—and I believe he was occasionally even called "Mike" around the STARbooks office (for reasons I am not privy to). I knew him as John, however, and that's the way I will refer to him here.

John Patrick wore many hats, figuratively, aside from his tam. He was the owner, publisher, editor, general factotum and what-you-will at STARbooks Press and the Florida Literary Foundation—both housed together and basically operating as one organization in Sarasota. He founded the house in the late 1980's. He developed a readership by writing and self-publishing a variety of gay novels and stories, beginning with such titles as "Deadly Minuet," The Bigger they Are," and "The Harder they Are." In 1990 he published "Angel," which, along with many others that followed, firmly established his international reputation as a talented writer of gay erotic fiction, and made STARbooks a major force in the field of erotic publishing.

In the same year he published "Angel" he also published "Legends," the prototype for the subsequent series of annual "Best of the Superstars" books, in which the facts, the gossip, and the reported scandal about the hottest among the male stars in the fields of pornography, movies, television, theatre, music, and even 'escorting' (hustling) are reported—often with accompanying photographs. The first of the thirteen "Superstar" volumes is for 1990, the last, published posthumously, is dated 2002.

In 1992 there appeared the first of the thirty-seven anthologies of erotic gay fiction he edited and published. He passed away before the last two of those anthologies were ready for publication, and I had the honor—unhappily made necessary—of completing work on them in his stead. I had also worked with John as an unofficial co-editor on the three anthologies that preceded those final two.

A complete list of John's works as published by his own firm appears at the head of the present volume, and considerably more detail about their appearance can be gleaned by accessing "STARbooks Press: A Brief

1

History" at the "Company Information" section of the STARbooks web page, *http://www.starbookspress.com.*

In a way, it seems odd for me to be introducing John Patrick to readers of this book, since I never met the man. I know his look only through the photographs published in his books; I never spoke to him, either in person, or by telephone. Yet, although our friendship was begun and continued through the medium of e-mail and occasional letters sent via 'snail mail,' I believe we were friends.

He discussed his sex life at length, and with astonishing candor, yet he seemed reticent to say much about other aspects of his life that one would normally think he might discuss freely. His sexual frankness aside, he struck me as a relatively taciturn man—an odd trait for one whose stock-in-trade was words.

He was not given to casual or insincere flattery, as far as I could tell. He never commented favorably on anything I wrote, but he published everything I submitted. Only once did he indicate he didn't like something of mine—a lengthy passage of intentionally 'purple' poetry in *model/escort,* the first thing I submitted to him. His disapproval was not couched in conciliatory language. I remember his comment well: "This is terrible!" I suspect his conveyance of similarly negative reaction to other writers was equally blunt.

Possibly as a result of the medium by which we communicated, I don't know much about his personal life, except what I could infer from statements he made in writing, what I read in various volumes of STARbooks, and information supplied after his death by people who knew his personally, *viz.*: Michael Huxley, his successor at the helm of STARbooks; Vincent Tozzi, who published a brief eulogy for John in the December 2001 issue of *The Blade*; and John Patrick's son.

John's son provided a few basic biographical facts about his father. He was born in Cleveland, Ohio, in 1943. He graduated from Kent State University in Business, and was a Vice President for Sales and Marketing with a major marketing firm before moving to Florida, where he was active in other business ventures before establishing STARbooks. His marriage, which produced two children, ended in the early 1970s.

Michael Huxley became well acquainted with John in the last year or two of his life, and John became something of a mentor to Michael, who is quoted in the Vincent Tozzi article mentioned above: "Although I did indeed see and speak with Pat [sic! Remember, John's actual *first* name was Patrick, not his last] most every day, and contributed to STARbooks Press as a writer, I wonder how well I actually knew him. Pat was an extremely private person who confided in few. I suppose he trusted me, alas his requesting—on his death bed—that I assist Anne Wellman in the 'downsizing' of STARbooks ....

"I remember [him] as having been an extremely intelligent and capable human being. He was well read, knew everything about film history,

2

loved good music (especially female jazz vocalists), was refined and handsome: an elegant man. Almost to the exclusion of all else, he was devoted to STARbooks Press. He was there easily seven days a week, for 12 hours a day.

"His response to (homo)sexuality was surely on the level of classical Greek adulation. One look at his personal library would tell you that. Add that fact to the overriding oppression of homosexuality in our current society and there you have his contribution: taboo, brilliantly suggested.

"As a publisher, he created one of the very few venues where others, like myself, could express themselves .... In that regard he was an archetype, and I thank his memory."

When I asked Michael to comment further for this introduction about John's tastes in the arts, to provide information that I was either unaware of, or could have only suspected, he told me:

"I cleared out his film, music and text libraries *at the office* .... His text library consisted of many, many reference books, especially concerning film (both porn and not). He had countless titles written by homosexual male authors, and we're talking Aristotle to Sedaris. ...Whitman, Williams, Isherwood, Rouse, Capote, Vidal, Baldwin, Burroughs, Wilde: You get the picture. I don't know if he actually read them or was looking for quotes or both." [Note that John Patrick's lengthy written introductions to his anthologies largely consisted of appropriate—and often lengthy—quotes from a broad variety of sources.] "Most of those volumes had zillions of sticky notes attached to the pages, indicating possible quotes. He had many volumes of erotica, both anthologies and single-author titles, current and classic, charting the history of erotica as a genre. There was Greek mythology and "The Front Runner" and Shakespeare, and Warhol, and Hockney, and Mapplethorpe, and other photo books, not all of them erotic.

"As for film, hands down the man *had* to be one of the world's authorities on male video and porn stars .... He was obsessed with film in general, and leaned toward the generic classics: Orson Welles, Sunset Blvd., Streetcar, Harold and Maud, Gone With the Wind, All About Eve... He had lots of reference books about the Oscars. [©]

"About music: Again, I can only judge from what he kept in the office, but seeing that he practically *lived* here ... He had a stack of records maybe three feet high and perhaps twenty-five, thirty cassette tapes. I never once heard anything but the radio playing background music whenever I had the occasion to be in his office, which was frequently enough, although the turntable and tape deck were perfectly functional. The entire collection was mostly female vocalists, many of them jazz-oriented. Ella F., Cleo Laine, lots of Streisand, Lena Horne, Roberta Flack, even Diana Ross and Donna Summer! .... He owned practically every album recorded by jazz pianist/vocalist Shirley Horn."

3

I was familiar with John's various publishing projects long before we ever communicated. I had enjoyed reading quite a number of the books he wrote and edited, and I was especially hooked on the "Best of the Superstars" series. It was in those latter volumes I learned a great deal I could not read about in other places concerning those hot young men who especially stimulated my libido—and apparently John's as well: movie stars Brad Pitt, Casper van Dien, James Marsden, Corey Haim and Ryan Phillippe; TV actors Mario Lopez and Randy Harrison; and, of course, those wonderful, wonderful porn stars Casey Donovan, Tom Steele, Michael Christopher, Jeff Stryker, Ryan Idol, Erik Houston, Tom Chase, Steve Fox, Lukas Ridgeston, Johan Paulik, Adam Hart, Gregor Yelson, Lane Fuller, Billy Brandt ...it's difficult to know when to stop naming the porn stars.

It was the indirect result of a disastrous love affair with one of those fabulous porn stars—a golden-haired, muscular Adonis, physically perfect in every way, whose name I will not mention here—that brought about my first contact with John Patrick. By the time the 1997 edition of "The Best of the Superstars" was due for publication, my golden-haired, physically perfect Adonis had proved to be much less than perfect mentally and morally; he was diagnosed by his psychiatrist as a paranoid schizophrenic, and I was reluctantly forced to diagnose him as an amoral, opportunistic con man.

I ordered the 1997 book direct from STARbooks, and John included a friendly note, apologizing for its late delivery—my first contact with him. That particular volume relayed surprising information about the porn star who had so recently made my life both ecstatically wonderful and abysmally miserable—in that order, unfortunately. Had I known the information earlier, I might have avoided the emotional and financial havoc he wreaked in my life.

For some reason I wrote John Patrick and thanked him for the information he had included about my former lover, pointing out the irony of my learning it too late. I also told him that I had recently begun writing erotic fiction—an interest that developed when I finished writing, for the purpose of catharsis, an autobiographical account of the tragic death of my partner of 24 years, and the abortive love affair with the porn star, which began after two-and-a-half years of celibacy following that.

We eventually negotiated the publication of the novel I had just completed, entitled *model/escort*. I began to submit some shorter fiction that STARbooks published, followed later by a couple of other novels and novellas. At the same time correspondence between John Patrick and me ranged further afield, embracing all manner of subject matter aside from writing and publishing—videos, porn stars, movies, etc. Our tastes seemed to be fundamentally in tune, particularly in regard to which porn and movie stars we found unusually attractive.

4

I cannot at this point remember why I offered to proof-read the galleys for a forthcoming STARbooks anthology ("Taboo!"), but John accepted my offer, and in addition to checking for errata, I could not resist recommending quite a number of editorial suggestions as I worked through the book. John apparently thought I did a good job, since from that point on I not only proof-read the anthologies, I did a considerable amount of editing as well. I worked on three more anthologies published before John's death ("Fever," "Any Boy Can" and "Virgins No More").

On October 31, 2001, in Sarasota, Florida, John passed away at the age of only fifty-eight. At the time of John's sudden death, I had worked through "Wild and Willing" twice, and once through "Seduced 2." I had also done the final work on my third novel, and it was ready to go to the printers, but the fate of the press seemed to be in doubt as November 2001 opened with John no longer there to guide it.

But Michael Huxley was still there.

John Patrick had become something of a mentor to Michael Huxley. Michael was himself a writer—of erotic stories as well as other things, like poetry and magazine articles. John encouraged his writing in the most welcome way any writer can know—he published two of his stories in the anthology "Fever!" He also accepted stories by Michael for the next two anthologies, which I was called on to finish editing. John entrusted the immediate fate of STARbooks to Michael and to Anne Wellman, a long-time employee of the press.

The ultimate fate of STARbooks was entrusted to John's son, and he decided to get my third novel released *(Boys Hard at Work—and Playing with Fire)* as well as the two anthologies that were in early stages of readiness for the printer *(Seduced 2 and Wild and Willing)*. He asked me to finish the two anthologies, and decided to keep the enterprise afloat, putting Michael Huxley in charge. At this writing, Michael has one new anthology ready for the printer, and another one well underway

John's son asked me to put together this "Best of John Patrick" anthology, and Michael Huxley suggested its title, "Living Vicariously." I spent endless hours reading through the published stories of John Patrick—as well as a few unpublished ones—and extracted those you are about to read. An enormously pleasant assignment, but made difficult by the task of winnowing through such an enormous amount of eligible material.

I believe the stories I have included are representative of John's output, and I have tried to provide variety for the reader by selecting both long and short stories. A considerable majority of John's stories published in the STARbooks anthologies are relatively short—five or six pages—and although a truly representative volume of his work should include mostly those short offerings, I felt it best to offer greater variety for the sake of avoiding too much similarity between the various stories.

The title "Living Vicariously" is, I think quite appropriate for the works of John Patrick. Of course I believe that any writer of intensely erotic fiction like that included herein is mentally participating in the sex acts he has his fictional characters take part in. I suspect that is true in John's case, and I know it is in much of my own writing. Often—usually, perhaps—I base characters and situations on real people I have known, and my actual interactions with them, but take them to places that I *wish* we had reached in real life, rather than where we actually went. If that's not living vicariously, I don't know what is—and it is great, great fun to finally have those feverishly desired sexual experiences with all those boys I wanted so badly, and so infrequently had, even if it is just in my imagination. Hopefully the readers of John's, and mine, and all those other erotic writers' stories will vicariously, and in their imaginations, experience the same joy and excitement.

A few words should be said here about John Patrick's *romans à clef*. The phrase literally means, in French, a novel with a key, but in usage it refers to fiction of whatever length in which real characters, or places, or events appear in disguise. The movie *Citizen Kane* is a good example; it is clearly the story of the publisher William Randolph Hearst, but since it was written as a *roman à clef*, the names are changed, and the author is able to take liberties with the facts—for dramatic purposes, or for any reason he sees fit.

Since such a vast amount of fiction is based on the authors' experiences, family, friends, etc., the *roman à clef* is *technically* one of the most common kinds of fiction. But in general, it is only when a piece of fiction is written about a well-known public figure that we call it a *roman à clef*, and that is how I believe John used the term—and how I surely do.

I have published a few *romans à clef* myself, and can well understand what fun it can be to write them. I have never had sex with, for instance, Brad Pitt, although I earnestly feel that the sexual union of Brad Pitt and myself would rank among the most perfectly splendid things that could happen in the history of mankind on the face of the planet—and the likelihood of that happening probably provides an excellent way of illustrating the most minuscule quantity conceivable by the human mind, of providing the statistician with a near-absolute-zero floor of probability. Yet, if I were to write a sexually oriented *roman à clef* about the divine Brad and me—which I most emphatically have not, I hasten to point out—I could, in a sense, realize that ultimate fantasy. Imagine how much fun that would be!

If John Patrick revealed the real-life subjects about whom he wrote the *romans* in this collection—"Mad About the Boy," "Love Lance," probably the "Prologue to *The Sex Trade*," and possibly "In the Heat of a Summer Night"—I do not know about it. He wrote quite a number of novels and stories in his form, but I only know who a few of them were

6

really written about, either because of my knowledge of the subject's real life, or because John himself told me. Because of the nature of the stories, it is reasonable to assume that most of them fictionalize actual porn stars.

John had many porn stars visit him, and I believe, based on many things he said, that he enjoyed talking with them at length, picking their brains, learning their stories—before and after having they had done what they were primarily there to do. We have pictorial evidence, published in many STARbooks publications, that he 'visited' with many of the great porn stars of the day. In no particular order: Tom Steele, Joey Stefano, the mono-named and megahung Roger, Tim Lowe, Ryan Idol, Tom Katt, Kris Lord, Rod Barry, Michel (now Michael) Lucas, Michael Vincenzo, Kevin Kramer, Pagan Prince, Alec Martinez, Sean Storm, Adam Hart— and finally, the one over whom John almost seemed to obsess in the last couple years of his life, Tony Cummings. I don't doubt there were a good many others whose meetings with John were not celebrated with published photographs. One of those, with whom he said he spent some 'quality time'—very high-quality time, according to report-- was the first of the widely renowned gay porn stars, the peerless Casey Donovan.

Perhaps the stories of many of those visiting porn stars fueled his *romans à clef;* I know some of them did. I strongly suspect that the series of related stories called "The Sex Trade: The Lives and Loves of Casey Cassidy," which appeared in Heatwave, and the Prologue to which is included in the volume, was a *roman à clef* inspired by Casey Donovan.

There was a relatively short period of time when I, too, engaged the services of porn stars for my personal satisfaction, roughly coinciding with the onset of my acquaintance with John Patrick. Three of them who spent at least one night in my bed were among those whose pictures with John in his publications. He and I compared notes!

As you will observe from the following pages—if you don't already know—John was a fine writer, able to bring great heat to the account of a sexual encounter, and at the same time create interesting and believable, three-dimensional characters and situations.

John had to take time for his own writing aside from his various duties with STARbooks press, a firm that not only published books, but which also offered books, magazine, videos,. etc. for sale. He wrote his annual "Best of the Superstars" volume and, in addition, edited no fewer than *four* anthologies every year for the press, and each of those books was five or six hundred pages in length. I can attest that writing a book, or the assembling and editing of a single volume is an enormous task; the prospect of doing five a year is staggering. Yet, John Patrick managed to do it, and at the same time produced a steady stream of stories—in addition to pursuing his personal interests.

Of necessity, then, he was unable to polish his writing as thoroughly as I am sure he would have liked before it went to press. As a result, while I worked on this collection I felt no compunction about making minor adjustments to the stories included here.

If you were to make a line-by-line comparison of the stories included in the following pages with their original incarnations in previous anthologies, you would find I have made a considerable number of minor changes. In most cases I have changed the text either to correct typographical errors or for the sake of clarification. Other minor additions, deletions, or re-arrangements of the text are the same sort of things I suggested to John when I worked through his stories (and those of others as well) in the last three anthologies he saw all the way through to publication—suggestions that he adopted.

So—read on, and for the space of the next few hundred pages, enjoy the work of a master story-teller while you share sexual excitement with a virtuoso of vicarious living!

I'M JUST WILD ABOUT HARRY

It seemed unlikely that sexual fantasies that were born while watching cowboy movies would come true—in Pittsburgh, of all places. And it was even stranger that cowboy star Harry Hunter would be anything but a straight shooter! Originally appeared in Lover Boys. *—JB*

As a boy growing up, I did the same things week after week, and Saturdays had a special place in my life: I got to go to the Palace. My afternoon at the movies. And I lived by the movies—not just *by* them, either, but *for* them and *in* them. Serials, cartoons and the feature film.

The features I loved most were the ones about cowboys and starring cowboys: Hopalong Cassidy, Gene Autry, Roy Rogers and, most of all, Harry Hunter.

Harry didn't achieve the great popularity of the other stars because he went to serve his country in the Second World War and, after the war, it seemed for a while he could only get supporting roles in other types of features. But eventually he returned to leading man roles in Westerns. Star-struck, I followed his progress through movie magazines. Harry was, to my mind, the perfect man. I had no idea in those days what that really meant. All I knew was, I wanted to be with him.

Later on, after my older brother initiated me into the pleasures of gay sex, I began fantasizing that it was Harry who was making me feel so good.

In his early Westerns, Harry was a nimble rider, and had a trick of throwing his right leg across the horse's neck in his comic dismounting scenes. I began to picture Harry pulling that same stunt with me.

When Harry was shooting somebody, he had a grim, deadpan expression, and after the Daisy Company put out a BB replica of his gun, called the "Harry Hunter Special," I just had to have one, so I could practice that same scowl while I plugged an outlaw mouse or rabbit.

In his Westerns, Harry wore a white hat and an air of lethal calm. When he took the hat off, his black hair was slicked back and parted as precisely as if it had been slashed by a razor. Of course, that was the way I had to wear mine.

His chiseled face was more handsome than any of the other actors of the era and, as I grew older and Harry's fame increased, people often commented that I looked like him. By that time, I was almost as tall as he was and I tried to maintain a year-round suntan, as he always did.

In 1956 I went to Hollywood myself and began working in television. I never expected to be in the cast of a film starring my boyhood idol but a few years later, that's what happened.

After reading for a director on the Universal lot, I was leaving his office when I saw a handsome man, just ambling along, wearing a tailored white suit, white Stetson hat, and cowboy boots. I did a double-take; it was Harry. He looked at me, too, and smiled. I introduced myself and just started walking along the street with him as if I had really been going in the same direction. I told him I was one of the kids on the "Sweethearts" series on CBS. I also told him they were now even letting me write parts of the scripts. "But not the funny stuff."

"Don't watch much TV," he said, shaking his head. "No actor in pictures does TV, let alone watches it."

"Oh."

He stopped, turned, and looked at me curiously. "Damn! You know, you look and act amazingly like I did when I was your age. It's almost like I've found a long-lost twin brother."

It was almost like I had found nirvana! Here I was, with Harry Hunter taking me to the Commissary, buying me coffee and a cookie if I wanted one. (I did, by the way, a chocolate chip.)

He had only coffee, which he slurped while smoking a Pall Mall. I went on and on about my passion for his films, recounting my favorite scenes in every one of them. Finally he stopped me and said, "Hey, some of those I don't even remember. I was drunk a lot of the time, you know."

No, I hadn't known, and I told him so. But he looked terrific. Whatever drinking he had done must have agreed with him. At just past forty, he appeared more distinguished, but carried himself with the same swagger he had in his early Westerns.

"Well, you're somethin' else, kid," he said, blowing a smoke ring. "I oughta get you to ghostwrite my autobiography."

I didn't want to write anything, I just wanted to go on talking to him, but he had an appointment with the production people for his new movie, "Life Sentence." He grinned. "You look like me and you're on TV, right?"

"Yes."

"Maybe you'd like to audition for the part of my son in this epic. There's only a couple of scenes ...."

"Tell me when."

The next thing I knew, I was on a plane to Pittsburgh. Pittsburgh? That was the setting of the movie and my scenes with Harry were to be filmed on location. Harry had already been there a week when I arrived.

In Pittsburgh, Harry took my arrival as an opportunity to escape the company filming at a prison and, as he put it, "coach me on my scenes." The night I arrived, after I had checked into my room at the Holiday Inn, Harry took me to a striptease joint in his rented Oldsmobile. He had two martinis and ended up with the lead stripper, Kitten, on his lap. "You're very nice," he said to her. But when she told him, "I also act," we left there in a hurry.

"Look at those kids," he said as we passed some teenage boys leaning against a building, their hands in their pockets, provocatively showing themselves off. "Youngsters standin' on street corners in the middle of the night."

It was close to midnight, but it apparently seemed much earlier than that to Harry. In the bar at the motel, he proceeded to down two more martinis, and I heard the full, sad story of his life—about the women he had been involved with and the ones he'd turned down. He talked about all the children he wished he'd fathered.

"There's still time," I said.

He nodded and stared into his empty martini glass. The more he drank, the more affectionate he became. I was astounded by the affectionate pats on my ass, the hugs, the fact that when we sat on bar stools our legs would press together and neither of us would move them. At two o'clock, I saw Harry to his room and then went to bed myself, dreaming of what it would be like to be in the room two floors up, in bed with Harry. He had noticed the boys on the corner before I had. There was still hope.

The next morning I went to Harry's room only to find him still in bed. He had ordered extra ice from room service along with his orange juice and Danish pastry, and had already started drinking. As he walked about the room, lighting cigarettes, pouring drinks, explaining the scenes we would have together, he was dressed only in his boxer shorts. I gazed adoringly at his beautiful physique, something that had never been fully displayed in a photograph or in a film. I was amazed at how fit he looked, considering his age and how much he drank. I longed to run my hands over his hairy chest, suck on his nipples, work my way down to his navel, and then ....

He was ranting and raving about how bad the film was, how the director stank, how awful the location was, and so on, and I begin to think what a shame it was he couldn't appreciate everything he had. Here he was starring in a new movie at Universal. He wasn't a star of the top rank, but his name was always above the title. He had a beautiful home in the Hollywood Hills, nice cars, money in the bank; seemingly, his every material need was met. I began to wonder what other kind of needs were not being met. Why the hasty retreat from the strip joint? Why the casual touching of my body? Why this 'coaching' business? Maybe all he needed was a push. That was all I had needed, and, since no one else could have done it at that time, it came from my brother. But here was a film star who had been kind enough to get me a role in his movie, one that involved getting me to the location ... Suddenly it all made sense. It was all coming together: Yes, he did need a push. He had pushed me about as far he could; now he was the one who needed a push. I began to feel special.

"Hey, let's get some lunch," I said, jumping up, interrupting his harangue.

11

"Oh, I'm sorry, I was ignoring you. I get so worked up."

I stepped over to him. "I'd never let you do that for long. " I stood before him as the adoring fan I was, yet I was bold enough to stroke the back of his hand as he brought the drink to his lips.

He held me in his gaze over the rim of the glass as he finished the drink. Slowly he put the glass down on the table next to the bed and took my hand in his. "You're on to me, aren't you?"

"Are you on to me?"

"From the first moment."

"I didn't mean it that way."

"But it was nice that I took it that way, wasn't it?"

I had never kissed a man before, but he had kissed women so often for the camera and for real that he knew just what to do, so I gave myself up to him. I felt as if I was being swallowed up by the most incredible force I had ever known. As our mouths locked, his arms crushed me to his chest and his hands squeezed my buttocks. This was not what I had expected. In my fantasies, I thought he would take me as my brother had, without any preliminaries. Just, "Here, suck it, you little shit."

Harry was making love to me, to every inch of my body, and sucking my cock. I couldn't believe it—and I couldn't keep from coming. The wonder of it was, he loved it. Took every drop, swallowed it and licked his lips.

Now I wanted to adore him in the many ways I had in countless dreams. At first he was reluctant to surrender completely to me, but I would accept nothing less. He lay on the bed on his back, watching me as I gorged myself on his beefy body. I got him so worked up that he begged me either to let him come, or to let him fuck me.

I had never been fucked by my brother. He had only showed me how to jack off, how to suck a dick. Anal sex was something I had learned about in high school, and then it was me doing the fucking—and it had been only once, one warm afternoon in my bedroom with the door locked. My partner, Jeffrey, a screaming faggot from the seventh grade, hadn't been able to take it for more than five minutes.

Harry was massively hung, and just looking at his penis standing straight up from his belly, I didn't see how it would be possible. But it was worth trying.

He was gentle with me, sucking at my hole for several minutes, tonguing it, then greasing his finger for a gentle probing. I came again while he was doing that. He couldn't believe it, and asked if I wanted to continue.

"Oh, yes," I sighed, "please."

Two fingers were next, still massaging gently. My cock was soon erect again and he sucked on it while he continued to slowly finger-fuck my ass. Before long I was begging for his dick.

"You have to get it ready first," he said, straddling my head with his thighs, his cock semi-hard and dangling lewdly before me. I licked the head for a while and then opened my mouth wide. He slid the cock in and began fucking my mouth, a pleasure so intense I didn't want it to stop. But after a few moments, he said, "God, I better do it now or I'll come sure as hell."

Lifting me up by the ankles, he brought the bulbous head of his cock to the well-prepared opening. I could not see how it would ever fit. The rigid shaft of what appeared to be purple-veined marble glistened with my spit as Harry began inserting it. He knew how to rub, and probe and slowly stretch so that it suddenly slid in without the pain I had expected. There was pain, yes, but it was quickly forgotten as Harry, totally in control of his fabulous instrument of pleasure, began his thrusting. I surrendered completely, locking him to me by crossing my ankles. He scooped me up in his strong arms and held me, rocking me back and forth, hardly moving his cock, settling in for a long fuck. We kissed, tentatively at first, and then with real passion, as if we were being filmed. My hands went to his head and I was holding him tightly when he came. He lifted up so that he could slam it in to the hilt as he filled me with his jism.

I dozed, lying close to him, feeling his incredible warmth. At one point I opened my eyes to find him sitting up, just staring at me. "What's wrong?" I asked.

"Nothing. Nothing at all," he said, taking me in his arms again. I reached down to guide him into me again. "Hey, I'm all fucked out," he said.

"Doesn't feel like it."

This time, being "all fucked out," he didn't come, but I did, and then it really was time for lunch.

The next morning it was raining, and the wipers beat back and forth against the windshield. "Jesus, what a crummy day," Harry said.

"Do you know the way? Do we need a map?" I asked as we passed a gas station.

"No. I know the way. Hell, I was out there all last week. Bastards, picking locations all to hell and gone. And for a black and white picture, at that. They told me that Otto Preminger is filming 'Anatomy of a Murder' in Michigan in black and white, so they guess we can do this thing in black and white and go to Pennsylvania, so I said, 'What do I know?' and they said, 'Right.' "

"It'll be fine," I said, patting his knee.

But it wasn't. Not really. "Look there," I said, pointing to a sign. It read "Steubenville, Ohio."

"Jesus, we're on the airport road. This isn't right. We're going in the wrong direction."

"I thought you said you always wanted to make a picture in Ohio."

This got him laughing, laughing so hard he had to stop the car. "You're the funniest little sonofabitch I've ever met."

"Maybe the littlest."

"Hey, it's big enough for me, boy. Big enough for me. Any bigger and I'd feel inferior."

"We'd never want that to happen."

What did happen was that he pulled into a gas station and we asked directions to the Allegheny County Workhouse. The guy at the pump looked at us as if we were planning on breaking someone out.

"The what?" he asked, scratching his head.

Harry repeated our destination, emphasizing every vowel.

"Well, buster, you're real lost."

"I know that," Harry said, shaking his head.

"Tell ya what, you turn around here and go right back to downtown. Then ask them there. Ask at any gas station. Yeah, you're thirty or forty miles from there."

"Jesus, I better call 'em," Harry said, getting out of the car.

In a few moments he was back and telling me that we could have the day off. It was raining anyway and they'd work around us, but we had better be there tomorrow, first thing. In fact, they were sending someone to pick us up.

"You know, they're not such bad guys. It could have been worse. I once had an offer to do this thing about a jazz musician in Harlem. Now that would have been something."

In a few minutes we were going into a tunnel, then out onto a cloverleaf and, as the rain started coming down in torrents, he just pulled over and started laughing again.

"Baby," he said finally, "I'm lost."

"No," I said, curling up to him. "You're found."

Our kiss lasted a good five minutes. I was ready to go down on him when there was a rapping on the window. It was the police!

Harry rolled down the window. "What's the problem?" the cop in the black rain gear asked.

"Hey, chief! Am I glad to see you. We're lost! We've been forty miles out in the country and now we're headed back that way again. "

The cop smiled. "Where are you headed?"

"We were going to the Allegheny County Workhouse but now all we want to do is get to the Holiday Inn."

"The Workhouse? Oh, yeah, aren't you that actor fella, Harry Hunter? Doin' that movie down there, aren't cha?"

"Yes, if we can ever get there."

"Any other time I'd lead you outta here, but not in this rain."

"Well, all I want is to get to the Holiday Inn."

The officer pointed to the tallest building in town and said, "Just go there. The Inn's right next door."

"Thanks, chief." Rolling up the window, Harry said, "This is what happens when you go on location. Nothing but a pain in the ass."

"That's for sure," I laughed, rubbing an asscheek.

"You shut up!"

As we were driving back to the hotel after dinner, we passed the Strand theater and I noticed "White Rapids" was on a double bill, starring none other than Harry Hunter. "Stop!" I shouted.

Harry slammed on the brakes. "Whoa! Now what?"

"C'mon," I said, "we're going to the movies." I pointed to the marquee.

"We can go to the movies at home. Here we can go to bed."

"We'll be going to bed a lot from now on."

"Promise?" he asked, groping me.

"Promise. Now, let's find a place to park. This is one of my favorite Harry Hunter pictures."

"Lord almighty! It's one of the worst pieces of shit ever made!"

"That's why I like it."

"You're crazy."

Crazy, yes. About Harry. And sitting in the dark with his image flickering on the screen and his one hand in mine and the other stroking my erection. Suddenly, I was back at the Palace, and I wasn't dreaming any more.

THE HAPPY HITCHHIKER

The death of a lover, even if the love has turned sour, leaves one lonely and vulnerable. And when a beautiful, sympathetic youth like Terry offers himself, the solace is even sweeter. First published in the anthology Dreamboys.—JB

Last night, as we parted, clouds overcast the sky and a mist was rising. "Tomorrow will be a miserable day," I said.

But the hitchhiker, a beautiful boy, said, "No, wait and see. You have to wait and see." He didn't want to think the future would be anything but bright and sunny. He wanted everyone and everything to laugh, to sparkle. And his joy had been so contagious last night, with so much tenderness, so much friendliness in his heart for me that I couldn't help but be as happy as he. A happy boy is always so full of seductive charm.

We made a date for the following night. I wanted to believe the next day would be wonderful, regardless of the weather, and that he would meet me, as promised, to provide the perfect ending to it.

And now, of course, he is here, standing on the same corner. He makes a mock gesture, as if hitching a ride. Last night he really was hitching a ride, and he was only a stranger—a beautiful, somehow mysterious stranger. I invited him back to my place but he said he had someone waiting, that he would meet me in the same spot the next night. And here he is.

This evening, strangely, Terry is doubling the amount of attention he showered on me last night, as if he wants instinctively to give me something he is longing for himself, something he fears he might not get. It is all so intense and concentrated.

I have come to meet him tense with emotion, hardly able to wait for the moment of meeting. I never expected to feel what I feel now, seeing him again. He is, if it is possible, even more luscious than he was last night.

At first, every word I utter makes him burst into nervous laughter. Finally he says, "Do you know why I'm so happy tonight?"

"No."

"Why I'm so pleased to see you?"

"No."

"Why I like you so much?"

"I have no idea." I'm beginning to shiver.

"I like you so much because you didn't force me last night. Someone else in your position might have started pestering me, become full of self-pity, laid it on thick," he moans. "But not you, you're so nice." He suddenly presses my hand so hard that I almost cry out. He laughs. "Yes,

16

God sent you to me. Really, I mean it. I can't imagine what would have become of me last night without you—my car in the shop, and appointments to keep. Damn, you've been so nice to me."

Somehow I feel awfully sad because being nice to him was really not all I wanted to do and he knows it, yet something resembling laughter stirs somewhere deep down inside me.

"You're overwrought," I say. "Whatever are you talking about?"

"Last night. I'm talking about last night."

"Oh."

He laughs. "I admit you're right. Yes, I'm not myself now, I'm all expectation, I feel a little too light-headed. I've had a wonderful time here, and ...."

"My God, what's this all about?" I interrupt him. "I don't understand a thing you're saying."

"I was trying to make you understand the strange feeling I ..."

"Stop," I interrupt again. This is making me crazy.

Laughing, he tickles me, trying to make me laugh, too. Every awkward, embarrassed word of mine sets off such long peals of laughter that I am soon on the point of losing my temper.

But then he becomes flirtatious. "Actually," he begins, "I'm a bit offended that you *didn't* try something last night. People aren't always so polite. You know, Mr. Cadillac Man, most guys wouldn't have let me leave this car so easy."

Now I feel sorry for him, and myself, but I don't know how to make up for my failure to attempt a seduction last night. I attempt to cheer him up, to find good reasons for my not having tried to put the make on him.

"It's really funny," he says heatedly, admiring the way his power-assisted seat can be adjusted independently of mine. He puts it all the way back and this prominently displays his crotch. I had not noticed his crotch before, so appealing was his face and his torso, tightly packed in jeans and tank top.

"What's funny?" My voice trembles as I contemplate his bulging basket, but I try to smile.

"All I want to tell you is that I'm grateful, very grateful, you met me tonight."

He falls silent and squeezes my hand. He draws it over, onto his crotch. "Yeah, I'm grateful, see?" He grins lewdly as he adds, "Or should I say 'feel'?"

Several minutes go by as I steer the car along the quiet streets with my left hand while my right hand learns just how grateful he is. I stroke the bulge. My mouth waters at the thought of how beautiful this cock must be.

This adorable lad has spared me. He has realized that I am lonely, although he cannot suspect that my loneliness is the result of my inability to deal with the loss of my lover Ralph to a lingering illness.

17

"Ah, my God, my God," he whispers as he opens his pants, lets me pull out his erection.

"Sweet boy," I cry, completely overcome now as I stroke it, "you're torturing me. But we'll be at my condo in just a few minutes."

Long before my lover died I had fallen out of love with him. He had made light of my feelings, he wounded me and slighted my love. I can only love one who is generous, understanding and kind; I think I myself am like that, so I came to feel he was unworthy of me. But I couldn't just let him die alone, I had to stay. It wasn't his fault that I had deluded myself and then discovered too late what sort of man he was.

Anyway, it was over. Like this, it had been a delusion; it began as a childish adventure: *you show me yours, I'll show you mine.*

But this is no child sitting here tonight, offering himself to me; this is a very mature youth.

Terry is short of breath in his excitement. He pushes my hand away from the throbbing member. "Enough, enough for now, that's definitely enough," he says, getting hold of himself. "By the way, where do you live?"

"Over there, in that building."

We park and walk to the elevator as if in a drunken haze, like walking through clouds, with no idea of what is going on around us. In the elevator, I sigh at the sight of him and a tear glistens in my eye; I become frightened, turn shy, but he immediately presses my hand and pulls me to his chest. We are about to kiss when the elevator door opens.

We go down the hallway and enter my rooms, where we move to the outside balcony, overlooking the beach. Terry says, "And look at the sky: it will be a wonderful day tomorrow. What a sky! What a moon! Look at that cloud about to veil the moon. Look at it! Look at it ... no, it just missed the moon. Look at it ...look!"

But am I not looking at the cloud, I am looking at Terry looking at the cloud—how beautiful he is in the moonlight! After a while he presses himself against me in a strange way. My hand is trembling in his. I look closely at him, scrutinizing him. My heart throbs. "Who are you?" I ask, very softly.

"Me. I am *me*," he whispers, pressing himself even more closely to me. I can hardly keep my balance. Then with the speed of lightning, his arms are around my neck, and before I know what is happening, I feel his passionate kiss. Still without uttering a word, I drop to my knees and bury my face in his crotch. I open his pants, then begin rubbing his cock across my lips and cheeks, helplessly nipping at his balls with my teeth.

"You are too hungry, Mr. Cadillac Man," he says, running his fingers through my hair.

He is right, of course, I am much too eager, too much in love with this boy, with this cock, for my own good.

18

He backs away, lets the swollen member throb in my face, dripping my saliva.

"Oh, please," I cry, lunging for it. He resigns himself to letting me have it, and I look up just in time to be a little startled by a look of almost demented malice on his young face as he ejaculates across my mouth and nose.

We get fully undressed and climb into bed. We lie in each other's arms for a long time. At this moment he exudes a succulent boyishness just faintly shaded with dim, inchoate cruelty, as though he just might kill me if he fucked me. Finally he spreads his legs to show me he's erect again. With his recuperative powers so aptly demonstrated, I feel very aware that I am so much older than he.

I go back down on his cock; I can't remember ever loving one this much. Ralph's was bigger, but not as beautiful. This is the most beautiful cock I have ever seen, I decide, letting it slip, hard and quivering, between my lips.

It is about eight o'clock in the morning, and warm autumn sunshine shows at the bedroom window when I wake up to a marvelous feeling of well-being. Sure, I blew him a second time and went to sleep with his cock in my mouth, but that circumstance alone has not produced this sense of euphoria. It is due, mostly, to the fact that he agreed to stay the night, and now as I roll over on my side and look at him sleeping beside me, I wonder what the day will bring. It is Sunday, after all, a day of rest—although not for us real-estate types, of course.

Today I should be showing the new apartments, but I'll wait and see what Terry wants to do, where he wants to go. The strange thing about this is that I am not usually attracted to boys as young as Terry. Ralph was a decade my senior, and I liked that, I needed that. But that was then, and this is now. I have always been attracted to older men who bring to love-making a wealth of skill, acquired over the years. They know what they want from a lover, they are not coy and do not pretend to be, and they are not surprised by pleasant little deviations. Yes, I adore older men. But every rule—if this is, in fact a rule—has its exceptions. And Terry is such an exception, radiating so much youthful sensuality that he is totally irresistible.

I make coffee and, when I bring it to the bedroom with delicious-smelling, fresh-baked croissants, Terry is already up and showered. He is sitting on the balcony with a towel wrapped about his waist.

I set the tray on the table and he shifts in his chair to make the bulge at his groin more prominent—or so I think. "Your beauty is truly devastating," I say, and I mean it, for I can not restrain a sigh of pleasure at the sight of him this morning, nearly nude.

19

"Thank you," he says. "This is really very nice of you," he says as he helps himself to a croissant.

I watch him eat, then feel between his warm thighs. Just to touch him sends little tremors of pleasure through my body. My softly moving fingers find his erection. I lift away the towel and fall to my knees.

He says, with only mild interest, "You are *so* hungry."

"Starved," I say. "You don't mind, do you?"

He laughs. "Obviously not."

He eats his croissant, and crumbs drop on the top of my head and into my face as I go back to sucking this most lovely of cocks.

I ask him to spread his legs—really telling him, rather than asking, although I speak in a soft voice without inflection. Asked or told, it doesn't matter in the least to Terry in his condition of arousal. He spreads his legs wide for me. His expression is one of tranquility, but not for long.

Soon he is pressing my head down deep into his crotch.

"Oh, yes," I exclaim in triumph as he starts to come.

Being a sentimental guy, I write him a card to take along: *So may the sky lie cloudless over you, and your smile be bright and carefree; be blessed for the moment of bliss and happiness you gave to another heart, a lonely and a grateful one.*

My God, such a moment of bliss. Why isn't that enough for a whole lifetime? It will have to be.

"You really shouldn't see me any more," he says as he's leaving. "I want only to tell you I love you. But I want you to keep our secret."

"I will."

THE DRIVER: A VIRGIN'S CONFESSION

The narrator of this little tale, which first appeared in Juniors, *had given up hope of getting what he wanted that night, but when he encountered the large, Italian cab driver, he discovered that sometimes when you despair of realizing a dream, it can still come true. —JB*

On this muggy, starless night the drivers stand around outside the Spike, chatting or smoking. Some just wait in their cabs. I watch as some boys climb into a long black limo; I wonder if they are celebrities. It is a strange moment, seeing the tallest one slide in beside the driver. A man I met earlier took me into the place with him, but he said leaving was the hard part. "Coming out of a gay club is coming out," he said, and I know he is right.

This cab driver knows about me. But, what the hell, he has *chosen* to be outside the bar, hoping for a fare. Maybe more.

"Where to?" he asks.

I look up, but it is too dark to tell anything much about him.

"The Summit Hotel," I tell him. My dad got me a room at his corporate rate.

The air conditioning had been turned all the way up inside the big old Mercury sedan, but I am still sweating. I regret that I have left the bar still a boy, only a boy, embarrassed and hopelessly confused. I will go home to Michigan having done *nothing*. But what did I expect? Did I expect New York would somehow celebrate me? I'm still feeling it in my stomach, a desire that coils around itself, knots itself up into a ball.

We stop at a light and I look for the picture of the driver that is supposed to be posted inside the cab, but there isn't any; I realize this is a gypsy cab. My father warned me: no gypsy cabs. What have I done? He'll drive me all over town and charge me double. He might even rob me! Now I'm starting to get the shakes, I can feel them coming, odd and sickening.

The driver is upright behind the wheel, staring straight ahead, but then he looks at me in the rear-view mirror. "You okay, kid?"

"Yeah, I'll be okay."

"What'd you tell your folks?" He has a heavy accent. Italian maybe.

"My folks?"

"Yeah. You're stayin' with your folks, right? At the Summit?"

"No. I'm alone. My last adventure till I go to college."

He chuckles. "And so, has it been an adventure?"

"Not really."

"Disappointing, huh?"

"Yeah." I don't feel like talking, but he obviously does. He's his own best audience.

It's eerie now in Manhattan. On the way uptown, everything is closed, dark, gated, locked, empty. But I get a running commentary on everything we pass. I didn't ask for a Gray Line tour, but I'm getting one anyway.

"Yeah," he says, finally, as we pull up in front of the hotel, "this is a nice place all right, 'cept for that fuckin' fire station next door. They keep you up?"

"What?"

"The fire trucks?"

I haven't been paying attention. "Fire trucks?" I know nothing of fire trucks. I begin to tremble. I have just realized the worst has happened.

The driver puts his arm across the seat and turns to face me.

"Somethin' wrong?"

I am madly searching my pockets, although I know now what has happened. "Yes. That man ...."

"What man?"

"The one who took me into the bar with him. I bought him a drink and he saw my money clip."

The driver breaks into a hearty laugh. "Dumb shit! Dumb shit!"

He really doesn't really need to keep saying that, but he does anyway. At least *he* finds it hysterically funny.

"I have my wallet locked in my suitcase in my room. I'll go up and get it."

"Hey, I know the score, kid. You go up there and you'll find out the maid fuckin' stole your fuckin' suitcase!"

"I'll just be a minute."

"Hold it!" he orders, slamming the car into reverse. He parks it, rather sloppily, in the cab stand. "I'm fuckin' goin' with you."

"No, no. That won't do. Look, I'll only be a minute."

"That's what they all say," he says, showing his perfect teeth in a wolfish grin. "Let's go."

In the elevator I get a really good look at my driver. Yes, Italian. Not particularly handsome, but not ugly either. And, at about six-two, he towers over me. He is huge; he should be working down on the docks, not driving a cab. He reeks of garlic. But I am too nervous to be repulsed.

He can't seem to stop chuckling. He looks over at me, cowering in the corner of the elevator. He shakes his head. His eyes take me in, from my new boots to my new jeans, my white T-shirt, my new haircut. I thought I looked pretty tough when I left the hotel, but now I feel puny, terribly out of place. He's wearing nearly the same outfit, but on him it looks so much better. He certainly fills out his jeans better than I do. My eyes can't leave the bulge at his crotch, and he catches me staring at it. He doesn't say anything, just adjusts it, making it loom even larger, chuckling all the while. I take a deep breath and finally pull my eyes away when we reach the 14th floor. He is still chuckling as we step from the elevator.

He follows me down the hall. "I'll bet they loved you at the Spike."

"Why?"

"That ass. You got one cute fuckin' ass."

Nobody had ever called my ass "cute" before, let alone call it a "cute fuckin' ass." Now I wonder what this goon has in mind. Images of the maid finding me in the morning flash through my mind: the desperate calls to my parents, the embarrassment over the newspaper headline "Recent Grad Stabbed in New York Hotel Room." I fumble with the key but finally get the door unlocked, and enter the room. I switch on the light and start to close the door, telling him I'll just be a second, but he's already pushing his way into the room.

He senses my uneasiness, and says "Cute fuckin' ass" as he rubs it.

"I'll get my wallet," I say, pulling away. But he will have none of that. He grabs my arm and tosses me on the bed.

"Why don't you just work off the fare?"

"What?"

"You're the fuckin' dumbest rich kid I ever met." He stands next to the bed, unbuckling his jeans. "But I know what you want."

I gulp. This is not what I intended at all, but…. There's no denying it, I crave him. He beams proudly at me without a word.

In a flash, he has it out, the biggest cock I have ever seen.

He smiles broadly as I stare at it while he plays with it. It grows even longer. Not only am I a virgin when it comes to butt-fucking, I am a novice regarding foreskin, which I see the driver has in abundance. I am fascinated by the look of it, and he chuckles as he kicks off his boots and shucks his jeans. Sweat and hair are everywhere, and his cock is lengthening as I stare at it hungrily.

He climbs on the bed and mounts me, putting the huge thing in my face. He takes off his T-shirt. More sweat, more hair. I reach out and pull the erection to my nose and breathe in its heady aroma. The eye of the cock is now staring me right in the face. The folds of skin wrap around the huge head. A long strand of precum drips from the iris. With his callused hands, he takes hold of the foreskin and stretches it back up the long, thick shaft.

My lips part as he brings it closer. Slowly he feeds it to me. Stretched tall above me, he groans as I work it into my mouth. He lets go of the shaft as I slide most of it inside. Now he takes hold of my head and begins.

I nurse his cock helmet. It dribbles some more precum. He moves it in, to the back of my throat, and I suck deep on it while I bury my nose in the fur above his hard-on.

Soon his thick thighs buckle and shudder, but suddenly he pulls out.

It's as if he has read my mind, because my own cock is aching for release. He runs his fingers over my crotch. He allows me to sit up and, in a flash, I am nude and back in position. He smiles and straddles me again. His balls swing about a foot over my face, then he drops them to my lips. I kiss them, suck them, then slide my tongue in his asshole and he moans with satisfaction.

Grabbing big chunks of my hair, he begins to fuck my face again. He's breathing heavily in no time, but then he stops once more. He gets up and walks across the room, pulling the long mirror off the wall and leaning it on top of the bed, which in this room is shoved into a corner. He angles the mirror to reflect the activity on the bed. He positions me where he wants me, then orders, "Lie back, babe, and suck me good and hard. Then I'm gonna fuck yer cute hairless ass."

I nod, but I know I'm not ready for things to go that far. I don't have time to reflect on it, however, because he aims his shaft at my hungry mouth; he fucks it like a wet pussy and his balls slap against my chin. I let my eyes wander to the mirror beside me to watch this stud use me as his little fucktoy. Another first for me: watching myself while I'm doing it. His cock throbs faster in my throat. He drips sweat from every pore of his skin and soaks me with it. The cold air blowing on me from the air conditioning has kept me fairly comfortable. His moans and panting get louder as he pumps long, hard strokes down my throat. I reach down and begin to masturbate. Then, just as I am peaking with desire for him, he pulls his cock out forcefully.

"Roll over," he barks.

I follow his order as he grabs the bottle of lotion from the nightstand. I watch in the mirror as he prepares my asshole and his cock. Then he mounts me and begins. He is surprisingly gentle now. Perhaps he knows I've never done this before. I cry out when he fingers it. He lets up for a moment, but then he has the head of it in. He pauses for a second, but then goes ahead; he keeps on shoving his hard cock into me, eventually lowering his large torso down on top of me in a final, sweaty lunge. His cock drives into me in rapid thrusts. I take deep breaths, getting used to it. He props himself over me and watches his cock going in and out. I look into the mirror myself to watch, and I squirm and moan in ecstasy. I feel my cock rubbing the sheets, ready to come. As if he is reading my mind while I am struggling for air under his heavy body, he rolls me over on top of him so I can breathe. This way, I can fuck the big cock and watch it penetrating me in the mirror. I sit up and swivel on his cock so I can watch his face while he fucks me. This sets me off and I come all over his hairy chest.

I keep at it, though, wanting him to come, now more than ever. God, I really like it here, him inside of me. This is the best sex I've ever had. Better than giving Jerry, the football center/hunk/moron, a blowjob occasionally—far better. I now know the kind of sex I was born to have. It is good for the driver, too. I can feel the end drawing near. I pull my buttcheeks farther apart, helping him. Soon I am being thrashed wildly around on his cock. His orgasm is quieter than mine, but no less intense.

There is no lingering, however, no after-sex cuddling. Instead, he bounds from the bed, still full of energy, and says, "Let's take a shower." I agree it's a good idea, since I have cum dripping from my asshole.

The shower barely holds his big body and mine. He lathers me all over with soap. He smiles the whole time but says nothing. Then he turns me around to wash my asshole. Gentle strokes soothe my ravaged pucker. Slowly, but firmly he runs his hands over me. He works his way to my front, slips his hand firmly around my cock, and squeezes. He works my cock in his hand, biting my neck. He is running the tip of his renewed hard-on up and down my crack. I shoot again in seconds.

I know he wants to fuck me again, but he senses I have had quite enough battering for one night. He turns me around and forces me down. I end up sitting in the tub while he fucks my face again.

Soon I am making him scream in ecstasy. He lets me take over, and my mouth fully encompasses him, my tightness holds him captive. He starts to shudder, but I keep him going, anticipating his inevitable orgasm. My eyes are closed, and in the darkness of my mind I see him enjoying this act to the fullest extent possible. Up and down I go, over and over again.

"Oh, kid," he sighs, "God!"

I don't respond, and the pace seems to quicken a bit. He is drawing nearer and nearer. Another few sucks on it and it will all be over.

"Oh, kid," he sighs again, his now voice seeming so warm and pleasant, just like his cock.

He suddenly pulls back, watching himself ejaculate in a stream, straight up in the air. The residue comes down on my face, only to be washed away by the spray of the shower. I pull him toward me again, kissing the slowly softening penis.

But he still is in no mood to linger. "Hey, I'm losin' fares hanging around here," he says, climbing out of the tub. "Back to work."

By the time I return to the bedroom, he's dressed and combing his hair. He's put the mirror back on the wall. He doesn't look at me.

I step over to the closet, crouch down to get at my suitcase. I unlock my suitcase, pull out my wallet. I still have a hundred dollars in cash, and some traveler's checks. My hand shakes as I offer him some bills.

"What's this?" he says.

"I don't want you losin' fares 'cause you were hangin' around here." The minute I say it, I regret my tone, and my mimicking of his heavy accent.

But he pays me no mind. He shrugs, shoves the bills in his pocket, and returns to combing his hair. "How long you here for?" he asks.

"I have a four o'clock flight."

"We should leave by two."

I have dropped to my knees and am busy returning my wallet to my suitcase, then locking it. "What?" I heard what he said but I want him to repeat it, just to make sure. "What did you say?"

"I said, we need to leave by two."

"I don't understand."

"You worked off your fare, and now you gave me enough to take you to the airport. Okay? That's not too hard to figure, is it, even for a little rich kid?"

"Okay." I smile and look at my watch. It is now four o'clock in the morning. "But what will we do between now and then?"

I look up, but now all I can see is blue denim as he takes my head in his hands and crushes my face into his crotch.

KING'S COCK

An older man and a young porn star on the make enjoy meet at a remote country house, an encounter that suggests their two very different lives might conceivably take a new direction together. Originally published in Huge 2. —JB

Seth cursed the rain and reached out the window again to wipe at the windshield with an already-drenched rag. The wiper on his side was working only in spurts, and the one on the other side had quit altogether. Icy rain soaked through his shirt sleeve as he held the wheel with one hand and cleared the windshield with the other. He cursed the day he bought the '62 'Vette, which looked like a dream and ran like a nightmare.

It could be worse, he told himself. He couldn't think of precisely how; but it probably could. After all, he was finally making enough money to get his own apartment out of Manhattan, away from Logan. Still, it had been fun while it lasted. It was never much strain to spend someone else's money. To shake free, you had to bleed a little. Then if you were smart, you took a hard look at the scars from time to time to remind yourself how life really worked.

Seth struggled with the map beside him, held it in front while steering with his elbows, then swore again. Yes, that had been his turnoff; he'd just missed it. With a quick glance up and down the stretch of rain-fogged road, he spun the little car into a U-turn. The wipers might be pitiful, but the 'Vette knew how to move.

He couldn't imagine why anyone would live way out here in the boondocks, but the client said he had bought the place as some sort of hideaway. "I'm hibernating," the man had told him. Just what kind of man was he? Well, Seth would soon find out. That was what was so interesting about his line of work now. And thanks to six videos, he was able to command a grand for an overnight. Two of those a week was all he needed.

He had to slow the 'Vette to a crawl to make it down the slushy, rut-filled lane marked by a battered mailbox with KING painted on the side. Obviously 'King' didn't believe in spending much money on driveway maintenance. Better to save it for a few hours of fun with a stud.

Seth wiped his window again and set his teeth against each jarring bump. When he heard his muffler scrape, he stopped cursing the rain and started cursing King. But when he saw the house, he perked up a bit. It was charming, homey. Though he could see it needed a paint job, it didn't look run-down, just lived-in. There was smoke trailing up from the chimney. He often thought of finding a place just like this for himself, a place away from crowds and noise where he could relax, unwind.

When his muffler scraped the road again, Seth was no longer charmed. He pulled up behind a pickup truck and shut off his engine. Dropping his rag on the floor mat, he rolled up his window and had started to open the door when a mass of wet fur leaped on it.

The dog was enormous. Maybe it had meant to give a friendly greeting, but in its current bedraggled state, it didn't look too pleasant. The animal slid two muddy paws down the window and barked.

"Dolly!"

Both Seth and the dog looked toward the house, where a man stood near the porch steps. *So this is King*, Seth thought. He was very slender, and looked very comfortable in jeans and boots and a bulky sweater. His face looked handsome through the rain. Seth couldn't see the color of his eyes, but he could see his mouth, full and snarly as he called to the dog again. "Dolly, get down now."

The dog let out a last halfhearted bark and obeyed. Cautious, Seth opened the door and stepped out. "Mr. King?"

"Hi, Seth. Sorry about the dog. Dolly doesn't bite. Very often."

"That's good news," Seth muttered, and pulled his bag out of the car.

King stood where he was while his nerves tightened. Seth was a stranger, and he was inviting him into his home, into his life. Maybe he should stop it now, right now, before it went one step further. Then Seth turned, bags in hand, and looked at King, rain streaming from his dark hair. King was amused to see it wet and plastered around Seth's adorable, boyish face. But it was not a kind face, King thought immediately as he rubbed his crotch, which was already swelling with the idea that Seth was here. There was too much living in it, too much knowledge, for a youth Seth's age. A man had to be crazy to let a kid like that into his life. Then King saw that Seth's clothes were drenched and his shoes coated with mud. "Looks like you could use a bath."

"Yeah." He gave the dog a last look as it sniffed around his ankles. "Your driveway's a bit of a mess."

"I know." He gave Seth a small, apologetic smile as he noted that his car had fared no better than he. "It's been a hard winter." He didn't step forward. With the rain pelting between them, he stood watching Seth—sizing him up, Seth decided—and he thrust his nervous hands in his pockets. He'd committed himself, and he'd go through with it. "Come inside." He went to the door to wait for Seth. His eyes looked dark, a soft green, and if Seth hadn't known better he'd have said they were frightened. King smelled of rain and wood smoke.

Pausing at the door, Seth pried off his shoes. "I don't think you want me tramping around the place in these."

"I appreciate it."

Seth stepped easily into King's house in his stockinged feet while King stood with his hand on the doorknob, feeling desperate and awkward. "Why don't you just leave your things here for now and come into the kitchen? It's warm; you can dry out."

"Fine." Seth found the inside of the house as homey as he suspected it would be from the outside. The floors were wood, their shine a bit dull. The furniture old, comfortable. He saw on a table by the staircase a vase of roses. As they walked, King said, "You drove down from New Jersey?"

"Yeah."

"Not a nice drive in this weather."

"No." He wasn't purposely being rude, though he could be when it suited his purpose. At the moment, the house interested him more than small talk. There were no dishes in the sink, and the floor was scrubbed clean, but the kitchen was hardly tidy. It appeared that King did a lot of work out of his house; there were piles of paper on the table. He pushed some files aside to make room for Seth.

If Seth wasn't going to bother to speak to him, King thought, they wouldn't get far. He turned for another look. King now decided he definitely loved Seth's looks: the turned-up nose and intense eyes that held a look of impish mischief, which matched the wicked grin on his luscious lips. His face wasn't kind, but it was intriguing, with those hypnotic eyes. King recalled he'd been fatally attracted to such intensity before. The boy named Chuck had brown eyes, but the message had been the same: "I get what I want because I don't give a damn what I have to do to get it," and he hadn't. King was very much afraid he had just opened his life to the same kind of man. But he was older and wiser now, he reminded himself, and this time he wasn't in love. This was just a porn star rented for the night.

"I'll take your shirt if you like." He held out his hands and waited until Seth slipped out of it. For the first time in years he found himself in awe of a male body. Seth was even hunkier than he had been in "Sex Watch," the last video he had seen, the one that had inspired him to call Seth when he saw his ad.

"The jeans?" King asked, anxious to have the boy nude. Seth moved with the easy grace of a supple cat, stretching languidly.

"Yeah, sure. They're soaked too." He casually opened the front of his denim jeans. Hooking his thumbs into the waistband, he dragged the snug jeans down his hips, twisting and bending down, riding them down his bare legs till he could step out of them.

"Now, how 'bout that warm bath?" King asked.

Seth grinned. "Why not?" Appearing nude before King was accepted with considerable ease; there was not the slightest trace of embarrassment at showing his young body, nor the least reluctance to follow King to the

29

bathroom. King smiled crookedly and slung a friendly arm over Seth's shoulder.

"This way," King said. He showed Seth the bathroom, the antique tub in the middle of the room, and began filling the tub with hot water.

Seth stood at the toilet and peed, glancing over his shoulder at King. "You gonna get in there with me? That's the biggest fuckin' bathtub I've ever seen."

"No, I'm going to just let you relax. In fact, I'm leaving now to get some more relaxants." He stepped over to Seth and ran his hand down the firm belly and into the pubic hairs. He smiled to see Seth's cock was semi-hard.

"All I need to relax me is this," Seth said, reaching behind him and groping King's crotch.

"That's on the menu, believe me." King squeezed Seth's cock and backed away. "You take your sweet time."

King was true to his word; he let Seth soak in the bath for twenty minutes, long enough that Seth dozed off. When King returned to the bathroom, he was smoking the biggest joint Seth had ever seen. "Here," King said. "Take a hit off this."

"I'm not much of a smoker," Seth said.

"Then just one hit is all you'll need." King handed him the joint, glanced quickly down at Seth's cock, bobbing in the soapy water, chuckled, and left the bathroom.

Seth lay back in the tub, finishing the joint, the hot water soaking his tired muscles; it had been a long day. He had looked like shit when he finally arrived, but King seemed to like him.

He spread his legs, letting the hot water push against him, watched it circle his cock, and he grinned. How men liked sucking it, he thought, and King would suck it tonight. He knew what King wanted and was more than willing to comply. In fact, he had a few new ideas. He let his head drop back against the tub's edge. Sometimes it was wonderful being paid for sex, and knowing clearly what the customer wanted. Not that it was rote by now; every time was different, at least in the beginning.

"Would you like your back washed?"

Seth looked up in surprise. King stood in the doorway.

"No, that's okay, I'll be out in a minute." Seth was a master; he knew that expectation was a wonderful sharpener of desire. They had only a short time together, and Seth knew that the best way of talking for him and his tricks was making love. He laughed to himself. He knew a hungry john when he saw one, but he also saw the kindness in King's eyes. He saw King as an open, uncomplicated man. King, Seth knew, wanted him, *all* of him. Seth wasn't sure if he was up to everything tonight but the grass had made him utterly relaxed. Maybe, if King wanted it....

He remembered the first time he had been fucked. He had been a virgin when he met Logan, and remained so for a full year afterward. The one night Logan got him drunk at dinner and shoved his legs back onto his chest, opening him up completely and then lying over him so he could feel Logan's erection against his own. He did not need Logan to tell him that something special was about to happen. They had been celebrating their first anniversary, and Logan was desperate to fuck Seth.

Logan stroked himself, bumping his cock into the entrance to Seth's ass, and then started making little moaning sounds. Soon he panted, "Please, please don't make me wait any longer."

Seth quickly got up and lowered himself onto Logan's cock; he thought this would be the best way to take it. He first moved his hips away and then slowly brought them back as if to test the promise of this new intrusion. Logan's pre-cum shone on Seth's ass and Seth trembled in anticipation of the entry to come. There was a pause, a silence in the room, and then the sound of a deep intake of breath as Seth lowered himself all the way. He bit into Logan's neck and cheek, he thrust his tongue into Logan's ear, and all the time Logan never stopped moving below him. Seth finally felt Logan's body strain under him, lifting them both up. After his cum had filled Seth, Logan told him he had never had a more intense orgasm.

Seth stepped from the bath and King was arrested by the beauty of the boy's toned body as he dried himself. King yearned to reach out, to touch the boy's limbs, to stroke them, to run his hands up along those marvelous sculpted curves, but he forced himself to wait. King was uncomfortably warm now, his brow shining with sweat. His straining cock, proudly erect, poked defiantly against the front of his loosely belted robe, threatening to break through the flaps at any moment. Standing in the semi-darkness, he wondered if Seth could see the obvious state of his arousal. He moved his hand in the shadows to brush aside the flaps of the robe, teasing Seth. He saw Seth's eyes follow the movement in the shadows, saw his moist lips part at the glimpse of King's cock.

King drew the robe down his dangling arms until his slim body was revealed, and Seth slowly nodded his approval, sending a secret shiver of pride up the spine of the tense older man. Silently, Seth approached King, then leaned over and kissed the head of his cock. He moved his lips down the full length of the monstrous organ to the pubic hairs, and let his lips linger there, just grazing the tiny hairs, while the pungent smell of sweat and pre-cum filled his nostrils. Now he shifted back so he could look up at King. He met his eyes and said, "God, it's so big." His hand was drawn irresistibly to it and, with gentle reverence; he let the pads of his fingertips move down over the hardness, caressing the cock as if it were some finely crafted piece of sculpture.

King's prick stiffened even more under Seth's touch and the frank admiration of his gaze. "My god," he croaked with a mouth that had gone suddenly dry.

King stroked himself and Seth savored the long sweep of that splendid torso as he dropped to his knees before him. King took a single hesitant step toward the youth; he could no longer resist the burning need to get his hands on Seth.

King pulled Seth to his feet, and the boy's outstretched hand trembled as he curved it around the jutting column of King's flesh till he heard King gasp with a sharp intake of breath. And then he pulled the prick closer, tightening his grip, savoring the solid feel of it as the older man's hand encircled his own prick and began to squeeze it.

Seth had a smooth, nicely cut cock. It was lovely, but more importantly, it was attached to someone King had been fantasizing about for months now. To be so close made him dizzy, brought a lump of emotion to his throat, but Seth was oblivious to King's reaction. "Ooooh," he whispered, exhaling sharply and closing his eyes. Seth opened his eyes as King dropped to his knees next to him. "Suck it," Seth taunted, his lips curling at the corners.

"Yes, I want to suck it," King gasped.

Seth's hard cock was aimed straight at King's mouth. The older man reached out and ran his forefinger up and down the silky shaft, around the smooth crown. Curious, King held it, studied it. It could belong to any man, but it didn't—and that made all the difference. Suddenly King became anxious. He realized that Seth had been sucked by the very best in the world, and he didn't know how he would measure up. Still, Seth had never been—could not have been— sucked by anyone who wanted it more.

King bent forward and planted kisses all over the prick that so many other men had also fantasized about. He caressed the head with his lips. He took his time licking it from base to crown, pausing to take each of his balls into his mouth and to gently suck on them. He returned to the head and took it in, relaxing the back of his throat so he could get it all down.

Seth's hands exerted pressure on King's head, his thumbs pushing hard against his temples. "Yeah, that's it," he whispered hoarsely. "Ooooh, that's the best, man. Keep suckin' it."

King looked up, nodding emphatically as he kept on sucking. He felt blessed, grateful and powerful all at once. "Better than Lucas?" King asked, recalling the scene in the woods in "Everhard," Seth's first video.

"Oh, yeah," Seth groaned. "He was really a nelly shit, man."

"You looked like you really enjoyed fucking him," King said.

"Yeah, he was into it, you know."

32

"Tell me about it while I suck you," King pleaded.

Seth continued talking about fucking Lucas for a few more minutes, his voice becoming softer and softer, until at last he was silent. King opened his eyes and gazed up. Seth's lips were hanging loose. All the muscles in his face had slackened. His eyes seemed to be covered with a gauzy film. With a rush of pride King realized that he was responsible for reducing this stud to a purring little kitten. His cocksucking skills were such that he had tamed the beast. He licked and sniffed Seth's balls; he squeezed his ass. A drop of pre-cum appeared on the head of his cock and King licked it away.

Seth's eyelids fluttered, and he swayed slightly as King clenched his hand, tightening his grip on the cock. Seth shut his eyes and curled his lower lip, biting down on it softly, as if afraid he might cry out. He arched his back, causing his cock to slap against King's lips.

King took the cock in his mouth again, then brought two fingers to Seth's ass. As he pressed upward, he heard a sudden shivering gasp through Seth's clenched teeth. He waited until the younger man relaxed, and then twisted his hand so he could finger-fuck him while he blew him. Seth groaned and swayed as the sex continued.

At one point, an abrupt grunt escaped Seth's compressed lips, and he arched his back expansively, like a great cat in heat. He twisted sensuously, pushing down on King's burrowing fingers. King glanced upward and was surprised to find Seth looking down at him, watching his cock-filled mouth through eyes that had narrowed into dark gleaming slits. Intently watching Seth's face, King smiled when he saw the boy's eyes close again as he appeared to slip into dreamy reverie. He seemed to purr, luxuriating in the pleasure of the suck and fuck.

Gently extricating his cock from King's mouth, Seth smiled down at him, and turned around slowly and very seductively, presenting his beautiful rounded ass for admiration and worship.

Seth's ass was unimaginably delightful to the eye and pleasing to the touch. King sucked on it until it was covered with saliva. Seth closed his eyes dreamily, luxuriated in the warm, comforting feel of those firm, masculine hands as they cupped his rounded mounds. He turned around again, and drew King to his feet. "Let's go to bed," he whispered.

King led Seth to his bedroom, where the boy lay face down on his bed, squirming sensually, and projecting his ass upward at the same time he arched his back in a gesture of feline pleasure. King knelt on the bed behind him and gasped in arousal as his powerful hands gently squeezed and caressed the perfect little bottom.

Seth reached back to grasp King's rigid prick, and began exploring its shape, its immense size, then clamping his fingers around it with surprising eagerness. "Get some lube," he panted.

King liberally coated his cock with the lubricant, then applied more to Seth's asshole as he positioned the tip of his cock at the opening. A wonderful mixture of excitement and tenderness gripped him as he gently penetrated Seth, who groaned in excitement as he felt the huge organ begin to enter him.

King's cock moved in and out, penetrating a little farther with each stroke. Seth's moans became louder; he tossed his head wildly, pushing the pillows up against the wall. His whole body was pointed at King's cock, and now his hunger took control. Seth's body rocked under King, until suddenly, he raised himself up to his knees, forcing King back. Now it was clear that Seth wanted it all. He was thrusting his ass back and forth onto King's cock with his own rhythm.

King looked down at the youthful body, gripped by the excitement of the fuck, watching and wondering at the strength of a whore's want. He reached under Seth and started playing with his cock; pre-cum dripped down onto the sheets. Seth was rocking quietly now, all hips and ass, and joy flowed through King's cock. Everything became quiet. Only the sound of movement could be heard, and then King felt all of Seth tighten around his cock, just as massive jets of his come exploded deep inside the boy. "Oh, God," Seth sighed, and fell forward, pulling King with him. "Man, it's so good, so good." King liked the sweat that trickled between them, the river of their desire, liked the feeling between them, the smell of them together. King could feel the lad's heat, the moisture between his thighs, the wetness of the balls that he rubbed gleefully before returning to the cock.

King was using his talented hand to pleasure the lad, flattening his palm and pressing it down his quivering shaft, electrifying him with tingling excitement. Seth gasped and tried to catch his breath just as King grabbed him viciously, tightening curled fingers on his rock-solid manhood. Jerking his fist upward, he sent a sudden shock of pure pleasure rocketing through Seth. King savored the boy's youthfulness, his power, the lusty urgency that infused his pulsating penis as it throbbed in his grip, alive and vibrant. He yanked on the cock again and again, forcing Seth into uncontrollable spasms of pleasure. A massive, violent tremor shook the youth to the core as his body stiffened. He arched back, forcing his hips against King, again burying the huge cock as deep as possible, and he came with a mind-shattering explosion that sent his penis erupting, spewing gobs of semen that cascaded down King's clenched fist, oozing over sticky fingers that after a time gave him up only reluctantly.

And a long night of passion and tenderness had just begun.

King faced the morning with a kind of dazed wonder. He'd discovered passion. So much had happened in twelve hours. He'd found affection, and maybe, just maybe, he was taking the first step toward finally severing his ties and obligations to the past. He had Seth to thank for that, but he didn't think the boy would tolerate hearing the phrase again. He couldn't express his gratitude without annoying him, and he couldn't tell him that he loved him without risking the loss of what might just conceivably have begun.

King forced himself to concentrate on his research papers and not think too deeply about what had happened the night before. What it had meant to Seth and what it had meant to him were two different things. He had to be wise enough to understand that. But Seth had given him something he'd never really had from a man before: respect, affection, passion.

When Seth came downstairs, clad only in a pair of King's briefs, he went straight for the coffee. He didn't usually wake up groggy, but his mind had been tense and active. What had happened between them hadn't been ordinary. Part of him wished it had been just another trick, while another—a part he hadn't yet explored—rejoiced that it hadn't. He wasn't a man who enjoyed contrasts within himself. He had considered himself trade, and with King he had become someone he detested. He'd begun to dissect the opinion he'd had of King before they'd met and compare it to the feelings he had about him now. Nothing added up.

"You said you didn't eat breakfast, but I have cereal there, milk in the fridge," King said, his eyes riveted on the papers before him.

"Thanks," Seth said. He poured himself a huge bowl of cornflakes, covered them with milk, and slid down on the stool at the counter to begin eating.

King looked at Seth's muscular back as the lad sat on the stool. He longed to go to him, to hold him. For the first time in his life, King's urge to protect was stronger than any other. He couldn't resolve what was happening inside him. He wanted Seth just as much as he had before—no, even more. There was a sweetness about Seth's lovemaking that he'd never tasted before, and he craved it again. But there was something else. He could close his eyes and hear the way Seth moaned as he sank his big cock deep inside him. He could see the way Seth worked at it, steadily and without bitterness, to make him happy with their lovemaking. How could there be such a whore on the face of the earth? King feared he was becoming a fool, after all these years. All he wanted to do now was to fuck Seth again in the daylight in the big, empty house. "I'm going upstairs. Come up when you're done, okay?"

"Sure," Seth said, his mouth full of cereal.

Shrugging, King poured a second cup of coffee and took it upstairs—to wait for Seth.

Seth took his coffee to the porch, looking out at the hills. He felt singularly wonderful this morning, having been so well-fucked the night before. He knew King adored him. The cup of coffee in his hand had gone cold, but he didn't notice. He was going over in his mind all the things he

35

had to do in the next few days. The dates he had, might have to break. He had to be strong, stronger than he had ever been in his entire life. It was early morning and the sun, shimmering like Jell-O, was starting to break through the early morning fog, a pale nimbus spreading across the low horizon.

The porch wrapped halfway around the house. King had said the house was a hundred and fifteen years old. It was a functional house, no frills. King said he owned all of the land he could see to the horizon, and even beyond. It would be a great place to "hibernate," as King put it.

Seth stroked his cock, which was tingling with the thought of going back upstairs and being fucked once more by King.

In the bedroom, Seth lay on his back on the bed. He wanted to watch King's cock enter him, and he grunted as he worked hard to take all of it in his ass. Finally King's furry pubes brushed against the bottom of Seth's hard-on, his balls getting smashed between the two of them, and King was holding Seth's asscheeks apart with his muscular hands. Now King once again pistoned his enormous hard-on into Seth, again and again, stretching him, filling him. Cum started oozing out of Seth's turgid cock; he couldn't help it. He was moving his ass up and down the long shaft to keep in harmony with King's movements, and the intense pleasure of it just made him want to explode.

As King looked at him with his wolfish eyes, Seth touched his cock and he began to come, slowly, in thick, ropy gobs, and King pushed his body down and slid his abs around in Seth's jizz. Then he kissed Seth fully on the mouth, and his erection started throbbing deep in the boy's ass. King held perfectly still and smiled a little as his cum again started to shoot deep inside Seth. Seth's ass muscles gripped the cock, trying to keep it in him as long as possible.

Breathing heavily, King lay atop Seth after they had disengaged, mashing his balls on either side of Seth's softening dick. Seth's thighs were still spread far apart. If King wanted to, Seth would have been glad to continue their lovemaking. "Well, it wasn't like you didn't wanna get fucked," King said eventually, smiling and stroking his cock.

"No," Seth told him, putting his hand over King's. "It wasn't like that at all. Not at all."

King lifted his hand away, allowing Seth to grip his cock. King wrapped the youthful hustler in his arms and held him tight, kissed his bare shoulder. As Seth squeezed the miraculous cock, everything was foreign yet oddly familiar. It was like a fever, the way the warmth enveloped him.

36

INFIDELITIES

This brief story of interlocking infidelities originally appeared under the title "The Infidels" in the anthology Huge 2. *—JB*

In the gusts of heat, we walk up and down in front of my apartment building, not knowing what to do with ourselves, not knowing whether to part or to prolong it. We both have been dreading it. It is heartbreaking for Hank, having to give me up. He has been unfaithful to his lover, Larry, for years, but upon learning of Larry's first infidelity, he went berserk and broke down—and then they fucked until dawn. Hank told his lover that if he had to have an affair, okay, but that he should try not to. And Larry swore not to. But Hank fears that somewhere along the way Larry might succumb, be sucked in—or sucked *on*, as it were. So to keep the peace and set an example, he has promised Larry that he will give me up.

Hank and I decide to walk along the teeming streets, remarking about how strangely suited we are. The right height for fucking, the dark-haired and the light, the young and the older. We talk of the first days of our affair. We were at the same party, and he looked across the room at me and smiled. When I came back from a trip to the gent's room, I was a bit taken aback at how jarring it was not to see Hank sitting where he had been. Then I saw him by the buffet; I began to make my way by a long route back to my friends—a detour that just happened to take me by Hank—so that I could talk to him. We became like star-crossed lovers in a fable. Just like that. I never went back to my friends that night.

We had to go back to my place because Hank's lover was calling often from the west coast in those days. Hank told me that night that he was afraid Larry was seeing someone in L.A., not just tending to business. Larry, who was beautiful and, I believe, rich, never really discussed things with Hank, but as it happened, he was not at that time being unfaithful to Hank. It was only later that he let Hank catch him in his infidelity.

Hank's talk of infidelity made me nervous that night, but once I had his big cock in my ass, I forgot all about it. I was so smitten that the next day I couldn't get the taste, the touch, the smell of him out of my mind.

As the weeks passed, I saw that falling for Hank was a mistake. He explained that it was not that he was promiscuous; it was just that he needed change. Then he said something very poignant: he said the reason love is so painful is that it always amounts to two people wanting more than two people can give. But after Hank, I never wanted more. I had never felt so alive, so ravenously alive, as when Hank was fucking me.

I wish now Hank was only a torso, only a big cock. No penetrating eyes to welcome me or send me packing. No little gifts after we quarrel.

The sky darkens and thunder begins to rumble as if marching in from the ocean. Hank says it's going to be a bad storm, that he had better go. Larry is back in town and he is waiting. "Of course," I say. He offers to return the key to my apartment. "No, no," I say. "You never know."

We smile, say we'll meet again—soon. "For lunch," Hank says.

On the way back to my apartment, I become aware that I am being followed. The youth has the stealth of a hunter. I pass a couple of rent boys huddling together, out of the rain. My stalker acknowledges them, but he keeps up with me.

The rain is by now coming down in buckets, and sadness is seeping into me by the time I at last arrive back at my building. The slender, dark-haired youth has followed me all the way home. He stands forlornly in the gutter, looking up at me. I open the front door, stop, motion to him.

Thunder shakes the foundation of the building but I am shaking anyhow. I feel myself to be at one with my visitor and his friends, to be an outsider even in a gay neighborhood, and I realize that ending my affair with Hank has stoked my hunger for sex.

In seconds, the boy stands next to me, wiping his face, rainwater dripping onto the tile floor of the foyer. I smile at him, "God, you look good, but I don't know you or where you've been...."

I'm sure this pisses him off, but he is too horny to leave now. I think of something to lighten the suddenly tense atmosphere: "C'mon, let's get out of these wet clothes."

The slow, sweaty ride in the elevator finds me in his arms, kissing him. Any serious concerns I had quickly melt when he engulfs me.

"I won't hurt you," he says.

"I know," I say. When his hand comes down on my crotch, I do not know how to stop him, and I feel at once I am no longer in my own realm, but into his, throwing caution to the wind. "No, wait," I mutter, but his hands are already moving freely to unzip my jeans. He seems not to have heard me. He has my cock out and is looking up at me. His face frightens me, the intense and worshipful expression on his features—as though he was kneeling to light a candle.

His mouth hangs open, his eyes are focused on my cock; "I'm not hurting you," he keeps repeating as he strokes it to hardness. "I'm not hurting you."

And all I can answer is, "No. You're not."

I close my eyes, thrilling at his technique. I feel myself grow dizzy, feeling each motion he makes, the starfish movements of his fingers as they slip into my jeans to tease my balls.

My cock glistens with his saliva as the elevator door slides open and I take him by the arms and guide him toward the door to my apartment. He seems unready to give up the taste of my cock. Still, once inside my apartment, he seems to know what I want and tosses his shirt aside as I kneel and unfasten his pants. Naked, he straddles me, biting his lip as his semi-hard cock is revealed and I begin stroking it. It looks so big and bold—a couple of inches longer than Hank's, and even thicker. I ease him forward so that my tongue reaches his heavy, wrinkled sac, savoring the musky scent of him and I tease his nuts one at time, as he does mine. He smells as if he has just had sex. His cock grows harder, pressing against my forehead. I greedily lick it end to end. It is a truly magnificent cock.

He rubs my shoulders as I explore him, then squeezes harder when I take him into my mouth. I close my eyes. He starts fucking my mouth with his splendid prick. The sensations are almost too much. I have tears in my eyes, my lips twitch around his shaft, and I am ready to explode.

I pull my head back. His cock bobs seductively in front of my face. My saliva has greased him, and I jerk him with both hands. He lets go a stream of milky semen, splattering my neck and cheek. My cock swells, and I come as well.

In the bathroom, I finally get nude. A shine of sweet passion seems to coat his delicious body, and he is soon flashing a mischievous smile, showing little white teeth. He tells me his name is Warren, and he's currently 'looking for work.' I wrap my arms around him and inhale him. To my shock, my dick is again rock-hard and dribbling as I kneel before him again and cleanse his cock with my spittle. Soon the huge prick is poking up against his heaving belly. A dot of pre-cum glistens on the tip.

We get into the shower, and he falls on his knees before me. As if he is starved, his teeth graze my cock at first. But then, tongue, throat and tonsils all ravish me. I pull back and ram it deep. He gulps and has to come up for air, then goes back for more. The tip of his tongue flutters anxiously on the head, then he moves down to my ballsac. He sucks my nuts and my knees wobble. He grabs my ass and pulls my cock deep into his throat again. His head begins bobbing up and down as his tongue coats my shaft. All I can do is shudder beneath his intense suction. And then he snakes his arms around me and jabs two wet fingers deep into my asshole.

"Oh, yes," I pant. "Yes!"

He shoves three fingers inside me. He finger-fucks me for quite a while, his mouth never leaving my cock.

Suddenly he stands, turns me around. He nestles up against me and kisses my back. I know what he wants, but a dick the size of his is something to be reckoned with; I am not sure I am ready. I try to push him away, but he is insistent. "It's okay. I'll be gentle," he assures me, kissing my neck, playing with my cock.

Then he shoves his dickhead in, very slowly, bending me over as he does so. I let out a long, slow groan as his thick cockhead is shoved into me, followed by the long, snaking shaft, flexing, burrowing deep into me.

I don't want it here; I want to be in bed. I manage to pull away, and soon we are embracing, moving together into the darkened apartment, clawing our way into the bedroom, into the shadows. I feel languid, and dangerously safe in his grip; I feel myself falling onto the bed, sinking into a softness that doesn't seem to stop. He straddles me, his great cock bobs before me as he shoves my legs apart, and begins furtively jabbing my ass. Now he's grunting, teeth bared, and his fucking is furious. I squirm under his grinding, and come again. Seeing my spurting prick turns him into a madman and he rams into me harder, harder, and then pulls out and shoots his cum all over my belly. He leans over and kisses me, then he's off the bed, back into the bathroom.

I close my eyes. I hear the shower running. When I look up again, I see him coming out of the bathroom, toweling himself off. He stands at the window. "I've passed this building so many times, wondering about the rich people who live here." He turns toward me. "So what's it like to live here?" he asks, looking around, taking it all in.

What it is like, I think, is like anything else. Like this was my dad's apartment when he was alive; he kept the apartment to keep from having to go home to Connecticut every night—and to have his liaisons with his various mistresses. He left it to me, figuring I would follow in his footsteps, which I did, in a way. Then, amazingly, the neighborhood turned gay, so I felt right at home.

Now I shrug. How I want to ask him a similar question, like what's it like to live on the streets, selling your body? He hasn't yet asked me for money. But he has his mouth open, ready to speak again. He isn't sure if I want him to re-join me in bed. "May I ask you something?" he asks finally, dropping his towel on the chair by the desk and looking for his briefs.

"Yeah?"

"Could I maybe stay here tonight?"

I nod solemnly.

He smiles and gives up the search for his underwear; he slides into the bed with me.

Soon one of Warren's fingers is pushing into me again, sliding up into my body. I feel a shiver of pain.

"Did I hurt you?"

"No, but you are now. Let's just go to sleep."

"You sure?" he asks, drawing my hand to his cock. He is hard again.

"My god...!"

This time I take him from behind, on my knees, the way Hank likes it. I'm amazed at how quickly I have become accustomed to the hugeness of Warren.

"Oh, man," he groans.

I am soon crying out loudly as he begins to fuck me brutally, the hard prick entering and retreating in quick thrusts. As he pummels my ass, I moan, jack my dick.

Then Warren pumps his cock deeper, and I ride along with him, sharing his pleasure as he comes. Then he pulls out of me and lies next to me, breathing hard. His cock is slick and wet as it hangs against his thigh. I lean down and kiss it, hold it against my cheek. I decide I love Warren's cock more than anything in the world.

It is still dark when I hear the key in the lock, the footfalls in the corridor, heading to the bedroom. I know who it is, and I can't move fast enough. Suddenly Hank is in the bedroom, turning on the lights before I can even get out of bed.

He says nothing, just stands there.

I want to fix this somehow, this new trouble, but I can tell from Hank's expression just how far away from him I have gone. I feel ashamed, almost ridiculous. I have a strange heat in my face and neck, and the ache in my bones make me wince.

"What...?" he finally begins to ask. It is almost a challenge, but he cannot finish his question.

I can't find the breath to answer him.

"Haven't I been good to you?" he asks, softly.

I nod my head that yes, he has. But it's not like that, I want to tell him, to say—as I had rehearsed it in case he found me in bed with someone—that having this boy in my bed doesn't mean a thing. But to say that would only sound stupid now.

Warren stirs, rolls over. Looking at how magnificent little Warren is, Hank's eyes become full of hurt, and he chokes up.

My choice is between total silence and rising to take Hank in my arms. I sit naked on the mattress, paralyzed.

"I'm a such fucking fool," Hank says. "You really are too young for me." And he steps out, quietly shutting the door behind him.

Warren moves next to me, and I put my hand on his erection. "No, Hank," I laugh, "you're not too old for me, you're just not big enough any more!"

TRUE BELIEVERS

From the anthology Dreamboys *we've included this titillating tale of interracial 'worship services' observed in the empty rooms of a motel by two youthful, admiring acolytes.* —JB

Nate was big and black, and he came to work at my ma's motel after my pa died. I was just a teenager then, confused by most things sexual, but I knew what I wanted: Nate. He had a big smile and a gold tooth in front, and showed a bulge in his paint-spattered overalls that tantalized me. Over the first summer he worked for Ma, he taught my pal William and me how to smoke, and, eventually, bribed us with Kool menthol cigarettes to suck his dick.

Technically, I guess he didn't actually teach us how to smoke, but one day at the market when he caught us stealing Uncle William's King Edward Deluxe Cigarillos with Plastic Filter Tips, he figured he could regulate our tobacco consumption and our behavior by becoming our supplier. It kept us from stealing and he made sure we did not inhale. That was about the best he could hope for. The cocksucking started when he caught me sucking off William one day when we thought he was busy painting one of the rooms.

William was leaning back on his elbows on the floor of one of the vacant rooms, partially nude, and I was on my knees doing as good a job of blowing him as I could, considering how big his dick was, and responding to his moans and groans. I guess we had been making quite a bit of noise, quiet as we had tried to be.

I had closed the door but I had been so excited about getting William's cock in my mouth again I had forgotten to lock the door. Nate burst right into the room, and when he saw us, he smiled and said, "I done thought so," which I suppose meant he'd known all along and was just waiting his chance. Anyhow, he told me not to stop and he stood over us, rubbing his bulge. William had gone limp so I was playing with him a bit, trying to get him hard again, but my eyes were on Nate's crotch.

My voice was shaking and my hands were shaking too as I said, "C'mon, Nate, lemme see it."

"Y'all sure?"

"Oh, yeah, Nate. Please."

The cock was so huge that Nate had a hard time freeing it from his overalls. When he finally did, after much slow fumbling with his great hands, his cock pointed up, pointing straight at my face at a forty-five-degree angle. He was unclipped, and his foreskin was much darker than the rest of his teak skin. The shaft resembled many things—a baseball bat, a fencepost, an arm, a leg—and it was also strong, powerful. I knew from then on I would be comparing all those things (baseball bats and the like) to Nate's cock, and not the other way around. The base of Nate's massive cock was buried in a forest of curly stiff hairs. His balls, what I could see of them, were the size of baseballs. My eyes returned to the cock; it was bobbing up and down.

I was speechless, but William, always the instigator, was urging me on. "Go on," he said, "see if it's real." William's cock was still quite a memorable one, long and tapering, uncut, as was Nate's, but it bent in a curious way, kind of down and to the left, and the head was bulbous, what I called a sucking head. I loved William's cock, but now I had another one that needed—demanded—my immediate attention.

"It's real all right, and it ain't even really hard yet," Nate said, obviously happy with his cock. A thick droplet of creamy pre-cum dotted the end, and, as I looked from it to Nate's slightly smiling face, William said, "See if you can get it really hard, Johnnie."

I let go of William's prick, which, before this, had been the biggest one I'd ever laid eyes on, and shuffled over on my knees to Nate. Shyly at first, I touched it, stroked it. Sure enough, it started to grow to an impossible length and thickness, and William gasped. I looked over at him. He was blushing. I'm sure he had his own fantasy going on because he often mentioned that he thought Nate was fucking my ma, and every white girl within fifty miles. I knew it aroused him to think about Nate fucking all those women with this huge thing.

I was shocked and fascinated at the same time. It was all so new and exciting that I didn't know what I should be doing. I looked up at Nate again, but he had closed his eyes and he seemed to have gone elsewhere. I continued stroking his cock and eventually it was fully hard. Now, seeing how huge Nate really was, William was getting turned on. He began wildly jerking his prick.

"Oh, man, ya gotta suck it," William demanded.

I was still dubious. "Kiss it maybe," I said. "I'll never get it all in my mouth."

"Yeah, kiss it," Nate said, running his hand through my hair.

Wrapping both hands around it, I kissed the shaft, then gave it a lick. Nate smelled strange, much different from William. It was a rich odor that was not entirely unpleasant. The cock stench was as exhilarating as it was foul. I kissed and cleaned the foreskin with wide swipes of my tongue. I licked all around the base of the head, tasting the sweat, the manliness of the cock, and then, finally (with a groan from Nate), I put my full lips on the tip and eagerly swallowed the cum that coated it.

I opened my mouth wider and wider till my teeth were oh-so-gently tapping against the ridge of the hidden cockhead. Then, slowly, I started to push myself onto Nate's cock and pull his foreskin back. In my wide-open mouth, Nate's cock was like a stone covered in silk. Nate growled and his musclebound body vibrated.

"Oh, yeah," he moaned.

Encouraged now, I really got down to work. Both my mouth and hands were working on his cock, coaxing the sperm from it. Then it was too late. The cum began gushing into my hungry mouth.

Just then, William came as well, sending jets of cum onto the floor while I gulped and swallowed every last bit of Nate's, letting it flow down my throat and into my belly. Above me, Nate was covered with a sheen of sweat, and groaned and moaned and cried with the stunning power of his orgasm.

Standing up and wiping my mouth, chin, and face with a large red handkerchief, I smiled at Nate. "Sometime I want you to fuck me," I said.

"Johnnie!" William chortled. "Nate'd kill you, man!"

I tugged at Nate's still half-hard penis. "What a way to die."

"You ain't come yet," Nate said. "I could fuck you now."

Nate inhaled deeply when I dropped my pants and got on the bed on my knees. I looked behind me to see the stud stroking his cock to a righteous state of incredible readiness, considering he had just had an orgasm.

And with that, he spat into his hand and started to lube up my asshole. Then he carefully positioned himself over me and asked, "Ready?"

"Do it, Nate," William cried, standing beside the bed, stroking his cock to hardness again.

The laborer's cock was like an iron shaft gliding in and out of my most tender and excited opening. I cried out with pleasure as Nate fucked me, slowly at first, then with faster and ever-longer strokes, gripping his tool tightly, eyes shut in concentration. After a few minutes, Nate's skillful use of his cock had me close to coming and I begged William to get on the bed and fuck my mouth with his lovely cock while Nate fucked my ass.

Sweat was again pouring off Nate, and his dark eyes were fluttering with anticipation of a second orgasm. I had no idea how many young white boys Nate had fucked in his time, but it was obvious he got off on this kind of worship. William's cock slipped between my lips just as Nate exploded with a spasming jerk unlike any I had ever felt. As Nate plunged into my depths, seeking my very heart, my legs seemed to give out, and I came. William's cock slipped from my mouth as I fell to the mattress.

Staggering to his feet, Nate hitched up his battered overalls. Now, after he and I had come, it was real quiet. All you could hear was the cars roaring past on the highway and William panting as his orgasm approached.

Suddenly, William broke the silence, screaming "Oh, oh," as he too came for a second time.

Nate's voice was like chocolate. "Next time, I want you both. On your knees, before me."

Just the thought of it got me so turned on, I could hardly speak. "Yeah," I answered obediently. William nodded, but said nothing.

Quickly, Nate was gone.

But when "next time" rolled around, William was nowhere to be found. It was just Nate and me. Nate was painting one of the rooms and Ma told me to watch the office while she went to town. It was nearly noon and everyone had checked out, so the only possible interruption would have been the arrival of a new guest, which was doubtful considering how early it was. I hung out the "Back in a Minute" sign and rushed to the room where Nate was working.

I was breathless with excitement, almost coming in my pants, but managed to tell him we had at least half an hour.

"Shut the door," he ordered.

After bolting the door, I turned and saw he had already removed his prick from his jeans. He stared right at me, like I was a target, a thing to attack. I stood, spellbound, watching him stroke his enormous cock. It appeared even bigger than I had remembered.

He loved his cock, that was clear; the way he massaged it, taking it in his hand at the base and working up to the big tip. Then he'd slam his hand right back down onto his nuts, making the whole thing seem magnified. Then he would grab both balls into a big sac and point his dick the opposite way. This turned him on, and me, as well.

His smile gleamed down at me and he jerked a little faster. "Yeah, get right down 'fore I blast, boy."

I have no idea how long I stayed on my knees before him, kissing it, licking it, sucking it, but I lost track of time altogether. I was rudely brought back to reality when Nate cried, "Oh, boy, your mama just drove in."

"Shit."

Nate stuffed the monster back in his pants and went back to rolling on the paint. I opened the door just in time. Ma was happy to see I was "helping Nate" and said I could stay. This got Nate laughing, and he led me into the little bathroom of the unit, where he sat me down on the toilet and then opened his pants again. The cock was still semi-hard, or maybe it was always semi-hard.

Now, as I peeled back the foreskin, clear cum dripped from the piss slit. Barely touching the semi-hard cock with my lips, I lowered my mouth over it until the foreskin was touching the back of my throat. Saliva ran from my mouth and down the shaft of the pole, into the wiry, sweat-grimy pubic hairs.

As his swollen cock bucked, I hacked, spit, gasped for air. He pulled it out of my mouth and came. I felt the hot gush of his cum against my chest, coating me as jet after jet shot out.

I had managed to fish my own cock out of my shorts and I jacked off while I stared at the exploding prick before me. All I could hear was our ragged breathing as we pumped our dicks dry.

We cleaned up and went back to work, saying nothing more about it.

A couple of days later, Nate took me and William fishing on the lake behind the motel.

Giving head was easier for me than smoking. Nate laughed at me when I smoked, but he was relatively silent when I gave him a blowjob.

"Lil' Johnnie," Nate said, "breathe out befo' you breathe in, and you won't be coughin' like a little fool. I know you think you got to do everything like yo' ol' buddy Nathan, but the only reason I breathe in when I smoke sometimes is because ya'll are enough to drive anybody crazy. I don't know whether to smoke or breathe, so I just do both at the same time. Yo' mama got the same problem I do, and I think y'all is the cause. You boys is just too much. Now breathe out, boy." Then he turned his venom on William, who was reaching for another cigarette. "No, William, you can't have another Kool because I saw you th'ow that last one in the creek."

"Give 'im somethin' to suck on, Nate," I said, and Nate was always happy to hear that. He had his shirt off and I admired his chest. I kneaded his tits, both hard knots of dark flesh, lightly covered with hair. I stroked his sweat-matted chest, then his hairy, hard belly. Nate's eyes got big and his lips got stiff over his teeth, and his head started going from side to side.

William followed my hand with his eyes as I unbuttoned Nate's jeans and let loose the monster. William leaned over as the cock began swelling.

As we began stroking his big dick, Nate held our heads and said, "I don't know if y'all do me that way cuz you crazy and full of the devil, or because I'm a black man and you think you can get away with it. But I loves y'all."

"We love you, too, Nate," I said, raising up, letting William suck on the head of Nate's prick for a while.

"Gonna sit you right down on it, William. You'll like this." Nate lifted William over his cock and we watched it go in. William let out a scream.

"Fuck him like you fuck your women. Fuck his sweet ass!" I shouted, as William shoved his foreskinned prick into my face, slapping me again and again with it. I grabbed for it, put it in my mouth and let him fuck my mouth while he bounced up and down on Nate's prick, till they both came. When they met at the peak of their respective orgasms, they rocked and rolled so much I thought they would tip over the rowboat.

"Oh, oh yeah!"

I lingered between William's shaky legs, enjoying his cock, which I hadn't sucked in a while. I figured William had made himself scarce because he was afraid of Nate, but whatever his fears, he was okay with it

46

now. More than okay with it, really. Behind him, Nate smiled, slowly removing the long prick from the tight tunnel of William's sweet, brave asshole. William grunted and I leaned in carefully and pressed my lips against his, tenderly, with feeling. William returned all of my affection and more.

When Nate was killed in an accident while he was driving the old church bus a year or so later, we were all very sad. He had the biggest cock I've ever known, and he was sweet about sharing it with us. He was one of the most gentle people we had ever met, and when he wasn't singing, he was laughing and joking, keeping the rhythm going. He sang in a high, powerful voice, and he could sing Soul like James Brown or Aretha Franklin, but the room rocked when he sang gospel. And that day he showed us his prick he made us into True Believers. And every time we held it in our hands, sucked it, or took it up our asses, we said, "Praise the Lord!"

HOT LOAD

Hauling a load down the interstate can be boring, and a little company can make the trip seem much shorter—especially if the hitchhiker is a cute young thing like Johnny. Pete had started out to deliver just one load, but by the time this haul was over, he had delivered an amazing number of them. —JB

"It's big." Johnny stared at the idling Peterbilt and the driver, nicknamed Pete after his truck. Johnny'd seen big trucks, sure, but this was the first time he'd ever stood next to one, ready to take a ride. He'd also seen big men before, but none as big as Pete, and he was ready to take a ride on Pete's cock, if he'd let him. Chances were good, though. He'd only known Pete for a few minutes and now he was about to climb into the cab and ride off into the sunset with him.

"Well, pretty boy," Pete said, breathing warmly on his neck, "I'll bring you home safe and sound. Just put your foot right there and reach for that bar and swing yourself up into the seat."

Soon Johnny was resting in the hydraulic passenger seat.

"What do you think of it?" Pete asked, flashing a big grin.

Johnny looked down at Pete's crotch and smiled. "It's big."

Pete went right on grinning as he fiddled with the CB, trying to clear the static from the nearby motors. Johnny held his hands over his ears.

"Soon as we get on the interstate we'll be fine," Pete said, shifting out of neutral.

Johnny noticed Pete's tight jeans were faded across the thighs. The sun coming through the windshield had done that, and his lizard-skin cowboy boots gleamed from a coat of polish applied during a layover the day before.

"A good boy and a good dog are always ready to go for a ride," Pete said as they roared onto the interstate. Johnny could feel his eyes glancing his way. "Let me know if you need anything."

"Okay," Johnny said, staring at the highway ahead of them. The yellow lines were mesmerizing and the cars they passed looked so small; Johnny'd never looked down on motorists before. The famous Sunshine State tourist traps slipped by, a kaleidoscope of tackiness, as Pete drove at a steady, efficient 70 mph. They flew past the Disney World exit and Johnny felt his stomach churn. He remembered the time his mother took him there. What a wonderful day they had. It was the only place she had ever taken him, except to the movies. He was beginning to feel homesick already. Johnny had always made a joke about running away, but actually doing it was something else again.

48

They stopped for supper outside Ocala.

"Order anything you like," Pete told the boy. He ordered chicken-fried steak, baked potato, tossed salad with blue cheese dressing, and headed for the john.

"I'll have the same," Johnny told the waitress.

Pete came out of the restroom with his sandy blond hair slicked back and a big grin on his face. He said the truck would be fueled by the time they were done with their food.

Pete cut into his steak. "So how do you like being on the road?"

"Fine so far," Johnny said. He finished his Mountain Dew and asked for more. Riding had made him thirsty.

Pete's eyes were clear, calm, kind. He smelled faintly of toothpaste and soap. He seemed like a nice man to Johnny. They had struck up a conversation at the Stuckey's just off the interstate near Fort Myers. Pete had seen Johnny's duffel bag sitting next to his stool at the counter and had asked him where he was headed.

"Home," Johnny answered matter-of-factly.

"Oh, you just visitin', are you?"

"Yeah, a friend of mine brought me down here, to see the sights and all, but he up and left me." Johnny shook his head. "It's a long story."

"Damn shame when you can't trust your friends," Pete had said.

They ate in silence for awhile, then, talking around mouthfuls of food, Pete said, "I hope we can drop this load early."

Johnny thought again of Pete's abundant crotch and nodded, "Yeah, I hope so too." He didn't want to appear too eager; maybe Pete wasn't gay after all, just friendly. Still, he'd heard stories about truckers who took their fun where they could find it. He'd never had a trucker and he figured it was about time.

"Take a nap," Pete suggested when they got back to the truck and he saw Johnny was yawning.

"Okay," Johnny said, moving over to the doghouse. Looking out, Johnny saw that the big rigs owned the night. They barreled past one another like giants in a race. With the vehicle's swaying movement, he soon fell fast asleep, only to be awakened by the clashing of gears. Pete was backing the truck up to a loading dock between an idling Mack and a silent Kenworth.

"Keep it warm for me, pretty boy," he said as he left the cab.

The cab began to sway as forklifts unloaded the trailer behind them and when the unloading was finished, Pete turned in his paperwork and they were back on the road. Pete steered smoothly onto a dark, silent street in Gainesville.

"You want something to eat?" he asked. "I have to make a call."

"Yeah," Johnny said; he was always at least a little bit hungry. Besides he was uncomfortable; the truck rode rough without a load.

They stopped near the interstate. Johnny found the restroom while Pete looked for the phones.

As Johnny came out of the john, he heard Pete on the phone, shouting to make himself heard over the video games by the bank of phones. "You know I love you, honey bunch. Don't I call every damn chance I get? Give the kids a big kiss for me."

Johnny grinned as he walked over to the counter and ordered a piece of apple pie with ice cream. He'd always wanted to be with a married man. Now he was with a married trucker with little kids! He smiled broadly as the waitress brought him his pie.

Soon Pete was sliding down on the stool next to him. "Well, you'll be back home before morning. You did say you were goin' to Tallahassee, right?"

"Well, no, not exactly."

"I coulda sworn that's what you said."

"No. Truth is, I'm runnin' away from home. I really don't care where I go as long as it's not back to Fort Myers."

Pete's eyes were wide. "You mean I got a hot load on my hands?"

Johnny chuckled. "Yeah, I guess."

Pete asked the waitress for a cup of coffee and he sat quietly drinking it, deep in thought. Finally, when he saw Johnny had finished his pie, he said, "Well, when a man's got a hot load, best thing he can do is move it fast. Let's go."

Once outside, Pete pulled the rig around to the back of the truck stop. "You know, I think we oughta get some shut-eye and think this thing through in the morning."

"Okay," Johnny said.

Pete told Johnny to wait in the truck while he registered at the motel office.

The room was sparse but adequate. There were two double beds, plenty of towels, a TV, and a Gideon bible on the table between the beds.

Pete went straight to the bathroom and began taking a shower. Johnny sat on the edge of a bed, fiddling with the remote control for the TV. Old movies, news headlines, religious programs, the weather. He settled on the horror movie, flipped off his sneakers and lay back on the bed, propping his head up with the pillows.

Pete came out of the bathroom with a towel wrapped around his waist. He was drying his hair with another towel. "What's on?" he asked, staring at the TV.

"I think it's 'The Bride of Frankenstein.'"

"I thought you were sleepy."

"This'll put me to sleep."

"You gonna sleep in those clothes?" Pete asked, dropping down on the edge of the other bed.

"No, I guess not."

"Bathroom's all yours."

"Thanks," Johnny said, lifting himself from the bed. He walked slowly toward the bathroom, his eyes on the screen. "This is a good part," he said, standing in front of the TV.

"Then get outta the way," Pete said, grabbing him and pushing him aside. But his meaty hands didn't leave Johnny's shoulders; they held him tightly and Pete breathed on his neck.

Johnny squirmed. "My neck hurts from sleeping in that doghouse."

"Oh? You want me to rub it for you?"

Johnny gulped. "Yeah, that'd be nice."

Pete began kneading Johnny's neck and shoulders.

"Oh, that feels so good," the boy sighed.

"It'd feel better if you'd take this damn shirt off."

Johnny was quick to comply. He already had an erection and he dangled the shirt in front of it.

As the massage continued Johnny dropped his shirt to the floor and brought his hands back, running his fingers along his thighs, and then groping Pete's crotch. His heart began to pound as he realized how well-hung the trucker was, measuring with his hands the long, thick cock throbbing under the towel.

"You like that, don't you?" Pete said, turning Johnny around, "Why don't you take a real good look?"

Johnny did what he was told, lifting the towel away, revealing the biggest penis he had ever seen. He held it in his hand, watching it twitch and swell even larger.

"Play with it," Pete growled, spreading his legs wide. Turned on by the older man's new coarseness, Johnny stroked the thick, vein-gnarled shaft. "You know what I wanna to do with that big dick?"

When Johnny shook his head, Pete chuckled. "Well, I wanna pull those pants down around your knees, and put it up your little butt, then fuck you till you howl for mercy. You'd like that, wouldn't you?"

"Yes," Johnny breathed, his voice barely a whisper.

"What?" he asked, bringing his hand to Johnny's face, caressing his cheek.

"Yes," Johnny said, louder now.

Pete crammed a finger into the boy's mouth, and Johnny sucked on it greedily, treating it as if it was Pete's hard cock.

"Oh, but first you want to suck it, is that it?"

Johnny nodded and dropped to his knees between Pete's massive thighs. The cock knob was ruddy, fat, helmet-shaped. Johnny probed the salty slit with his tongue, savoring the taste of the stud. Then he took him deep in his throat. Pete leaned over him, massaged his ass through the fabric of his jeans.

Pete was hung long and thick and the slight curve of the shaft allowed it to slip easily down Johnny's hungry throat. Johnny lunged forward, swallowing him till Pete's balls bounced against his chin, then slowly pulled back. His lips were tight and his tongue moved slowly all along the tender underbelly of the cock.

Johnny swirled his mouth over it, not really sure of what to do with it. Pete grabbed the back of his neck and showed the boy what he wanted. He slowly fed the cock into Johnny's mouth, a little at a time, telling him to take it slow and easy when the boy took too much at once. Finally Johnny developed a good rhythm and Pete howled, "Hey, you've done this before," as he leaned back onto the mattress and watched Johnny go at it feverishly. "Damned if you haven't. Here I thought you was a virgin boy."

After a few minutes, Pete said, "And you've probably been fucked before, too, eh?"

Johnny nodded and, letting the cock pop out of his mouth, he said, "But it wasn't as big as this."

"Some little squirt at school, eh?"

Johnny nodded.

"Well, then you're ready for a man-sized piece of meat, ain'tcha?"

Johnny had to admit he'd been ready for *this* meat when he first saw the bulge in Pete's jeans at Stuckey's.

Johnny took one last suck, swallowing convulsively, tightening his throat along the shaft of the cock, then he stood up and unbuckled his pants. As he slipped them off, Pete's appraising eyes lingered on the slender, nearly hairless body, the respectable six-inch, cut prick jutting up high in the air from a small patch of pubic hair. Pete made room on the bed for Johnny and took him into his arms as he climbed on. He tweaked the boy's nipples and tenderly ran his hands up and down the firm young torso.

"You're a pretty boy all right," he said, his hands coming to rest on the asscheeks. He shifted so that Johnny could lie on his stomach.

Soon Johnny felt Pete's sweaty hands being replaced by his lips on his ass, his tongue occasionally plunging in. Johnny shivered and groaned when Pete inserted his finger. As Pete kissed his neck and fingered his hole, Johnny's hard cock was rubbing against the sheet.

"You want my cock up there?"

"Please. Yes, please," Johnny begged, his big brown eyes flashing.

"Okay, pretty boy." Pete positioned the knob of his cock against the throbbing hole, grabbed both cheeks and slowly inserted it. Johnny squirmed. Pete took it slow, not letting up the pressure until their balls banged together and his enormous prick was in to the hilt.

Johnny had never felt anything quite like the sensation of Pete's big dick pumping in and out of his body.

"Keep squeezin' it," Pete growled, smacking the boy's butt with his open palm several times as he pounded rhythmically. After a while, he pulled out and rolled Johnny over, slipping his big hands under the boy's arms; he pulled him up against him, and took his head in his hands.

He pressed the head of his cock into the hole and hunched his hips forward. At first, only the head and a couple of inches of the shaft were in Johnny. Finally, his thrusts became more powerful, driving inch after inch of the thick shaft up into the boy's ass until it was again all the way in. Then he slipped his arms around Johnny and sat up, pulling the boy along with him. He leaned back, bracing his hands on the bed behind him. "Now you fuck it," he moaned, his eyelids fluttering as Johnny clenched his ass ring down tight around the base of the prick. Johnny crouched over Pete, gripped his shoulders tight, and began to gyrate his hips.

Johnny looked into the mirror to watch Pete pistoning in and out of his hole as he bounced up and down on it, impaling himself ecstatically. He jacked off in this position, sending glistening white droplets flying. Then he lifted himself away from the cock, wanting to take it while he knelt.

Pete got behind him and Johnny reached down to guide the monster dick back into his ass. He rubbed his back against Pete's torso as the older man's arms encircled his chest and he started to fuck him.

Pete pushed Johnny down and, pressing his face against the boy's neck, his breath was soon coming in labored snorts. "Oh, shit!" he cried, hips pounding, eyelashes fluttering as he began shooting bursts of cum deep into the boy's quivering ass. When he finished, he collapsed on top of Johnny and held him tight. Johnny fell asleep with Pete's glorious cock still deep in his ass, swimming in the cum that filled it.

In the morning, when Pete came from the bathroom, a towel wrapped around his waist, he saw Johnny, dressed in a clean pair of powder-blue shorts and a Mickey Mouse T-shirt, a souvenir of his trip to Disney World, perched on the edge of the bed ready to go to breakfast.

"God, you're pretty this morning," Pete said, pushing him back onto the sagging mattress.

The boy moaned softly as Pete began playing with his curving pecs and, in just seconds, his pointy nipples were trying to poke holes in his T-shirt. A quick glance told Pete that the bulge in Johnny's crotch was beginning to swell up nicely as well.

Johnny responded immediately to the tit play, and in less than two minutes Pete had his T-shirt pushed up under his armpits. With one hand cupping and fondling his smooth chest, Pete used his free hand to unzip the boy's fly and open it wide. Johnny's cock rose up tall and proud through the open gap. Ignoring it, Pete forced his hand down between his thighs. Curving his fingers under Johnny's balls, he found the still-moist asshole and eased two fingers right in. Johnny got wide-eyed at this quick action, and he groaned as the speed of the finger-fucking increased. He looked startled when Pete abruptly pulled his fingers out and took off his tennis shoes and tugged his shorts off over his feet, throwing them into the corner.

"I thought we were going to eat breakfast," Johnny said.

"Breakfast can wait."

Johnny whimpered when he felt Pete's naked body pressing him onto his back.

Pete's hands cupped Johnny's wondrous buttocks, lifting his body off the mattress slightly, squeezing and fondling the lush mounds. Pete's cock nudged into the crack, his hardness separating the trembling buttocks with ease. He plowed into him with one steady slide. To torment him a little, he drew out again until just the enormous head was captured by the boy's tight ass ring. He held himself motionless, waiting for Johnny to thrust his hips to get more of the cock back inside.

"Oh," Johnny sighed, humping up against Pete.

When all ten inches were lodged inside Johnny, Pete began to pump. Johnny turned his head and Pete could see him grimacing as he writhed beneath him, moaning as he plunged his cock steadily in and out.

After a while, Pete got on his back with Johnny on top. Johnny straddled him and began riding Pete's prick wildly. With a steady rhythm, his ass kept rising and falling, working the full length of the cock up and down. Soon he was squealing, then gasping, coming with a mighty spurt, splattering Pete's chest, squeezing Pete's cock so tight that Pete came himself, without much cum but with considerable relief.

Johnny stayed in the saddle and, rubbing his cum into Pete's skin, he asked, "Can we have breakfast now?"

At breakfast, Pete listened patiently as Johnny told him all about his troubles at school and at home with his mother. Johnny was too pretty to be a boy, Pete decided, and it didn't help matters that he liked art, music and books more than football, or that his mother was hardly ever home, having to work two jobs to support them since his father died when he was five. It was a tough life. Pete had heard similar woeful litanies before, but no one had spoken quite so heart-wrenchingly as Johnny.

Pete had gotten so he wouldn't bother with hitchers, especially ones over twenty-five. They could be downright dangerous. He'd begun to prefer the young runaways but even then, most of them were just too much trouble. Still, he got horny and he kept telling himself he was being faithful to his wife by fucking only boys on the road. Besides, they appreciated it more than the waitresses at the truck stops. The gay guys really got off on his muscular six foot-four frame and when they saw his dick, well, there was no stopping them.

Now Pete had a deal for Johnny. He told him if he went back home, returned to school, he'd stop in Fort Myers every time he passed through and they'd spend a few hours together. "I know that's not much of a reward for finishing school, but.... "

"It's good enough for me."

Pete was pleased Johnny had seen the light. He had two daughters at home and his wife had lost the boy she was carrying. He could never have a son now, and Johnny brought out the daddy in him. Besides, if Johnny agreed to go home, Pete wouldn't have to go out of his way to take him to Tallahassee, which he was fully prepared to do, and could probably pick up a load in Ocala to take back to Miami. Yeah, Pete thought, the day was starting out pretty good.

Pete grinned and suggested, "Why don't we go back to the room for a few minutes before we shove off?"

Johnny's eyes sparkled and he said, "Sounds good to me."

Back in the room, Pete was again aiming his prick at Johnny's butthole, amazed at how easily it slid in, how the boy practically sucked him inside.

Pete sat back on his heels. He always liked to watch his meat slide in and out of a cunt or butthole. Now the contrast of his leathery dark skin against the lily white of Johnny's buns was thrilling him beyond belief.

"You've been a bad boy, haven't you, lying to me like that." *Slap!* Pete whacked Johnny's ass. *Slap! Slap!* He whacked it some more.

"Oh, yeah, spank me. I've been a bad boy. I deserve it."

Soon Johnny's butt was rosy red and Pete could see his imprints of his hands where he'd bruised the skin. He got up on his haunches like an animal and began fucking the boy wildly.

Johnny started bucking underneath him, his butt muscles clamped around Pete's cock. Pete was sweating profusely, breathing hard. Johnny's back glistened as Pete's sweat dripped onto it. Suddenly, close to coming, Pete stopped. He rolled Johnny over and fucked him with his legs flailing in the air.

With his ankles riding on Pete's shoulders, Johnny moaned, "Oh, God," as Pete hovered over him and buried his cock balls-deep up Johnny's spasming anus. Pete firmly gripped a buttock in each hand, slowly raising and lowering the boy's butt while he smoothly worked the full length of his cock in and out of his ass. Soon Pete could feel the intense contractions of the boy's ass around his cock and soon Johnny was having another orgasm, jerking away as Pete plunged into him again, coming himself, this time no more than a dribble. Then, reluctantly, he slid it out.

They slept until noon and Johnny was groggy with sleep when Pete pulled him up on all fours in the middle of the messy bed. He held the boy's hips in a tight grip while his cock entered again and began slamming against the jiggling ass cheeks. Johnny's ass was soon rotating and Pete wrapped his arm around his throat, resting his hand on his opposite shoulder. Pete could feel Johnny swallow hard as the inside of his arm pulled the boy more upright. Johnny's heels pressed against Pete's big buttocks, as Pete's hand moved slowly up and down his back.

Pete smiled and pressed his lips against the back of the boy's neck as Johnny began quivering in agony while the fucking continued. Pete looked down to see Johnny's cock was hard and he was stroking it feverishly. Johnny wiggled around on the cock inside his ass as he came again, to the pleasure of an astonished Pete. The older man had never been with anyone who could take him so repeatedly. Johnny could, he decided, take everything he had to offer and perhaps even more.

As much as Pete wanted to keep the boy with him the entire day, he knew their idyll had to come to an end. By the time they reached Fort Myers, the sun was setting and they stopped for supper. Before getting out of the cab, Johnny brought his hands to Pete's crotch and started kneading it. Pete cleared his throat and moved the truck to the far end of the parking lot. There, as it turned dark, Johnny gave him a blowjob that he would not soon forget.

Johnny started by taking hold of the big penis, pumping it slowly with a tight grip of his fingers. Then he took Pete's balls in his hand and rolled them inside the sack with his fingers. Johnny rubbed his nose in Pete's crotch, inhaling the rich, musky smell of him. Pete pushed his penis inside Johnny's mouth and began rocking back and forth, ramming Johnny's face with a steady rhythm. After a few moments, he rested, wanting to prolong it. Johnny worked his tongue back and forth on the erect cock, licked the pre-cum from the head, sucked it, drawing it out, twisting it with his mouth. When he took it deep, Pete moaned, his thighs opening and closing in ecstasy. In another moment he exploded, crying out as his eyes rolled up in his head. He started squirting into Johnny's mouth. Johnny's cheeks bulged as he tried to force Pete back, a gob of semen spurting out from one corner of his lips as the pressure became too great.

Johnny continued gulping, his mouth pulling at the cock until it was completely drained. When at last the cock left his mouth it was limp and wet.

Pete considered that no one had sucked him like that in years. The boy laid his head on Pete's thigh and idly toyed with the massive penis he had just drained. Pete ran his fingers through Johnny's tousled brown hair and, with the other hand, he hugged the youngster to him.

Pete brought the rig to a halt on U.S. 41 about two blocks from Johnny's house. "Always take good advice," Pete said, pressing his hand against Johnny's back and pushing him out of the cab.

"I will. Thanks for the ride."

Pete reached over to touch him on the cheek. "Catch you on the flip flop."

"Ten-four," Johnny said, grinning.

Pete sat in the truck watching the boy trudge wearily down the street, illuminated by the headlights. When the boy was finally out of sight, Pete smiled. "Ten-four, little buddy," he said, and smacked his lips.

SATIN

The narrator of this short story from the anthology Come Again *is troubled by his inability to understand his sublimated, unwelcome fascination with a drag queen.* —JB

I lose out on the dark, sexy hunk and I don't think my luck can get much worse, but I am wrong. I offer to give Eddie a ride home from the bar. He too lost out on the one he'd been pursuing and, as always, I take pity on Eddie. Once I took so much pity on him I let him blow me in the john. It wasn't a bad blowjob—rather good, as a matter of fact—but nothing I wanted to repeat. The very nelly Eddie is simply not my type.

"Steve-ee," Eddie says softly. I turn and look at him. His face is a crumbling, ashy white, except for the reddened lips. He's sunken down in the leather seat of my black Lincoln Towncar and he has the most bizarre expression on his face; it is hard to place at first, looking up at me, eyebrows raised, a hint of a smile, the hint of a tongue at the back of his open mouth, until I realize that he has slipped into his drag mode again. Then I see the rest of it: His shirt and pants are open and he is wearing red satin panties, too small to hold his balls, which are slipping out the sides; the head of his now hard uncut cock seems to be winking at me; and he's fingering the red satin. "I put these on just for you," he says.

"C'mon, Eddie," I say.

"Tell me what you're wearing," he says.

"Eddie, this isn't my scene." I'm edging myself as close as possible to the door.

"I bet you have on those same white cotton Calvins you had on that night you let me…" He puts a hand around my wrist and locks on. With the other one he's rubbing himself. "Just touch it. Just touch it and see how much I want you."

"Eddie, you're really fuckin' out of line," I shout.

"I just wantcha to touch it, Steve-ee." He's strong as hell, for a nelly shit, and pulls on my wrist. I yank back hard, dragging his body closer to mine. He starts to half-slide, half-crawl toward me. I'm practically up on my feet in the car to avoid having to touch him. Eddie's head slides down into my lap with a kind of whining and grunting noise, like an infant.

I slow the car to a crawl and yank him off me. He slams against the door, stunned. I hit him in the rib cage, hard. He's still making that noise, like a child; it enrages me. I hit him again, and again, just bringing my fist down like a gavel on his side. Something seems to crack a little bit. He groans. I pull the car to a stop. I reach over him and push open the door. I shove, hard. It takes some doing but I manage to get him off the seat and onto the soft shoulder of the road. He cries out, begging me not to leave him.

Suddenly a car passes, its lights putting Eddie in the spotlight, as if back at the bar, on the stage. I gasp at the pitiful sight. He reminds me of that dethroned queen Cookie, sitting alone night after night, having seen far better nights, waiting to be picked up. I once made the mistake of sitting down next to her (or, rather, him, because his real name is Clyde) when I first moved down here. In those days I hadn't made up my mind about drag. I was both fascinated and repelled. Maybe it went back to when my dad paid for me to see a psychiatrist. The doc said, "You should be seeing a boyish girl, not a girlish boy." Well, I tried that, but it didn't work out. My dad said the girl was a lesbian.

Cookie seemed to have more brains than any psychiatrist I saw. She told me about the guy who wouldn't take her out because she was from London. "Honey, a queen is a queen," Cookie said, lighting up a Marlboro Light with a theatrical flair, "no matter where you're from." I told her about my bad times with my dad. She said, "When I told my parents I was a drag queen, I could just see their faces over the phone. Being gay is one thing, but a drag queen on top of it? My, oh my!"

Cookie tried to set me straight, as it were: "Drag is an art form," she said. "And just the same as an artist paints a picture, we paint and present ourselves as a form of art, our canvas being ourselves."

Eddie does not look at all artful now, on his knees in the ditch crying out to me. Maybe if he were in full drag I'd like him better. He's a kinda cute boy in some respects, but he's wearing red satin underpants, for God's sake!

But there I go, making judgments again. "Let's not criticize all the time," Cookie had once told me, "let's harmonize." I'll always regret never letting her harmonize over my body.

I blink back to the present. I am out of the car, standing over Eddie, and for some reason I am unable to move. Then he grabs my legs. "Please, Steve-ee," he coos.

"Okay, bitch. I'll take you home. But I want you to put on a show for me. I want to see you in drag. None of this half-assed playin' around in satin underpants."

"Oh, no, Steve-ee, no more half-assed anything."

Fucking can lead to enlightenment, Marco Vassi said once. Fucking can lead to many things. It can also be a bummer sometimes. I am thinking this is one of those times. I am waiting for Eddie in his bedroom, sitting on his brass double bed with the red satin sheets. It's all very comfortable. He says his parents pay him to live here, to stay away from them.

A dress like one Carol Channing wore in "Hello, Dolly!" is hanging in the closet. I remember what someone at the bar had once told me: that Eddie played a great Channing. He lip-synched to "Before the Parade

Passes By" in a drag contest at the bar one night, and won second place. That was his one time in the spotlight, I guess. Nothing since—and a year in hiding, because he didn't win first prize.

I strip to my briefs, begin to wonder what's taking him so long. I get up and go into the bathroom. He shuts off the water and reaches over the stall for his towel. He emerges from the shower wrapped in terrycloth from his armpits down.

"You want the shower?" he asks.

"No," I say, "I want to talk to you."

He looks at me with his large brown eyes. He's taken his shiny brown hair out of the ponytail and it now frames his face. He flutters his long lashes at me and slides a hand across my arm. "What, Steve-ee? What did you want to talk about?"

I feel a silly thickness in my throat as I eye this boy, who is a boy but not really a boy. A thing. I lean forward and take Eddie by the shoulders. I kiss him quickly on the lips, just to see what it would be like. He's got sweet breath and there's a strange shudder between my legs, one that I immediately feel guilty about. This is a queen, I tell myself, what the fuck am I doing?

Eddie giggles and I watch his butt as he drops the towel and walks away, his firm, hairless little cheeks moving in a disturbing rhythm. I stand looking after him for a few moments, even after he's gone.

I can't believe it but my tongue is up Eddie's butt, or what he calls his *pussy*, and he is groaning in gratitude. This is an acquired taste, but a delicious one. I must admit I really like licking between his legs, first the butthole, then the balls, then the cock. Then back again, deeper and deeper, until he's begging. I can't imagine any of my friends would understand this; it's a rush that I can't quite comprehend myself. But it's hard to concentrate on such questions when Eddie is sucking your cock. He makes me come, but he isn't done. Not by a long shot. And thank god because, as exquisite as the blowjob was, I do want to fuck him. This is raw, vital sex. Pure sex.

Desire coming from a bottom, waiting for me, eager for me, has always gotten me hard and kept me hard. But this is new to me, talking sweetly to a boy as if he were a girl. He's on his knees, presenting his glorious ass, "Fuck my pussy," he begs. "Fuck it."

My dick slides into him as if we were built for each other. No one has ever appreciated my cock more than Eddie, if all his moaning and groaning can be believed. He comes, but tells me to stay in, to keep on, come myself. And I do.

I feel the satin sheet under us become steadily more soaked with sweat, saliva, and cum. Eddie gets up. "Just for a sec, Steve-e," and he goes into the bathroom.

My heart is pounding in my ears after he returns and gets into position again. There is no end to this, I have found; Eddie can take it all and beg for more. The head of my dick pops into his ass and he whimpers, as if it's hurting him, and slowly, carefully, I press my entire length into him again. I pull almost all the way out, then slam back in. He's stopped whimpering; now he seems to be actually crying, but still begging for me to continue. We're like a fucking machine, two parts moving together perfectly. His hands are all over me now as he begins to come. He has a fierce, shuddering orgasm that seems to go on forever as I stare into his eyes.

"Yeah, come for me, Eddie." Eddie. It's the first time I've said his name.

"Steve-ee!" he shrieks as the last of the cum is ejected from his little cock.

But damned if he's still not through. He wants to suck me again. I love having him on his knees in front of me, his throat milking me. I grab his hair, relax and enjoy his incredible ability. He can take the full length of me without gagging. He watches me the entire time, lets me see the tears that fill his eyes and roll down his cheeks as my cock-head fills his throat and presses even further while he sucks. Where it comes from I have no idea, but more sperm eventually spurts from me and he takes it all.

"Maybe I'll see you again?" Eddie asks hopefully as I later pull my clothes on. I shrug, as if not to rule out the possibility.

*   *   *

I see him leave the apartment building, follow his Volkswagen to the bar. They let me go backstage. I am transfixed as I watch him from the door of his dressing room. He has transformed himself into Carol Channing again, the Channing of the '60s, not the self-caricature of the '90s. Now that I have seen him in full drag I am impressed. "Eddie," I finally manage to whisper.

He is surprised to see me, interrupts his primping. "How do I look?"

"Fine, hon ....," I say, terrified now. I nearly called him "honey," a term I despise. I have come too close to this scene. It is a nightmare from which I must shake myself awake. I run out of the room, out of the bar, into the street.

I sit in my car smoking a joint, coming to terms with this crazy attraction we have for one another. I decide I will go back to the bar, take him from that place and bring him back to his room. And we'll fuck again, there in that satin-sheeted bed. And we'll sleep together this time. And in the morning we'll talk about what it all means.

Yes, that's what we'll do.

THE KIDS AT THE MALL - AND KENNY FROM KENTUCKY

The mall rats weren't doing anything for him, and besides that hot Texas masseur was waiting. But it was young Kenny from Kentucky that really made his day. First published in the collection In the Boy Zone. *—JB*

"Oh those kids at the mall, I just love 'em," my friend Steve gushed over the phone. He'd just returned from 'shopping,' but Steve never buys anything when he goes to the mall, he just cruises the shoppers. More accurately, he cruises the kids. "Why don't you write about 'em?" he asked.

"I write about what I know. I don't know any kids at the mall. In fact, I hate malls. I hate to shop, period."

"Well, you're missing something."

So, not wanting to miss anything in this short life, on my next trip to Fort Lauderdale I decided to go shopping. The weather conspired to convince me to do it; it was raining and I decided to go to the upscale mall called The Galleria, where at least I could park under the building and not get soaked.

Not too many kids seemed to go to Saks or Cartier, the shops that might interest me, so I walked the entire length of The Galleria and back again, just so I wouldn't miss anything. I found the most horrifying thing about the kids I did see was their hair. The youngsters in every generation seem to display their rebellion in the way they treat their hair, but these latest ones, I thought, were going a bit too far. Some shaved it completely, some had it shaved in funny ways but, thankfully, most wore baseball caps— mostly turned backward—so it was difficult to tell. At least no kid at The Galleria had dyed his hair magenta like Macaulay Culkin had recently. Now that would have been the limit.

Another horrifying thing was that kids today certainly don't want to show anything off. They wear baggy shorts and oversized T-shirts, usually commemorating the last rock concert they went to. (And why do their sneakers have to be so big and black?) I decided what I'd really like to see was some of these kids naked in the showers at school. Now that would be *awesome*, as they like to say.

On the way back to my hotel, I drove along the Ocean. I was dismayed to find that the site of many of my more decadent revels in the Seventies and the Eighties, the Marlin Beach Hotel—which had once towered over its neighbors—was now just a dirt field. A sign informed me that this site would soon be occupied by "Beachplace," with more places to shop, including a Gap and a Banana Republic. Now that's progress!

After this revelation, I was badly in need of a drink, but wanted to try the new masseur from Texas I had discovered. J.R.—that's how he advertised himself—claimed to give a wonderful massage and, wouldn't you know it, had a "hankerin' for big, uncut cocks." He proved to be true to his word. When he finished, I felt refreshed but still in need of a drink.

The Bus Stop Bar was practically deserted at five on a Friday afternoon. I wondered where all the boys had gone but was too polite to ask. Suddenly the door opened and in popped a youth who could easily have been one of those kids from the mall, and his oversized T-shirt was emblazoned, "I'll Do Anything, Just Ask." It was doubtful that any kid at the mall would have been bold enough to wear that! Unfortunately, he was accompanied by a gent wearing a tie, who was at least 75. They sat across from me and the boy lit a cigarette. Now I noticed he had a loop and two studs in his left ear. I forgave him both those transgressions because he was cute and seemed so friendly, chatting up all the older gents near them. I figured him for a regular. Just as their drinks were served, he returned to talking with the man wearing the tie and ignored me. Suddenly, almost as quickly as they had come it seemed, they were gone.

A few minutes later, clutching the latest issue of *Hot Spots*, I made my own exit. No one urged me to stay or even to "come back soon."

I left the parking lot and was forced by the signs to turn right. As I approached the next intersection, who should be waiting at a *real* bus stop but "I'll Do Anything"! I made a quick turn into the parking lot and lowered the window.

He looked over at me and smiled. He seemed to recognize me from the bar. He was now carrying a boom box—blessedly, turned off.

"Need a lift?" I offered.

"Yeah, sure," he said with a wide grin, ambling over.

He was a bit taller than I usually go for but he did have the dirty blond hair and slender body I prefer.

When he was seated in the car, with his boom box stowed in the back seat, I said, "I thought you were with the guy with the tie."

"Hank? Oh, no. A friend of mine borrowed my radio, brought it up here and pawned it."

"Nice friends."

"Well, Hank helped me get it out of hock."

"Now he *is* a friend. But no sex?"

"No. He says he's too old, that he might have a heart attack."

"Boys need at least one friend like that."

By this time I was headed back to my hotel. Still, I wanted to get things straight, so to speak. "How much do you charge?"

"Depends. What do you like to do?"

"Oh, I'm easy."

He smiled. "I usually get forty."

Forty? Oh, yes, it was off-season, I hastened to remind myself. You always get a bargain in the off-season. "Do you have a regular job?"

"During the season, at the Sheraton. Now I just hang out."

Now he was massaging my groin. He was either in a hurry or he really got into this.

I pulled into the hotel's parking lot as he was unzipping my pants, eager to get to the hard-on he had caused.

"Wait," I said. "We're here."

I needed to know his name. I asked.

"Kenny."

Perfect.

Moments later, he was on the bed, me kneeling over his naked chest.

"Hmmm, I love uncut cocks," he sighed, pulling the foreskin back and closely examining the head of my erection. The second 'natural man' fan that day. Truly amazing. He began nibbling on my cock. He was hungry. Soon he was sucking like there was no tomorrow.

"Where did you learn to do that?" I finally asked.

"You know how it is back in the hills of Kentucky."

"No, not really, but I wish I did. When did you start suckin' dick?"

"When I was six."

"*Six?*"

"Yeah. It was a lot of fun until my brothers discovered they were straight."

"That occurs at about fourteen or fifteen. Older if you're lucky."

Talk about luck! An incredible spark of lust and excitement jolted up through my cock. He reamed and twisted and slammed my dick deep down his throat until I felt my load quickly boiling up. I was so close, yet I held back, feeling swept away by a maelstrom of fears and joys beyond my understanding. A low groan of pleasure escaped my lips and I knew for certain I wanted this Kentucky babe to do more than just this.

His hand on my thigh slid slowly upward, sending shivers up my spine. He stopped inches from my balls and started backing down again, murmuring something to himself about softness. Next his left hand reached out to glide across my hairy chest. His own nearly hairless chest was dappled with sweat. His eyes slipped shut as he tweaked my nipples while he continued sucking my cock with world-class fervor, as if he was determined to suck out every possible ounce of cum I could muster. He kept screwing my right tit and then my left until they both were numb.

I felt my body shiver and thrash, my hips convulsing upward as they fucked his mouth. The more I moaned and groaned, the faster his mouth worked and the more self-satisfied his grunts of pleasure became. Finally, I stopped resisting the inevitable and began coming. His grunts of appreciation grew louder as he released my cock from his mouth and watched it spurt on his chest. My own groans of pleasure rivaled his, and then, exhausted, I lifted myself from him and lay on my back next to him. He gave my spent cock one last squeeze and then bounded off the bed and hurried into the bathroom.

I heard the shower running and then, in seconds it seemed, he was back, nude this time, with what at that moment I thought was the hardest, meanest-looking uncut dick I'd ever seen. His huge balls hung low and heavy between his legs, swaying slightly as he stood silently before me— waiting for further instructions.

I am selective when it comes to cocksucking but I am always ready to be butt-fucked, and Kenny had the perfect tool for the job. I rolled over onto my stomach, saying, "You know where I want that, Kenny."

I had several condoms on the nightstand and he helped himself.

Suddenly, one thrust followed another, each fiercer, more sadistic than the last. My ass arched upward, driving his dick even deeper into me. I looked behind me to see that he had closed his eyes, tilted his head back, and had slipped into a world of his own. He shivered in a spasm of shattering sensuality so intense it made me jealous for a moment. His huge prick changed its angle of entry just enough to slam hard into me on nearly every stroke, and I ground my ass into his crotch. Suddenly, it seemed he was having a seizure as his massive manmeat exploded. As he came down from his high, he continued ramming my butt, hugging me to him.

Finally, slowly, as though relishing a slight delay to intensify his ultimate pleasure, his cock popped from the opening and I dropped to the mattress.

"Wow, you sure learned a lot back in Kentucky," I said.

"You liked it?"

"Loved it."

He took another shower and quickly dressed. He didn't say so, but I assumed I was to return him to the bus stop. I threw on a pair of shorts and followed him to my car as he carried his radio.

When we arrived at our destination, I asked, "Haven't you forgotten something?" I pulled a fifty out of my pocket.

He chuckled. "Oh, sometimes I have such a good time I forget."

I still couldn't believe this. Was he for real, or was I only dreaming?

"How long you in town for?" he asked.

"Just tonight." I really didn't know, but it was better to play it safe.

He said he'd take the bus south. He drew the boom box from its resting place in the back.

"Uh …. " I started.

"Yeah?" he asked hopefully, his big brown cow eyes meeting mine. Damn, I liked him. I wanted to ask him to stay, and yet …. I'd had what I came to town for—in spades. I didn't need any more.

"Do you ever go to the mall?" I asked.

"Which mall?"

"Any mall."

He shook his head. "No, not if I can help it."

I smiled and handed him another fifty. "Good boy."

THE YOUNG & THE BEAUTIFUL

John Patrick wrote a number of stories about Terry, "The Saint," and his adventures on Earth. In this one, from Dreamboys, *Terry restores an older, widowed man to a life of sexual activity, but of a different kind than he had known before. —JB*

The scene: heaven. The time: All-Souls' Eve.

"Before we get carried away," Peter said, "we thought we might just remind you of the rules for All Soul's Day."

Terry shook his head. "I know the rules..."

"Yes, of course. But just to remind you, you must ascend after sundown on November the 2nd and all worldly possessions must be left behind. Please don't take a bottle with you."

"For goodness sake..."

"Don't get huffy! Do you remember Evangelina? She went down for All Soul's Day. Had a good time. Drank as much as she could before ascending to the blue. Poor thing forgot all the rules of the holiday and tried to bring back a bottle of champagne."

Terry chuckled. This was goodhearted sport on Peter's part, but there was a seriousness to it as well. Terry had been through this many times. No matter where he was, it seemed, no one had any real confidence in him, mainly, he felt, because he was so young and so beautiful. But, they conceded, his attributes certainly made his job easier.

*   *   *

It was All Souls' Day, 1975, a day of solemn prayer for all dead persons, and the bells rang. But Terry didn't hear them. He was sitting on a stool in a Bourbon Street bar in New Orleans.

The man next to him, Archer, was "drinking his lunch" and expounding on sainthood. Terry had told the man he was named after Mother Teresa. This always got a good conversation going, but this one today was an especially lively one.

"It seems to me," Archer was railing, "saints are a fraud by definition: once called saints, they cease to be."

"Oh?"

"You know, become known, like on TV."

"I don't watch much TV," Terry said, staring at the TV over the bar, now playing a music video.

"I think saintliness should be unrecognized," Archer said, "and *that,*" he concluded, "is the longest speech I have ever made on a religious subject in my life. The longest and, I promise you, the last."

"Good." Terry had the bartender bring Archer a cup of strong coffee. "Sainthood bores me," Terry said, "and that's a fact."

"I don't know what the fuck got into me," Archer said.

"If I didn't know better," Terry remarked, "I'd say you had too much to drink."

"I'm sorry. It's my birthday, such as it is. Oh, I don't want to make myself out as some pitiful object. My wife, may she rest in peace, had a theory about hitting forty. She thought of it as a time to begin again, if one would just let it happen."

Terry smiled. "She sounds like my kind of woman."

"Oh, she was. She was the best."

Terry saluted Archer with his coffee mug, "Happy birthday."

"Thank you. And Happy All Soul's to you," Archer said.

Archer had loved his dead wife madly, entirely, had promised to be hers alone till he died. But now, he couldn't help himself; all thoughts of her—the little fair beauty, all demure delicacy—were obliterated by Terry, with his bold radiance, his promise of a good time.

Archer took Terry back to his dreary rooms on Frenchmen Street in the Faubourg-Marigny district.

They had brandies and Terry told Archer how he wanted to celebrate this feast day: being fucked by Archer's ten-inch dick.

"How did you know I have a ten-incher?"

"Your hands, your fingers. I've had practice."

How *much* practice Archer could never have imagined, but Terry in the nude with his ass high in the air was a sight that would have gotten many a man going, even a tired-out old drunk like Archer.

Terry played with his hole, applied some grease. He was teasing Archer unmercifully and Archer was loving it. Archer stripped and climbed on the bed.

"Oh, Jesus," he said, sinking his finger in the hole, "don't let me have a heart attack! Let me live to see my next birthday party!" Tensing his legs, he could feel the power thrust in his muscular thighs as he began. Soon he had the massive head and a couple of inches of his shaft in, and Terry was taking it really well. And with Terry squirming, Archer lunged, deep.

"I try to come, but I can't. Nobody can get me off. No woman, no man, not even myself, so you just go ahead, enjoy yourself."

"Don't worry so much," came Terry's voice, deep. He rolled over and Archer hung Terry's legs over his shoulders. Terry caressed Archer's back, and Archer began humping even harder, tears of sweat sliding down his face.

Then something miraculous began to happen. Archer felt a change come over him. It started like a slow-moving train, pulling him inexorably, building evenly, coming on, coming on, coming on—as if wheels were rolling, rolling, and actually going somewhere! There was an incredible *feeling* coursing through him. And a bright lightbulb of realization snapped on inside his brain. "This is it! I'm actually gonna come! It ain't gonna stop!" It was an incredibly uplifting experience. A fullness. An intense heat. Each of his thrusts brought him further ecstasy, his cock working inside Terry, hard. Soon he was at the height of heights, reaching Satisfaction Unlimited! "I'm having a birthday party!"

Terry laughed at Archer's quaint way of describing his orgasm.

After he finished coming, Archer lifted up and stared down at Terry's cock bouncing around as he continued to poke him. Then he pulled out his own cock, glistening with cum. "I got something for you." He hopped out of bed, went to the dresser, got a huge pink plastic cock.

He had tried for years to get off with others. When he was with himself, he would use the Pink One, playing with himself, teasing his anus with the Pink One. But lately, not even that worked. But this night was proving different. Archer fingered Terry's butthole. He stuck one finger in, then two, in and out. Then Terry took the faux cock and guided it in with his hand while Terry gasped for breath as Archer inserted the Pink One; he began a slow thrust of his hips as the old man jammed it in, hard and firm.

Archer leaned over Terry, watching the boy's bouncing erection. The expression on Archer's face meant business now. The orgasm he had enjoyed had broken his resistance. His body let go, and so did his mind. Archer had another man's cock in his mouth for the first time and he loved it. Terry knew it wouldn't be the last time, either; Archer was busting out!

Terry took over pushing the Pink One in and out of his boy-pussy. With each thrust he got hotter and humped up his hips to meet Archer's suddenly eager mouth. Then he spread his legs wider, and began a volley of his own.

After the first spurt of Terry's orgasm burst inside his mouth, Archer pulled away to watch in admiration as further gobs erupted. "Atta boy," Archer muttered blissfully, body tense. "Come for Poppa!"

The cock, flowing its juice onto Terry's washboard stomach, then onto the sheets, was glorious, Archer thought. He had never experienced this satisfaction. He had been like a kite tied to the earth, his wife's memory a lead weight that wouldn't release him. Now he was free.

Aggressively he hooked his hands around Terry's thighs and pulled his cock, covered with cum, back into his mouth. He started to suck it again. Working his lips, tongue hot on the kid's sex, licking, lapping, making a wet sound that caused Terry to scream, "Ohhhh!"

A low moan came from Archer as he lifted up to take the prick in his hand, once again hard. "So good!" he said, and quickly returned to his work. Soon another intense orgasm exploded from Terry's cock, and this time, Archer took it all. Finished, Archer wiped his mouth, went to the bathroom.

Terry heard noises: coughs and spitting.

When Archer came back out, Terry was dressed, ready to depart. "What's this? You're leaving me?"

"I must."

"No, please."

"Yes. My job is done."

"Job?"

"I was sent to persuade you."

"Sent?"

"For your birthday."

Archer didn't have time to reflect on this notion because Terry had wrapped him in his arms.

"Do you know," Terry whispered, his tongue flicking at Archer's ear, "why I was chosen to persuade you?"

"Because you're the best?"

"Oh, no." He laughed, a rippling breath on his neck. "Oh, no. I got this job early in life, and I was never properly trained. See what I did with you? I slipped off into my own pleasure, when I should think only of yours."

"Oh, but I was pleased, really. Really, really pleased."

Somewhere here was an answer to a question Terry had never thought to ask. "It is the same, isn't it? The pleasure, the joy? It's for both of us."

"You can say that again."

Terry glanced up at him, a slanted look through those long, shadowy lashes. "You are too kind, Archer. No. I was chosen not because I am the best, but because I am the worst. The youngest, the most naïve, the most distracted," he gulped. "The least adept at the arts of love."

"What? Man, that was the best sex I've ever had!"

"Really?"

Then Archer spoke aloud the thought that had formed in his mind: "My god, imagine what the others are like."

The others, Archer thought. The other hustlers who worked for this service that had sent Terry, what were *they* like? It had never occurred to him that there might be men available for such things. Before his marriage, he had picked up a tart or two in his prime, just for intermittent loving, an occasional spell of peace, a few moments of sweet passion and tenderness. But these were never enough, always just an interlude, and soon forgotten. But this, *this* would never be forgotten.

"Must you go?" Archer protested as Terry began to leave him standing in the middle of the bedroom, bewildered.

"Yes, I must. It's nearly dawn and I have to be in... uh, Rio by nightfall."

"Rio?" Archer was totally confused. "Like in Brazil?"

Terry nodded. Now Archer imagined Terry worked for a worldwide escort service, wandering the world an orphan, alone in life as he had been alone at birth, and he imagined that solitude was Terry's destiny. Archer could never have imagined the truth: that Terry, when he was offered another destiny, one that was his for the believing, had taken it. And that now he could spend his life—or life after death, as it were—saving souls through sex.

ON A BED OF GRASS

Adrian was mentally retarded, but he was extremely gifted in the cock department, And the way he dressed made that gift obvious to the adults, who deplored his special asset, but not to his young friend Jody Tinsley, who especially appreciated the way Adrian could show the depth *of his friendship—literally! An excerpt from the anthology* Heatwave. *—JB*

Around noon on a burning, bruising summer day, Mrs. Tinsley heard the roar of a motor in the yard. She looked out. A convertible drove up outside, the exhaust from the tailpipe raising a little dust.

"Your friend is out there," she said.

Jody turned around slowly. He was just getting over a cold and had a headache from all the dust.

Outside, Adrian, dressed only in worn denim shorts, slid out of the car and came rushing toward the door of the farmhouse with a smile. His dust still floated over the road.

Mrs. Tinsley gazed at Adrian as he approached the house. "There's some around, you know, who'd as soon cut him and make sure he don't breed no more half-wits, maybe calm him down some."

"He ain't no half-wit," Jody said. "I told you, he was in a bad car wreck. There's no harm in him, but he was hurt bad."

"Well, I understand all that. And I'm sorry about it. But it seems like there's a part a him that ain't hurt, don't it, he's so eager to show it off."

"Whaddya mean, Ma?" Jody giggled, playing dumb.

"You know damn well what I mean. He can't hide that thing of his."

Jody stopped giggling when he saw Adrian, standing outside on the porch, peering into the kitchen. Yes, it certainly was obvious to anyone with two eyes that young Adrian was hung like a horse. Today, the shorts he was wearing were so short that the head of his cock hung out under the torn hem. "He was hurt but he's a boy like anybody else."

"I don't know any boy that's...."

"That's what?"

"That's, well, got what he's got. Man, either. He's a freak of nature, that boy is."

Adrian tapped on the door. Jody hesitated. The only pleasure the boy had in life was his time with Adrian. Adrian and his big dick. Jody *lived* for Adrian and his dick.

Mrs. Tinsley served them iced tea as they sat in rocking chairs on the porch. Adrian looked wretched, hair matted, hands and arms dirty, but he was, as always, oblivious to it.

71

"Adrian," Jody whispered, "I need to talk to you. Now you pay attention. You can't go on doin' like you been doin'."

"How's that?"

"Look," Jody said, pointing to the cockhead that lay against Adrian's deeply tanned thigh.

"You can't show yourself like that. You're scarin' people."

Adrian blushed, tried to pull the denim over the cockhead. "I guess I've just outgrown these shorts all of a sudden."

Jody chuckled, remembering the swimsuit Adrian wore the week before when they went to the pond, and the jeans that would be baggy on anybody else that Adrian wore to the movies the week before that. Mrs. Tinsley had said that Adrian showing off like that was downright obscene, but now, seeing the huge cockhead poking out, the old woman was speechless.

They stood up and while Jody delivered the empty tea glasses to the kitchen, Adrian pulled his shorts down as far as he could, to cover himself.

Moments later, the boys were in the old convertible, heading to the pond. They were bathed by the sun, which forced its way through the trees, dazzled by the fierce glare off the tall grass, and their bodies were covered with perspiration by the time they reached the pond. They were, as always, alone in this idyllic place.

After only ten minutes or so of swimming naked in the refreshingly cool water, Adrian's eyes became cloudy with desire. His flesh throbbed languidly. He did not know why, but he could stay here no longer. He got out of the water. He had to get out. He had to get rid of the feeling. And he had to do it right away. Jody followed Adrian to *the place*, their place, behind the trees.

Jody's diligently combed hair was now wet and glistening. The tanned cheeks of his long, oval face were covered with thick, long hairs, like weeds. Now their voices buzzed with an intimacy few teenagers could ever approach.

Jody was trembling now in anticipation of being hurt, fiercely desiring to be hurt once again by Adrian's enormous cock. "Oh my god!" Jody cried out over and over, and he shivered. But his cock never lost its hardness, and Adrian skinned it back, licking the wet crown as it pulsated on his tongue.

Adrian slurped slowly down the tapered shaft, and swallowed hard. He could take all Jody had and not gag, and he was proud of this; he loved sucking on Jody's cock—it was like everybody else's, not a freakish thing like his own.

Jody could take only a few inches of Adrian's cock when, a few minutes later, he started sucking it. He gagged, took a breath, and tried it again, groping mounds of Adrian's taut, tan assflesh. He took more of it than he ever had, but still it was too much for him. He pried his lips away to lap the dark sac of Adrian's low-swinging balls. He was so hungry for him, there was no limit to what he would do for Adrian. Adrian dragged Jody's mouth back to his bobbing dick. Jody's tongue suctioned its large, juicy head as two fingers tapped and drummed the long, dark, rubbery shaft. The spittle-soaked nuts kept slapping at Jody's chin, and they established a rhythm. Jody was bobbing his head and sucking with such vigor, with such an expert pause at the bottom of his stroke, and another, longer, kissing pause at the top, that Adrian was soon ready to come.

Unattended, Jody's cock poked the hot air. As Jody continued sucking Adrian off, Adrian reached behind him and stroked Jody's ass. Jody took a deep breath, flexed his throat muscles and burrowed down the long, choking shaft until he gagged. Jody's gagging only made the monstrous prick throb more, and the bloat of Jody's cheeks seemed to set something off in Adrian. He pulled away, the long, wet meat tumbling from Jody's lips.

Jody knew it did no good to tell Adrian to take it easy now. He got on his hands and knees and lifted his ass to Adrian. There was no other way Jody could take Adrian's enormous prick up his ass.

Adrian laid the huge, throbbing shaft on Jody's back, where it looked like a swan's neck. Then, smearing the moist tip of it between Jody's buttocks, he grinned at Jody again as he placed it against the asshole. He put one hand on Jody's shoulder to pull his body back toward him so he could embed the whole purple bulb of his cockhead in the boy's ass. Then, having thus carefully set it, like a screw, he put both hands on Jody's shoulders and gripping them, pulled, driving his cock all the way home. Just as this was the only way Jody could accept all of Adrian's cock inside his ass, there was no other way Adrian could sink it in there; it had to be accomplished like this, in one swift, furious plunge; to do otherwise would mean a loss of some of the hardness, and it would hurt the boy even more.

The dickhead went in, then inch after inch of the shaft. Jody let out a gasp of mixed pleasure and pain as the shaft flexed, burrowing in to the hilt. Adrian nestled up against Jody and gently kissed his young lover's shoulders. He dipped his hands down to curl his fingers around Jody's cock, which stiffened with his urgent touch, and he quickened the pace of his stroking, doing it in time with his thrusting in Jody's ass.

Jody began to moan; his knees were shaking, his shoulders trembling as he came, cum spurting out of him onto the bed of grass. Adrian seemed to pause now, holding his cock at the root to give it extra rigidity—as if it needed it! Then he sent it back in to the hilt. "Oh," Jody sighed, his sun-burnished body coated in a sheen of sweat.

Moments later, Adrian's cum flowed into Jody. When he was finished and his cock slid from the opening, Adrian affectionately rubbed the boy's ass and closed his eyes. They lay silently together on the cum-spattered grass, catching their breath and taking pleasure in the hope that it might always be like this.

When the boys returned to the farmhouse, Mrs. Tinsley was jabbing at a boiling pot full of halved potatoes.

"Dinner!" Mr. Tinsley shouted at the boys, taking a last long swallow of his whiskey. "Dinner! Eat it or go hungry."

They ate without talking, finishing all of the pot roast.

Over coffee and freshly baked chocolate cookies, Mr. Tinsley, scratching his salt-and-pepper beard, finally confronted Adrian. "Boy, they are gonna hurt you one day. I've been told they got the word out they'll cut you if you don't quit pesterin' the girls. You understand what I mean?"

Adrian blushed, stared at his plate.

Mr. Tinsley went on, "You understand what I'm sayin' to you when I say *cut*?" He snapped a cookie in half to make his point.

Adrian nodded, oblivious, but Jody found it disconcerting. Jody shot Adrian a sly look and began to laugh. Adrian joined in then, and the Tinsleys had no choice but to laugh too, even though they had no idea what was so funny.

In the dark that night, Mr. Tinsley confessed, "I don't know if that boy understood a thing I said. I don't think he did. He laughed his head off. Christ, I wish there was some way you could tell what goes on in that poor boy's mind."

There was a silence and Mrs. Tinsley whispered, barely audible, "Well, you could take him down to Laramie. You know, visit one of those houses." In the dark, she blushed just to speak of it.

"Why, no," her husband said, truly shocked that his wife would even think it. "I couldn't do no such thing."

74

MISSING YOU

It shouldn't have ended. Jeff gave everything to Stefan, who took it with such enthusiasm and passion that when he later married Rita, and fathered a baby with her, it didn't seem possible to Jeff. Now, after a long separation, they reunite, and the spark is obviously still there. So it couldn't have ended. Could it? *A story from the anthology* Beautiful Boys.—JB

Jeff:
You're right on time. Walk in and look around, smile when you see me, come to the table, slide into the booth.

"Hi," you say, your eyes avoiding mine.

You touch your fingers to the menu, and the waitress comes right over. You order coffee and pie, pecan pie. We always used to come here for the pie. You love pecan pie.

But still, you have to ask the slutty, peroxided blonde waitress if it is good. My teeth are clenched so tight they hurt, watching you smile at that cheap bitch, play with her, flirt. She takes your menu, turns, and leaves, and you look at me, waiting for me to speak. I am biting the inside of my mouth, trying to get control, not wanting to cry.

"You're disgusting," I mutter, finally.

"What?"

"You and pussy."

You glare at me. "*What?*"

Something snaps inside me. "You never change."

"*What?*"

"You know what I'm talkin' about! I'm talkin' about you and *pussy.*"

You gulp. "Why did you invite me here?"

"To see you. I miss you."

"Look, Jeff, I've got obligations now."

"Of course. And how is the new Mrs. Andersen?"

"She's fine."

"You're happy then?"

"Sure."

Yeah, sure. But I knew that if you accepted my invitation to meet me over pie and coffee, you couldn't be all *that* happy.

The pie and coffee arrives. You flirt with the waitress again. She's smitten with you, like everyone.

I sip my coffee while you enjoy the pie. You eat the whole piece without stopping. When you're done, you push the plate away and wipe your fingers with your paper napkin. "Man, that's the best damn pecan pie in the world!"

"Glad you enjoyed it."

"You know what else I'd enjoy?" Suddenly you are all sweetness and light. Must have been the pie.

"Yeah, but I don't have a pussy."

Your eyes search mine, concerned, as if I have lost my mind, as if *I* was the one. I sit here stock-still. "C'mon, let's go back to your place."

"You're crazy," I say.

The waitress won't leave us alone for a second; she refills our coffee. I dip my paper napkin in my water glass and wipe my face, trying to get control of myself.

"Well, thank you, sweetheart," you say to the waitress. "That was just fine." She smiles back, pleased you're happy. Then she walks away. She never glances my way. Not once!

"I love Rita and the baby," you say, quietly. You put your coffee cup down. Something about the set of your shoulders scares me. I don't know what it is, but I can feel something about to happen that I won't be able to stop. Tears are blurring everything. I want to touch your hand, but I don't. I pick up my car keys. They're making a racket, my hand is shaking so. I stand up. Your big dark eyes stay right on mine. My knees are trembling.

"Well, let's go then," I say.

In my car, you say, "I never said I was perfect. Never." A little smile crosses the corners of your mouth. You put your hand over my fingers as they clutch the wheel, cover them with your hand, and then push down on them heavily. I try to pull my hand out from under yours, but you won't let me. Like when I was a kid playing that game where you slide your hand out from under the other person's hand. Only when you and I played it, you would grab my hand and hold on to it until you'd hurt me, until you'd make me yell.

"I'm gonna fuck the hell out of you today. You fuckin' deserve it." Your fingers are white on mine, you are pushing down so hard.

I am trying so hard not to cry out, my tooth bites into my lip. I want you so badly, sweat stands out on my face.

"What do you mean, Stefan?" I say.

Breathing hard, you say, "Keeping me waiting six months for it."

"But you're a married man now."

"So?"

I don't answer you. I have no answer. If it doesn't make any difference to you, why should it to me? You take your fingers away and begin massaging my thigh.

I start the car. "You said you'd given up things like that."

You sigh. "I've decided, the way I look at it, that what she doesn't know won't hurt her."

I want to go into a 'but what about me?' rant, but I can't, not now. I want you too much to let anything change what is about to happen.

You have always had me right where you want me. You were my first. Most people lose touch, forget, move on. But not us. You wouldn't let me. There were always girls, but I could handle it, because you always came back. But then there came the time you didn't.

"You've played hard to get right from the start," I go on, reminiscing. It's always turned you on to remember it, so you let me go on.

Stefan:
Jeff had a certain appeal that fascinated me for several months before I first let him suck me off. He had just moved into the neighborhood, and I said to my football squad teammates that if he were a girl, I'd be in love. They all laughed.

Jeff did act kinda nelly, but that was part of his charm for me. He was everything I thought a gay kid would be. He was pretty, short, soft, sang in the school chorus, kinda swished when he walked—and he wore tight, tailored clothes, pants that accentuated his ass. I had never noticed another guy's ass before, and I couldn't explain why it turned me on to see Jeff's ass filling out those tight pants, but I knew it did.

One night we were all over at Rosie's house. Everybody was invited, including Jeff, since Jeff was Rosie's new best friend. I was sitting with my football teammate Bud near the pool table, watching the object of my secret crazy desire play pool. He was incredible! I asked Rosie where the kid learned to play like that. She said his father bought him a pool table when he was very little and he'd discovered something he could do without leaving the house—and something he could play by himself. He and Rosie often had matches that lasted all night.

In between Jeff's pool shots Bud was calling him names. Bud was a genius at creating scenes and I guess he thought this was to be his biggest triumph. He was making lewd remarks about how Jeff used his "stick," and other suggestive comments.

Watching the tip of his cue while he chalked it with detachment, Jeff finally asked, "What'd you just say, Bud?"

"I said, I've been wondering if you've had any other experience getting in holes," Bud prodded.

"I'll bet more than you have, Bud," Jeff kidded back.

I laughed, much too loudly, trying to ease the tension that seemed to be developing between them.

Finally, my gang left the party, but not before I took Jeff aside and made a date for the next night, to go over to his house and shoot some pool. Of course, pool was the last thing I wanted to shoot.

That next night, we went into the basement where he had his pool table. We shot a game and he let me beat him. He said he couldn't concentrate. I said I understood, and as he walked past me to rack the balls again, I trapped him between the wall and the table, taking his hand and forcing it down onto my bulge.

He opened my belt buckle, then undid the buttons of my jeans. My breathing became deep and labored; I knew what would happen next, and I had worn no underwear, hoping that it might. The base of my cock was exposed as Jeff pulled the flaps of my jeans wide apart. It was already hard, and he could not miss seeing the bulging tube of hard flesh extending down into my left pants leg—quite far down, I am proud to say—and pressing against it from within. He pushed my shirt up with one hand, and pressed the palm of one hand against my stomach.

His first touch was electric and suddenly my head began to ring with an excitement so intense it seemed to resound throughout the room. Even as my mind cried out against this seeming perversion, I was filled with such feverish desire I began to moan. I had learned much earlier to act on my impulses when presented with an opportunity for erotic satisfaction—and although this one had presented itself much more quickly than others, my reaction was immediate, and my sexual urge fully as hungry for satisfaction as it had ever been. There had been none of the usual preparation or elaborate talk, this was pure surrender.

I was doing battle with myself. A battle I knew I would lose—knew I *wanted* to lose—but couldn't live with myself if I didn't fight. As Jeff pulled my cock completely from my jeans and began fondling my balls, my body became stronger in its demand for the pleasure and release the kid could give me. Jeff was absorbed by the enormous size of my erection and by the writhing of my body as one of his hands caressed my ass and the other traveled up into my shirt and explored my chest. He dragged my jeans down to my knees, so that my ass was bare, and he resumed fondling it with one hand as his other took the shaft of my cock gently, and he licked it, kissed the head, then opened his mouth wide to admit it. My passion, already almost as great as it had ever been, mounted as I watched his lips moving up and down my shaft, and my cock moving in and out of the hot suction of his mouth.

When he released my cock and silently studied it in apparent admiration, its saliva-coated length glistened in the bright light coming from the fixture over the pool table. I watched the throbbing hardness with new interest, trying to see it as Jeff was viewing it.

I had never seen my cock adored this much. No girl had ever sucked it, really sucked it, at least not like Jeff had been doing. I bit my lip trying to stifle my moans. I was actually weak-kneed with excitement, and with one hand I supported myself on the pool table. My other crept around to the back of Jeff's skull and he quickly opened his mouth to take me inside again as I forced his lips all the way down into my pubic hairs. He gagged, but managed to contain it as I suddenly exploded with a screaming, godless orgasm. I all but doubled over with the force of it, but Jeff didn't let a single drop escape his mouth. He sucked hungrily, and moaned with pleasure as he swallowed what had to be he biggest load of cum I had ever produced.

I had cried in appreciation as I filled his mouth with my cum, "Oh god! Oh, Jeff!" But as he continued to nurse on my cock while my excitement subsided, I realized I had never had a more enjoyable, or more *meaningful* sexual experience. I perceived the first inkling of where my sexual appetites might really lie—and that I might possibly be one of those *queers* my buddies and I ridiculed so often. I cursed Jeff, quietly and gently, because I didn't really want him to hear; he wasn't at fault for showing me what I really wanted. "Oh Jeff, damn you!" But I was already looking forward to blowing another load down his throat.

Jeff ignored me and kept on sucking, holding me tight as I caught my breath and recovered from the assault. At the same time, he unbuttoned his own pants, pulled his dick out, and beat himself off—blowing his load on the floor. By the time the excitement of his orgasm caused him to pant heavily around my cock—still inside his mouth—I was fully hard again.

I wanted to seize his head and take the initiative—to *fuck* his mouth hard, not just left him suck me off. But I wasn't ready for him to know how completely his blowjob had excited me, for him to think that I might be more like him than he could suspect. So I gently pulled my prick from his mouth, and restored it to my jeans—with quite a bit of difficulty, as it was still huge and fully erect.

Jeff's cock was still protruding from his pants, with a string of cum hanging from the tip, leading to an impressive pool of it on the floor. His prick was obviously no longer fully erect, but I was amazed to see that it was larger than I would have thought, and—the thought surprised me— quite beautiful. I had seen plenty of big dicks, but I had never before had an impulse to reach out and fondle one as I did then. I suppressed the unwelcome, but undeniable, desire, and was glad that I already had a hard-on when I put my cock back in my pants, so he couldn't tell it had grown even harder when I looked at his cum-dripping monster.

I knew Jeff had a good memory and he would play this scene out in his mind again and again, jerking off to the thought of it day after day. But later that night, and the next morning when I woke up, I found that was exactly what *I* did! I knew the memory of what we had shared was not enough; I had to have more of the real thing.

The next day, we were at it again. We went to his basement, where Jeff dragged my pants down immediately, pushed me to my back on the pool table. He leaned over me and just slurped my entire cock into his mouth. Then he settled down to work on it for a good long time.

I tried to delay my orgasm as long as possible, to enjoy Jeff's wonderful cocksucking to the fullest, and he helped by varying his speed and strength, and the motions of his head. Finally, I could hold back no longer, and I came, shooting so hard I couldn't keep from shouting my

79

excitement. For a long time his sucking, swallowing mouth continued to gently surround my cock, licking the glans, and finally releasing it to let it fall slowly back against my thigh.

"I could really get used to this," I told him.

And I did get used to it. I'm not sure how many times Jeff blew me, but I remember I was reluctant every time at first. I had my upbringing in America to overcome. My relatives back in Europe have a different attitude, and some had tried things with me when they visited. In their view, "sex is just sex," but as much as I liked that idea, doing anything about it made me nervous. Jeff helped me overcome my hesitation by saying it was our secret; no one would ever know.

The place for our sex was always the same: in the basement at his folks' house, where Jeff had his pool table. I always knew we were going to do it beforehand, of course, but I never acted as if I were eager for it, although I invariably was.

It amused me how Jeff wore a mask of innocence, so that his parents would not suspect what was going on in their basement. I didn't feel comfortable when Jeff's father was in town, though, watching TV in the living room above us. I sensed he was curious why a jock was hanging out with his fruity son.

"We'll have to hurry now," Jeff said one night when he took me downstairs, which was dark except for the light over the pool table. He didn't suggest we shoot a game, as we often did. He went right to his knees in front of me, pulling my pants down to my ankles, and holding them as I stepped out of them, at his request. I was quickly aroused and then Jeff stood, kicked off his shoes, and removed all of his clothing, revealing himself to me for the first time. I had seen his cock many, many times by then; he almost always beat off while he was blowing me—and I was reminded all over again, as I always was, how beautiful it was. It was fully hard, bobbing in front of him as he turned around to show me his ass for the first time. He turned slowly, seductively, *presenting* his ass, *displaying* it for me—and displaying it proudly, I thought, as if he was aware of the effect the sight of it would have on me. And he had every right to show it proudly. Although it was his ass that had attracted me initially, I had almost forgotten about it, so entranced was I by his skill as a cocksucker, but on seeing it bare, I caught my breath; if his prick was beautiful, his ass was *glorious!*

He stepped over to a table and got some grease. He leaned down and looked back over his shoulder at me while he applied some lube to his fingers. and then began fucking his asshole with them. "I want you to try this," he said.

I began stroking my erection, fully huge and hard now, actually throbbing with my desire to possess him. "Have you ever ....?" I began to ask.

"Yeah, a couple of times. But never with one as big as yours."

I never thought my cock was anything special until I had started playing around with Jeff, until I saw how much he admired it and craved it. He still looked back at me over his shoulder, and our eyes stayed locked together as I stepped forward to stand directly behind him, letting the tip my pulsating dick rest against his back, just above his ass. He reached behind to take hold of my shaft, and I could feel his desire as he pressed the tip down below the rounded globes of his perfect ass. He faced forward and bent his knees just a bit, spreading his legs enough that the shaft of my throbbing cock went in between them. He used both hands to spread the cheeks of his ass wide, parting the lips of his asshole. I rubbed my cock up and down his asscrack for a while, finally allowing the tip to rest right at the opening he was offering me. I was almost staggering with desire as he pressed his ass back toward me, and his greased sphincter pressed so tightly against my cockhead that it began to slip inside. Sighing in pleasure, he reached behind himself to keep me in place as he pulled me along and leaned over, bracing himself on the pool table.

I'd fucked maybe a dozen girls, usually in my car, in one of several secluded places around town, but this was like the time I fucked Chrissie in the woods—standing, from behind. Jeff turned to look at me over his shoulder, and snarled, "Stick it in!" He reached between his legs, grabbed my penis by its length, and hung on to it as long as he could while it slid into him without stopping. I held his buttocks and I moved into him. He welcomed me by gripping and squeezing my cock inside his ass. We gasped together.

I folded my arms around his waist, drawing his arched back into my stomach as I began to thrust in and out. I bent over him, and my teeth found the back of his neck. He flexed all at once and then began to change the tempo, coming back to meet my thrusts with such determined force that I had to stand again to brace myself. He pounded back into me and began to moan. Then I convulsed, gasping, my belly slipping on his now-sweaty back as my cum erupted deep inside him. He'd taken more than I ever knew I had to give.

I pulled out and leaned back against the table. In my thick, sensual stupor, I couldn't resist watching and feeling him sucking my cock again, as he fell to his knees before me and began to do so, stroking my thighs at the same time. I could feel my cock, still slick from before, begin to throb heavily once more, and return to the fierce hardness that had lessened after I came inside him. He stood, turned, and again bent forward slightly, rubbing his ass against my groin, and I could feel, with each movement, my cock growing still harder. I put my arms around his waist, and pushed my crotch deeply against his ass, putting my throbbing dick between his legs. My hands worked their way upward, starting at his thighs, moving across his pubes, over his smooth stomach, to his taut nipples. I rubbed his nipples until he let out a deep moan, and his knees buckled.

I lifted him up and turned him around to face me. I smiled at him, then pulled him to my chest and kissed him. I don't know what possessed me to do that, but I was treating him as if he was a girl—and I loved kissing my girlfriends. He kissed me back, but it was a brief kiss, broken as I gently eased him down to the cold concrete floor.

Crouching on top of him, sweaty and feverish, I stroked my cock. He took my balls in his hand and began to nibble on the tip of my cock. I moaned as he eased it deep into his mouth, and shouted when he suddenly took the last few inches in and gave me a tremendous upward suck. My body shook as he licked the exposed base of my dick with his tongue. I straddled his face with my legs while he continued sucking hard on my cock and fondling my balls. He twitched as I reached behind me to massage his asshole and then enter it with my fingers slowly, surely forcing their way inside. He threw his pelvis onto my fingers, grinding himself against them, and let out a little cry. I pushed him away and positioned him on all fours in front of me, spreading his legs from behind.

Holding my cock in my hands, I rubbed the head in the asscrack. Jeff was shaking with pleasure as I inserted the first several inches of my dick with a slow, deft push. Inch after inch slid into him, not stopping until my bush was against his ass. I began to fuck him again, retreating and entering in long motions, my balls slapping against his butt as I pumped, my fingers biting into his skin where I held his thighs.

I thrust harder, forcing my cock deep into his asshole, pulling almost all of the way out before sinking in again. Then I rolled him over and knelt between his thighs, pulling his legs up over my shoulders.

As I shoved into him in this new position, Jeff cried out in pain. My hungry cock was now buried deeper inside him than it had been before. The thick shaft tore at his insides, and he started to cry. He looked up at me and his blue eyes remained clear and bright, even as I plowed into the tender ass beneath me. I touched his face with a tenderness completely at odds with the ferocity of my fucking, let him take my hand, suck my fingers. He spread his legs wider to give me better access, and, a few moments later, I came deep inside him again.

I kissed him again, taking him in my arms and rolling on the cold floor with him, my cock still inside him. But this time our kiss was long and impassioned, and our tongues invaded each other's mouths hungrily. I started fucking him again but I could tell I was hurting him, so I pulled out and lay quietly beside him.

After a few moments, I said, "I remember when I was a little kid, I saw a bunch of the older kids in a circle in the playground. I went over to see what they were doing." Jeff got up on one elbow to listen. "There was this big beetle. The kids were poking it with a stick. The bug just kind of curled up to protect itself."

Jeff snorted, "God knows I been poked with enough sticks."

I smiled, then kissed him on the forehead, as if he is one of my girlfriends. He had followed my train of thought.

"God," he went on, "by the time you're really old enough to have sex, you're already fucked, you know what I mean?"

I shrugged. No, I didn't know what he meant, not at first hand, anyway. But I smiled, remembering his secret story, the one he had shared with me earlier. As he began licking me, slowly, teasingly, moving in small circles with his lips and tongue, his kisses pelting me, gentle as the rain that had started to fall outside, I recalled what he had told me:

"I had gone to Catholic schools until my father was transferred and we moved into your neighborhood," Jeff had begun. "If truth be known, my father had asked for the transfer, and he understood it would be best that I attend public school. We had left a scandal behind, or what would have become a scandal if they had not sent Father John away to a place where he could be 'rehabilitated.' I laughed when I heard that, sensing he loved what he was doing with the boys far too much to ever give it up. I knew that when he did it with me, he was in heaven

"But Father John wasn't the only one; there were others, too. I had been passed from priest to priest and even between a few lay brothers. I was godless, they said, and everyone had to try to save me—but to me, being fucked or sucked by them, or giving them blowjobs, seemed a strange way for them to do so. For me, it became a simple journey from religious to sexual ecstasy.

"After the move, we stopped going to church altogether. I was struggling with my emerging gay identity in those days, desperate for an older brother or a friend in whom I could confess my secrets, as I had with my priests.

"Later, I began to fantasize that you might like me the way the priests had, and recently I started to hope that you might be just like me; because you loved fucking me so much, I thought you might be gay. Shows you what I know."

I fucked Jeff regularly for over a year before I met Rita, and in all that time, no one found out about us. There were a couple of close calls, but for the most part it was a blissful time, and the happiest moments of that period were when I felt Jeff sucking my dick and swallowing my cum, or his beautiful, tight ass working my cock so expertly he was almost sucking me off that way, and the thrilling moments when my cum shot into his eager mouth or his hungry ass. The sight of hot cum shooting from his beautiful prick while I fucked him was almost as exciting as the feel of our lips pressed together while our tongues danced inside each other's mouth and we frantically pawed each other's bodies.

Jeff:

83

Now, for the first time since your marriage, we're back in the basement, the little place where we made love so often, and you say you want to play a game of pool. I go to the bathroom, but when I come back you're standing next to the table, naked, jacking off. I knew pool was the last thing on your mind.

"You're beautiful," I say reflexively before I really look at you. You grin, keep jacking off.

Now I stare at you. You are quite a beauty, though not in the way I have learned about beauty from the gay magazines. You're dark, your nose is crooked, your eyes heavy-lidded. And your penis is uncut. Maybe that's why I find it so exotic, so sublime. Certainly it is the biggest cock I have ever sucked. You've grown a lot more pubic hair, which is lustrous and coarse, and you give a surprised, pleased cry as I suddenly bury my face in it. I suck your huge cock for a good ten minutes before I hear you say, "Now, let me see you—see if you've grown any."

I stand and you motion me away a few steps. "There," you say, as though I have reached center stage. "Go ahead and pull 'em down."

I am a little embarrassed, but I quickly get out of my clothing. I stand before you, a little chilly, looking down at myself, then looking over at your incredible cock, which looks bigger than ever.

"You're beautiful, too," you say, and I can tell that you mean it. "For a boy." You have to add that. I understand that.

What I can't understand is why, when I get on my knees again, and am about to take your cock in my mouth once more, you push me away.

You look at me as if I am a stranger, as if you hate me. I feel your anger like a physical blow. I shake, watching as you jerk your shorts on, tearing them in your haste. You look at me once more, your expression becoming gentler as you see my hurt and confusion. "It's not you, Jeff," you say gently, "it's my fault. I shouldn't have tried this."

I start to cry, and you stand still. "Oh, god, don't do that."

I can't speak. I feel so stupid, kneeling here, my cock losing its hardness, tears streaming down my face.

"Oh, fuck!" you scream, as if cursing a fate you can't resist. You take my hand, none too gently, and with hardly any effort lift me up and lay me across the pool table. You strip off your shorts and bend over me.

As your naked body covers mine, I feel the thrill of our two cocks pressed together. Your lips find mine. You suck deeply at my mouth while your hands reach up and gently stroke my hair, tugging on it, pulling my head back to expose my neck. Those big, soft lips devour the tender flesh of my neck and ears as they travel all over my body—slowly moving down to kiss and suck my chest, my nipples, my armpits. Your hands and lips seem to be everywhere as they burn a trail across my yearning flesh, the weight of your body keeping me pinned helpless beneath you. One hand works its way down beneath my balls and into the sweaty hollow between my asscheeks. Your fingers probe my hole.

Without warning you shove two fingers deep into me. At the shock of the penetration, my body arches up - lifting us both off the pool table.

In an instant you tear your mouth from mine and you bury your head between my legs. I am stunned as your tongue replaces your fingers and you use it to probe feverishly into my aching hole. You are using me as you would Rita's pussy ....and I don't mind a bit.

You stand, and I can see your cock is hard again, ready for me, as if it has nothing to do with your brain. My hips shift slightly and my heart beats fast. How I have waited for this! You are perfect—physically at least.

You love my low moans, my sighs, my silent mouthing of your name with my head thrown back, loving it as you kneel on the pool table straddling my waist. And I won't disappoint you today. No sense arguing anymore. No sense at all. You are the most beautiful man ever created. In fact, now, after six months apart, you are even more beautiful than I remember, if that is possible. There's not an ounce of fat on your six-foot frame. Lifting all those cartons every day at your father's wine shop must agree with you. I'll admit that you put on a few pounds while you were away, flunking out at college, only learning how to fuck better, as you used to say, not that you needed to know anything about that. All that fat is gone now; in fact, you've added some definition in six months.

Six months! Why did you make me wait so long? This is the driest spell we've ever had. Of course, I wasn't faithful. I don't want to tell you how many times I've moaned your name around a fat cock I was sucking, or said it as others have rubbed against me, taken my dick into their mouths, drove their cocks into my ass. But they don't count. Not really.

The last one was taller than you, a bear of a man really. I knew he was following me, but I didn't speed up. I let him catch up with me at the corner. He smiled and led the way. I followed him to an open garage. When he got out of his pick-up, I saw he was wearing tight blue jeans and black boots. He had a tremendous bulge at the crotch. I wanted him so bad!

I smelled old oil, gasoline, dust and the sweat under his arms. He was rough with me; I knew he would be. I could tell by the way he drove his pick-up. It's what I wanted. What I needed after you got married and said you couldn't see me anymore.

He shoved me all the way to the back of the garage and slammed me, face down, onto the hood of an old Ford station wagon. He pulled my pants down, down to my ankles. I wasn't wearing any underwear; my ass was bare. He spread my legs with the toe of his boot. He unbuttoned his jeans and laid his cock inside the crack of my ass. Pre-cum dripped down from his cock hole onto my pants.

He spread my cheeks and tried to push his dick into me, but my ass was too tight and too dry. His dick wouldn't go in, not even the tip. He spit in the crack, then on his cock. He tried a finger. Then two. Finally he jammed his cock into me, hard. His cock was not as big as yours, of course, but it was big, and I felt as if I were being ripped apart. I whimpered. He slapped his hand over my mouth and pulled me up to his chest. Sweat dripped off his forehead onto my face. "Quiet, asshole. We have to be quiet."

He started to groan like he was about to come. I felt him pull out. Warm cum shot onto my ass and dripped onto my trousers. But he was not through. He wiped his cum off my ass and lubricated his cock with it before he shoved it back inside me.

God, it was incredible! The second fuck was even more savage than the first. When he began that now-familiar groaning, I reached down and jacked off. This time he came inside me, pulled out and left me in the garage. I pulled myself together as best I could. I stood, trembling from the shock of it. I pulled my pants up and buttoned them before I stumbled out to the street, to my car.

A couple of days later, I drove by the house and the garage door was closed. I did see him, though, mowing the lawn. His wife and two kids were playing in the yard. I slowed down, but I didn't stop.

Oh, but you're making up for it now, you gorgeous stud, shoving that nine-incher into my face, making me raise my head to lick it, fondling your balls while I begin to suck. You position a pillow from the old couch beneath my head. I know what is coming: You're going to fuck my face first. Today you'll probably even come, then want me to keep sucking till you're hard again, and I won't mind. Not a bit.

Oh, yeah, hold my head while you slide it in! God, I've missed it. It tastes so good. I chew on the foreskin. Now I'm sorry I've cheated on you. I remember when I admitted the long affair with the man who owned the florist shop where I worked after I graduated from high school, but you forgave me the moment I opened my mouth. You said all the practice blowing the boss had made me even better.

Yeah, that's it, get it good and hard. Rita doesn't do this, I know. And even if she did, it wouldn't be the same—there is no way she could want you as much as I do.

Oh, don't come, not so soon! Oh, shit!

There, I swallowed it all. Make you happy?

I love it when you move your hand down there and stick those fingers in. You don't have to prepare it, but you like to anyway. Yes, three fingers. Yes, yes.

You're hard again; it's just fantastic, that cock of yours. You position your knees between my legs and guide it in, right to the edge of its head. It is only just inside my sloppy ass. Then out again. Then a little farther in next time. I don't move. Now it's coming again.

I lift myself up a little, and press my ass up towards your prick. I screw it firm, with thighs and muscles, and you fuck me ferociously, endlessly, moaning in passion as drive your big cock in and out of me. I want to feel you. I get a hand in and hold two fingers to the underside of your prick, just at the root, where the balls knock against my ass at each movement. Under my fingers I suddenly feel the semen coursing through your dick as it explodes far inside me. I have to scream. I come, also. We can breathe again.

I try to get up, but I can't. My legs shake under me, so I continue to lie there on my back. You succeed in standing, but you stagger.

Still, I can see you want more. I lift my legs and put my knees on my chest, near my neck. My asshole is open, right in front of the eye of your enormous prick. A drop of cum emerges from the crack in the prick-head and falls straight down onto my asshole, which is already wet, your hot cum probably oozing out. My asslips close, trapping the falling drop of cum, and your cock throbs as it moves toward the target. Then you push it down into me in one movement, right to the bottom. It does not move but is so big that my ass is almost splitting. I am almost out of my mind.

After you fuck me for a few minutes, we roll on our sides, my ass against your groin. I lift my leg, as I love to do. Your cock slips out of my ass, and you take hold of your prick and rub it along the crack. This will have to be the last one. Your wife will be holding dinner.

I turn, and roll you onto your back. I tug at your prick. It stands up at once, and I sit up on it. I feel as if it's the last time in my life I'm going to be fucked. It's the last chance, I think, and slam down hard on your prick. You grab my buttocks with your callused hands and massage them like balls. I will come soon, I can feel it. You scratch my back with your nails. That's just what is needed: now I come You kiss, suck on my neck while my cum flows and spurts. Gobs of it.

You lift me off and up on my knees and enter me again from behind. You are merciless as you shove it in, completely savage now, desperate for my ass.

I reach behind me, through my legs, to grab your balls from below. I hold on to them so hard you have to yell.

You tear at my ass. It hurts. You scratch my back and my sides. You hold on to my hips, lift up my ass, and shove your prick in all the way. When you come, you howl.

You ask if you can take a shower.

I tell you my mom is upstairs, somewhere. You understand and do the best you can in the lavatory I helped my father build in the basement.

You stand hard by the door and thank me for the pie and coffee. I laugh. You laugh.

I start to tell you how beautiful you are, and how much I love you, but I stop myself.

It is late. I lie in the jumble of my filthy sheets. I am alone again, but filled with you. I no longer miss you. You are gone, but you are coming back. Everything will be all right.

From now on I will say that to myself every morning when I wake up, missing you.

FANTASIES OF PRETTY BOYS

The previously unpublished story of a young man who cannot avoid fantasizing about Cody, his sister's former boyfriend—who not only dished out what he claimed queer boys wanted, but was equally thrilled to take it as well! —JB

I'd been perfectly happy for several months with my fantasies and my fist. But with a stranger on top of me, his big, cut cock deep inside me, I was reminded of what I'd been missing. It was good to feel a youthful stud's tremendous energy again as he pounded his hard flesh into me.

My fingers moved through his soft blond hair and I felt his muscles straining, blood coursing. My ass muscles clutched involuntarily and suddenly I shivered, despite the night's heat and humidity.

The blond boy's forehead glistened with sweat as he rammed his cock deep into me. He balanced his lean body forward on his hands and poised himself. He slid easily in and out. His thrusting was so expert that I lost all sense of place and time. I fastened my legs around his neck and I was soon screaming in desperation. He shuddered as he came inside me. He slowed, as if he was ready to leave me, but he realized I hadn't come and continued to thrust, long and slow now. He began to jack my cock, watching with fascination as I climbed higher and higher. He plunged deep as my cries became violent and I came all over his hand. Slowly, he withdrew. His cum dribbled between my damp thighs as he leaned right over me and his face hovered above mine. "You okay?" he asked.

"Yes," I sighed, wondering what had come over me, acting like this with a stranger. I had come to the beach to take a walk, not get fucked. But it was great; I hadn't come like that in months.

"Who's Cody?" the stranger asked, pulling on his swimming trunks.

"Cody?"

"Yeah, you whispered his name when you were coming," he said.

"I didn't realize ... Oh, he's nobody special."

In truth, Cody *was* somebody very special. And the young man who had just fucked me reminded me of Cody. I suppose that was why I agreed to walk all the way down to the gay end of the beach with him, agreed to sit on his blanket and....

Cody was my sister Carole's boyfriend, and he sponged off her shamelessly. While she went out to work, he stayed at home and drank beer. I had often told Carole I didn't know what she saw in him, but I did: He was a brute—and easily the sexiest man I had ever laid eyes on. And I'd despised him with a passion since the moment we'd met over dinner at an elegant place downtown when they were here for a visit.

"Great ass," were the first words he said to me the minute Carole left us alone to go to the powder room. He had not watched my sister's ass as she left us, and his eyes bored into mine as he said it, so I assumed he was complimenting *my* ass. Stunned, I could only blush helplessly as he leered at me. He got so much pleasure from my discomfort that he got an erection—and he told me so. By the time I caught my breath, Carole had returned and we went on with the dinner. I didn't stay for dessert, feigning a headache. I made up my mind to steer clear of my sister and her new boyfriend.

Carole would call, inviting me to drive up for a visit and I would tell her I didn't want to interfere with her new relationship. It was awkward because she had never had a boyfriend who attracted me in the slightest, but this one, well, it was obvious he might welcome anything I might want to give him.

My quick, anonymous fuck on the beach reminded me that what I really wanted was Cody, so when Carole called and invited me up for the next weekend, I accepted.

As the weekend neared, I became incredibly excited, wanting to see once again the face that had filled my thoughts as I'd come on the beach, with my legs wrapped around a young stranger. I still couldn't believe that, at the ecstatic moment of orgasm, my thoughts were of Cody, and I had even blurted out his name.

I pulled into Carole's driveway late Friday afternoon. As I expected, she hadn't come home from work yet. I was pleased, because I wanted a few minutes alone with Cody.

Cody asked me in, poured me a drink. I felt him staring, laughing at me. He smirked as he sat down next to me on the couch. "Carole says you don't like me."

"I never said that...."

"No?"

"No. What I said was, I didn't approve of you."

"Oh ... well, I'm fuckin' glad I don't need your approval for anything." He gulped his drink. Then we sat silent for a few moments.

I looked him up and down. He was tall and too skinny. He had blondish, lank hair that was cut in an affected way so that it flopped over his face. He put his feet up on the coffee table and leaned back. His crotch bulge was obscene. I wanted to unzip his jeans, straddle his hips and devour his cock. And he knew it too.

Instead, I said, "You told me I had a great ass." I never should have said it, but it was too late to take it back. He did that to me, he made me nervous. And horny.

"Well, you do." Cody stared at his drink for a long minute. When he raised his head, his expression had changed. The hardness had gone and his green eyes were sparkling. "See, through my teens, I always wanted pussy ...always. But because girls are so hard to get with, and when I did get one ...well, they were afraid of me."

"Afraid?"

He smirked, patted his crotch, and winked—conveying the impression that his dick was a monster. "But I would also start fantasizing, would have, like, fantasies of pretty boys—girls with dicks, really. I would take a shower and jerk off, and I would think, 'What's it like to fuck some little boy's butt?'"

"My God...!"

"Well, what *is* it like to fuck some kid's butt?"

"I don't know," I stammered.

"Well, then, what's it like to have something up your butt?"

"What?"

"Oh, c'mon. I can tell a fudge packer when I see one. I've been around."

"Yeah, I know."

He chuckled. "I'm interested, you know?"

"Curious?" I asked, incredulous.

"Yeah, curious."

"You've gotta be putting me on."

Now, I wasn't sure of anything. What I did know was that he had once been a Marine, stayed in for three years, and he told Carole he got kicked out for some drug-related offense. He became a cook, and worked for a couple of restaurants and screwed a lot of the waitresses.

"See, I've been curious for a long time. But I never knew any queers, at least anybody that I knew was queer."

"Okay." I finished my drink.

He jumped up, poured me another, and as he handed it to me, he said, "Yeah, I even got close once."

I practically dropped the drink. "What?"

"Yeah, serious as a heart-attack. This young busboy came to work at the restaurant. He was cute as a button; in fact, he reminded me of you. Well, I wouldn't leave him alone. I'd make hints, then one day I cornered him in the john, put my hands on his butt. I knew I shouldn't have, but.... Well, he blew up. He went to the boss and I lost my job."

"So you gave up?"

"Well, till I saw you. Brought back all those memories, all those fantasies." He leaned over and stroked my arm.

"Look, I think I better just go back home." I set my drink on the coffee table.

"Carole's working late tonight. She told me to keep you company."

"How late?"

"Dunno."

"I can't do this. Not here." I jumped up, lost my balance, and dropped back down on the couch. He was all over me. I couldn't resist him—and didn't want to, in a way. I would at least get to see what his cock was like. While he tore the clothes off my body, I managed to yank down his zipper and spread his worn denim shorts apart. He obviously wanted me to have him as much as I wanted to. His semi-hard cock flopped in my face; it was very thick, uncut. I stroked it.

"Suck me," he begged, mounting me.

He had a huge pair of balls beneath his swelling cock. My own dick sprang to attention, and my legs actually shook.

He grasped my hair, not roughly, but very firmly. His dick slipped between my eager lips. It swelled and fattened to an enormous length and girth, throbbing steadily as I mouthed and tongued it. He moaned softly above me, his hand in my hair manipulating my head up and down on his mammoth prick. He smelled musky, but clean. I rolled his big balls in my hands. He groaned, raising his crotch to meet my mouth and hands. His free hand roamed over my back, sliding back into my crack. Then he grunted, and he came in my mouth. It was sudden and unexpected. A river of cum flooded my throat. That huge dick pulsed in a steady rhythm, filling me. I sucked and swallowed without losing a drop.

I could feel his body relax, fall back against the cushions. I released his dick and sat up, my own breathing heavy. He led me to the darkened bedroom.

He got on the bed. I stared down at him. He lay back, gazing up at me with an easy grin. He was covered in sweat. He ran a lazy hand over his stomach, then lifted a thigh and rolled over on his side. He sensually ran a hand over his asscheek. He continued to grin while his hand explored his own ass. I stood over him with my cock jutting out in a raging erection, and I began stroking it while staring down at his body. His pale, thin body was surprisingly sensual in its near androgyny. He should never have tried being straight. Against everything I held dear, and contrary to all the fantasies I had had about being fucked by him, all I wanted at that moment was to do the fucking. I gazed down at the slender ass that was so close, so oddly inviting. He pulled his cheeks open for me. The light fur covering his buttocks disappeared into the smooth flesh between them. The crack was bare, and a small pulsing hole seemed to wink at me.

I fell to my knees again and rammed my face into that crack. My tongue snaked out and explored, my mouth opened wide to embrace the center of his being.

His moans were now louder than ever. He rolled over a bit farther and again parted his asscheeks with his hands, to allow me easier access. He raised one of his thick thighs, his fat balls dropping down for one of my hands to grasp. He grunted as I squeezed eagerly. His asshole opened to my tongue as I rolled his nuts in my hand. I dove deep, licking him as he had probably never been licked before, opening him up with rapid stabs of my tongue. He lay there, writhing in ecstasy, moaning and groaning. I sucked and licked and he raised his butt up, begging for more.

For a few fleeting moments I worried about our being discovered by Carole, here in the bed they shared, but I was too far gone to allow that fear to stop me.

I pulled up and got in position.

"Oh ... no ...don't stop." He looked over his shoulder. "Oh, shit."

"This'll feel so good. Trust me." I pointed my erection at his well-prepared hole. My cockhead slid inside easily.

"No, no," he begged, but he didn't move.

I rammed forward to the hilt, my balls slapping against his widespread asscheeks.

I gasped out loud, and so did he.

"Oh, shit!" he cried.

He had taken all of me in one thrust. I lay over him, my hands roaming his body as I fucked him steadily, going all the way in, then nearly all the way out, then all the way back in again. My pace was slow, sure. He grunted every time I was all the way in. Eventually he raised up so that he could jack off while I fucked him.

"Oh, yeah," he sighed, "just keep doin' it. Oh God!"

He came all over the sheets—a huge volume, I thought. Maybe he was saving it up.

Moments later, I trembled from head to toe as my dick began to spew cum into him. I pulled out of his ass and shot the remainder of my load across his backside. Then he rolled over and pulled me down into his arms.

He licked my lips, my teeth, my chin. His long, sloppy tongue caressed my face, my ears, my neck.

"No one must ever know," I told him as I pulled away.

"I know."

"We can never do this again."

"I know."

I jumped up and ran to the shower.

In a few moments, I was back, and hurriedly gathered up my clothes. As I dressed, I asked, "Are you all right?"

He was staring vacantly at me, stroking his semi-hard cock. "I'm fine," he said.

I turned my back to him so he wouldn't see my tears. I started pulling up my pants. I was crying—crying, not because I'd messed up my life, but because I wanted Cody, and I knew I couldn't have him.

I heard him get up and move behind me.

He stood by my side. He kissed my bare shoulder.

I turned my face slowly. His eyes had changed. The usual sneer had disappeared. "Stay," he begged. "Don't go."

"No. I can't stay after this."

He took me in his arms. "But how would it look? She comes home and finds you gone...."

He was right, of course. I pulled away and went to the couch in the living room where I slept when I visited.

He followed me, bringing a pillow.

He wished me goodnight. He was sweet, really, but I knew that when Carole arrived home he would revert to his sneering, obnoxious self.

The next morning, I lay on the couch as long as I dared The previous night's exhilaration was dulled by nagging guilt and an intensifying apprehension. I heard Carole and Cody talking in the kitchen. I could not make out their words but they were laughing. Well, that was a good sign, at least. As I lay there, stroking my morning hard-on, I suddenly realized that for the rest of my life, or at least as long as Carole was with Cody, every time I came here to visit I would have to worry about last night's events slipping out in conversation. The thought made me shudder.

Then I heard Carole about to leave the kitchen and I threw the covers over my head. I couldn't face her, not just yet. I heard her tell Cody that she had to hurry, she was already late for a closing at the real estate office where she worked. She told him she would be back sometime late in the afternoon And, here is the best part: On the way out the door she told him, "Take care of my little brother."

Moments later Cody was tugging the blanket off me. I fought back. "Leave me alone."

"C'mon. Let's go back to bed."

I let go of the blanket and my throbbing erection was revealed.

"Ha!" He said that with that sneer I had come to despise. "Looks like you've been expecting me."

"You know what I was expecting!"

"What?"

"You know."

"What you didn't get last night? Is that it?" He reached down, stroked my cock. "Is that what all fairy boys want?"

"Yeah, and some straight boys too, if last night is any indication. Well I'm gonna get it now." I reached for the bulge at his crotch. He backed away.

"Let's go back into the bedroom."

"No, here. I want you to fuck me right here."

He sneered. "Let me get some lube."

I made myself comfortable, with my legs spread wide so all he had to do was kneel on the floor and he could shove it right in. And that was exactly what he did. He slipped it deep inside, pressing, loving. In moments, trembling, I came; I couldn't help myself. I told him not to stop, to keep on, that I could come again. He pulled me to him. I felt he wanted to kiss me on the lips, so I let him. It was a sloppy, wonderful kiss. Then he just held me while he fucked.

That morning, Cody ravaged me, as I had never been ravaged before, and as he pulled up for his final assault on my asshole, the angry, almost ugly beauty of him brought a lump to my throat. I squeezed him within the walls of my ass, and my semi-hard cock bounced in his face.

"God, this is good, kid," he whispered, his thin frame tangled around mine, his long white fingers on my waist, and he came inside me, groaning. He bit my neck as I jacked off and came again.

"Yeah," I said as he lifted himself away from me. "It's too good." I took his sopping, semi-hard cock in my hand and stroked it. I sighed as I felt the lingering power there. It was as if I was saying goodbye to it, which, in fact, I was, because I did the decent thing and disappeared before Carole got home.

In the weeks that followed, depression merged into obsession. Then one day, Carole called me out of the blue to tell me that Cody had, in her words, 'moved on.' I went to see her, comfort her, but I couldn't stay there, not after what I'd done in her living room and in her bedroom.

I never saw him again; and yet I saw him everywhere. I craved another fuck from him. Mostly I jacked off to my memories of him, but sometimes I would see men who reminded me of him and I went with them, but it just wasn't the same. They just weren't Cody—my fantasy lover made flesh.

MAD ABOUT THE BOY
An Erotic Roman à Clef

A novella, first published in the anthology Mad About the Boys. *The story of Johnny Lawrence, son of a famous actress, a boy whose appetite for sex with other boys matures when he goes to bed with his teacher, Steve Parker. Steve and Johnny fall in love, but Steve's wife fails to understand her husband's obsession with his amazingly sexy student. A* roman à clef *is, of course, a story in which actual persons, places or events are presented in the guise of fiction. Whose actual life is fictionalized in this account is up to the reader to discover, since John Patrick never publicly revealed that information.* —JB

Prologue

"You're on the hot seat," Pierce said to Johnny.

Johnny looked at him out of the corner of his eye. He rocked forward and planted his spread hands on the carpet and tried to do a headstand.

"Getting upside down won't help," Pierce said.

Maggie picked a cigarette from a lacquered box on the table. She said, "Johnny, go get Mommy's lighter from the bedroom."

"You send a nine-year-old kid for a cigarette lighter?" Pierce asked. He gestured to Johnny to stay where he was. Johnny ignored him.

"I do it all the time," Maggie said. "It never occurred to me not to."

"Well, when you come home and the apartment is a charred black hole, it'll occur to you," Pierce said.

"I just wanted to shoo him off," Maggie said, putting down the cigarette. "I'm going to discuss this stealing thing with him, but not now. He's embarrassed about the scene at supper and being on the spot."

"He's always on the spot. He gives Johnny-on-the-spot new meaning."

Johnny was back in a flash. "Aren't you, Johnny?" Maggie leaned over and looked at her son. "Aren't you Johnny-on-the-spot?"

"No," Johnny said.

"What, are you crying? Do I see tears?"

"No," Johnny said. He was biting on his lip.

"Neither do I," Pierce said. "Frankly, Johnny, I could wring your pretty little neck."

Maggie said, "Thank you very much, Pierce. Now I think it's time for Johnny to take a bath."

95

"I wouldn't know what time it is," Pierce said. "I don't have my watch. Johnny must have stolen it."

"Pierce, please." Maggie refilled her glass and tasted her drink. "My, this is strong," she said. "Excuse me, Pierce." She took the cocktail and left the room with Johnny.

Maggie balanced her drink on the side of the tub in Johnny's bathroom and turned on the gold-plated faucets. Johnny came into the room on tiptoes.

"A bath, and then I'm tucking you in," Maggie said.

"Now?" Johnny said. "It's so early. I don't even see the moon."

"What I see is you," Maggie said. "And unless I'm mistaken, you need a bath. Now, get out of those underpants and hop in."

"I'm so hungry," Johnny said, turning his back to his mother and dropping his underpants.

"Didn't we offer you dinner downtown? Would you eat it? No, you wouldn't."

Maggie left Johnny in the bathroom. A few minutes later, she came back carrying a tray with a dish of sliced fruit and cheese and a glass of lemonade on it. She put the tray down on the closed toilet seat. Johnny had poured half the bottle of bubble bath in the water and had become virtually invisible behind the froth. She retrieved her gimlet and stepped over to the tub.

Johnny pushed the bubbles off his face, twisted around and sniffed. "God," he said, "why are you drinking that?"

"Don't say 'God' to me, Johnny Lawrence," Maggie said. "You're in enough trouble. Pierce has had it with you, in case you don't know. He thinks you made off with his watch. And you walked off with Dr. Hanley's paperweight. Then you brought home poor Freddy's baseball glove. And you stole seventy-four dollars from somebody. Think about it."

"I'm sorry," Johnny said.

Maggie finished her drink and submerged her glass in the bath water. "You've got one last chance," she said. "I think you'll agree it's better for us if you stay out of sight and under the blankets tonight. Do I hear a 'yes'?"

Johnny heaved a sigh and nodded.

Maggie's face was flushed. She said, "So you see, if you watch a little TV and go to sleep in a while, or even pretend to go to sleep, I'll buy you a car tomorrow."

"What kind of car?" Johnny said.

"A big Caddy like your Uncle Bennett's. You can drive around town and get some new friends."

"Yeah, sure," Johnny laughed. "What will you *really* buy me?"

"It depends," Maggie said. "How 'bout tickets to see that cute David Cassidy at the Garden?"

Johnny made a little shiver of pleasure. "I Think I Love You" was his favorite song and he even had a pillowcase with David's picture on it. He had abandoned hope of seeing his idol at Madison Square Garden; the concert had been sold out for months. "Would you really?" Johnny asked, eyes shining.

"Really," Maggie said. "Stay out of sight tonight, and tomorrow I'll find us some tickets."

Ordinarily Johnny didn't mind staying out of sight. He was good at it. But tonight he would have preferred being downstairs with Mommy and Pierce. Pierce was the latest, and, at 28, the youngest, in Maggie's never-ending stream of boyfriends. Besides, he was tall, dark and handsome. He just looked like a movie star, which, in a way, he was. Pierce had a featured role in Maggie's latest film, a costume epic filmed in Rome, and they had carried on a torrid affair off the screen as well as on. Their romance continued even after Maggie returned to New York to prepare for her part in a new William Inge play. Pierce, having no other commitments, stayed on with her in New York.

But Johnny had one consolation: he had Pierce's watch, which he had stolen, in fact. He would wear it tonight as he slept, taking it off before he dressed in the morning, putting it back in the cigar box hidden in his suitcase, which contained all his treasures, souvenirs of the boys and men he idolized.

He hadn't been able to hide his sexy, exciting schoolmate Freddy's baseball glove, however, and when it was reported to the school office that Johnny had swiped it, he had to return it. But Johnny did get something out of that as well: After school Freddy jumped him, pushing him to the ground and throttling him until Johnny, reluctantly, was able to squirm out from under the older boy's powerful body and run away.

Just thinking about Freddy on top of him, sweaty from softball practice, slugging him, excited Johnny in his bath and he reached down and began playing with himself. In moments, he was gasping, his chest heaving, and then he relaxed, his head on the edge of the tub. He didn't know why boys like Freddy excited him so, he just knew the minutes spent thinking about them were the most pleasurable of his days.

1.

As he had five years before, when he had taken Freddy's baseball glove in grammar school, Johnny stole something from the boy he liked the most. He stole Luke Maxwell's catcher's mitt. And like Freddy, Luke was pissed. He knew Johnny had taken it, but rather than go to the principal's office as Freddy did, Luke took matters into his own hands.

One afternoon as Johnny was walking home from school, he had the feeling he was being followed. He ducked into an alleyway and waited. Sure enough, Luke was behind him. When Luke saw Johnny cowering in the shadows, he began to laugh. "I won't hurt you, squirt. I just want my mitt back."

At first, Johnny denied he was a thief. Luke pressed him against the wall. "Don't lie to me you little fairy. I know what you're up to."

As Luke took the smaller boy in his arms and shook him, Johnny was overcome. He couldn't believe how fixated he had become on Luke. He admired him as a rebel, like the one Marlon Brando played in "The Wild One," a film that had fascinated Johnny. Luke had been set back two grades during his early years because he was continually in trouble, and that endeared him to Johnny. And because he was older, Luke was much more developed than his classmates, which turned Johnny on. He had surreptitiously checked Luke out in the showers after Phys. Ed. on several occasions. Johnny would sit on the bench nearest the shower room so that he could watch Luke soaping himself, getting a near-erection. Johnny would start to get hard himself and have to turn away.

There was no turning away now. Luke clutched Johnny's arms and began pounding him against the wall. "Please," Johnny begged. "You said you wouldn't hurt me."

"I won't, if you give me my mitt back."

"It's at home. I'll go get it."

"*We'll* go get it."

Johnny agreed to take Luke to the place he called home, the Lawrence's penthouse, which occupied one full floor high in a thirty-two-story tower. Johnny smiled at the perfect timing: Maggie was at a rehearsal for a new play and the maid had the day off.

As they passed through the living room, Luke was awed by the stunning wrap-around view of Central Park—the trees, rocks, and ponds, edged with skyscrapers in the distance—and he stopped just to take it all in.

"Come on," Johnny urged, shaking with anticipation.

No other boy had ever been in his room and Johnny felt a rush of excitement as Luke locked the door behind him. Johnny was glad he had picked everything up.

"Neat," was all Luke said, his eyes wide at the sight of Johnny's huge satinwood-and-mahogany bed, desk and night tables. He picked up a baseball bat that was leaning against the desk. "You steal this, too?"

"No," Johnny said. "One of my mom's boyfriends gave it to me."

"Never been used," Luke said, stroking it lewdly. "Like your dick I'll bet."

Johnny blushed and turned away, dropping to the edge of the bed.

"You ever had anybody suck your dick?"

"No," Johnny mumbled.

"I have. Lots of times. I just go down to Third Avenue and they pay me $50 to suck my dick."

Johnny blinked. "Really?"

"Oh, shit, I shouldn't have told you, you little pervert. You'll go down there and steal all my tricks." He looked at Johnny appraisingly, then chuckled. "Nah, nobody'd want you. You're too puny. Shit, you're no competition. Zero." He shoved Johnny back so that he sat on the edge of the bed, with Luke standing over him. He said nothing as he unbuckled his belt and unzipped his chinos.

Johnny's confusion was now giving way to tremendous excitement. He could hardly believe this was actually happening.

"Well?" Luke said.

Johnny reached down inside Luke's underwear to feel his nakedness. The head of his dick was oozing with precum, which Johnny smeared down the thick shaft as Luke let his pants drop to the floor. The electricity Johnny felt from touching Luke's skin was incredible, and as he pulled the cock from the briefs, he continued stroking it. He sighed in admiration when it was finally completely revealed, because it was everything he had hoped for—and more. Johnny was dazzled by the incredible thickness, the glowing whiteness, the enormity of it.

"Kiss it," Luke commanded.

Johnny obeyed.

Within a few moments, Luke showed Johnny exactly what he wanted. And Johnny was getting good at it, taking nearly all of it in his mouth, but Luke wanted more. He told Johnny to get undressed. He nonchalantly stroked his cock as he watched Johnny shed his clothes, all but his briefs. Johnny was not about to let the older boy see his cock, which he saw would suffer terribly in comparison with Luke's huge, beautiful dick.

Luke pushed Johnny back on the bed as he climbed up on it, and knelt, straddling the younger boy, who lay flat on his back looking up at the sexy object of his fantasies. Luke rolled Johnny over onto his stomach, seized the waistband of his underwear, and began to drag it down. Johnny raised his body enough that Luke could easily slip the shorts down his legs, then he collapsed flat on the bed again as Luke pulled them over his feet and threw them to the floor. Luke whispered, "Yeah!" then slid his heavy cock between Johnny's legs.

Johnny giggled. "No way you're going to get that in."

"I only want to tease you." He rubbed a generous wad of saliva on his cock and Johnny's asscrack and for a long time just barely nudged his swollen head against the asshole. Luke pushed his foreskin all the way back, and pressed the hot, sticky tip of his cock against the back of Johnny's legs, then began massaging the younger boy's ass. His fingers dug deep into the tissue. When three fingers were inside him, in a brief moment of panic, Johnny cried out, overwhelmed by the pain. Johnny gradually relaxed and Luke brought his cockhead to the opening again, pressing more aggressively this time.

Luke's pushing became ever more ardent, and as Johnny relaxed further, lessening the resistance Luke was meeting, the lubricating mixture of saliva and precum allowed the tip of the older boy's prick to begin sliding inside. Before Johnny knew it, the entire head was going in and out of him. His breathing became erratic and shallow, his heartbeat completely wild. Luke kept driving in slightly deeper with each thrust.

Johnny reached back to feel Luke's balls and realized that Luke was only about halfway in, so he spread his legs farther apart and surrendered completely. Luke slowly bore down until his balls were hitting the base of Johnny's. Johnny felt totally *filled* with his idol's big prick. Luke pulled almost his entire length out and then eased it back in, over and over, with rapidly growing excitement. Johnny couldn't believe how amazing this felt, both sexually and emotionally. By the time Luke's thrusts had grown ferocious, Johnny was delirious with the sensation, and he cried out, "I'm coming!"

Without losing a beat in his assault on Johnny's ass, Luke reached beneath the boy and cupped his cock just as Johnny's orgasm gushed relentlessly from his penis, filling Luke's hand with the boy's hot cum.

Luke wrapped his arms tightly around Johnny's chest and fucked even harder, and much faster, until he moaned, "Oh, yeah, here it is!" just as he pulled his cock out and seized it with the hand full of Johnny's cum. He pumped his cock wildly into his cum-slick hand until Johnny's back was being sprayed with his own burning semen. After a few moments of shaking the last drop of his orgasm from his dick, Luke collapsed on top of the boy, languorously sliding his chest in the slipperiness of Johnny's cum-coated chest.

They lay there for several minutes, two sweaty, spent bodies. Finally, Luke rolled off Johnny and lay on his side next to him, still panting. Johnny turned to his side, and wrapped Luke's body in his arms. He opened Luke's mouth with his tongue and pulled him tightly against him. He hadn't kissed any boy before, and he found it delightful—fully as exciting as he had anticipated. The softness of Luke's mouth contrasted sharply with the hardness of his chest pressing tightly against him. Before long, Johnny was sucking and licking Luke's chin, nose and ears.

"Hey, I gotta get outta here," Luke said, pushing Johnny away.

Johnny lay still, watching the young stud yank his chinos on and pull his T-shirt over his head. He was beautiful, Johnny thought, the most beautiful boy at school. Some boys were more handsome, had even better bodies, but Luke was more beautiful than any of them because he had let his body speak for him in a way Johnny could only envy.

"Going to Third Avenue?" Johnny asked snidely.

"So what if I am?"

"Take me with you."

"Maybe. Some day, when your pecker is bigger," he sneered as he stepped into his shoes.

Johnny pulled a sheet over his lower body. "Don't forget your mitt."

"You can keep the mitt. I got what I wanted."

But Luke acted as though he wasn't sure about letting Johnny keep the mitt. He would spot him in the halls between classes and ask if there was anyone home at his house. If Johnny said no, then he'd tell him he was coming over to get his mitt. And he would go home with Johnny, and within a few minutes of their arriving there, he would have his cock planted deep inside Johnny's ever-more hungry ass, filling it with his hot load. The mitt would never be mentioned

This went on for weeks. Then one afternoon while Johnny was lying face down on his bed, and Luke lay on top of him, fucking him furiously, Luke suddenly pulled out and rolled the younger boy over. Johnny was no longer embarrassed about showing Luke his cock—in fact, he thought it had actually grown some since the older boy had begun fucking him. Now he stroked his dick proudly, while he lay his back between the kneeling Luke's legs, and it stood high and proud, bending precariously to the left. Luke stroked his own cock eagerly as he looked down and watched Johnny masturbate; he ran his free hand over Johnny's hairless chest, then down to the navel and beyond. Johnny released his throbbing cock as Luke took it in his hand and leaned over. Luke opened his mouth wide and inhaled Johnny's cock in one swoop, pressing his lips against the base of it as he began to suck profoundly.

The sight of his hero engulfing his erection practically caused Johnny to come. He grabbed Luke's head to stop him, but it was too late: his cum erupted inside Luke's mouth, and Luke swallowed it hungrily. Luke reluctantly stopped sucking after a few moments, and let go of Johnny's prick, tonguing his way up to his face, kissing him hard on the lips. As he did, Johnny's legs parted and Luke's sex slipped back inside the welcoming heat of his ass. They fucked this way for several minutes, as lovers, locked in each other's arms, until Luke came.

After pulling out, Luke leaned back and took Johnny's cock in his hands. "You know, this isn't a bad dick, squirt. Not bad at all. I think we could do some business with this dick."

He turned Johnny over and slapped his buttocks. "God knows we could do some business with this ass."

And so it secretly began.

2.

Luke was from the privileged class; his father worked in Wall Street, but he was street-smart, and Johnny discovered he could ask him anything. Johnny had been looking for a friend like Luke all his life.

People would ask Johnny, "Who is your girl?" And he would say, "I have no girl," and they would laugh and his mother would say, "Johnny doesn't care for girls." "All that will change," they'd say, but Maggie knew it wouldn't and she had accepted it.

People said, "Johnny is a good boy," and Johnny knew they said that because they didn't really know him. He didn't look or act different from other boys his age, but he knew he was a bad boy, a misfit, an outcast. Johnny stopped asking questions, though his mind was teeming with them; it was no use. The questions he wanted to ask were the questions grownups and even older boys did not want to answer—until Luke came along.

When Johnny went to the New York Public Library and read Darwin, he got a shock: "'...the hair is chiefly retained in the male sex on the chest and face, and in both sexes at the juncture of all four limbs with the trunk....'" There was more, but he heard someone coming and had to replace the book on the shelf. He found another book, called "What Every Boy Should Know" and it told him nothing that he didn't know already. It made it clear that he was a sinner, but that much he was already aware of.

His mother played sinners on the screen, and as far as he could tell there was little difference between the real Maggie and the *reel* one.

Once when Uncle Bennett was in Manhattan, he took Johnny to church. There, wearing his blue serge Sunday suit, Johnny heard the minister say solemnly from the pulpit that everyone—which clearly included Johnny—was conceived in sin. But afterward, at the church door, in the brilliant sunshine, the Reverend shook hands with Johnny and said he was happy to have the boy with them in their church.

Before Luke, Johnny was sometimes a child, sometimes an adult in an uncomfortably small size. He blushed and had his feelings hurt easily. His jokes were rarely successful, the point of them escaping most people—except Luke. Luke seemed to know everything; he even told him it was okay to be homosexual—*gay*, he called it—"Just don't advertise it."

When he was around, which wasn't often, Uncle Bennett would try to discipline the boy, telling him to sit up straight in his chair, to stand with his shoulders back, to pick up his clothes, read in a better light, stop chewing his nails, stop sniffing and go get a Kleenex. Uncle Bennett often teased him about his thinness, his pallor, his poor posture, his moodiness, and concluded that the boy did not spend enough time out-of-doors. Johnny took that as an admonition to hit the streets—but not at all in the way his uncle had in mind.

After weeks of being fucked by Luke, Johnny had his plans made, and his startling green eyes became a mask of innocence while he waited for his mother and the maid to leave the apartment. Then the mirror became his accomplice. He practiced looking like the person he wanted to become. He could slip into roles as easily as his mother did, and he soon became stuck in one role: the pretty blond-boy hustler.

Even though Maggie had accepted Johnny's homosexuality, little did she know what Johnny was thinking when, on those rare occasions, she would take him out.

One day they were walking through Greenwich Village when they were stopped on the street by a man who invited them into his shop, *Ron's Then and Now*. The eye contact between Johnny and Ron began immediately. The walls of the shop were covered with posters and photographs of film and theatre stars. Ron brought out a box and began to show Maggie photographs of herself from her early films.

"Look at this one," Ron enthused. "It's from 'The Cattle Queen.' It's my favorite. It was taken in 1960." Maggie looked horrified.

"No it wasn't," she told him. "That's a mistake. It should be 1966." Maggie autographed the picture just the same.

Johnny smiled; he knew all of her films, and she had made that horrible western in 1960. It was released in 1961, the year he was born, and she had moved to New York to be with his father. She bought Johnny a few of the other photographs, and they quickly left, but not before Johnny had surreptitiously written, "I'll be back," on one of Ron's business cards. Ron saw the card as they were leaving the shop and raced after them. He stood in the doorway and when Johnny looked around, Ron waved. Johnny winked back.

Johnny went back to the shop a week later. Ron, a slender man in his mid-thirties with wire-rim glasses, was overjoyed to see the boy. The thought that he could spend some time with Maggie Lawrence's son was inconceivable to him. Johnny lingered over a bin containing stills of David Cassidy while Ron finished waiting on a customer.

Finally the customer left and Ron came over to Johnny. "May I help you, young man?"

"I think so," Johnny said, turning to face the man, his hand on his crotch.

Ron looked down to where Johnny had brought his hand to rest. He gulped. "You are even more beautiful than your mother."

Johnny smiled. How was it that everyone else was always finding fault with him, but with Luke and this older men he could do no wrong? In fact, all he had to do was stand there and be worshipped. It was the most incredible thing.

"Just a minute," Ron said, stepping to the front of the store. "I've been thinking about you every minute," he said, swinging the sign around to CLOSED and pulling the shades.

Johnny stepped up behind him and tugged at the ribbon holding his ponytail; Ron's brown hair fell around his shoulders. When the man turned around, Johnny stood back, considering him. He found him more attractive than he had first thought, laugh-lines around his eyes the only tell-tale sign of his age.

To Ron, Johnny was a luscious temptation. "Such forbidden fruit," he muttered, sinking to his knees before Johnny and cupping the boy's buttocks as he brought his mouth to his groin. It was an incredible fantasy come true; he had never had sex with a movie star's son before. A moan of intense longing growled deep within his throat. His tongue explored the growing bulge in Johnny's chinos. He could not get enough of the boy.

Johnny began to breathe fast and hard, his chest heaving. Ron went on sucking on the bulge now protruding from Johnny's groin. Ron's fingers grappled with the zipper, spreading the pants open, reaching into the white briefs underneath, finally revealing the cock. "Hmmmm," was all Ron could say as he plopped it in his mouth.

"Yes... God, yes," Johnny moaned.

Ron ran his teeth lightly along the entire length of the cock. His thumb played with the throbbing vein on the underside of the shaft, while the other hand kneaded the lightly-furred balls. Soon Ron began sucking with relish. It would not take long for Johnny to come, Ron feared, and sure enough, an excruciating groan filled the store, Johnny grabbing fistfuls of Ron's hair, holding him fast, plunging his sex into Ron's mouth as it erupted. Ron accepted the steady stream of cum down his throat as he slid his hands down to undo his own pants and take out his prick. He jerked himself off, and as he shot his semen out onto the floor, his spasms were so intense his whole body ached.

Panting, his cock still enveloped in the heat of Ron's mouth, Johnny opened his eyes and looked down at Ron's head as he began running his fingers gently through the older man's hair.

Even though they both had come, Ron was reluctant to give up Johnny's cock, but when he finally did, Johnny zipped up. With a big grin on his face, he went back to the David Cassidy bin and picked three stills that he did not have in his collection.

At the counter, slipping the photos in a brown bag, Ron said, "They're on the house."

Escorting Johnny to the door, Ron rubbed Johnny's shoulders and said, "Your name is Johnny, isn't it?"

"Yeah."

"I finally found it in a story in one of the old magazines. Johnny Lawrence." He said the name as if he was sucking it.

Johnny stopped and put his arm around Ron's waist. "That's not my real name, of course."

"Oh, of course," Ron said, with a giggle.

That night, before they went to dinner, Maggie and Johnny sat in the living room together, the vast panorama of the New York skyline in shadows and neon before them. Johnny had always been captivated, mesmerized by the view—the continuous performance, the scenes, the comings and goings far below them.

Maggie had two martinis and then they went to "21" because Johnny loved their corned-beef hash. Lydia Lester, the gossip columnist for the Tribune syndicate, was table-hopping and stopped to chat. Johnny once again found himself reveling in the glamour associated with being a movie star's son. Maggie brought Lydia up-to-date on the play she was going to do in London, and a guest shot on *Kojak*. Then she said, "But the public doesn't care about me anymore. It's always Ryan O'Neal! Always Tatum! Always McQueen, Nicholson, Beatty, Candy B., Sylvia Miles and Andy Warhol ... even Tony and Berry for godsakes!"

"Times change," was all Lydia would say.

"But not New York," Maggie said. "The electricity of Manhattan never goes away. The city is always changing and some of the changes are large, but they're not distracting. The excitement of the city never, ever diminishes; the speed with which it moves. And the people, the cab drivers yelling--none of that changes. It's such a wonderful place! People here act like they grew up with you or they helped you to get to where you are. They're very supportive; they make me feel terribly welcome." Maggie had her publicist's lines down pat. She could change them to suit whatever city she happened to be in.

"Can I quote you?" Lydia asked, her eyes flashing as she scanned the room for more familiar faces.

"Of course," Maggie said.

They bussed each other's cheeks and Lydia patted Johnny on the head before dashing to a table across the room where Bob Evans was sitting with a starlet whose name Maggie couldn't recall. "The next Maggie Lawrence," she said with a shrug. "God help her."

Before going home they window-shopped along Madison Avenue. When they returned to the penthouse, Maggie was tired and Johnny went with her to her bedroom. Only a few of her things were scattered about the room but it seemed as if she'd always been there. She'd come home, but only temporarily. Now she was taking her son to California for Christmas.

Johnny stood at the end of her bed watching her get comfortable. When he was sure she was asleep he switched off the light but left the door open in case she called out in the night, then went to his own room. He sat by the window, dialed Luke's number. He wanted to tell him about his encounter in the Village. There was no answer, and holding the telephone, lost in thought, he just let it ring.

A few days after they arrived in California, Maggie said, "Let's go and take a look at where I used to live." They put the top down on the rented, baby-blue Cadillac convertible, and took off.

For the first few days of their stay in California the weather had been dreary. It was drizzly and everything looked gray. Now, the sky was a diamond; the buildings and the roads, the cars and the people all glistened. Palm trees, plants and flowers were colors right out of a paint box. Johnny recalled the names of the roads which had always excited him: Sunset Boulevard, La Cienega, La Brea and Vine. Everything was even more enchanting now than he remembered. And the people all looked beautiful, healthy and clean, dry-cleaned—and rich, very rich.

As they were driving through Brentwood, Maggie spotted the house. She slammed on the brakes and threw the car into reverse. Johnny gripped the leather seat. He couldn't remember a time when he had actually seen her driving—other than in a movie—and it was unnerving.

They shot across to the other side of the road, managing to miss a truck that appeared from around the bend, and then the car stalled on a small ridge at the entrance to a driveway. They rolled back down onto the street.

Johnny panicked. The traffic was coming at them from every side. Suddenly they stopped rolling, and Maggie hit the gas. They veered back across the road, bumped up a ridge and ended safely in another driveway, leading steeply upward to a mansion.

"Mother, why'd you do that?"

"It's not my fault, honey. It's that stupid gateway. It's at the top of a mountain!"

They drove up the driveway, and Maggie stopped the car and shut off the motor—several yards short of a gateway across the road. She said she didn't want to be "seen" unannounced. Johnny felt that at any moment they might be set upon by a pack of hounds and arrested on suspicion of being robbers.

It was wonderful to get out of the car. Johnny thought they were only going on a short trip, but so far it had ended up being a three-hour journey.

Seen up close, through the iron grillwork and a protective screen of tall trees, the house was impressive. Maggie said it was owned by Sam Spear, an RKO line producer who had been her third husband. Howard Hughes, owner of RKO, had wanted to put her under contract after she left Metro, but Sam had a better idea: he'd marry her. Their union had lasted for a year.

She said once that Spear had married her so he could put her in his pictures for free. He was a wealthy purveyor of monster-movie cheapies, drive-in-circuit turkeys that raked in considerable cash. Marrying Maggie would also, he thought, bring him prestige.

"What do you think of the house, honey? Do you like it?" Maggie whispered quickly.

"Yes. I do like it," Johnny whispered back. "It's so big."

"Sam was a dreadful man, but living here was so much fun in those days." Maggie took his arm and they began to walk back to the car. "Betty and Bogey lived right over there," she added, pointing to the mansion across the street.

"It must have been great."

"'Just keep it in the shadows, Maggie,' Bogie used to tell me, 'let the camera come to you.'" His mother did a pretty fair Bogart impression, Johnny thought. "Oh, I liked him. We used to go out on his boat, the Santana. And Betty ... you know, I still see her when I'm in New York."

"Yes, I know," Johnny said, rolling his eyes.

Maggie clicked her tongue against the roof of her mouth. "Hmm," she winced. "That Betty. She always looks so good."

They got back in the car and Maggie took a last look as she switched on the ignition. "Why did you leave?" Johnny asked.

She thought for awhile and then, while she miraculously negotiated a three-point turn to aim the Cadillac back down the driveway, she said, "Why to have you, of course." She chuckled. "Sam and I wanted different things from life. Who knows why?" She bumped the car back out of the difficult entrance to the driveway. "I'm sure glad that I got that divorce, honey, 'cause I got you."

The car squealed and tilted to one side as she turned and careered on down the winding roads that led to the coast.

They stopped to have dinner, then went to the house Johnny's maternal grandmother owned in Huntington Beach. It had a stunning view of the ocean, but it was small. In the back was a little garden where his Grandmother grew tomatoes and flowers. The swimming pool was outside the kitchen window. Johnny thought it idyllic.

Grandma was excited to see them but the conversation soon degenerated into nastiness. Grandma tilted her head at Maggie. "You want to be a good person, and you work at it, but your brother's the real article. Goodness comes to him without any effort at all."

Maggie nodded. Bennett had made a fortune in New York real estate, never married, and doted on his beautiful young sister. He said he was devoted to his mother, but most of the year he lived three thousand miles away, in splendid semi-retirement in Palm Beach.

"Bennett says you have a new boyfriend."

"He's always a bit behind the times. I used to have one," Maggie snorted. "I'm between engagements right now."

"Why do people your age always have to find the right person?" Grandma went on. "Why can't you learn to live with the wrong person?

107

Sooner or later everyone's wrong. Love isn't the most important thing. Why can't you see that? I still don't understand why you couldn't live with Jack. He seemed like such a nice young man."

"Come on, Mother," Maggie said, finding some Christmas music on the radio. "Over and done with, gone and gone."

"You live with somebody so that you have somebody to live with, and then you go out and do the work of the world. I don't understand all this pickiness about lovers. In a pinch anybody'll do, believe me."

On the side table was a picture of Grandfather. Maggie glanced at the picture and let the silence hang between them before asking, "How are you, Mother, really?"

"I'm all right." She leaned back in the sofa, whose springs made a strange, almost human groan. "But I want to get out. I spend too much time in this place. You should expand my horizons. Take me somewhere. Take me back to New York with you."

"I can't. I'm starting a play—in London."

"You should do a movie. You're a movie star."

Maggie was growing more agitated by the minute. She looked at Johnny and said, "Maybe we should go."

"No!" Grandma said, much more loudly than she'd intended. Then more softly, "Please stay a while. I hardly ever see Johnny, and it's Christmas Eve."

Maggie disappeared into the kitchen while Johnny talked to his grandmother. He told her about New York, then made one-sided small talk about the snowstorm that had hit the city before they left for Los Angeles, thinking the thought of snow might spark some memories from Grandma.

Grandma was well over eighty. Wearing a mauve house dress and a row of beads, with her hair waved and rouge on her cheeks. Her voice was high-pitched and seemed to demand great effort; she reminded Johnny of a little bird, a little operatic songbird. Her accent changed in varying degrees from a lowland Scottish brogue to proper English pronunciation, but sometimes fell into West Coast American slang.

"Have you ever come across my friend Violet Fairbrother back there in England?" she called to Maggie.

"No, I've never come across her."

Grandma had been born Jean MacDougall. She was a native of Scotland but moved to England in her teens, where she studied acting at the Royal Academy of Dramatic Art. Along with her best friend Violet Fairbrother, she was, she told Johnny, a star pupil, and went on to play Puck at a London theatre before being asked to join the Benson Players, a forerunner of the Royal Shakespeare Company, at Stratford-upon-Avon.

When she married Maggie's father, Michael Lawrence, she gave up the theatre and they emigrated to Canada, where Bennett was born. The family then moved to Pasadena where Jean gave birth to Maggie. When

Michael divorced her, Jean started teaching acting and elocution at her home to keep the family going. Her own daughter was her "star" pupil, and she was determined that Maggie would become a film star.

After acting in high school plays, Maggie become enamored of the theater. Jean's encouragement and determination for her daughter to succeed were rewarded when Maggie, after leaving high school, began appearing in local productions.

Mother chaperoned her daughter everywhere, so when Maggie was asked to understudy Sabina in "The Skin of Our Teeth" at the Plymouth Theatre in New York, Mother went with her. She coached Maggie in the part that gave her that first important 'break': When Maggie was signed to replace the star during the run of the show, she was spotted by an MGM talent scout, taken back to California and put under contract.

"I wish your mother would have tried harder," Grandmother said to Johnny.

"Oh, Mother," Maggie shouted from the kitchen, agitated by having to listen to her reminiscences.

Mother leaned forward and spoke to Johnny confidentially. "Maggie would never apply herself properly. She'd never talk to the columnists. I used to get them on the phone, and they'd be going crazy. 'That girl's going to ruin her career if she won't talk to me,' they used to say. But Maggie would never talk. She always hated gossip; even though she created quite a lot of it. And she'd never dress herself properly. When we used to go over to Zsa Zsa's house, her mother would say, 'Oh that Maggie! She could make something of herself if she'd only fix herself up a bit.' But that's Maggie. She's impossible. She didn't even wear a new dress when she won her Tony! She just threw on her mink. Maggie likes to do things her way."

"That's enough talking about me," Maggie called out, bringing Grandma a cup of tea and some cookies from the kitchen.

"I like tea," Grandma said with such a satisfied smile that it made Johnny's eyes get misty.

"All these Christmas cards," Johnny said, standing at the mirror and fingering them one by one, flipping them open to read the messages. "So many people love you, Grandma. Look, here's one from Mrs. Stone. I remember her. She was your crazy old neighbor. She must be in her nineties now."

"Yes, she's in a rest home," Maggie said.

"Hated her," Grandma sighed, lifting the teacup again, letting the last drops slip onto her tongue. "That was good tea."

"Would you like more, Grandma?" Johnny asked, but the question stumped his grandmother, who was busy examining the sugar cookies on the plate. She picked up each one as if considering its shape, turning it over, and replacing it carefully.

"We'd better go now, Johnny," Maggie said finally. "We'll be back tomorrow, Mother, and take you to dinner."

"I'd like that. I never go out anymore."

Johnny kissed his grandmother's cheek, which was surprisingly smooth and silky. He whispered, "I miss you" into the wisps of white hair that brushed across Grandma's ear. "Merry Christmas."

"Bye-bye," Grandma answered, holding up a Santa Claus cookie and waving it at them.

"Let's go for a drive along the coast," Maggie said as they got into the convertible. "It's a beautiful night." Johnny's face lit up.

They stopped in a parking lot on the Pacific and sat on the hood, looking out across the ocean. There were little bonfires burning along the beach where people were having parties and somewhere, someone was playing a guitar. The sky was a magenta color and seemed to be lit from behind with golden rays. The moon was full and seemed to be sitting on the surface of the ocean. It was a stunning evening sky. Even if there was no snow, Johnny could not imagine a more wonderful Christmas Eve.

"Why don't you like people talking about your career?" Johnny asked. "Don't you like being a movie star?"

"I'm not a movie star anymore, honey, I got too old. Now I'm finally an actress. And I like being an actress. That's why I love it when I'm in England. It means something there. I just never liked all that movie star stuff. It's nothing. Sometimes I wish I'd have continued on the New York stage instead of going to Metro. Maybe that might have worked out better. Who knows?" She shrugged and nestled her head on Johnny's shoulder.

It was at times like this that Johnny wished everybody had a mother as wonderful as his.

3.

Sooner or later, Luke warned, Johnny would get into trouble. To Johnny, whoring had been a lark because he hadn't needed the money but, after awhile, the men who were picking him up began to bore him. Johnny had become fascinated by the other hustlers on the streets.

Of all the street boys he met, it was one named Eric who titillated Johnny the most. But Eric wanted nothing to do with Johnny. Finally Johnny agreed to pay him and the two went off to a place where Eric said he was staying temporarily. It was July and the heat was unrelenting. Johnny paid for a cab.

The neighborhood was vaguely familiar. Johnny had tricked once with a businessman who lived nearby. He waited on the tiny concrete stoop as Eric unlocked the door. Inside, it was too dim to see anything, but Eric seemed to know what he was doing. He immediately stepped into a side room as Johnny stood just inside the door, letting his eyes adjust. There wasn't much to see: a cramped front room with old pictures hung on one wall. Beneath the pictures was a fold-up frame and mattress, stripped of its sheets. The fan was on, humming softly. Eric switched the control setting to maximum cool.

When Eric took off his tight black T-shirt, Johnny saw his broad torso was slick with sweat.

"Lick me," Eric commanded.

Eric guided Johnny's mouth over his hard stomach and pecs, then into his armpits. The stud unbuckled his pants, pulled out a cock even larger than Luke's. Eric pushed Johnny down to his knees, made him worship the cock until it was fully hard.

"Turn around," Eric ordered, unfolding the bed.

Johnny got on all fours on the bed and the stud pulled down his shorts.

Eric greased Johnny, calling his ass a "boy pussy." He told Johnny to back up on his cock. Johnny pushed his ass against the shaft. It felt like a fist. Johnny pushed hard, but couldn't even slip the head in.

Eric broke a popper under Johnny's nose and pushed. The head slid in. Johnny cried out. A couple of inches of the shaft went in. Johnny wanted it, but at the same time he didn't. The pain was too much, but the sexual rush from the popper made it feel wonderful at the same time.

Eric took the belt from his jeans and lashed at Johnny's ass.

The crack of the wide belt slapping his flesh sounded fierce, and the pain that accompanied it made Johnny begin to tremble.

"Just a little more," Eric demanded, shoving his cock back in.

"No, I can't," Johnny pleaded. "I can't take any more."

Eric broke another popper under the boy's nose and shoved. It was at last all the way in.

"Fuck it," Eric commanded, and Johnny began moving his hips very slowly, sliding the cock in and out. As the lashing continued, Johnny worked harder and harder, riding the stud's shaft.

Johnny, through clenched teeth, began to groan as Eric's eruption began filling him, at last. He loved the fucking, but welcomed an end to the pain.

"So what do we have here?"

Johnny turned to see a tall, brutish-looking man standing in the doorway, clad only in a studded leather jockstrap, holding a sweating beer bottle.

"Just having a little fun, Doc."

Doc entered the room. "Save anything for me?"

Eric pulled out. "Plenty to go 'round. Plenty." Eric moved around to Johnny's face while Doc gripped Johnny from behind.

"Did this boy know he was messing with my lover?"

"Of course."

"Well, fair is fair, Eric. You had your fun, now I'll have mine."

111

His hands clutching Eric's thighs, Johnny took Eric's sopping cock into his mouth, concentrating simply on fellating the monster prick. Then he felt a heavy hand lightly cup first one asscheek, then the other. Then he felt the sting of an open palm land square on his ass. *Thwaaack!* He jerked at the impact. It was followed by another and another and another, a rain of blistering blows. Soon the warmth spread over his ass and he seemed to find the spanking pleasurable for a while, until Doc changed from his hand to Eric's wide leather belt. Johnny's whimpers became groans, then muffled screams. Tears were flowing down his cheeks before Doc finally eased off, going back to moderate smacks with his hands before changing over into gentle caresses that quickly had Johnny moaning again with desire.

"He's a pretty one, Eric, I'll have to say that," Doc said while his busy fingers stroked and tickled and pinched the boy everywhere he could reach. Johnny began gyrating frantically when he felt Eric was about to come again.

"No," Doc ordered, "hold it, Eric. We're just gettin' this one warmed up."

Eric withdrew momentarily, then slammed his cock back into Johnny's gaping mouth.

"Yeah, and now I'm going to stick so much dick up this pretty little butt that he'll really have somethin' to think about."

Johnny felt a cold and greasy finger poke at his hole. Doc shoved it in slowly and moved it around, then pulled it out and paused a moment before he put it back in, rolling it around inside Johnny, pressing on his prostate. The slowness of the entry started to relax Johnny, and soon his ass was squirming around the invading digit. It was joined by another, and then another, twisting around inside him, opening him up, making his groans of pain turn into moans of pleasure.

"Oh, yeah, give your ass to me...give it up...let go...relax....That's right, you're getting it....I'm going to give you what you need...."

Suddenly a greased cock replaced the fingers and Johnny bucked back to take more of it with each thrust. Doc had a nice-size cock, not small and not terribly large like Eric's, but still he managed to hit Johnny's prostate with almost every stroke. Eric came, pulling out and dumping his load all over Johnny's face and shoulders, then slamming his prick back in again.

Johnny gave himself over to ecstasy as Doc continued to fuck him and play with his smooth skin. He was moaning and chewing on Eric's semi-hard cock in his mouth when Doc finally shouted that he was coming. Johnny's ass spasmed around the thrusting dick, and while Doc was filling his ass with cum, he shot his load, too.

Johnny was happily wasted by the time Doc pulled out. Doc stood for awhile with his arms around the boy, gently fondling his nipples. A bell sounded. Doc lifted himself from Johnny and left the room. Dazed,

Johnny turned to see what was happening but Eric forced him back down on his cock. Doc entered the room again, accompanied by another man. Again Johnny tried to turn his head to see the visitor but Eric held his head steady, his cock hard again, enjoying the blowjob too much to let Johnny stop.

Once more Johnny felt fingers at his asshole. Gently the visitor began to lick and kiss the now-scarlet mounds and the boy moaned and wriggled with excitement.

"My God, what a beauty," the visitor remarked, and his lips moved to the boy's throbbing asshole. Very gently he nibbled around the inside of Johnny's cheeks, inhaling the musky scent. Slowly he flicked the open hole with his tongue.

"Aaaaah!" Johnny was sobbing with ecstasy. The visitor began to slowly slip his fingers up and down the shaft of the boy's cock milking it, all the time feeling the lips of the boy's anus pulsing against his tongue.

"And a pretty cock, too, Joe," Doc said. "Aren't you glad you came by?"

"Hmmmm," groaned Joe, then sank his tongue deep inside Johnny, covering the whole asshole with his mouth. As Johnny tightened his hole instinctively, Joe sucked and nibbled. Johnny writhed and squirmed. He longed for release but his cock was gripped by Joe's powerful, hairy hands.

Joe rose and pulled down his pants. Johnny uttered a muffled cry around Eric's dick and the load of come that suddenly filled his mouth as Eric came yet again. Then Eric pulled his huge dick free and began stroking it proudly. Doc moved and knelt in front of Johnny, taking Eric's place. Johnny turned to take a look at Joe but Doc seized his head and forced it back so he could press his dick against Johnny's forehead. The boy's mouth opened and his tongue began to lick the man's heavy balls and then faster and faster it moved up the shaft towards the knob, glistening with cum.

Meanwhile, Joe had put on a pair of thin rubber gloves and he began applying cold cream to the boy's scarlet buttocks. Slowly the fingers moved over the defenseless tender flesh, rubbing and probing at will. Johnny's tongue moved in a frenzy along Doc's cock—sucking, licking, biting. Johnny's sphincter spread for Joe's fingers. The finger-fucking continued for several minutes and at times Johnny thought he would pass out from the pain, but Joe knew exactly when to stop. Then he positioned his dick against Johnny's gaping, juicy hole. Slowly he pushed forward. His cock, about seven inches long and thick, slipped in easily. Reaching beneath him he found Johnny's nipples and he began squeezing them until Johnny cried out, his buttocks gripping Joe's cock as it drove in and out. Joe moved his hands down under Johnny's body and grasped the boy's stiff cock. Johnny moved his flanks in time with Joe's fuck-rhythm. His breathing quickened and he thrust his body back, opening his asshole as wide as he could. He couldn't speak because Doc's cock filled his mouth, but he was groaning.

Firmly holding Johnny down, Joe suddenly pulled out and replaced his cock with the gloved fingers of his hand. Johnny rode back more eagerly still, his ass muscles gripping the fingers, which slipped deeper and deeper inside him. Johnny suddenly felt his bowels opening at the same time his orgasm exploded uncontrollably. Joe began jacking his cock and soon was spraying his cum across Johnny's smooth young cheeks. Slowly, gently, Joe removed his hand and the hot juices dripped from the throbbing, bloated asslips. Seeing this, Doc could take no more and began charging into Johnny's mouth, his cum soon blasting down the boy's throat.

Doc ordered Eric to clean up the mess and to help get Johnny dressed, then he and Joe left the room. Witnessing the scene had turned Eric on again and he began applying more hard licks to Johnny's ass.

"Messy boy," he scolded. "Messy, messy."

Johnny cried out. Eric's hard lashes continued until Johnny was sobbing. Then Eric rolled him over and lifted Johnny's legs over his shoulders. Johnny was now more vulnerable than ever and all Eric had to do was push forward and his erection slid right in all the way. With his hands clasped tightly on Johnny's forearms, Eric held the boy down as he ravaged him. Johnny could hear the other men returning to the room and laughing. "Eric can never get enough boy pussy," Doc said.

"Look at him go," Joe laughed.

Later, when Johnny returned to the apartment, he went straight to bed. The next morning, the red welts on his buttocks were still hurting him and it was painful for him to sit. Worse still, his anus was bleeding.

The next day, at school, he went to see the nurse, a woman who had been friendly and helpful in the past. He begged her not to tell his mother, but the woman betrayed him, calling Maggie with the news that Johnny had been raped.

Johnny refused to tell his mother who had hurt him. Her reaction was to call Bennett, who was at his summer place in Rhode Island, preparing to return to Florida. He agreed to come into the city and meet Maggie for lunch. His reaction to the rape of Johnny was typically swift. He wanted to take the boy with him, enroll him in a Christian school in Florida he had helped bankroll.

"I don't want him to go to Florida," Maggie said, shrugging sadly, then lighting a cigarette. "I don't expect you to understand this entirely, but for so many years that boy has been part of everything I've done. I tried to organize my life in order to spend as much time with him as I could. Now I've done all that and Johnny is just reaching the age where he can fend for himself."

"What's so hard to understand about that?"

"I know, you're worried about the way I live, you worry about the effect on him."

"Well, I worry that you've never spanked him. My feeling is: spare the rod and spoil the child." Bennett loved his sister; he knew that she loved life, loved what she did, offered no apologies, and took responsibility for her actions. Still, he knew the secret about Johnny's father. He went on: "You can't let him grow up to be what his father was. I just hope it's not too late."

Although she had talked with her older brother on the phone many times recently, she hadn't seen him in a year. Bennett had grown heavier, almost ponderous, and his hair was thinning at the top. He'd always looked younger than he was, often looked to be the youngest man in the room, even among those younger than he; now, he looked older. Maggie appreciated the fact that at least he didn't dye his hair or wear double knits.

Bennett had always been a decisive man, and now his manner was weightier than she remembered. "You've done very well, Maggie," he said in his careful voice. "And it must be quite a lot of fun, and profitable too, I suppose. Yes, I think you've done damn well. Really damn well in this acting business, but .... "

"To have Johnny in Florida would mean quite a change in my life," she interrupted.

"Mine, too."

"Understand this," she went on. "For the first time in a long time my life is ordered the way I want it. Johnny is an important part of it, part and parcel. Perhaps in some ways Johnny is responsible for it."

He stared at her; she thought he was about to press an advantage. Instead, he said, "Well, it's not important." She saw him watching her, a slight smile on his face. The smile irritated her, it was almost a smirk; it was the smile he used when dealing with his tenants.

"Think about *his* life for a moment. Not mine. Not yours. *His*."

"I am," she said.

"For one thing, he can be troublesome."

"Of course," she said. "He's only a teenager."

Johnny was a teenager whom she provided for, who was part of her life. He was as happy as any of the other children she knew, mostly the progeny of cheerful, durable marriages. Seeing Bennett looking more and more like her father, she recalled her own childhood. She saw her father sitting in a leather chair, her big, careless father, who seemed to gulp life like a swimmer perpetually surfacing from under water. He was the source of her energy and her pride and her ambition. He was the source, but not the sustenance. She wished she could still ask his advice; he had always given her good advice. She would not be bound to follow it, but at least she would have it. She concentrated, recalling various typical pronouncements of her father's, but at the moment she mostly recalled only his jokes. Her father thought a good dose of humor could solve everything, and perhaps it might. No, she thought, it was impossible; for Johnny, Palm Beach would be like a death sentence.

That night, she sat in the library at the apartment, drinking brandy, surrounded by photos of her family, and her eyes welled up. She saw her life captured in an 8 x 10 photograph: her son had his arm lightly around her waist, they were clowning together. His head was high, her hand rested on his shoulder. They were unconfined, separate centers of gravity, but they were connected, too. They depended, each on the other—not for support alone, but for love. That boy was hers, no one else's.

No, she thought. She could not do it. She knew how to fight and she would fight like hell. She would give in to Bennett only so far; she would agree to move her son to the summer house in Rhode Island, near Newport.

She turned back to the photograph, crying freely now. God, she loved it, she loved her life and what it meant. In this life you have to take what you want. She turned toward the stairs, momentarily confused. You took what you wanted, when you wanted it badly enough. That was what you had to do.

"I will survive," she said aloud, as if she were rehearsing a scene from a play. She said it over and over, differently each time. She raised her voice one last time, putting what she thought was at last the right emphasis on the line.

She hurried up the stairs, stumbling once, then moved down the long hallway to her bedroom, pausing first to look in on Johnny, who was resting peacefully. He'd be fine in Rhode Island, she decided, in a regular school, with ordinary kids and good-hearted, well-meaning teachers.

4.

An ass like Johnny's shouldn't have been legal, Steve Parker thought. And then there was the rest of him: the perfect proportions, the flawless skin, the mischievous smile. Oh, but that ass!

Steve often wondered if the other students noticed him watching Johnny every day as he made his way to the same spot: back seat, middle row. Of course, Johnny himself must have known. Just as he passed Steve's desk each day, he'd dig his hands in his pockets, spreading the fabric tight over his ass for his walk to the back of the room.

It was difficult enough for Steve to watch Johnny in his classroom and not be able to touch him, but then he began showing up during his office hours. *Orifice* hours, he began to think of them, because that's where he wanted to apply his talents on those days when Johnny scooted his chair up close to his.

He was always the proper, respectful student, but most of the time his questions were pretty lame; Steve began to think he just wanted attention, and, like most beautiful people, couldn't resist watching the impact he had on others. Steve tried hard to maintain his polite-but-firm classroom persona, but it was rough. All he could think about was locking the door and grabbing that ass and....

But Steve just lusted for Johnny in silence until one day just before the Thanksgiving holiday recess. Figuring that Johnny would be coming in later that afternoon, Steve had been reviewing his file. The report saddened him. After Johnny had been thrown out of every private school his mother put him in, it was decided public school was the place for her so-called incorrigible son. He would live with a housekeeper at their "cottage by the sea" and on holidays he would join his mother wherever she happened to be in the world. Of his father, nothing was mentioned.

There was a knock on the office door. Steve put down the report, stood and stretched, taking his time to let the boy in. When he did, Johnny entered slowly and stood by Steve's desk, shifting from foot to foot.

"Yes, Johnny," Steve said, as he sat back down, trying to keep his eyes on the latest progress report about Johnny when all he wanted to do was gaze at his crotch—which today was bulging even more enticingly than usual in his always-well-packed chinos.

"There's something I want to show you," Johnny said.

A brief, but dizzying thought crossed Steve's mind—that Johnny wanted to drag his cock out those well-packed chinos to show to him. But Johnny told him he wanted to show him something at his home, and that they would need to drive there. Both disappointed and excited at the same time, Steve volunteered to drive.

They piled into the tight quarters of Steve's white Volvo. For a quarter-hour they journeyed up along the highway edging the sea that defined the landscape. Sometimes, while adjusting the clutch, Steve's hand brushed Johnny's knee, causing him to feel a tingle of intense pleasure. They took a road that seemed somehow familiar, yet many of the roads around there resembled each other.

"I live up this way," the boy said, pointing to the left. Suddenly, Steve saw it: a sprawling, whitewashed house, framed by a broad stretch of cloudless sky.

Inside, it was fashionably decorated, with white leather chairs and sofas, soft as sponges. The mosaic floor was a sea of alternating swirls of blues and yellows. Steve thought a camera crew from *Architectural Digest* could have come right in and started snapping, but at the same time it had a friendly, lived-in air.

The housekeeper, Nell, a small, grandmotherly type, greeted them. Johnny introduced Steve as his "counselor," ordered by the school administration to get a report on his living conditions.

This was all coming as a shock to Steve; he swallowed hard and continued to glance about the immense living room.

"Is Johnny in trouble again?" Nell asked.

Steve blinked. "Oh, no, not exactly. It's just that …."

"It's just that I'm a transfer student," Johnny interjected. "They do this with all the transfers."

Nell seemed to accept this feeble explanation. "Well, make yourself at home," she said. "I have to go to town to do some shopping. I was planning on going when I picked Johnny up at school but now here he is."

"Yeah, here I am," Johnny said, smirking. "Come on, Mr. Parker, I'll show you my room."

Johnny's room was a private suite overlooking the bay. It had the best views of any room in the house. He had every conceivable toy a boy his age could want, most of which looked unused. As soon as Johnny had closed the door and locked it, his impatient hands caressed Steve's crotch. Steve let him revel for a moment in the glory of his swelling, aroused by simply being in forbidden territory: *his* bedroom. Then Steve pulled away. "Whoa! What's going on?"

By then Steve was almost mindless with frustration. By sheer force of will, he kept his arms at his sides as Johnny came on to him, pressing against him, warm and hard. Johnny hugged the older man, who hugged him back—first hesitatingly, then with increasing excitement. Then Johnny kissed Steve. Suddenly sure of himself, Steve relaxed and let the boy continue. As Steve's tongue slid across the boy's full lower lip, savoring the sweetness of him, his cock rose, pressing against Johnny's thigh. Johnny moaned softly, deep in his throat, and closed his eyes as Steve took over, kissing his neck, hearing both his own and Johnny's ever-more passionate breathing all but drowning out the sound of the crashing surf below them. What joy it was to Steve to feel the boy stirring sensuously against him, to imagine they could be this way always—two lost souls, finding themselves cast up on this shore together, finding a home they could share. He couldn't help himself; in that moment, he loved Johnny madly, entirely.

"Take off your shirt," Johnny commanded.

Steve was pleasantly stunned by Johnny's directness. He did as he was told. Soon the boy was covering him with kisses and tiny bites, the tickling of his headful of uncontrollable blond curls adding to the excitement of the moment.

Soon Johnny was unzipping Steve's pants, and Steve's penis, dangling free, excited him enormously. "Wow!" he cried as he dropped to his knees, and began licking and sucking.

Soon Steve couldn't tell if it was Johnny's hands or his lips working him over. He knew only that he felt like a squashed fruit whose skin has burst in the heat—suddenly, and totally liberated. The boy's eagerness to pursue this lovemaking freed Steve to indulge in sensations he had only

118

dreamed about experiencing. Looking down to watch the golden-haired boy's lips traveling up and down the shaft of his cock was almost as enjoyable to see as it was to feel.

Johnny pleaded, in muffled cries, that Steve come in his mouth. At that moment—he didn't know why—Steve was reminded of his wife, Susan, of how she would never do this for him. And he thought how unfortunate it was that no boy had done this for him—until then—and how thrilled he was to be granted the opportunity at long last.

As Steve came, Johnny's hands pressed tightly against his firm, hairy buns, and the boy took everything Steve had to give him before he swallowed it; it was the most intense orgasm Steve ever had. As he reached down and tilted Johnny's chin up to look at him, his glistening, cum-coated cock, slipped out of the boy's mouth. He looked lovingly into those beautiful eyes for a long time before he asked, simply, "Why?"

"You thought I didn't know?"

Steve shrugged. "I don't know how you could know."

Johnny smiled slightly. "How could I not know?"

Steve shook his head. "But I hadn't even dreamed of this."

"But you had thought of it. From the first day, you've been thinking about it."

Steve raised his eyebrows at him. "But this can only happen this one time. No more. This is wrong." He used a stern tone.

Johnny stood, and gazed levelly into Steve's eyes as he stepped out of his shoes and slowly removed his shirt. He turned around and slid his pants and underwear down to the floor, bent at the waist and presented the older man with the lightly muscled expanse of his back, his magnificent ass, the sight of which gave Steve's cock a renewed twinge. Straightening up, he turned to smile at Steve over his shoulder as he stepped out of the wad of fabric at his feet. He was so astonishingly beautiful that Steve suddenly felt his worries dissolve—being here with this sexy, naked boy felt *right* somehow. He was tempted to think that he wasn't himself, but he knew that what he was doing was as true to his *real* nature as anything he'd ever done.

Johnny lay on the bed, on his back, and stretched himself lengthwise, putting his hands behind his head on the pillow. He provocatively raised one knee, and studied the ceiling.

As he moved in and leaned over the boy, Steve's eyes consumed his every part. He fondled Johnny's nipples until they popped out in sharp, half-inch points. After sucking and flicking them around with his tongue, Steve worked them over with his thumbs and forefingers. Soon Johnny's stiff cock poked straight up, and Steve's hand encircled the shaft and gently played with it. Although not unusually large, the cock was in perfect proportion with the rest of him, and beautifully cut. Johnny spread his legs and Steve knelt between them as he started moving his tongue up and down Johnny's throbbing cock, then worked over his balls with

119

gentle lapping. After a few minutes, he licked his way farther down between the boy's legs, his hands firmly planted on his buttocks.

"Show me your beautiful ass again," Steve said. Johnny smiled, and rolled to his stomach. Steve sighed; it was the most perfect ass God ever created. He spread Johnny's plump buttocks apart with his thumbs. The boy's hole was tight and puckered, and when Steve gently blew against it, it tightened even more.

Johnny groaned. Steve began to kiss and nibble on his firm buttocks, first one, then the other. Raising his ass higher, Johnny spread his thighs wider while Steve licked and kissed more urgently, causing the boy to shudder with delight. Steve stuck the tip of his tongue into the narrow, pink opening. Johnny started to protest, but he couldn't find the words— and instantaneously did not want to find words of objection. His cock immediately went rigid again when Steve's tongue moved around slowly, thoroughly exploring the sensitive opening.

Johnny began rocking his butt back and forth on Steve's spearing tongue, humping his ass more firmly up into his face. Steve's hands gripped the globes as the tip of his tongue tortured the clenched asshole, flicking around it with feathery strokes.

Soon Johnny was rolling his head from side to side, his asscheeks contracting with pleasure. Steve kept pulling his tongue out and plunging it back in, then swirling it around in the tight hole until he knew Johnny was ready. He brought his thick dick up against the frantically squirming butt. Nudging the mushroom head firmly between the writhing globes, he separated the boy's asscheeks. He rubbed his erection smoothly back and forth over the fluttering hole, and the pucker opened like a delicate flower. With steady pressure, he managed to stuff most of his nine inches into the willing boy.

As Johnny whimpered beneath him, Steve leaned down over his back and began kissing his neck, nibbling on his ear, caressing the back of his head while plunging his cock in and out of him.

The day had been clear and sunny but also windy and cool. The bright light outside had been changing from a pale gold to a deep coppery tint while they made love—making Johnny's room so dazzlingly beautiful that Steve thought he had truly found paradise in that bed, with that boy. Or maybe one thinks like that only if one is, like Steve, an unhappily married man—and a dedicated teacher.

Steve had heard remarks about certain of his colleagues who were thought to be lecherous, but he had never thought that he, himself, was numbered among them. As an instructor of English, he considered himself sensitive to nuances of dialogue, and innuendo, and had gone out of his way to avoid any suggestive or erotic content in his remarks to students. But even though he had never verbalized his attraction to Johnny, the boy sensed how he felt. It taught Steve a lesson.

Now, with his cock hammering into Johnny's beautiful ass, Steve came in another glorious rush. Pulling his prick out, he rolled off of Johnny and stretched an arm across his warm back. He turned the boy's face to his. "I hope I didn't hurt you," he panted.

"I love you," Johnny whispered.

"Oh, you're just a boy," Steve chuckled.

"Yeah, but I know what I like," he said, groping Steve.

Steve turned away. "So do I."

Steve's torment began the next day. He ached to see the boy, and when he did, it was frustrating not to be able to touch him, hold him, make love to him. School let out early for a faculty meeting. After it was over, for relief, Steve went with a few of his faculty friends to a restaurant for dinner and tried to join in conversation, tried to find interest in things around him, especially one of the cute waiters, but it was no use. All his thoughts seemed to return to Johnny. Scowling fiercely, he left after coffee was served.

He took the longest possible route home and by the time he reached his house he was even more keenly aware of the difficulties of his situation than before. He wished over and over that some solution would offer itself, that he could see his way out, but nothing came. He was in a greater quandary than ever. What had he gotten into? How could things have gone so quickly out of control?

He quietly entered the house and went to the den, not wanting to make his wife aware of the fact that he had returned. At first he got some vague comfort out of a good cigar, but as he sucked on it, it reminded him too much of sucking on Johnny and he put it out. Every once in a while he would clench his fingers and tap his foot.

He fixed a brandy and soda, and as he sipped it, he brooded over his position until long after midnight, when the sheer loneliness of his situation closed in on him. He got up, locked the door to the den. He undid his pants and took out his erection. Leaning against the door, his eyes shut tight, he massaged his balls, then stroked his cock. Visions of Johnny stretched out before him, wiggling his ass at him, consuming him. As he came, all he could hear was Johnny saying, "I love you."

As desperately as he wanted to tell Johnny it was over, that they would never have sex again, when Steve saw the boy, he simply could not.

They invented the need for special tutoring sessions in Johnny's room, which lasted three hours. Johnny would greet Steve in his briefs, or sometimes wrapped in a towel, still wet from his shower, his body aroma mingling with that of scented soap and shampoo. Sometimes he was nude, his slender body appeared at the doorway like a forbidden delight tempting the older man.

Steve would close the door with a sigh, all control vanishing, and bury his face in Johnny's crotch, his mouth frantic for his cock, his hands trembling with the desire to feel the silken smoothness of his flesh.

Johnny remained in control. There was something predatory about him as he orchestrated the spasms of Steve's pleasure with sure hands, sly murmurs, and words of encouragement. He kept Steve utterly off-balance until, with a last little gasp, he begged the older man to come inside him.

After Johnny had taken Steve's cock and his load in his ass, he would mount him and make love to him with such mastery that Steve would climax a second time before Johnny's first orgasm. Steve realized for the first time in his life that his ass had become an organ of sensitivity, a receptacle to provide him and his partner mutual joy, a toy manipulated by a boy's caresses, its spasms ordained by the youngster's heated probing.

Sometimes, when he felt Johnny's sex disappear into him, followed by the incredibly energetic thrusting, it seemed as though he finally understood what it meant to be fucked senseless. Steve was astonished. The thought of this had never occurred to him. Still, he did not protest. Typically, Johnny's attack on Steve's ass was savage. It seemed as if he literally intended to impale Steve, tear him apart.

Steve's roommate at college, Roger, was the only one who had ever fucked him before, and Johnny was better than Roger ever thought of being. Johnny would thrust hard and pull partway out, and then slam into him again with incredible force. Steve would lift himself up to meet Johnny's cock as the boy drove it all the way in and continued his energetic pumping for several minutes. Steve's moans would grow more intense with each thrust, until he reached down and brought himself off. Hearing Steve's groans of ecstasy as his orgasm erupted, Johnny would ram his dick into his lover for the final time, while his own orgasm filled Steve's hungry ass.

Where did Johnny learn this stuff? Steve asked himself. The kid was far more experienced than he, and it showed. In that moment when the boy was finishing, furiously pressing down on him, and deeply into him, Steve only wished he could fuck as well as the much younger man driving his exciting cock into him.

As the days passed, Steve found he was spending so much time worrying about Johnny, fantasizing about him, and losing himself in the beauty of his body and his ceaseless caresses, that he hadn't really noticed that his wife, Susan, had now taken to spending as much time as she could away from home, leaving a babysitter in charge. She was always out with friends, shopping, playing tennis or bridge, visiting, or going to the movies. She left him dinners to warm up when he chose to come home, and curt notes letting him know where she was.

On the rare occasions when he spent time with her, they got into quarrels. They fought about money, about the kids, about school. Both of

122

them seemed to know what they were really fighting about, but neither wished to address it directly.

So as not to arouse Nell's suspicion, Johnny suggested they go for a drive. Merely the thought of having sex out in the open turned Steve on. The first time they ventured out, Steve headed out of the city, past Johnny's house, to a point on the shore where there were no more houses.

As they drove along, Johnny reached over and unbuttoned Steve's shirt. He brushed his fingers across Steve's chest, then dropped his head to it and began rooting through the chest hair with his nose, licking all around his nipples with his tongue. He took Steve's right hand off the wheel and placed it on his hard-on. Steve kneaded the bulge in Johnny's pants.

Johnny undid Steve's belt and pulled down the zipper. He put his hand around Steve's cock to pull it free, up and out. He blew on it, then began sucking it. Steve shivered, lifting up his hips and squirming. Johnny slipped Steve's pants and briefs down so that his balls were exposed. The boy began squeezing them and licking them, finally taking them in his mouth and sucking them while he jacked Steve.

Steve's hand left Johnny's crotch and grabbed hold of the back of the boy's head. He left the main road and slowly took a rutted path down near the shore. Finally he stopped and turned off the engine. He lay his head back on the top of the seat and lifted Johnny's face from his crotch with both hands. Johnny sat up, wiping the precum from his chin. He pulled his clothes off while Steve watched, and then climbed into the back seat. Steve stripped off his own clothes and climbed into the back seat with the naked boy.

"Oh god, that's beautiful," Steve sighed, sitting back and spreading his thighs as he held Johnny's waist and raised the youngster's body so that he was leaning forward into the front seat and presenting his luscious ass for the older man's appreciation. Steve put a copious load of spit on his cock and stroked it. Johnny lowered his ass over Steve's cock and, pressing down and judging his angle, sat down hard, impaling himself. Steve's cock went all the way in, in one long, incredible thrust. Johnny clamped hard on the prick and started fucking it while he jacked himself off. When Johnny's load splattered forcefully against the back of the front seat, it was Steve's turn to come. He pumped and shoved and ground inside Johnny's tight, eager ass. He fell into the rhythm he knew the boy loved. Johnny dropped his head and shook it, side to side, sending sweat flying across the front seat as Steve's orgasm burst inside him, and Steve gasped while he nibbled Johnny's shoulder.

Hugging Johnny to him, Steve finally came up for air. The boy's butthole quivered as the older man removed his dick. Johnny fell back onto the seat and took Steve's dripping cock in his hands. He nibbled on the head, then opened wide and swallowed it all the way down. After a few moments, he began fingering Steve's asshole just the way Steve had fingered his, spreading him, massaging the muscle, forcing him to come again.

"Oh, I love you, Johnny," Steve screamed at the height of his orgasm.

As the days passed, they would repeat the scene many times, with variations, sometimes not stopping the car at all while one drove and the other sucked him off before they changed places.

Steve was playing with fire, but he could not seem to stop himself.

Finally, with the afternoon sunlight streaming through their living room windows, Susan and Steve had a quiet but definitely unpleasant chat.

"Steve," she said with her lips tightening, "I know you're seeing somebody, and I know these things happen. But I'm not just going to stand by any longer. You make your choice. Either you're in or you're out."

Marriage is so damned fragile and complicated, Steve thought, but he knew he had to stay in. He had his career to think about. They had two young girls. They agreed that he would cease seeing '*somebody*,' effective immediately. But, Steve knew, *somebody* would have something to say about that.

5.

Driving to school the next morning, the day before the Christmas recess, Steve knew his situation was impossible. He knew that the minute he saw Johnny he would desire him. His goal that day was to avoid him, but Johnny would not be denied; he insisted on going for yet another drive.

As they headed to the lonely spot on the shore that had become their favorite, Johnny was not smiling. He announced he would be flying to London to spend the holidays with his mother, who was performing on stage there in the West End.

Johnny asked Steve to take him to the airport; he had managed to change his reservation so that there would be time for them to rent a motel room. He wanted to make the most of the time remaining.

Naked on the bed in the dim light of the motel room, Johnny was intoxicating to Steve. He had never been with anyone so passionate, so inexhaustible. Or so beautiful.

After the initial, obligatory nervousness of being in a strange motel room, Steve surprised himself by managing erection after erection, fucking the boy repeatedly.

"Oh, Johnny," Steve moaned as he entered the boy for the last time. His body convulsed as he came inside the boy, as if it were the first time. Now, Steve wanted it to last for eternity; he realized this was it, he had done it, he truly had a lover—someone he could not live without. He could no longer fight the pleasure coursing through his body.

They were speechless for a long time after the orgasm; Steve finally disengaged from Johnny, pulling his now-limp and moist penis from the warmth of the boy's ass. He kissed him on the lips with all the tenderness he could muster, even as he knew that neither gestures nor words could properly express what he had just experienced. The bedspread was rumpled, soaked with sweat and sperm; they had not even bothered pulling it down to uncover the sheets.

Steve got up, led the way to the shower. He soaped Johnny, his fingers lingering in the gaping crack of his ass longer than hygiene necessitated, caressing the boy's erect cock with lather until it shone like a wet jewel. He realized he had been selfish: Johnny had not come a third time, or even a second time. He had come only when Steve was fucking him moments after they entered the room.

Johnny rubbed Steve's back and manipulated himself into a position where he could enter the older man, and his fuck was masterful.

Steve stayed in the shower several minutes after Johnny had left, letting the jets of water soothe his ravaged ass. "Have you got my shorts?" he asked as he emerged from the shower, finding Johnny curled into a ball on the bed, with the sheet pulled over him..

"No. What would I do with your baggy old shorts?"

"I don't believe you."

"Tough. If you don't believe me check it out."

Steve flipped the sheet off Johnny's body: blond curly hair, bony shoulder blades, vertebrae, then the ass. That incredible ass—more truth, there alone, than was dreamed of in all the philosophy classes he had taken at the university. But Johnny wasn't wearing Steve's shorts. "Turn over. I want to see the rest of you."

"You've seen all you're gonna see today."

Steve knelt on the floor by the bedside, leaned across, and touched the boy's shoulders. "Come on, give them to me. We have to go."

Johnny rolled over and gazed at Steve's semi-flaccid cock. "No, but if we can stay, I'll give 'em back."

Steve said, "No, we have to go. Your plane is leaving."

Steve's underpants flew into his face as Johnny pulled the sheet over his head and disappeared from sight. His voice muffled, he cried, "I don't want to go. I want us to stay here forever."

"Hey, come on. Come on."

"Why? You say you love me, so why can't we stay?"

"We can't. You know why."

"All I know is what you say."

"Please, I do love you, I really do."

Suddenly Steve was ripping the sheet away and was back in the bed he had left only minutes before, wrapping the boy tightly in his arms.

"Let me go. I'll scream." But Johnny's voice was filled with happiness. It sounded like Christmas morning, the biggest present of all saved for last.

"No. Not until you behave. Stealing my shorts. Playing tricks on me."

"Talk about tricks—what's this supposed to be?" He turned so that his ass bumped the tip of Steve's now erect cock, then he bumped it a second time. Ten minutes earlier, Steve had been sure he was fucked-out.

"'Supposed to be?' What do you *think* it is?"

"It's another of your big old nasty hard-ons. You always have a big old nasty hard-on when you're with me."

"So do you, except I wouldn't call it nasty," Steve said, grabbing Johnny's cock and kissing him full on the mouth.

Steve twisted them up in the sitting position, Johnny straddling him. They pushed back against the flimsy headboard, then humped a little to position Steve's prick for an easy entry. The moment it was in, Johnny pressed down on it, impaling himself. Johnny bobbed up and down, fucking himself, while Steve masturbated him. After a few minutes, he slid down and off Steve, onto his back, freeing Steve's prick. "I just want to show you how much I love you," Johnny murmured.

A little pre-cum seeped out of the slit of Steve's prick and Johnny licked it off, giving it a generous squeeze with his hand before devouring it. Steve thought he might come again this way but Johnny had other ideas; he slithered his legs around Steve's hips and locked his ankles in the small of Steve's back as the older man entered him again.

Taking Johnny in his arms, Steve looked into his adorable face one last time while he fucked him. He wanted to hold the image in his mind, thinking, *There will never be anything again as beautiful as this.*

On the way to the airport, Johnny's hand never left Steve's crotch. The cock was easily accessible now, since Johnny had Steve's underpants in his suitcase.

Steve parked the car in the garage and kissed Johnny one last time. "I love you, Johnny. I'll miss you."

Tears began to flow from Johnny's eyes and Steve wiped them away as he caressed the boy's smooth, rosy cheeks.

"I'll miss you too, Steve," Johnny snuffled, "but I'll be back."

6.

When she first appeared on the London stage, it was obvious that most of the audience for plays in which Maggie Lawrence appeared came to the performances just to see her. She was inundated with fan mail and her telephone rang constantly. Reporters wanted interviews, and photographers started turning up at the house she had rented. The interest shown by the press was surprising. There was a double page spread of photographs of her in one of the Sunday magazines, and a national newspaper ran an article calling her a "legendary floozie."

Invitations to cocktail parties, film premieres and first nights at West End theatres arrived in the post daily. It was as if she had been rediscovered and was *the* new celebrity around town, mobbed by photographers flashing cameras as soon as she stepped out of a taxi.

Now, after performing in London steadily for almost five years, she could move about without attracting much attention and Johnny was looking forward to Christmas there with her this year.

Maggie was starring in a revival of Ruth and Augustus Goetz's adaptation of "The Heiress," based on Henry James' "Washington Square," in which a domineering and oppressive father squelches his shy daughter's attempt at romance. Johnny was keenly interested in the young actor who played opposite his mother, Jeffrey Lyndon. Photographs his mother had sent of Jeffrey stirred Johnny's imagination. Jeffrey was an American television actor who had made a success on the London stage in recent years and bore a striking resemblance to Montgomery Clift, who had played the role in the 1949 film version of the play.

But Johnny found things were not happy in London. The play had suspended performances indefinitely because of Maggie's recurrent illnesses. She told Johnny she had a virus she couldn't kick. When he asked about Jeffrey, she didn't want to talk about him. He asked about a few of her other beaus, but she didn't want to talk about them either. Finally, in desperation, Johnny asked about his father.

"You know it hurts me to talk about him," Maggie sniffled, blotting her face with a linen handkerchief.

"All I did was mention his name. Can't I even mention his name? You never let me talk about him! Never!"

Johnny's mother said something into her brandy snifter that sounded like "It wasn't my fault." Johnny wanted to say he knew that, that no one blamed her, but he was sure Maggie would never believe it. Parents must always think they can save their children, even when they have no control over what happens to them. Johnny put a consoling hand on her shoulder, thinking about the burden she had carried around all these years.

To escape a revolting marriage to Sam Spear, she had married Jack Wilson, a choreographer on the MGM lot. He soon quit the studio and went to New York to stage a show on Broadway. As much as Maggie loved New York, she had her film career to think of, and she spent more time in California than in New York during the first months of their marriage. When she did return to Manhattan, she discovered her husband's secret nature: he was bisexual. She could have lived with that, but her prolonged absences put an even more severe strain on the marriage.

Then she discovered she was pregnant. At first she planned to get an abortion, but changed her mind. She had been making one movie after the other, and she thought that staying in New York to have a child might renew her marriage as well as give her a much-needed rest. By the time she made this decision, Jack had already taken a young dancer as a lover, but the thought of having a child so delighted Jack that he agreed to a reconciliation with Maggie, provided she would permit his lover to live with them. Maggie thought she could deal with it; after all, she was pregnant and at least she would have company. But in the end she found that she couldn't deal with seeing her husband with a man, and returned to California, where her mother cared for her during her pregnancy.

Shortly after Johnny was born, she went to New York with the baby to see Jack. He was still living with his lover and the quarrels began all over again. Maggie stayed only a month, then returned to California.

Now Johnny was again asking about his father. "Tell me," Johnny kept saying.

She said, "Your father was dancing when he died."

"You told me."

"But now I want you to hear it all. He was rehearsing a show about ballroom dancing..." And then she went on to tell Johnny as much as she was ever able to learn about the incident.

Jack Wilson had stayed at the theatre one night after everyone had left, and shot himself on stage with a service revolver. They never found out where he had bought it, or when. He was found in his warm-up clothes, a pullover sweater and pleated pants. He was wearing his tap shoes, and he had a short towel folded around his neck. He had aimed the gun barrel down his mouth, so the bullet would not shatter the wall of mirrors behind him. "He was always so considerate of everyone," Maggie said, breaking down.

Johnny sat on the bed and his mother took him in her arms. They didn't stop crying for several minutes.

"Let's go out," Johnny coaxed. "It's Christmas Eve, and it's snowing. Let's go for a walk, okay?" He reminded her that the previous Christmas Eve they had visited his grandmother together, in California.

Maggie dried her eyes with the handkerchief again and blew her nose. Her eyes were red. "I'd like that," she said.

Johnny had been left, so far, to discover London on his own. He found that, like New York, it is a great city that reveres its traditions. In the capital's quiet residential corners, wreaths adorned the lacquered doors of row houses, and on street corners everywhere, there was the smoky aroma of hot chestnuts, roasted over open fires and dispensed in warm, steamy paper packets. He shopped with the crowds along Oxford and Regent Streets, becoming especially fond of Hamleys with its seven stories of dolls, games and model trains, and an arcade of video machines and games in the basement. In Leicester Square and Covent Garden, he enjoyed the amusement rides and side-show barkers. Everywhere there was music, and he especially enjoyed the carolers warbling beneath the giant tree in Trafalgar Square. Now, he wanted to show it all to his mother.

After pulling on their coats, they stood at the mirror in the hall. "What do you think I'll look like when I get old?" Johnny asked. The top of his head reached Maggie's nose, but aside from their height difference, they looked remarkably the same. Johnny's body was leaner, but their faces were almost identical, round and pink with deepset green eyes. "I mean, when I'm thirty."

For Johnny it was hard to imagine thirty. Steve was thirty, and on him it looked good, but Johnny never wanted to be thirty.

She ran her hands through Johnny's hair lightly, always surprised at the feel of it, so much like her own. She mumbled that she loved Johnny more than anything in the world, and for some reason was always glad he was a boy, not a girl.

"Maybe someday," Johnny said, "you'll stop getting older and I'll pass you up!"

"Im-possible," Maggie declared. "When elephants fly."

With her illness, Maggie had grown more depressed, and at the recommendation of her doctor, she had consulted a psychiatrist. She asked the shrink seriously about her son, what effect would her illness have on him? And what about the effect of the way she lived? The psychiatrist had shrugged, saying he didn't know anything about the boy, but from what Maggie had told him, it sounded to him as though Johnny would be able to handle things.

He had said, "I'm sure there are dozens of unresolved conflicts, and you've got a pretty good case of guilt about the child. But I don't believe the conflicts are serious or in any way out of the ordinary; you're an attentive mother and the guilty feelings, therefore, are not warranted. You know that. You're not some silly housewife with only her orgasms or her bridge games to worry about. You've lived, you've been around."

"I appreciate the thought," she had said dryly.

A couple of days later, Maggie told Johnny that Jeffrey had returned to London after doing a television show in New York and wanted to take them to dinner at the hotel where he was staying, the Connaught. But later that afternoon, she said she didn't feel up to going out, that Johnny was to go with Jeffrey alone.

Ordinarily, this would have excited Johnny beyond measure but he had become anxious about his mother. "I don't understand what's happening to her," Johnny said to Jeffrey that evening at the Connaught dining room, after the waiter had taken their order.

129

"I don't really understand it either," Jeffrey said. "I was staying with her for a while, and one day everything turned strange. She told me she had an appointment with her agent, which I found out afterwards wasn't true. When she returned a few hours later, she closed herself in her room. At first I assumed that she was just 'thinking' and would eventually confront me with some fantastical idea, so I didn't take much notice. Then after a while I started to wonder and thought that, perhaps, she was indulging in one of her childlike, petulant sulks. But it was apparently more than that; she seemed to have been taken over by some terrible mood.

"We didn't go out that night as we'd planned. We hardly spoke, in fact. Maggie just wanted to be left alone, And she smoked a great deal. I'd never known her to smoke so much. I remember having to go to the store across the street because she'd finished all the cigarettes. The air was thick with smoke. Maggie was lying in the dark; I couldn't make out the look on her face, but she told me to get out and never come back. But I did, of course.

"Over the next few weeks she became demanding and possessive, even secretive, taking to disappearing for hours at a time without giving any clue as to where she was going. There were times when we got along quite well, we had fun and the relationship was like it had been, but those instances were getting few and far between.

"But Maggie still looked beautiful, radiant, and she started to take more interest in her appearance. She stepped up her health regimen, going regularly to the gym and becoming even more picky about her food. But still she smoked with unusual regularity.

"One day, I found myself back on her street and I dialed her number from the callbox across the way. When she picked up the receiver I said, 'It's me,' but she immediately put it back down.

"Eventually she did see me again but it was never the same."

"But why didn't she tell me?" Johnny asked. "Why didn't she let me know she was sick?"

"She didn't want anyone to know. You can't blame yourself for anything that's happened. Maggie must have had her reasons for not telling us she was ill. What's happened has happened. We can't change that. Things don't always go the way we'd like them to. Something will always go wrong, things will always get fucked up. Life's like that. Maggie just kept this secret; I don't know why. Anyway, let's not get depressed, let's not get upset." He raised his wine glass. "Let's drink to Maggie, to life."

After dinner was over, Johnny realized he had consumed too much wine during the meal, so Jeffrey suggested he spend the night with him at the hotel.

Too many shocks had jolted Johnny into a daze recently. His mother's strange behavior, her turning Jeffrey away, Jeffrey turning up. It was all too much. Jeffrey had merely suggested Johnny spend the night with him,

130

but Johnny was pretty sure the actor had more than merely sleeping together in mind. As much as he was attracted to Jeffrey, Johnny was dubious about having sex with a man who had been having sex with his mother. Jeffrey seemed blasé about it all, as if he did this sort of thing every day—which, Johnny considered, was perhaps the case.

Johnny had noticed that his mother seemed to gravitate toward men who could go one way or another, sexually. Perhaps, Johnny mused, that was the *normal* thing. After all, it seemed perfectly natural for Steve to go from being in bed with his wife to being in bed with him. But as eager as Johnny was for sex, he made the conscious decision to spend the night with Jeffrey, but to do nothing sexual with him unless the older man seduced him.

While Jeffrey went to the bathroom, Johnny got naked and turned out the light as he slipped into bed. Jeffrey, after entering the bedroom, undressed in the dark, but Johnny could see from the bathroom light spilling through the door that he was extremely well-made. He reminded Johnny a bit of Steve—the nicely-furred chest, the trim body—but he was even more handsome.

By the time the actor reached the bed, Johnny had an erection and he exposed it to Jeffrey, who said nothing, but knelt on the bed beside the naked boy. Bending over Johnny, Jeffrey's tongue darted and licked and stroked Johnny's cock, driving the boy to a shuddering pinnacle, then tethering him there with rapid flicks. It was all so directed, so accurate, so patient that it took Johnny's breath away.

Johnny clutched at Jeffrey's long brown hair as his urgency built, and as the actor took his cock inside his mouth and began to suck methodically, but with obvious relish, he ignored the boy's demands for him to suck harder and more wildly. Even after he had sucked out and swallowed a massive orgasm from the boy, he continued to fondle him and nurse on his cock.

"Have you ever been ....?" he began to ask, gently probing Johnny's anus.

"A long time ago," Johnny breathed.

"I'm a big man and you're very small inside," he murmured. "I don't want you to be uncomfortable when I put my cock in."

"I won't be," Johnny said, almost giggling.

Johnny rested his heels against Jeffrey's broad shoulders, and Jeffrey pushed against them, forcing Johnny's hips up, his legs awkwardly bent and spread. The boy was vulnerable, helpless.

As he began to enter Johnny, the boy shoved his fist into his mouth, stifling the scream that threatened when Jeffrey began fucking, but he rode it through, bucking, begging.

Jeffrey dug his fingers into Johnny's ass and pressed it against himself, clearly enjoying the ride. "Oh, Johnny," he cried, urging Johnny's legs around his neck, and Johnny instinctively tightened the embrace. "That's it, beautiful little boy, hold on tight."

"Please... It's too much..."

"Not nearly."

Jeffrey thrust in and out until he too was a trembling mass of exposed nerves, and as he came, Johnny started to cry.

"Tell me what I did wrong," Jeffrey said.

Johnny giggled. "Oh, nothing. You were perfect, it's just that I never thought this would happen."

"Me neither," Jeffrey chuckled and untangled Johnny's legs from around his shoulders, then slid up to cover Johnny's body with his own. "You're so soft." He nestled the head of his cock against Johnny's and captured one of the boy's nipples in his mouth. Johnny arched toward his mouth and Jeffrey began sucking hungrily on one nipple, then the other.

Before long, Jeffrey was hard again and put the head of his cock at the entrance. "Pull me in," he said.

"I need to rest a minute."

"No, you're ready." He tugged on Johnny's swelling erection.

"Please...wait...." But Johnny's words were choked off as Jeffrey inched the head of his cock into the boy's sweaty body.

"No, now. Oh, yes, see, you want it. Such a greedy little boy." He nudged Johnny's legs wider. "That's it, take it all."

"Wait...oh, please...."

Jeffrey nipped at Johnny's bottom lip, demanding his acquiescence while he fucked deeper, Then, his voice low and dark with emotion, he moaned, "Shit, I've never had a woman drive me this crazy."

"You're so...big."

"Yes. Big enough to take good care of you." The heavy ridge of his cockhead rubbed against Johnny's aching anal lips. Then he started jabbing—short and quick, different from before. Johnny dug his fingers into Jeffrey's hard ass, trying to pull him in deeper.

"Oh, yes," Jeffrey growled, nearing orgasm once again.

Johnny crushed his body against Jeffrey, whose tongue darted into Johnny's ear as he came.

Jeffrey relaxed, rolled off Johnny and lay on his back gasping. Johnny turned and looked at him. In many ways, he reminded Johnny of Steve, desperate in his need for sexual adventure. He tried to imagine his mother with Jeffrey on top of her but he could not. After Jeffrey was asleep, Johnny let himself out and took a cab back to the apartment.

Jessie, Maggie's maid, whispered "Johnny!" from the bottom of the stairs as Johnny was about to go into his mother's bedroom late the following morning. "Don't go in there. Not just yet. The doctor doesn't want her to be disturbed. Come down. I've made a pot of tea."

Reluctantly he followed Jessie to the kitchen. "What's going on? What's happened to Mother? Why didn't you wake me up?"

"Nothing's happened. Everything will be fine." Jessie pulled up the flaps of a carton of milk, only from the wrong end. "Oh look what I've gone and done," she said and wiped away the splash. "It's just that the doctor came round again to visit Miss Maggie and we didn't think to wake you. Anyway we thought you needed the sleep. You got in so late."

"How long has he been here?" Johnny asked.

"Oh, not long. It can't be more than half an hour. Don't be so agitated. Sit down and have a drink of tea."

Johnny sat on the edge of a chair, leaning his elbows on the table.

"Oh, I forgot," Jessie said. "You like a mug, don't you? I've gone and poured a cup."

"That doesn't matter, I don't care."

Johnny looked around the kitchen. The sink was piled with dishes, mostly cups and saucers, needing to be washed. The room looked miserable, he thought. "Everything's a bit of a mess," he said.

Jessie pointed at him with a spoon. "Now, I've been awake all night and your mother's been up since five. Anyway you look a bit of a mess yourself. If I was you I'd have a bath."

"You're right. I think that's what I'll do."

Later, Jessie, sweeping a stray gray hair away from her tired eyes, told Johnny, "The doctor's just gone. We couldn't call you because you were in the bath." Jessie attempted to change the subject. "But he's coming back later today."

"What did he have to say?"

"He's never known anything like it in his life! Hollywood's got nothing on this," she cried and threw her hands in the air. "I feel as though I'm living in a picture—and I've got the lousy part." She began sorting laundry. "And I don't think you should go up to Miss Maggie, because she needs to be left alone. The doctor says she needs to be kept quiet and not get too excited. She's losing all her body fluids. There's nothing you can do."

Jessie went to do the laundry, leaving Johnny alone.

7.

With Johnny in London, Steve was able to focus his attention on Susan. As her anger subsided, he began remembering what an attractive person he had married—blonde, tall, very thin and willowy. Suddenly he noticed what subtle taste she had in clothes—or perhaps she had bought some new outfits? Whatever, he decided she was very pleasant to look at. It seemed as if his time with Johnny had revitalized his interest in Susan. And when he had sex with her, although he was thinking of Johnny, and only him, he performed very well.

"Things are better, aren't they?" Steve asked her one evening when they were lingering at the table after dinner. The girls were in the basement watching television.

"They're not so bad," she said, turning her head towards the dining room window in a way that he knew meant she was thinking about it, that she would always think about it, wondering who the somebody was who had threatened their marriage. Then she got up and walked around the table, stood behind him and ran her fingers along his shoulders. "In fact," she said, "it's really better than it's ever been."

What Susan did not know was that what had never been better were Steve's sexual fantasies. He had even begun to fantasize about bringing Johnny into his home, to create a *ménage à trois*.

Some of his fantasies had Susan accepting Johnny without hesitation. Others found her flinching and backing pathetically away like a wounded animal, trying to hide her face from the bestial truth of her husband's unnatural desire for the boy. He imagined that as he would leave the house for what she was sure was another tryst with his male lover, she would beg him with clumsy girlish pleas to stay. He instinctively moved away from her, toward the door.

Steve's favorite fantasy involved Susan's finally agreeing to meet Johnny, but when he brought him home, they found Susan lying on the kitchen floor, wearing a bikini. She had been drinking and had passed out. Seeing Steve's wife, despite her condition, aroused Johnny, and he desired Steve even more greatly than before. But Steve was disgusted with his wife's condition, so he moved away from Johnny, going to Susan, kneeling next to her as she lay there, her mouth open. Johnny realized now Steve loved his wife, and his hunger for him was somehow wrong. Still, there was the moment to be seized.

"Fuck me," Johnny said in the fantasy, walking toward Steve.

"What?" Steve said, shocked, not moving from his wife's side.

"Fuck me right now. In front of her. Fuck me," Johnny whispered, smiling a little, feeling the potency of his allure. He began taking off his clothes.

Steve tried desperately to lead Johnny away from her, out of the kitchen. "No. I want to do it here. Now." Johnny was naked, his cock hard. Steve put his tongue on the throbbing prick, licking it, then sucking it. Johnny pulled him up, away from it and they kissed. Steve knelt again in front of Johnny, his face resting on his hard belly, nipping gently at the head of Johnny's cock.

Suddenly Steve pulled Johnny down on top of him. They fell to the floor, next to his wife, and, as their bodies clashed and sparked, they rolled and tumbled against her inert body. Johnny's ass rested on her ass.

He bit Steve on the neck, forcing him to focus on the pain. Johnny tore at Steve's clothes until he was naked, and he spread his legs and lay on his back while his lover entered him.

After a few moments, Johnny looked down to watch with almost clinical detachment as Steve's cock disappeared into him. Steve opened his eyes and looked at Johnny very intensely, fucking him slowly but more forcefully with every thrust. He dug into him as though he was seeking reassurance that with every graceful push of his hips, with the arch and bend of his tight belly, that he was pleasing the boy. His wife still lay motionless as his and Johnny's bodies fused.

Johnny began coaxing him, holding them together with his thighs, feeling his body filling more and more with him, with his smell, his sounds, his sex. Steve closed his eyes, close to orgasm while Johnny turned and looked at Susan, still unconscious, and impulsively reached over and touched her. He touched her skin, her cheek. He put his hand in her hair.

Steve opened his eyes and saw that Johnny was touching his wife, tracing her lips with the tip of his finger. "Don't do that," he said helplessly, knowing that tonight Johnny would do whatever he pleased, to both him and his wife.

Johnny dragged his finger down Susan's chin and over the soft, sexy grotto of her neck. She didn't respond at all. Still Johnny was excited, filled with limitless possibilities—and also still filled with Steve's cock, fucking him harder, heading to orgasm.

"He's fucking me," Johnny whispered into Susan's face. He was close enough to smell her boozy breath.

Steve pulled at him, trying to draw his body away from her.

Johnny fell to the side and put his lips over her mouth. He kissed her slowly, letting his tongue caress her lips, feeling the creases of her soft, dead mouth. Steve was holding Johnny tightly, reaching for his cock, and Johnny could feel his warm breath in his hair. Johnny took Susan's hand and brought it to his mouth, began sucking her fingers as Steve entered him from behind. The more fiercely Steve fucked Johnny, the harder Johnny sucked his wife's fingers.

Steve was fucking Johnny's body up against her when Johnny tore his mouth from Susan's fingers just as he started to come, and Steve pulled him back against his thrusting cock. Johnny braced himself on Susan and trapped Steve's exploding cock with the clenching muscles of his ass; he came with a scream so violent that it should have awakened her, but it did not.

8.

From the beginning of her public life, Maggie was often happy to tell her story to interviewers, and she never varnished the truth when she did. She spoke of her professional life with impetuous candor, fully describing both her achievements and her mistakes. She did not neglect her personal life either, and that was what the reporters were usually most interested in. Questions about her son Johnny usually came at the end of the interview, and were asked out of a sense of politeness. Yes, she had one son, a teenager. No, she was not currently married nor did she believe in marriage any longer. Her apparent frankness was frequently deceptive, and she managed to conceal many important things about her personal life.

She had, for instance, never mentioned her illness, and once her cancer was diagnosed, she refused further interviews, so she and Johnny were able to escape London without being detected. As her condition worsened, Bennett insisted she come to Florida to see some specialists. This time, she did not argue with her brother.

Johnny had rarely visited Bennett's mansion on North Ocean Boulevard. He had purchased the property at considerably below market value from the estate of a dowager who had let it deteriorate, and he was slowly restoring it to its original splendor. It was a two-story Spanish-style house hidden from the street by enormous banyan trees. In the back an expansive lawn reached to the ocean and was covered with avocado, grapefruit, orange, and coconut palm trees. Pink and salmon bougainvillea bloomed everywhere along the fences. Under other circumstances, Johnny felt he might actually enjoy living there.

Since retiring to Palm Beach, Bennett had 'got religion' in a big way, and became a major contributor to the Good News ministry of James P. Gifford, based in West Palm Beach. The second night Maggie and Johnny were at the mansion, Gifford came to dinner. Maggie said she was too ill to go downstairs. Johnny wanted to have supper with her but Uncle Bennett insisted Johnny meet the man he called The Pastor.

Bennett told Johnny to dress for dinner in his Sunday best, while he, himself, wore a navy blue blazer. His skin was deeply tanned from playing golf every day, and although he was nearly bald, a few strands of dark hair crossed the glossy dome of his scalp with precision and order. Johnny thought he looked just like Captain Kangaroo.

Before dinner, they entertained The Pastor in the living room, where ceiling fans revolved slowly. There were two deep-tufted sofas piled high with tapestry pillows, and bookcases along one wall, full of volumes bound in red Moroccan leather with gold lettering.

Johnny couldn't believe the discussion as they ate their filet mignon in the cavernous dining room. Bennett started right out by saying how Johnny was being tempted with evil at every turn in today's society.

"I think most of us lose sight of our goal at times and listen to Satan and his temptations," Gifford said. There was a feverish sparkle in his eyes.

"We get in a church and want to love, but lose sight of the goal. We have to be so careful to keep the proper goal in mind and not get sidetracked. We have to make sure that we put love first just like Jesus did. And, believe me, putting love first isn't always easy. But God has always told us to forgive and not to judge.

"You see, Johnny, Christ stands up to Satan and goes on to carry out His Father's will. He wants to tell the world the 'Good News' that God loves them, and what happens? John 1:11 says, 'He came unto his own, and his own received him not.' He was rejected. Jesus himself was rejected!

"The fear of rejection is one of the biggest fears Satan tries to instill in the Christian today. Believe me, I know what rejection means—I live with it daily. People we are trying to love turn on us or misunderstand us. And that hurts. At times it feels like we don't have a friend in the world."

"Johnny doesn't have many friends," Bennett interjected. "He's moved around so much because he's the son of somebody who's in the limelight. He's been hurt a lot."

"You know," The Pastor went on, "Satan can puff us up to make us think we're somebody, and then he bursts the bubble by making us feel rejected so that we feel like we're nobody. Satan is always playing his tricks on us."

"Yes, we need to follow Jesus's example," Bennett said. "He got hurt. The religious leaders of His day scoffed and laughed at him. Do you think that didn't hurt? They tried to stone Him and even plotted His death. But did Jesus give up? No. He knew that at the end of everything would be His victory."

"Yes," Gifford said. "I think all of us have experienced rejection at one time or another when we were simply trying to love. I know many people who have been so hurt that they're afraid to get up and try to love again."

"Satan would just love to keep us afraid to expose ourselves to others for fear of being hurt. He wants to keep us separated from each other and feeling all alone. When the devil comes upon us, all we have to say is, 'Go away, Devil, in Jesus' name.' We don't need to cry out in anger, but, according to the Word, say simply, 'Go away, Devil. Go away, right now.'"

"Johnny, you should heed what The Pastor is saying," Bennett said. "I think God wants us to protect our sexual urges from Satan's influence. I know you are constantly bombarded with Satan's sexual traps—and you're not alone. Satan gets housewives to watch soap operas on TV that show broken marriages and sexual fantasies. Satan gets men to hide their strong sexual drives, and he makes them live in fear that they may not be normal and that someone might find out that they do not have totally 'pure' minds."

"Yes, Johnny," Gifford interjected, "girding our loins with truth means we go to The Word for answers instead of going to the TV, the movies, or some magazine that might excite us. God will protect us from Satan's evil sexual urging as long as we live and walk in His truth, as we flood our minds with The Word.

"All through the Bible, God condemns lust. Fornication's a sin and breaks the Seventh Commandment. Homosexuality is condemned in the Bible as sin: sodomites shall not inherit the Kingdom of God! Any use of sex, except as an expression of love in marriage, or for the purpose of procreation in marriage, is a sin, and breaks the Seventh Commandment! Totally refraining from sexual intercourse, masturbation or other sexual outlets does no harm whatsoever, and the self-discipline of such continence develops character!"

As he railed on and on, in his excitement swallowing the final consonant of almost every word, The Pastor's hands punctuated each sentence. At first, Johnny tried to follow the monologue, but soon found himself thinking the man was crazy, deranged, over the line. In appearance, the Pastor reminded Johnny of the evangelist Jim Bakker; he wondered if the Pastor had a wife as ugly as Bakker's and was perhaps screwing boys on the side. He couldn't help but wonder if all holy men were guilty of the very things they railed against.

Gifford stopped to take a drink of the Ca' del Bosco Chardonnay Bennett had picked from his extensive wine cellar just for the occasion. This finally gave Johnny an opportunity to say something, but he never said a word, just sat there with his eyes closed, still as a mouse. A boy couldn't make it through an evening like that just on dinner; what he needed was a drink. So, tired as he was, Johnny went to his bathroom before going to bed in order to find one. He grabbed around under the sink, behind the Windex and Comet and came up with the bottle he'd seen Uncle Bennett's maid Millie sneak drinks from, and he dusted it off. He poured out a good two fingers in a glass and drank it down. Neat.

He remembered something he'd heard one of his mother's lovers say and changed it to suit the occasion: "Age will be served, but youth has its privileges." Those bastards don't know everything, he thought.

Bennett found Maggie sitting at the dressing table in the suite that was always reserved for her. He smiled at her, patiently, serenely. He commented about the weather, about how nice the golf course looked at dawn, how he almost had a hole in one, how nice the dinner was, how attentive Johnny was to The Pastor.

"Take care of my little boy," she said finally, interrupting him.

"Don't worry about a thing," he told her.

"I don't. I have my insurance."

"Insurance?"

"Yes, I wrote it all down. It took me months, but once I was diagnosed I knew I had to do it. To protect Johnny."

"To protect him?"

"From you."

138

"How can you say that?"

"How could I *not* say that?"

"I've spent thirty years making amends … "

"I know. Well, just so you don't stop, so you don't forget what happened, I wrote it all out and I sent it to someone I trust. I told Johnny if you give him any trouble, he's to call that person. Then the envelope will be opened. That person will know what to do."

"How could you do that to me? How can you do that to us?"

"You've often made life comfortable for me, Bennett. But that's all, just comfortable."

"I've always been there for you."

"You can say that again." She looked away, growing more frustrated with him with each moment.

Bennett remained silent, listing in his mind all the things he had done for her in the name of love. She was eight and he was fifteen when it had started, and it lasted three years.

Maggie had her own memories of what Bennett was thinking: *I was outside, playing. I guess I must have fallen asleep. Suddenly he was over me, his huge eyes staring down at me, so close I could feel his eyelashes on my face, and they were tickling me... I didn't know what it was but it felt good, somehow. He began to run his fingers through my hair. I'd never really had anyone touch me like that before except my mother... I knew there was something wrong but ...I don't know, I liked it. He just kept repeating, "You're so beautiful." Then I got nervous and embarrassed, and tried to get up. He started to laugh, and soon he was pulling me down, pinning me to the ground, and I heard this screaming. And I finally realized it was my voice, and then I started to hear my clothes rip. Now I was scared, and hoped nobody would find us because I was so embarrassed.*

Long before she took to her deathbed, which would happen much sooner than anyone might have anticipated, Maggie would reveal her biggest secret. If it would not explain everything about her life, her behavior, at least it would illuminate some of it.

To Bennett, their secret was vague, indistinct and shadowy, a half-remembered dream. But he did recall a time when he bought her ice cream and took her to the playground. As they were leaving, he swung her up from the ground and kissed her cheek, savoring the feel of her palm against his back—a touch so gentle it made his eyes burn with sudden tears.

"It's so funny, really," she said in a faint voice.

"Funny?"

"Yes, how you were always there, like you said. That morning, just before Johnny was born—that last hour or so when I wondered if it might all be over—I thought, 'If I live through this, I can live through anything; nothing else can ever be as hard as this.' " She looked into the mirror and up at her brother again, her face puffy with weariness. "I want to know what you were thinking at that time." Her voice grew stronger. "I want to know."

What she remembered was the moment of birth, the surprising violence of it, the vividness of color, the blood everywhere, the boy looking almost blue-gray, looking like something unearthly.

What Bennett remembered was being choked with fear that she was in mortal danger and that he might lose her. And now that concern seemed to be approaching again, only this time it seemed it would actually happen. Gathering her hair behind her shoulders, fine as a baby's now, he weighed it delicately in his hands with his eyes closed. Maggie held her breath, waiting for his answer.

He let go of her hair, letting it fall without a sound against her shoulders. "I can't remember what I was thinking," he said, and quietly left the room.

Maggie began combing her hair again. Her brother had become even more contemptible to her. But she didn't hate him—remarkably, she had never truly hated anyone. With a little effort, she could almost feel sorry for Bennett, a man who'd let his whole life slip through his fingers. He devoted himself to making money—a lot of money—almost if to prove he could. And now this Good News business. It was pitiful, really. She thought how there had been many women, all of whom he dismissed as not being good enough. How sad that there had been only one girl good enough for Bennett, and that was his little sister.

9.

"I hate this place."

"Johnny, where are you?" Steve held the phone tightly as he got up and quietly shut the door to his study.

"In Palm Beach, at my Uncle Bennett's. I hate Uncle Bennett."

"Palm Beach? I thought you were in London."

"Mom's sick. She's real sick."

"I'm sorry."

"Uncle Bennett has nurses, everything." He held back a sob. "But I don't think …."

There was a prolonged silence. Finally, Steve asked, "Johnny? What's wrong?"

"Oh Steve, please come down here. Please come get me. I miss you so much."

"I miss you too."

"I hate this place. Come down, please."

"But I can't come right now. There are exams, and …."

The phone went dead. Steve could not call Johnny back, he didn't have the number. He shut his eyes to hold back the tears. What had he done? For weeks he had wanted to call Johnny, to speak to Johnny, to hold him, kiss him, caress him, fuck him. And now he had failed him. Johnny needed him and he had refused him. Finally, the tears came. He couldn't help it.

Susan knocked and burst into the room, saw her agonized husband sitting at his desk, still holding the phone. She asked what was wrong.

As usual, Steve remained stoic. "Trouble at school. Kids these days …."

But the kids were not the problem, Susan knew, instinctively. It was her husband who had the problem.

The students were caught up in the frantic stillness that accompanies preparation for finals. There was a hushed tension in the corridors, the packed silent libraries, the rooms stunned by collective worry. Many students already suspected their grades could not be saved by final exams, and that their grade point averages would sink well below what was needed to get any scholarships.

But among all these struggling, terrified young people, Steve walked the corridors with his heart soaring. Spring break would see Susan taking the girls to visit their grandmother, and Steve had formed a plan. While ordinarily he would look forward to some peace during the recess, he knew solitude would bring only more thoughts of Johnny. He had still not heard again from the boy, and he had gone so far as to check for Bennett Lawrence's number in the Palm Beach phone directory. There was no entry in the phone book, but he realized the number was most probably unlisted.

Bennett was at one time one of New York's most successful developers. He had retired to Florida but still maintained offices in New York. Steve's plan was to contact his offices in New York, represent himself to someone in authority as Johnny's teacher and counselor, and have them contact the boy for him.

10.

Other than the times when his mother was awake and ready to talk, Palm Beach had become a place of torment for Johnny.

Bennett took it upon himself to set up a rigid schedule for the boy: studies with his school books from nine to noon, then a swim, followed by lunch. By then, Bennett would be back from his round of golf at the country club ready to quiz Johnny on what he had studied earlier. This regimen was to Johnny far worse than actually being in school.

Then Bennett decided that this time would be an ideal one for Johnny to get his driver's license. He took the boy out in the older of the two Cadillac Fleetwood Broughams he owned. Johnny couldn't tell the difference between the two huge cars but Bennett assured him the white one was three years older than the yellow one. Once satisfied that Johnny knew how to handle himself behind the wheel, Bennett began coaching the boy for the test. Still, that wasn't enough. There had to be time in a formal driver's education course, and every day Johnny would be driven to the school. This was even more frustrating because the instructor was a woman. There was a male instructor at the school, a rather attractive young man, but he was busy.

Johnny's sexual frustration during this period was unprecedented for him. His nights and early mornings were filled with his memories of Jimmy and Steve, with a few memorable bouts with Luke thrown in for good measure. There was one consolation, although it was a meager one: The gardener at the mansion across the street was a beautifully built Latin in his late twenties. Johnny would stand at his second-floor window while the stud pruned the bushes and mowed the lawn in the muggy, eighty-degree heat of the afternoon. He took Bennett's binoculars from the living room and used them to get a better look at the man. His blue work shirt was soaked with sweat and rolled up to his elbows, showing his tanned, muscular forearms and large, strong hands. His unbuttoned shirt gaped open, exposing his well-muscled chest beneath curly black hair. His long legs were hugged casually by well-worn Levi's.

The gardener moved about with consummate grace. The fact that he tended to the yard all by himself made him even more attractive, as if he was saying he didn't need any help. But Johnny knew the man needed *somebody* for at least one thing: sex. No man like that could go for long without it, Johnny thought. He put down the binoculars and dropped his shorts to the floor. He often stood there stroking his erection as he watched the sexy Latino, imagining what it would be like to run his hands across every inch of that tight body, to take that penis in his mouth and suck it to orgasm. The vision of being on his knees in front of the man, who was fucking his face with a monster dick quickly brought Johnny off.

So desperate was Johnny for closeness to a man that on occasion, dressed only in his white Speedos, he would go over to the laborer as he was loading his equipment into his rig and ask him some off-the-wall questions. The man, who said his name was Jose, spoke broken English and seemed to be very shy. Up close, Johnny found the stud even more attractive and, one day, Johnny could feel his dark eyes studying and seeming to penetrate his skimpy, tight Speedos as Johnny turned to pick up a loose branch, partially exposing his buttocks. When he handed Jose the branch, Jose was smiling. Johnny looked away, feigning indifference, but felt his cock begin to harden. As he scurried across the street, he turned to look behind him and saw Jose was leaning against his truck, smiling broadly, insolently at him as he broke the fallen branch in half.

Usually, by late afternoon, Maggie was ready to see Johnny. He would go to her when Millie served tea and quietly sit with his mother and listen to her.

She was his captain, laying out the line of march. "If you don't learn anything else from me, Johnny, learn this." Drawing herself up, she created a hush into which she let the next words fall: "No matter what happens to you, *you can't afford to let it show.*"

Now Johnny was listening carefully. He knelt beside the bed and smiled at this beautiful woman. He knew his mother had, for whatever reason, always understood everything.

"Listen," she said, "the worse things are, the better you have to look. You see, it's not what happens to you that makes the difference, it's the way you handle it."

Johnny waited for some more advice. But Maggie had given all she had to offer. "That's all," she said. "That's all you have to know."

Johnny dropped his head into his mother's hands and she caressed his hair. "After I change, we're going shopping."

"Shopping," Johnny muttered, holding back the tears. "Of course we will. We'll go shopping."

The next day, when the doctors said the time was at hand, Bennett, Johnny, the servants, and the Pastor came and went from Maggie's room, holding flowers, candy, new bedroom slippers—anything to take her mind off dying. But in her mind she had already left them—as she did in actuality a few hours later.

Confused and distraught by his mother's death, Johnny told Bennett he was going shopping after Maggie's body had been taken to the funeral home. As he accelerated onto the street from the driveway, he saw Jose's rig pulling away. He had no intention of following it, but that's what he ended up doing, all the way to West Palm Beach and beyond, to a trailer park in a seedy part of town. Jose made no attempt to lose his stalker; rather, he slowed so that the white Cadillac would be able to catch up with him in case Johnny was detained by a traffic signal. By the time the truck stopped at the far end of the trailer park, Johnny was desperate, pre-cum already staining his tight white walking shorts.

Jose got out of the truck and slammed the door. Johnny pulled up behind the rig and turned off the ignition. Jose passed the Cadillac without saying a word. Johnny followed.

Jose unlocked the door of his trailer and left it open. Johnny tentatively entered the darkened room. The air conditioning was on full blast and Johnny shivered.

"Close the door," Jose instructed. He was standing in the tiny kitchen, opening a can of beer. Johnny did as he was told.

"Something wrong at the house today?" Jose asked, carrying the beer into the living room where Johnny was still standing by the door. "Many cars."

"Yes, my mother died."

"I sorry. She very sexy. I see her pictures on the TV."

Tears started to flow from Johnny's eyes.

"But you even sexier," Jose said, running his hand down Johnny's arm.

Johnny smiled. He remembered what his mother had said and wiped away the tears. "She's in a better place now."

"And you are here, at Jose's. Why you at Jose's?" The Latino took a long drag on the beer.

Johnny stared at his sneakers. "I just wanted to be with somebody."

Jose put his arm around Johnny's tiny waist. "Well, now you with somebody. You with Jose."

Jose reached over and found Johnny's hand; he brought it to his crotch. There was no mistaking that under his jeans Jose had a mammoth dick. He pressed Johnny's hand onto that mound of flesh; then, leaving Johnny's hand to its excited exploration, he peeled off his shirt and let it drop to the floor.

Jose's beefy pecs held coffee-colored nipples that grew erect as Johnny's fingers grazed them. Johnny felt the wisps of damp black hair in the hollow under his arm. He brought his hand back to the ridges that ran across his stomach, then headed down to the heat between his legs.

Jose finished his beer and tossed the can into the kitchen. He let out his breath slowly.

Johnny felt the cock. It was hard. Terribly hard. It was pretty obvious to Johnny that Jose wanted this just as much as he did.

Johnny roughly jerked Jose's jeans down around his ankles, spread his thighs, and knelt between his legs. Johnny thumped the big dick with his nose and rolled it over his eyes. He pressed soft wet kisses against the thick, fleshy base and ran his tongue flat against it, up and down the sides, as it stretched and jerked about. Jose ran his fingers through Johnny's hair as the boy reveled in the exquisite, satiny texture of Jose's delicate shroud.

When Jose's cock was fully extended, the pink glans blossomed out of its sheath. His balls hung close to the base of his dick, one on each side, and the pink and brown skin of his scrotum was tight with expectation. Johnny marveled at it; he had never seen such a huge prick. It was so large that it was, in fact, pretty ugly. But Johnny loved it.

The boy put his lips around the massive cock and bathed the entire length of it with his tongue, pausing to lavish extra attention to the cockhead. He sucked hard and fast, savoring the salty taste and milking pre-cum from the slit. Every time he went down on Jose he inhaled deeply

144

the warm and pungent aroma rising from between his legs. He let up just long enough to take the heavy balls in his mouth, bathing them in saliva and coaxing them to release their cum. Then he licked the soft and tender skin between his scrotum and thighs, until Jose pleaded with him to suck him some more.

Johnny's lips were stretched thin around the cock and he felt its heat on his tongue as he lapped around the glans, causing Jose to squirm and moan. Johnny felt its heat on the back of his throat as he took him in and buried his lips in Jose's pubic hair.

It didn't take Johnny long to bring Jose right to the edge. He was bucking and moaning, grabbing at Johnny's head, pushing the boy down on his cock. Johnny felt Jose's balls draw up tight against the root of his shaft and heard his gasps become more insistent.

Jose pulled Johnny's head into his crotch violently, at the same instant that he thrust his dick deep into Johnny's throat. A strangled moan, then he exploded in the boy's mouth. A torrent of cum spurted out, filling Johnny past overflowing. Cum trickled from the corners of Johnny's mouth as he sucked the last creamy drop from Jose's dick.

Without saying a word, Jose pulled his sopping cock from Johnny's mouth, hitched up his jeans and walked to the back of the trailer. Johnny leaned against the door, his hand on his own erection, his eyes closed. He could hear water running. He got up and made his way to where Jose was showering. On his right he saw an unkempt double bed that filled the room. He took off his shorts and lay face down on the bed. His hand went to his cock and he played with himself, his head pushed into the pillows. He heard the shower being turned off and then Jose entering the room. Johnny raised up onto his knees. Jose snickered and reached under the bed. He took a tube of Vaseline and squirted some on his cock and began stroking it. Soon it was erect again and Jose climbed on the bed. He dabbed some of the grease on Johnny's puckered hole, then got into position.

Jose began by rubbing his dick up and down Johnny's ass-crack, and Johnny's mind matched images to the sensations he felt: the swollen, red head and the fat shaft sliding past his hole, and the ridge at the base of the enormous cockhead adding friction as it slid back. Johnny recalled all the times he had take furtive looks at that cock, packed into the dirty work jeans—a tantalizing mound that he never thought he would get to see, let alone touch. Now that thick shaft was grazing his tight, puckered butt, wanting to punch through the ring of muscle and plunge itself deep up inside him. Johnny began to loosen up, and with a long growl of satisfaction, Jose slid into the boy. Johnny cried out, jacking off furiously as first the head then an inch or so of the shaft entered him. "Oh, yeah," he groaned. This was what he had been needing since he came to Florida.

"Easy, baby, easy," Jose cooed.

Johnny could feel the fur on Jose's legs graze his ass-cheeks and thighs as the older man drove his cock in deep, to the hilt. He started pumping faster and his growls became shorter. Johnny felt like he was on fire, like this fuck was the greatest he'd ever had and he just couldn't stand any more. He started to jerk and squirm in spite of Jose's grip on him.

"Oh, yeah. *Oh,* yeah. Uh, huh!" Jose's voice was deep and gravelly. He was pounding so violently now that Johnny was nearly hitting the wall with his head. It was almost more than the boy could stand. Flailing his legs as much as he could in that position, he shot out several long streams of cum. Jose roared and shoved his cock into Johnny with a horrendous jab, and Johnny felt warm squirts way up in his gut. Jose backed up, and jabbed again. And again, and again.

Everything became a blur for a moment or two; Johnny felt weak and lightheaded. Jose remained inside him, but he was still. All Johnny heard was his heavy breathing.

Finally Jose slid out, and gently laid the bulk of his body across Johnny's back. Jose caressed his shoulders and kissed his neck. "You feel better now?" he whispered.

"Oh, yes," Johnny moaned. "Oh, yes."

11.

The hustler's brutal skill was bringing an orgasm from Steve's loins quicker than Steve had expected. Sensing Steve was near, the hustler murmured encouragement and worked faster at him.

At that instant the phone rang. "Damn."

It was too late. The final spasm had come, but the shock of the sudden noise had ruined his pleasure. Steve cursed himself for not having unplugged the phone. He had not expected it to ring tonight. He had left the number of the Summit Hotel with the secretary at Bennett Lawrence's office, telling her he would be staying overnight, then returning to Rhode Island. He had underestimated the efficiency of a millionaire's secretary.

"Yes?" he said irritably into the receiver, looking down at the young man who had just sucked his cock.

"Steve?"

It was Johnny, calling back at last.

Steve listened for a moment, through the labored breath of his abortive orgasm, then all at once he turned pale.

Johnny was telling him his mother had died and he would be returning to Manhattan with his uncle for the memorial service. Steve went to the desk, made a few notes, then hung up the phone. For a moment he seemed lost in thought, his eyes on the night sky outside the window.

Then he glanced back at the bed and the hustler. The young man looked at once resigned and reproachful. He knew his performance was forgotten now. Tragedy had eclipsed pleasure.

"Put your clothes on," Steve said, "and go." The brusque command was tempered by a note of appreciation—the hustler had done his best, after all.

And it had started out so right. Earlier that evening, Steve had gotten an irresistible urge to find the gay bar he remembered from years ago. While he was in college and still with Roger, he had wanted to visit one, just to see what it was like. Still it had been difficult to get up the nerve to actually enter the place. He had walked down the street but kept going right past the door, too nervous to actually open it.

Now, tonight, alone in the city, he decided that it was time to stop being silly and to take control of his life. He took a deep breath, and pulled open the door to the bar. When he stepped through it, he felt as if he were moving slowly through water. The blood pounded in his ears and he actually felt dizzy for a moment. Then his eyes adjusted to the dim light and he looked around. Amazingly, it looked no different from any other bars he had been in before, except that all of the patrons and the staff were men.

He ordered a drink. The jukebox was playing "Your Love Is So Good to Me" by Diana Ross; it was so loud he sought a quiet corner. Trying to act as cool as possible, he sat down at a small table. It was difficult, for his stomach was in knots, and he had to take a deep breath and try to stop his hands from shaking. Every time he picked up the glass, he thought he might drop it. He hadn't planned on being a hunter, but at the same time, he couldn't help but return the glances that came his way.

Eventually a young man came by and looked at the empty stool on the other side of the table. "You waitin' for someone? he asked.

"No, I'm not."

"Mind if I sit down then?"

Hardly believing his own newfound calm, Steve had said, "Please do," and watched as his new companion slid onto the stool across from him. The young man seemed eager to please, and after two drinks, Steve was ready to leave. He had taken the hustler back to his hotel room

Now Steve found a hundred-dollar bill in his wallet and put it on the desk as the hustler pulled his jeans on. Watching him dress, Steve's heart sank. The hustler, who said his name was Ken, was in his early 20s, long-haired, dark-eyed, attractive in a brutish sort of way, and wonderfully skilled at fellatio. But he wasn't Johnny.

Ken opened the door and turned to Steve, his hand still on the knob.

"I hope everything'll be okay," Ken said, moving into the hallway.

Steve stood in the doorway, close to him, prepared to watch him go down the corridor to the elevator. In his white jeans, the hustler was a studly apparition in stark contrast to the dim hallway.

The look in Steve's eyes had changed somehow, seeming to ask the hustler to stay, even as his position urged him to leave. Steve stepped towards him. "It wasn't you. It's just that his mother died and he needs me and I'm not there. And I'm so lonely without him."

"Lonely," Ken murmured, a husky note in his voice. "I know what you mean."

Some note of sadness in his voice stopped Steve cold. He opened the door a few inches wider. "Life can be awfully cruel sometimes," Steve said. "It can happen to any of us."

Once again Steve was deep under the spell that had taken possession of him earlier, in the bar. And again it was simply impossible to resist. He wanted so much to hold someone, to have someone hold him at that moment. And even though Ken was just a hustler he did not know where he was going to find the strength to let this quick and easy sex go.

To Steve's enormous relief, Ken came back into the room, closing the door slowly behind him until the lock clicked shut. Ken's hands slipped to Steve's waist, and with the subtlest of movements he was drawing Steve back into the room.

Steve moved like a sleepwalker, his gaze studying the stud's perfectly shaped lips, which were fixed in a smile. He tried to reach out to kiss them, but Ken began moving away. Steve followed him deeper into the room. Ken looked back at him and Steve saw his smile curl a bit more.

At last, in front of the rumpled bed, Ken stopped Steve with two hands on his shoulders and kissed him deeply, hungrily. The smooth, inquiring tongue reminded Steve of Johnny's in his mouth, caressing and inflaming. Ken's hands rested on Steve's ribs, his hips shoving the hot bulge of his sex against Steve as he swayed with him in the shadows.

What happened next was the greatest combination of ecstasy and frustration Steve had known since that first time with Johnny. He remained shy and hesitant, slowly letting the hustler kiss him again and again, allowing him to touch more and more of him, so that the stud was always the aggressor.

It was Steve's little shrug of acquiescence that allowed Ken's hands once more to enfold and caress his cock, pulling his hips forward onto his own sex. And it was Ken's sigh as Steve tore at the buttons of Ken's shirt that told him he would be allowed to bend in worship, to kiss the hard pecs, suck on the nipples. As with Johnny, Steve was being driven mad with excitement.

Every step of the way the hustler was in control, encouraging Steve with a tremor, a returned kiss, a moan, until, despite Steve's fumbling, Ken's clothes had fallen away, his cock slapping hard against his belly.

At last Steve fell before the stud like his slave and, holding him by the back of his muscular thighs, kissed his hairy stomach, his navel, his hips, and finally became hypnotized by the throbbing cock, oozing precum. He felt a small shudder along the inside of Ken's thighs. A harsh groan came from him, and Steve buried himself against the russet pubic hair before him.

Great sadness was overwhelmed by passion now. Steve was not entirely aware of the sequence of events as Ken pulled him down on the bed beside him and began making love to him. The whole hard length of the stud was caressing Steve all over now, gentle calves on his thighs, their loins pressed together. And somehow in all this madness of contact, Steve retained his shyness, yielding only with hesitation to the hustler.

He did not need to guide the hustler's cock inside his ass. Ken roughly turned him around, and pushed his upper body down onto the bed. For Steve, feeling Ken entering him was like going into a nether world of unbearable pleasure. Nothing in his life had ever been so perfect as Johnny welcoming his frantic thrusts, and now he was welcoming this virtual stranger the same way. He also remembered how much Roger said he had loved it when Steve fucked him. Somehow, it seemed so *right*.

Steve was chagrined to be doing this at a time when his lover was suffering so greatly. But his shame only made the sexual pleasure all the more intoxicating. He loved the sensual grace of Ken's kisses, and the touch of his fingers as he became a heedless animal crouched atop him, pushing and groaning and working with all his might. Steve's hands now encouraged him, until at last Ken was torn by the final spasm, and his cum exploded inside Steve.

Utterly spent, Ken fell atop Steve, who listened to the gasps of his exhaustion as his hands caressed his back and shoulders. He lay in the thrall of Ken's touch, his sweaty skin, his robust smell, and the fresh smile he could even now feel on his lips, as Ken once again brought them to Steve's erection. In moments, Steve was coming and Ken held his cock and squeezed the last drops of cum onto Steve's belly.

But Steve's mind again returned to Johnny. Ken was good, but so was Johnny—and he *loved* Johnny. He would do anything, risk anything to have him again. Without that hope his future held only death. It was that simple.

Ken got up, a studly, statuesque marvel slipping like a ghost through the darkness, and into the bathroom. The hustler returned a moment later with a wet towel, which he handed to Steve. He dressed quickly, saying nothing until he looked in the mirror as he combed his hair, catching Steve's eye in the reflection, and saying, "That'll be another hundred."

12.

Steve had told the school he was attending a friend's funeral. But he didn't go to Maggie Lawrence's memorial service. Instead, he again rented a room at the Summit Hotel, and then got a cab to take him to the Lawrence penthouse on the upper east side. Johnny was waiting in front of the building and came running to the car when he saw Steve arrive.

The half-hour ride to the hotel was agonizing for both of them. They could only hold hands in the cab, and then only discreetly. Once alone in the elevator, they kissed until they reached the seventeenth floor. In the room, Steve closed the curtains while Johnny went to the bathroom. Over the sound of Johnny peeing, Steve offered the boy a drink.

"I could sure use one," Johnny said.

Steve poured two shots of vodka into two glasses over ice. He added a bit of vermouth to his, a shot of vermouth to Johnny's. "I only have vodka."

"That's fine," Johnny said, coming from the bathroom. He had left his pants unzipped and sagging. Johnny sipped the martini, pursed his lips. "Wow, I needed that."

Steve had turned shy again—eager for Johnny, but also wanting to take his time, to savor their time together as he was savoring his drink. Johnny went to the bed and, after setting his drink on the nightstand, took off his clothes. Steve stood across the room by the bureau watching the boy. He was again astounded by the youthful beauty before him, and tears of wonder came to his eyes at the sight of Johnny's ass. As he sipped his martini, Steve drank in the sight. No matter how many times he had seen Johnny nude, he was still transfixed.

He now gulped his drink and set the empty glass on the bureau. Undressing as he moved, he slowly walked across the room. Johnny got into the bed and Steve cuddled against him for a long while as the liquor warmed his insides. The feel of Johnny's young body against his was so natural and wholesome that some of his fear was assuaged. How could this perfect experience of love, this holy fulfillment, be wrong?

He did not know how long they stayed that way, while Johnny placed moist, tender kisses on his lips, his neck, his chest, and his fingers, and gently stroked his erection. He only knew that in what seemed no time at all the boy's feathery touch alone was making him come. As he cried out, "I'm coming!" Johnny's mouth went to his erupting prick, sucking, licking, sucking some more—draining it and swallowing what he had sucked out.

"Oh, Steve, I've missed it so much." Johnny brought his cum-slickened lips to Steve's and they shared long, tender kisses. Steve crushed the boy to him. His breath was hot against Johnny's ear, and the silky, dark hairs on his sinewy forearms tickled the boy's bare skin. All the while, Johnny squirmed against Steve's hard body in agonized horniness, begging Steve to fuck him.

Finally, Steve could contain himself no longer. He cupped Johnny's ass. His long fingers traced the crack, coming to rest at the puckering asshole. Steve tickled and probed, and when his finger slipped inside the boy, Johnny made no protest. Steve flipped him over so that he was on his hands and knees on the bed. Steve began kissing his ass and sticking his tongue inside. Johnny moaned, "I've missed this so much."

At last Steve mounted him and began entering him. Johnny didn't cry out, despite the sharp pain; he was lost in the purely sensual pleasure of the entry. Soon Steve was bucking and grunting, and his arms tightened around the boy's chest, pulling him back against his heaving body, sending his cock in to the hilt. Johnny jerked himself off, feeling Steve's balls slap against his ass, his vodka-breath on his neck, the hairy bulk of him pressed against his back. Johnny whimpered helplessly as his cum splattered the bedcover.

Steve rolled him over and spread the boy's legs apart, baring his asshole to his will. In a single, gut-wrenching thrust, he entered him again. His arms tightened around Johnny, who put his hands on Steve's back and started to trace the curves of bone and muscle slowly, feeling the heat of his skin beneath his hands. He ran his fingers up to where Steve's closely cropped hair had been shaved on his neck, brushing his fingertips along the line where skin met hair. He could feel Steve shiver as he did this.

Leaning down, Steve took one tit between his lips, fluttering his tongue over it lightly, and cooling it by blowing on it. He gently moved his mouth over the mound of his breast, slipped his tongue into his armpit, licked and sucked at the tiny damp hairs. When he drew away, he saw that Johnny was looking lovingly at him. Gripping the boy around the waist, Steve kissed him as he slammed into his ass.

Johnny began to whimper almost immediately, and as Steve fucked his ass harder and harder, he let out groan after groan, his voice rolling through the dimly lit hotel room. Johnny took every thrust of Steve's prick with a whimper of pleasure. As Steve jacked the boy off, his head was swimming from the heat of it all, and after several more pumps of his cock he started to blast away inside him. Johnny came too, his sphincter tightening around Steve's still-spewing cock as he came, and Steve felt his body convulse. Spent, Steve lay next to Johnny on the bed. Johnny kissed his stomach and began to lick his lover clean.

Suddenly, a whisper of reproach was in Johnny's ear. "You have to go. Your uncle will be worried."

"And your wife..." Johnny spat, bitterly. "Don't forget how worried *she* will be."

With shaking hands, Johnny put on his clothes. He was crying. He did his best in the bathroom to wash Steve's marvelous scent off himself. At the door, he hugged Steve close, intimately close, pelvis pressed to his, arms curled passionately around his back. Steve could feel Johnny's heart beating against his chest. His hands furled his hair, losing themselves in its magic softness as he kissed him goodbye.

He searched for words that would tell him how he felt, but they seemed ugly and insufficient after what had just happened between them. He wiped a tear on Johnny's cheek and Johnny's smile, warm and languid, reappeared.

"I have good news, Steve. Uncle Bennett says I can go back to Rhode Island to finish the semester. But then he's selling the place and I'll have to go somewhere else next year."

"It's wonderful that you'll be coming back, even for a little while."

"Yeah, and see if you can fix it so I have to spend the summer there making up all the work I've missed."

"I don't see that as a problem."

Hearing this news lifted Steve above all care or worry. He held in his arms the most beautiful boy in the world—and he was coming back to Rhode Island.

13.

So anxious was Steve to see Johnny that he arrived at the shore an hour early, only to find a strange car in the driveway. At first he drove by, then he came back and waited. Finally, he saw Johnny, dressed only in skimpy yellow shorts, leave the house with another boy, who wore blue jeans and a white T-shirt.. The other boy was taller, older, dark and attractive, but mean-looking. He and Johnny kissed briefly and the older boy got in his car, a sixties vintage Chevy coupe, and started the engine. Steve sped away, waited a few minutes, then went back.

"I saw you down the road. Why didn't you pull in?" Johnny asked when Steve finally rang the bell.

"I think that's obvious."

"Oh, you mean Luke?'

"If that's his name."

Johnny nodded. "He's a friend of mine from when I lived in New York. He's going to a special school in Boston now and was passing through on his way back home. He just stopped to say hello, that's all."

"Oh."

Johnny let Steve into the foyer and closed the door. "Aren't I allowed to have any friends?"

Steve didn't answer as he followed Johnny into the living room. Finally he said, "I'm sorry. I'm being silly."

"Yeah, you are. But there's a lot about me you don't know, Steve."

"Oh?"

"Yeah, I'm a whore. You'd probably say slut. Yeah, I'm a *terrible* slut. It runs in the family."

"You're not."

"Oh, yes I am."

"If you say so." Steve wanted a drink desperately. He glanced about the room.

Johnny went on, pacing back and forth. "It's just a fact. I never promised you I'd never *ever* have sex with anyone else."

"No, you never did."

"Then what are you getting so upset about?"

"I'm not upset," he said, clasping his hands behind his back to keep them from shaking.

"Yes, you are. You want me all for yourself."

"No ...." He started toward the kitchen. "What I'd like is a drink."

"No booze here, Steve. Nelly sees to that. I can't hide anything from Nelly." He chuckled. "Can you imagine, my uncle has a maid named Nelly?"

Steve stopped and walked back to Johnny. "I better go. "

"You came to fuck. Don't you want to fuck?" Johnny reached out to him. "Luke's fun but you're better."

Steve backed away. "Why are you talking to me like this? I don't want to hear this."

"What do you want to hear, Steve, that you're the only one?"

Steve threw up his hands. "I can't believe I'm having this discussion with one of my students."

Johnny plopped into a chair. "There you go, like all the others. First of all, I'm not just one of your students any longer."

"No, but you're still just a teenager."

"What's age got to do with it? I was born old. Mom always said so."

"Age has a lot to do with it."

"Please don't change on me, Steve. What I have liked about you is that you treat me like I was somebody."

"You are somebody. believe me."

"I mean, you treat me like I was an adult. A real person, not just a kid that has to be bossed around. You treat me like Mom treated me."

Steve slapped his hands together. "Oh, god, Johnny I'm sorry. You miss her terribly. This has all been very difficult for you. That's what it is."

"What *what* is?"

"Why you're acting like this."

Johnny jumped up, started to go up the stairs. "How am I acting?"

Steve followed the boy. "Like a whore."

"So it's back to that again." Johnny shook his head. "But I am a whore."

As Johnny bounded up the stairs, his ass was in Steve's face. "Okay then, whore, let's fuck."

"Let me take a shower first."

"No. I want you with his sweat on you."

"His cum up my ass, you mean."

"All right," Steve said, grabbing him, pulling him down on the landing. He tore Johnny's shorts away and shoved his finger in the boy's ass. It was wet, ready. The kid who had just left had indeed fucked him. Steve hurriedly unzipped his chinos and pulled out his cock. What had attracted him to Johnny in the first place was his sexual aggressiveness. And he had admired more than anything the boy's prowess. The only way to learn how to please a man the way Johnny did was to have many experiences. Steve could deal with the past, but confronting the prospect of competition in the present had unnerved him. Still, the boy was saying Luke was good but he, Steve, was better—and Steve was determined to prove it once again.

"Oh yeah," Johnny murmured, watching intently as Steve parted his thighs and sank his cock deep into his ass. It was a vigorous fuck for a few minutes, as Steve ran his tongue slowly up Johnny's neck to his earlobe. Already Johnny was responding, begging Steve not to stop. Steve nibbled gently, then darted his tongue in and out in a flurry of probes into the boy's ear. Steve lifted up and took Johnny's pecs in his hands, massaging them, then bringing his lips to the nipples, sucking them, teasing them. Johnny moaned and began writhing uncontrollably.

Slowly, generously Steve licked his way down Johnny's stomach, pausing at his belly-button to tickle it. His cock slipped out of the asshole as Johnny lowered his legs. Steve repositioned himself between Johnny's velvety thighs and began flicking, licking, and lashing each inch of

Johnny's erection with his tongue. Johnny started to come, wave after wave of ecstatic bliss now overtaking him completely. He grabbed Steve's wavy brown head of hair and drove Steve's face deeper onto his cock. Steve grabbed the tightened buttocks and plunged three fingers into the boy's gaping asshole as he drank every drop of Johnny's hot cum.

Finally Steve lifted his face away and Johnny pulled his body down on top of him as Steve slid his erection back into Johnny's asshole. Johnny clutched at the hard-driving cock with the muscles of his ass, realizing how extraordinary the fuck was, so different from the mechanical fuck Luke had given him that morning. Steve would withdraw most of his cock, then grind back in, building Johnny's desire to a fever pitch. Soon Johnny came again and this time Steve did too.

For a long while, they lay on the landing, Steve cuddling Johnny in his arms, nuzzling his ear and saying, "God, what a whore."

After the last bell, Johnny went to Steve's office. The door had been left partially open, and Steve was not there. He closed the door behind him and before he even lifted one box, ruffled through one drawer, he looked around the place for something to take with him. Something small. Something he could slip into his pocket without anyone noticing.

Not that it mattered, he realized; no one would notice anyway, and if they had, he didn't think they would care. Just as Johnny picked up a freshly sharpened pencil from Steve's desk, the door opened. It was another teacher, Mr. Allen. "What are you doing?"

Johnny had learned much earlier that being in Steve's office alone was apparently not something to cause suspicion on the part of someone who might find him there. The teachers all thought Johnny was "a marvelous boy." If he hadn't had any business to take care of when he went in, he managed to invent something as an explanation before he left. Frequently, whoever found him would give him something to deliver to someone, or have an errand that needed to be run—and Johnny was always so trustworthy, they said.

Now, making a big show of rolling back his sleeve to check his watch, Johnny answered he was waiting for Mr. Parker.

"He's gone."

"What?"

"He's gone."

"Really?" Johnny had seen Mr. Allen around the office a lot. He was in his early thirties, slim, good-looking, a nice guy, the kind who always filled the fluid cartridge bottle in the Ditto machine when he was done with it. Johnny wondered what he would be like to fuck. Mr. Allen slipped into the duplicating room next to Steve's office. Soon the very Ditto machine he was so conscientious about was clunking away. Johnny consulted his watch again, and just for good measure, went to the door and checked the clock above the secretary's desk.

The teacher was apparently beginning to wonder why Johnny was still there when he came out of the duplicating room, holding a sheaf of paper against his chest. "I said, he's gone."

"Oh, yeah. But for how long?"

"The rest of the day. He said he was taking his wife on a long weekend."

"Oh, okay," Johnny said, slipping a pencil from Steve's desk behind his ear and heading for the door.

While Nell drove him home, Johnny took the pencil from behind his ear and studied it. There was nothing extraordinary about its design. Faber-Castell American No. 2. It was yellow, with an eraser at one end and a fresh point at the other. This wasn't a mitt or anything terribly symbolic. Yet, to Johnny, it was an instrument of creation and was weighted with potential. Of course, since it served as a metaphor to him, he wouldn't actually write with it. Not this pencil. And he carefully stashed it in his notebook.

*   *   *

In her dream, they were dancing, but Susan kept stepping on his feet and the music was all wrong. "Wasting away in Margaritaville, looking for..."

"Susan!"

"Umm," she turned in her seat and slowly opened her eyes. His left arm rested on the steering wheel, his right hand caressed her.

"Susan, you're beautiful and I love you."

"I know you do," she said, reaching for his hand. "We've stopped."

"You've been sleeping the last fifty miles."

"I've been dreaming."

"Good dreams I hope."

"Strange." She looked around her. "Where are we?"

"At the hotel, finally. I'll go check us in," he said reaching for the door.

"Steve, darling ..."

"Huh?"

"I do love you."

"I'll see if they have a vacancy," he said planting a kiss on her forehead. He jumped out of the car, his white pants flapping against his bare ankles, taking two steps at a time toward the hotel lobby. Susan settled into the seat and closed her eyes.

After Steve tipped the young bellboy, far too generously Susan thought, they unpacked the liquor from the grocery bag and Steve went to get ice. When he returned to the room, he took off his pants and tossed them over the frayed upholstered chair. Susan had slipped into a silk negligee.

They sipped vodka martinis on the small balcony and watched the sun go down over the lake. Susan eased into Steve's lap, placing her drink on the table that separated them. "I'm so glad you got this idea for a second honeymoon."

"It's comfortable, isn't it?" Steve savagely shoved a finger in her cunt. She pushed him away. She wanted to take her time and tried to get up but he held her firmly and kissed her.

She finally pulled away, grabbed her glass and stood at the railing, finishing her drink, went into the room and made another. "You want any more?" she asked.

He followed her and encircled her in his arms, kissing her neck. "No, and you've had enough." She set her glass down and turned, pressing herself against him.

"Let's go to bed," he said and lifted her in his arms to kiss her.

It was a short kiss. She pulled away again. Steve was refusing to take his time. Suddenly, the chenille bedspread looked like she felt, faded and frazzled. Susan reached for the phone and called home to check with the babysitter. Everything was fine.

"No one said this was going to be easy. C'mon Susan..." He nuzzled her. He had stripped off his briefs while she had been calling. He had lost his erection. He brought her hand to it.

"No, Steve, I can't," she pulled away from him. "Look at this place. It's a dump. It's nothing like it was. Nothing is!"

"We were lucky to find any room at all."

She started to get up. "I hate it here."

"Don't pout. I hate it when you pout."

"I'm not pouting. I'm... I'm just frustrated."

"What happened? It started out so nice."

"When I see you nude, I can't stop thinking about you with somebody else. I just can't."

"It's always *somebody*." If she only knew, Steve thought. But then, if she did, it would really be over. "Have another drink," Steve offered.

He got up and fixed another martini for himself. Raising the glass, he said, "Cheers!"

"There's nothing cheery in this whole situation." She folded her arms and glared at him. "And getting boozed up won't help, Steve," she scolded.

"Neither will nagging," Steve said, dropping to his side of the bed. The mattress creaked.

"I'm not nagging."

"Methinks she protests too much."

"Oh, get out of your teacher mode."

"Hey, you used to love that. Now that things are a little tough..."

"Steve, things are more than a little tough. They're rotten."

She saw the hurt in his face, the same look she had seen when he failed to get tenure at the university and left to teach in the public school system. "Why can't I please you?" she asked.

"You do."

"No, or you wouldn't be seeing somebody else."

"The somebody I'm seeing has nothing to do with us."

"So you admit it, you are seeing somebody."

"Correction: *was* seeing somebody. And not in the way you think."

"Oh?"

"No."

She got up, stood over him. "I want to leave."

"You're out of control," he said calmly. "I must say I'm surprised. It's a side of you I've never seen before."

"If I'm out of control, it's your fault." She stood over him as he sipped his drink.

"Of course," he smirked. "Everything's always my fault."

"I don't understand this at all."

The martinis finally had their effect on Steve. He had lost his patience. "Okay, if you must know, the *somebody* I'm seeing is a man."

At first, Susan stood perfectly still. Then she slapped his face. The last of the vodka sloshed on his crotch. Unruffled, he placed the glass on the bed stand. She stood there, trembling, her hands on her face, sobbing. Steve reached up, grabbed her and tossed her on the bed. Then he mounted her, grinding himself into her, lifting her negligee. She gasped.

"No, I can't. Not now," she said softly, but her protests were smothered by his lips. His hands melted her anger, like always. But it was terrible; Susan cried all the way through it.

They checked out of the hotel early the next morning. Susan waited until they stopped for breakfast before bringing up the inevitable.

"How did it happen?" she asked finally, pushing away a half-eaten plate of eggs and sausage.

"It just did."

Steve knew Susan was fighting down two competing impulses in her gut, the first one total disapproval, the second total fascination. He watched this conflict reflected on Susan's face and said, "It didn't mean anything."

Susan was silent for awhile, trying to understand what this situation meant. She had never been a promiscuous person. Steve, as far as she knew, never had been either. She stared at her husband's face across the table and looked for any perceptible signs of distress. There were none. Then she said, "How could it happen? I simply don't understand you."

He sighed. "Of course I'd never done anything like that before. It was strange—like a compulsion. Inevitable. Dangerous, but compulsive. I don't know. I can't understand it myself. There was something explosive about the situation, the confrontation, something strangely...well, strange. Erotic."

158

Steve looked down at his hands gripping his coffee cup. He had never used the word erotic with Susan before. Using it was fun; he suddenly felt like he was lecturing on D. H. Lawrence.

Susan was devastated. She looked at Steve and he knew she couldn't understand him, couldn't sort out what he had done in the relevant compartments of her brain. Her perception of him had now been so radically altered that any coherent discussion about motivation and intent seemed utterly fruitless. But she wanted to know the details. Eventually, trembling, she asked, "So, how was he?"

Steve looked for a moment like he wasn't going to reply, then said, "Strange." He was silent for a long moment and then added, "How can we even discuss it? How can we talk about it? There's nothing to say."

Susan looked away. "So you won't be seeing him again?"

Steve nodded. He realized it was as though nothing could be expressed between them that would make sense, which they could both understand. And yet something so incredible had happened. He felt sad, almost bitter, but in his heart he knew that the space that had sprung up between them, the vacuum, had now opened up and it was a positive space that could be filled with many things—ideas, possibilities. He remembered something he had read once, "Words are like gifts, some people are generous and some frugal," and decided to make himself a present by keeping quiet the rest of the way home.

14.

After their weekend away, Susan got Steve to agree to see a marriage counselor. They went to Providence and saw a man highly recommended by one of Steve's former colleagues at the university.

Steve liked the rotund Dr. Harris immediately; he appeared to be a thoughtful, kind man, talking to each of them separately, then together. During his session, after some preliminary discussion, Steve relaxed and felt no qualms about recounting his sexual history.

"Tell me about your sex life," Dr. Harris said. "When did you first experience sex?"

"When I was two or three. I actually remember getting this great feeling when I played with myself. I began playing around with girls when I was about eleven or twelve. Nothing heavy but lots of feeling and kissing."

"Did you like it?"

"Yes."

"Did you experience anything of a sexual nature with males at that time, or even consider it?"

"Not unless you count circle-jerks at camp, and then there was this kid at school who used to blow everybody."

"Did you like that?"

"Yes, but I didn't admit it, even to myself."

"Why not?"

"I didn't want to be thought of as queer. I didn't want to think of myself that way."

"How old were you when you had your first sexual encounter with a woman?"

"It was a gangbang. My brother arranged it. He's three years older than me. He's a lawyer like my father—married, living in Arizona, and straight as an arrow. I haven't seen him in four or five years. He's been married three times, by the way, whatever that says about him.

"Anyway, at this party, this gangbang, I was probably something like tenth in line. I never saw the girl's face. She was kneeling up on a bed and taking it from behind. When I finished, my brother drove me home and told my father I was a man, and that made my father happy."

"But did it make you happy?"

"No. I'm terribly romantic when you get right down to it. The thing is, with a woman I have to *know* her. I have to care about her. Susan was the only one I have ever really cared about. We met in college. Her family has money, she had a good background. She was shy, had never dated much. It took us a long time before we had sex. Like I said, I have to care about a woman."

"Do you see that as a hang-up?"

"Yes, but it's a good one. It means I value sex with women."

"But not with men?"

"It's different with men. I was only with Roger, except one time, when I was walking the dog in the park at night a couple of years ago. This guy approached me and we went into the bushes. He blew me. It was very exciting. He gave me his phone number, but I didn't call him back, and I stayed away from the park."

"Why?"

"I felt rotten afterwards. Because I enjoyed it, I was sure that I must be a homosexual. There was no other way to look at it, I thought. Every book on the subject, every expert, said that if a man engaged in homosexual acts, no matter how much heterosexual sex he enjoyed, he *was* homosexual. I hated the idea of being homosexual, a closet queen. I didn't feel homosexual. As a matter of fact, I didn't feel heterosexual. I just felt sexual. I wanted sex and I wanted *all* I could get. It relaxed me. Made me feel better. I now realize that of course I was attracted to both men and women from the beginning. Even in camp as a kid during the circle jerks I wanted the other boys, and I wanted them to want me. Of course I never admitted it to myself, or to anyone."

"Until now."

"Yes. Now, I can see I'm bisexual. I think each person has to have areas that are private to himself. It doesn't matter what they are, but you

160

have to have something of your own that is private to you, uniquely your own."

"What does Susan have?"

"I don't know. She has something, though; otherwise she couldn't have kept me so intensely interested all these years."

"Would you like to know what it is?"

"I would ... and yet, somehow I wouldn't."

Two days later, Steve went to see the therapist alone.

"Susan appears to be able to cope with this better now," Steve said.

"Yes, she seems to be doing well. But I don't know what she would think if she knew it was really a *boy* you're seeing."

"*Was* seeing."

"All right. But if Susan knew how old he was ...."

"He was born old."

"I'm sure of that. But still he's a child, and prone to foolishness. And you have your career to consider."

"Yes, and I suppose this must all appear as if I'm the one who's prone to foolishness."

"And you see no way out of this ... foolishness, as you call it?"

"That's right. I want him every minute. When I don't see him I miss him terribly."

"Even though you know he is seeing others?"

"I'm afraid the fact of his cheating makes him even more desirable." It was true. Steve's fantasies when he was masturbating and having sex with Susan now included mental images of Johnny with Luke.

The therapist said, "She wants to meet this boy—who she thinks is a man, of course."

Steve shook his head. "What?"

"That's what she said. She wants to meet him. She doesn't look upon him as competition. He is giving you something you can't get from her. If it were another woman, like she thought it was, that would be something else, but *this* ..."

"*This* is private."

"Fuck me in the ass," Susan pleaded that night, "if that's what it is that turns you on now."

"No, that isn't what it is."

Susan told Steve she couldn't even *imagine* two men having sex together, but she had heard that's what they did. "Then what *is* it?" she asked.

"Stop this! I told you, it's over. You're ruining everything."

Their situation had gone from bad to worse. Steve thought Susan had begun obsessing on the man her husband was seeing, and at times he was sure he was being followed. Then a colleague at school told him a man, a

161

private investigator, was asking some of his associates questions about him. Steve feared Susan was spending her family's money on preparations for a messy divorce that could destroy him.

Finding Steve uncharacteristically moody and reluctant to meet him, Johnny abandoned the pretense of going to summer school altogether and followed Luke to New York. But before leaving, he got Steve to agree to come to the city as soon as he could arrange it.

15.

When Johnny arrived at the penthouse, he was surprised to find Uncle Bennett in residence. He made up an excuse for his sudden appearance, saying he had come to the city to see a friend.

This infuriated Bennett. "It's time we talked," he said.

If there was one thing Bennett had learned in the competitive world it was that one could not defeat people by hating them. Hatred brought them too close for one to control. Only by viewing them from afar, like insects surveyed from a great height, could one manipulate and destroy them without putting one's self at risk.

Bennett's meddling in his sister's affairs had begun with her marriage to Jack, and his hatred of Jack was so severe that he had gotten careless. He had Jack investigated, and presented him with the evidence he had gathered. He also presented him with an ultimatum: either go back to Hollywood to his wife and son or be destroyed. The confrontation with Bennett was more than Jack could bear. No one, least of all Maggie, ever learned of their meeting.

Now Bennett was having Steve Parker investigated. He had been told by Nell about the unusual amount of "tutoring" Johnny was getting, and sent detectives to Rhode Island. From the evidence they gathered, Bennett saw Parker as a man whose unnatural passion threatened to ruin him. He felt a mixture of contempt and pity for Steve, but was not about to confront him personally, as he had Jack. No, as long as he was Johnny's guardian, he would work subtly by simply removing the temptation that had driven Parker to these acts.

Bennett insisted on meeting Johnny's so-called "friend." Johnny called Luke, who came right over. Bennett made them lunch and seemed satisfied that Johnny was not in New York to meet his older lover. He gave the boys money to go to the movies.

"You still do it?" Johnny asked Luke as they passed a couple of hustlers on the street.

"Sometimes, just to keep my hand in. But I'm too old for the street, man. Now I go to the bar." The bar, as Luke called it, was *Rounds,* on East 53rd Street.

"You'll get in if you're with me, but for you to go alone, we'll have to get you a fake ID. "

"Okay," Johnny said.

Luke said the man at the bar was named Chet, but to Johnny it sounded more like "Cheat." Whatever his name, he spoke very little English. Luke seemed to know what the man wanted, though: two boys. This had never happened before. Luke wasn't sure he wanted to be in the same room with Johnny while the boy was being fucked. But when the man handed him a hundred-dollar bill as his bond, Luke acquiesced.

The man was staying at one of the diplomatic hotels and took them to his suite. In the bedroom, Luke touched Johnny's perfectly shaped ass and made certain Chet admired it too. Chet sat on the other bed and watched while Luke ate Johnny's ass.

Johnny turned around and rubbed his swollen cock against Luke's lips. "Look at this, Chet," Luke gasped. And Luke studied the glistening rod of pleasure while he pursed his lips around it and sucked. Johnny looked at Chet while he was being blown. Chet was nodding.

At first Luke thought Chet was going to just watch them fuck, but suddenly he stood and started taking off his clothes. His neck, arms and chest were huge and well-muscled, the skin dark. Hair tufted from both armpits and from his groin and spread in an eagle-shaped design across his chest. His thighs were enormous, knotted with muscle; his uncut cock, which rose out of a mass of wiry black hair, was the size of a baby's arm.

"God almighty," Luke gasped. Johnny was speechless.

Chet made strange noises deep in his throat, and said something in a language that made no sense to them whatsoever. But Luke figured the man wanted Johnny and let Johnny get up. Chet moved up slowly, took Johnny by the waist, and gently pulled him close. He ran his fingers over the blond hair tumbled around his shoulders and smoothed his hands over the small patch of pubic hair, which was as blond as the hair on his head. He stuck a fat finger into Johnny's ass, as Johnny grasped his dick with his hand.

Chet withdrew his finger and smelled it. A smile appeared on his face, and Johnny found himself smiling back. Chet idly began to stroke his member as his big, hairy balls swung back and forth. Then he started to moan a little. He shifted from foot to foot and cupped the boy's ass, giving smart little tweaks to his nipples from time to time. Then his surprisingly smooth hands ran down Johnny's hard belly to his cock, and Chet's fingers went to work on it. Johnny began moaning with him and pulled him closer, all the while keeping a tight grip on Chet's enormous prick.

163

Chet picked him up and tossed him onto the bed. Johnny lay spread-eagle on his back and waited while Chet hovered over him. Johnny began blinking wildly as Chet pulled the boy's legs over his massive shoulders and, with a tongue that felt as wide as a washcloth, licked and teased Johnny's anus.

Pulling him by the hips, Chet took Johnny's buttocks in his hands and lifted them up to drive his penis right into them. Johnny let out a huge moan. The man was so large that for a moment Johnny thought he would pass out, but he wiggled and struggled to get comfortable. Finally it started to feel good—and then *damn* good! Johnny wrapped his legs around the man's waist and caressed him with both hands.

Chet continued to mumble and moan in his strange language for about ten minutes of the most arduous fucking Johnny had ever experienced. Suddenly, Chet raised up and pulled out. Johnny sighed as the man motioned to Luke, and Luke climbed on, slamming his cock into Johnny.

Then Chet got behind Luke and entered him. It felt to Johnny as if the man's cock reached right through Luke, so that both men were fucking him. Luke was grunting, making animal sounds Johnny had never heard from him before. He felt Luke's cock stiffen and he gripped it hard with his anal muscles. As Luke shot his load into Johnny, spasms rocked his ass. At the same time, Chet came inside Luke, letting out a loud grunt that was almost a lion's roar, and the three of them shook together as one organism, desperately holding onto each other. Then they collapsed in a sweaty, exhausted heap.

On the street, Luke hailed a cab. Johnny was still shaking. In the cab, Luke handed him two hundreds. "Wow," Johnny said, "to be paid to get fucked like that."

"Only in New York," Luke said.

16.

Johnny was desperate. For days, he had tried to get Steve to come to New York. Finally he called him and told him he *had* to come, that there was some news he could deliver only in person. Steve relented at last—he simply had to see Johnny. They agreed to meet at the Summit Hotel at nine o'clock the next evening. Johnny told his uncle he was going to spend the night with Luke.

So anxious was Steve to see Johnny he caught an earlier train and arrived in mid-town at six. He decided to have a drink before meeting Johnny. He entered the bar and saw Johnny immediately, but Johnny was with Luke; they were talking to a well-dressed man with gray hair, and they didn't see him. Steve stayed in the shadows, finding a stool at one of the little tables. It was seven o'clock and the place was packed.

He moved to the bar to refill his drink. It was then that Johnny finally saw him and left Luke and the other man at the bar. "You're early. You're always early."

"I didn't want to be late."

"I'm surprised to see you here."

"Likewise." Steve lead Johnny to the little table.

"I told you I was a whore."

"But you're also underage."

"Shhh," Johnny said, bringing his forefinger to his lips. "I'm too old for the street and too young for the bars." He placed a firm hand on Steve's thigh, stroking the fabric. "Loosen up, Teach."

"Shhh!" Steve mimicked.

"Do you want me to stop?"

"No," Steve replied, so happy to see the boy he could hardly refuse him anything.

Johnny moved his hand over Steve's thigh, grazing the hardness concealed between his legs. He pulled Steve's jacket over it discreetly, and they giggled over the naughtiness of the situation.

They chatted as Johnny continued stroking Steve. Johnny told Steve about the johns seated across from them, about the hustlers who cruised about. Johnny unsnapped Steve's trousers and eased the zipper down under the cover of his jacket, allowing his fingertips to skate over the head of the stiff cock, rolling a thumb over the creamy drop at the end, his head dropping to Steve's shoulder. Johnny wanted to look at Steve's cock again, so he briefly lifted the jacket and turned his face up to Steve's. Their eyes locked in a gaze of desperation. Steve felt they were causing a scene. They had to leave.

In the gleaming hotel elevator, they were alone. All the way up to the 17th floor of the Summit Steve's hands roamed Johnny's body, forcefully, insistently. Steve had become crazed, like a hungry beast. Johnny opened Steve's pants and his cock sprang free. He sighed. Johnny's eyes, misty with desire, locked on Steve's, and he wrapped his hand around the pulsating cock.

"Oh, God..." Steve moaned as Johnny dropped to his knees and began sucking it. The elevator doors were about to open. Steve pushed the boy away and turned to zip up his pants. No one was in the corridor, so Steve encircled the boy with his arms and pulled him against his chest. He caressed Johnny's hair, running his hands over his back, sending waves of anticipation shivering through the boy. He tilted Johnny's chin up to meet his face, and their lips met. Johnny whimpered and pressed himself even more insistently against his older lover. Steve held Johnny tighter and slipped his tongue into his mouth. The elevator doors shut behind them and Steve broke free, leading the way to his room.

Steve stripped while Johnny used the bathroom. His cock was fully erect when Johnny returned to the room, with his pants undone, and started to undress. But Steve stopped him. "Let me do that." He caressed the nape of Johnny's neck while he removed his shirt. Then he got down on his knees and pulled the jeans down, his tongue flickering over him, tracing the tan line. The jeans fell in a pool at Johnny's feet and he gasped as Steve's fingers softly stroked his cock.

Johnny went to lie on the bed and Steve knelt over him, smiling gently as he parted the boy's thighs. Johnny arched himself up to meet Steve's embraces. His hands reached out to fondle Steve's hair as the older man continued to explore every part of Johnny's body with his mouth. Trembling, Johnny took Steve's cock in his mouth and, as he flicked his tongue over the balls, he felt Steve's hands on his ears, clutching them as he groaned out his pleasure. Johnny took the cockhead completely in his mouth and as he slid the shaft in, he felt it grow even more rigid and fiery. Steve arched to meet Johnny's lips. He let out a howl of pleasure as he got close.

Lying back, Steve gasped as Johnny climbed over him and impaled his ass on Steve's cock. His hungry bobbing up and down brought Steve off in moments. Leaving Steve's wilting erection in his cum-filled ass, he played with his own cock, his eyes locked on Steve's, and came harder than he had in weeks.

*   *   *

Steve slept soundly and it was nearly noon when he awoke. Johnny was in the shower. When he came out, scrubbed and fresh, with an incredible hard-on, Steve blew him. Then they decided to go down to the coffee shop for breakfast.

"So, you never did tell me the news," Steve said after they had ordered. "Why did you have me come down here?"

"I wanted to say goodbye."

A sudden, brief stab of alarm racked Steve. "Oh?"

"Uncle Bennett's letting me go live with my grandma."

"Where's that?"

"Los Angeles. Huntington Beach. Those were my choices, either live with him and go to that 'Good News' school of his, or live with grandma."

"Nice options, Palm Beach or Huntington Beach. Not everyone is so blessed."

"Will you come to see me?"

"I'd love to, you know that. I'll just have to figure out a way."

"You got down here, you can get out there."

"Well, I *am* a married man, remember."

Johnny looked away. "How could I forget?"

"I love my wife, Johnny."

166

"Yeah, I know. You're a bisexual. You love everything."

"I'll ignore that. Do you like your grandma?"

"She's crazy. I mean, she had my mother and my uncle. She'd have to be crazy, right?"

They took a cab to 42nd Street. New York was baking. Even the nightmare sounds of fire truck sirens were muffled by the heat; cops chewing gum hung around the sidewalks bartering with criminals; athletes on skateboards livened up the traffic; narcotics were available on every corner of 42nd Street. New York was on parade.

"I'll miss this," Johnny said.

"You'll be back," Steve said.

They played games at the amusement arcade. Before they left, they went into the Quik Foto booth and had their picture taken together. Steve handed the strip of four poses to Johnny. Johnny tore it in half. "Two for you, two for me," he said.

Steve shoved the pictures in his wallet, wondering just where he would hide them when he got home.

"I'd like to have you see me off but Uncle Bennett's taking me. He said he wants to make damned sure I get on that plane.

We'll have to say our goodbyes at the hotel."

Back at the hotel, Steve disappeared momentarily through the bathroom door, then reemerged, naked.

He looked at Johnny kneeling on the bed, naked, presenting his ass for him. Steve's heart beat faster at the always breathtaking sight of the boy's magnificent bottom.

Johnny rolled over and looked up at Steve. "Say goodbye to it," Johnny begged, spreading his legs wide apart.

Steve didn't know quite how, but he was determined to make this final fuck the very best they had ever enjoyed. He got on the bed between Johnny's thighs, kissing his moist skin, breathing in the aroma of him and the heady, lingering smell of the fuck they had shared so recently. Steve ran his hand over the smooth surface of Johnny's cheek. Johnny pulled Steve to him, kissing him passionately, their bodies again alive with the promise of the greatest pleasure either of them had known.

Johnny's eyes were bright, bold, and clear as he looked back into Steve's. Steve smiled, not catching the thoughtful expression on Johnny's face, which suggested he was going to say something. Before Johnny had a chance to say what was on his mind, Steve kissed him, and their bodies moved in tight against each other—strong arms, legs entwined.

Steve began gyrating his hips, grinding his cock against Johnny's crotch. Soon he rose to his knees, his tongue gliding down Johnny's smooth chest and hard abdomen as he went lower to worship the boy's cock.

167

Johnny's cock was rigid now. After Steve took his first tentative taste of Johnny's dick, Johnny began to thrust his hips upward, fucking Steve's mouth fiercely..

Relinquishing Johnny's cock after a few minutes, Steve buried his face between Johnny's thighs, burrowing into the lad's ass with his tongue. Johnny's body began to writhe, and he placed both hands on Steve's head, pulling his mouth tightly up against his ass while Steve tongue-fucked him feverishly.

After a few more minutes, Steve raised up and squeezed a large amount of lotion into his hand. He first greased his cock, then reached between Johnny's spread legs and greased his ass, sliding his fingers inside Johnny's hole. After Steve loosened the boy up with his fingers, he entered him, then began to pump slowly, soothing him with a probing kiss, then building to an exciting staccato fuck that had Johnny humping and twisting beneath the weight of the older man's body. Steve came hard, shooting deep inside Johnny's writhing ass, over and over again.

Panting, Steve lifted himself up and straddled Johnny. Soon he was clamping his anus around Johnny's stiff prick, which was oozing pre-cum, sliding up and down on it. Within moments, Johnny was enjoying a thunderous orgasm that seemed to roar through every fiber of his body. Steve lifted up and Johnny's cock slipped out of his ass with an audible 'plop.' Panting, he lay next to Johnny and closed his eyes.

Johnny propped up on an elbow and looked at him, eyes bright, amused, and a little guilty. "I'm sorry for getting you in so much trouble with your wife."

"It wasn't your fault," Steve offered, kissing away the crease in the boy's forehead.

Johnny was silent, his face more serious than ever before as he lost himself in thought. Steve felt the boy pull away from him, felt something shift between them as Johnny announced, "It's time for me to go."

"I know," Steve said, and kissed Johnny deeply, holding him. With a sigh, he hugged the boy to him. How comfortable he'd become with him. "Damn, I'll miss you," he whispered as matter-of-factly as he could, but the softness and the hoarseness in his voice betrayed his sorrow at their imminent parting. He inhaled the smell of their sex still lingering on the boy's young body.

Himself overcome, Johnny covered Steve's face with kisses. They cuddled for a moment on the bed. But neither was really present, both of them having already parted, anticipating the strange emptiness of the times that lay ahead, preparing for them.

Steve watched Johnny dress, his sleek body exposed and still incredibly tempting. "You're so beautiful," he said, sincerely, now completely present in the moment.

Johnny was silent, his mind full of a million feelings and thoughts. Suddenly he moved swiftly back to the bed, leaned down and kissed Steve one last time, soft lips, gentle tongues. Steve leaned up toward the boy, wrapped his arms around him.

The kiss finished, they held their faces close.

"Good-bye," Steve said, touching the tip of his finger to Johnny's soft lips as he looked at them, his eyes sad. "You know where to find me."

Johnny stood again, proud and strong at the bedside. "Come down to the lobby with me. See me off."

After Steve hurriedly dressed, Johnny handed him an envelope. "I have a present for you," Johnny said,

Steve opened it. It contained the pencil Johnny had stolen from his desk. "Why, thank you, Johnny. It's what I've always wanted."

"I thought you were going to say you've been wondering what the hell happened to it."

"Oh, you mean you stole it?"

Johnny nodded in mock sheepishness.

"Well, I really hadn't missed it. I mean, I have a whole drawer full of them."

"But there was only one on the desk. And I had to have it."

"You're crazy," Steve laughed. "First my heart, then my shorts, now my pencil."

Johnny snatched the pencil back. "Okay, if you have so many, I'll keep it. It means nothing to you, but to me …."

"Okay, now my heart. Can I have my heart back?"

"No, never." Johnny giggled, clutching the pencil to his chest.

"I was afraid of that."

Watching Johnny turn and smile at him before he passed through the revolving glass doors to the street, Steve couldn't help thinking about how he had never been to California. How could he arrange it? Nothing came to him. He shrugged. He would think of something.

From a distance, he followed Johnny out onto the street. Johnny hailed a cab and told the driver take him to Bennett's apartment.

Dusk had begun to settle over Lexington Avenue and, with his hands in his pockets, Steve stood there under the hotel's canopy until he could no longer see the yellow cab that carried Johnny away.

Epilogue

A lot can happen in almost a year.

Steve surveyed Johnny thoroughly. Then he said, "You're looking great, Johnny, you know? All that time at the gym has been good for you."

Johnny smiled and nodded. "I know."

Steve was surprised by Johnny's new confidence, his calm assurance. In a year the boy seemed to have changed incalculably. Steve felt rather piqued by this but also attracted. Johnny seemed so happy. He had become a man.

Suddenly it struck Steve that he must have a lover; there was something about him that was so serene and fulfilled. The idea of his being incredibly happy with another man made his stomach churn. He said, "Well, I bet you've been having fun."

Johnny laughed. "Why?"

Steve shrugged. "I dunno. You seem different."

Johnny had picked the restaurant, a vegetarian place with abundant hanging ferns, and said he would meet Steve there. Steve noticed how other men stared at the boy as he walked in, but he seemed aloof, and oblivious to their stares.

They chatted about school and Johnny asked how Steve's wife and kids were. He said everybody was fine. They had stopped in Phoenix to see his brother and then come to Los Angeles. Steve had Susan take the girls to Disneyland. He had told her he was going to relax by the pool at the hotel.

"Still fuckin' her pussy, eh?"

Steve looked away. "I'll ignore that."

"Oh, I know. Duty calls."

"I love my wife."

"So you've said. Well, I wondered what pussy was like, so I tried some. I can't say I was impressed."

Johnny had Steve's full attention now. "Oh?"

"Yeah. I fucked a girl. That make you happy?"

"No. I mean, yes, it does. Whatever you want, Johnny."

"I fucked her but I wanted you."

"That happens to me sometimes too. I'll be with Susan but I'll be thinking of you."

"And I'm three thousand miles away."

"Sad, but true."

Now it all felt rather odd and unnatural. He had imagined that Johnny would be tense when he saw him, but in fact he seemed perfectly relaxed and at ease. If anything Steve was the one who felt uncomfortable. He knew that Johnny needed to be with someone, and he knew it couldn't be him. Steve felt curious and jealous, but he neither asked questions of Johnny nor did he say anything.

The nelly young waiter flirted with Johnny as they ordered their meal. Steve noticed their eye contact and it made his stomach churn. After the waiter had left their table with the order, Johnny played with his cutlery, making his finger into a flat, straight scale and trying to balance his knife on the finger, then his fork, then his spoon. Steve watched him with a half-smile flickering around the corners of his lips.

Eventually Steve said, "You said over the phone you were being a good boy."

"It's a business decision. You know, Uncle Bennett laid it all out for me. It's all mine if I want it."

"If you do as he says."

"No. He agreed I could do as I wished. I just had to graduate, which I have, and go to college—any college, he didn't give a shit, which surprised me—and go back to New York and give real estate management, or whatever it is, a try."

"And you ....?"

Johnny grinned. "Well, I love New York."

"And money. Lots of money."

"I've never known anything else, Steve. I don't think I want to."

Steve sipped his water. "So there's no one special?"

Johnny looked out the window. "I've been seeing some guys, but it's rough. I mean, they're all into drugs, or drinking, or hanging out and I've got my future to think of." He caressed a bicep, flexed.

"You look wonderful. Better than ever."

"Does that mean you'll fuck me after lunch?"

Steve smiled. "Now *that's* my Johnny."

At a motel on Selma near where they had eaten lunch, Steve let Johnny undress him, push him onto the bed. It was the same Johnny, all right. Why the boy wanted him, Steve could never figure out; he did not think of himself as handsome. He was not unattractive, but hardly one to make heads turn the way Johnny did. From the beginning, he had been astounded by Johnny's hunger for him, and today was no exception. Johnny kissed him with deep, passionate, probing strokes of his tongue, delving into Steve's mouth. Steve's tongue met his, entwined in soul kissing in a way he never had experienced before: Johnny sucked Steve's tongue deeply into his mouth as he squiggled his own all around it. When he pulled his tongue from the depths of Steve's mouth, he planted tiny kisses on his lips, nose, and cheeks, and then worked his way down his neck, to his pecs. By the time he took the right nipple between his lips, Steve was delirious with lust. When he gently gnawed and bit the hardened bud, Steve was moaning, louder and louder with every delicious bite. Then Johnny went to work on the other nipple, totally disregarding Steve's cock, which was pressing against him for some attention.

171

Johnny stood and began stripping off his clothes. With the shirt gone, Steve saw the boy had grown some golden hairs on his now-sculpted chest. When Johnny removed his pants and underwear, all Steve could focus on was the incredible fact that the boy's ass was even more delectable than before. His hard-on was just as Steve remembered it, scrumptious-looking and standing up close to his navel.

He came back to the bed, straddled Steve and stuffed Steve's mouth with his cock. The face-fucking, with Johnny reaching behind him occasionally to tease Steve's erection, lasted several minutes until Steve's head was reeling from pleasure. Johnny was ready to come, but he had just begun. He switched places with Steve and permitted the older man to fuck his mouth with his erection. All the while Johnny's hands were moving, probing, touching, exposing. Steve's face was flushed and he was breathing hard. For a moment Johnny had the full length of him in his mouth; he gave him a smooth, tight suck at the back of his throat before he pulled out. "Fuck me," Johnny begged.

In no time, Steve had mounted Johnny and expertly drew the boy's legs over his shoulders so he could fuck him with the deepest penetration.

"This is what I've been waiting for," Johnny said, as the big head was pressed past the clenching ass muscle. Steve glided into Johnny with ease. As he began to pump, the bed shook.

"Oh, fuck it, man! Everybody out here wants to get fucked," Johnny admitted. "I've needed this for so long."

Steve's eyes glazed over and the passion raged in him, amplifying the speed and depth of his thrusts. He grabbed Johnny by the hips and pressed his legs way back as he continued to fill his ass.

"I'm gonna explode," he panted as he fucked. And soon he was rocking, pressing, fucking in shorter, harder, stronger thrusts until Johnny felt his ejaculations shooting through his cock and into him. Steve pressed himself inside Johnny until he could press no more, filling Johnny. Johnny's ass muscles twitched around Steve's cock until the very last drop of jism had been expended inside him.

Steve collapsed next to Johnny and brought the boy's cock to his mouth once more. He kissed it, stroked it, adored it. "Will you fuck me with this?"

"If that's what you want."

"Yes, I want it. I guess I'm like all the others," Steve said.

"No, you aren't, or you wouldn't be here."

"What makes me so special anyway?"

"You're just a nice man, Steve. A very nice man. You're the only man who's treated me right. And, besides, you'll always be special to me, *Mr. Parker*." Johnny mussed Steve's hair. "I mean, you're the only teacher I've ever fucked."

As Steve got into position, his legs spread wide, he smiled. "And you're the only student I've ever fucked."

172

"So," Johnny said, greasing his cock, then sliding it into his former teacher, "that makes us even."

And the thought of being "even" with Johnny Lawrence, the beautiful boy whose cock was inching into him, made Steve shudder with delight.

IN THE HEAT OF A SUMMER NIGHT

I would like to think that this was another roman à clef, *with the Johan of the story actually the breathtakingly sexy Czech porn star Johan Paulik, since John Patrick was endlessly charmed by the beauty and impish charm of that young man. But I have no reason to be sure he had the real Johan in mind when he wrote this unpublished story about an older man realizing his fantasies in bed with a young, famous sex symbol—JB*

I left the theater and stepped into the heat of the summer night, which was already beginning to seem oppressive. I wondered how the couple I had seen at the bar during intermission had enjoyed the play. The thin, dark-haired, comely lad, obviously bored, allowed the older man, probably a john, to fetch him a glass of champagne. The lad stood there, leafing through his Playbill, while the man waited in line to buy the bubbly. Suddenly two other men appeared, greeted the lad—nervously I thought—and then presented their Playbills for him to autograph. He was obviously a celebrity of some sort, but I just couldn't place him.

Living in Manhattan for a couple of years, I had become used to seeing celebrities on occasion, but I frequently had difficulty placing them. Such was the case again, although I knew I should be able to identify this boy. I watched him and his escort guzzling the bubbly as the lights flickered, signaling the second act was about to begin. I quickly stepped closer and my eyes met those of the lad; he smiled, then lowered his eyes and turned away as I passed them on my way back into the auditorium. I felt as if I had wronged the older man in some way, as if I had something to atone for.

As I walked along, like a detective, like a lover, I returned relentlessly to the image of the lad I retained in my mind. He was unquestionably one of the sexiest boys I had ever laid eyes on, and his shy, yet sly, smile was totally disarming. I felt an inner shaking or trembling, as if I were on the verge of an overwhelming revelation. Then it came to me, I finally knew: it was Johan, the dancer who became a star in all those sexy videos from Europe. But what on earth was he doing in New York?

My revelations didn't end when I arrived at The Revolver, my destination following the show, because, against all odds, I encountered them again at the popular bar/restaurant. Johan and his john had obviously taken a taxi and bested my time on foot. I arrived there soaked with perspiration from my long walk.

I ducked into the men's room immediately, feeling wilted, to pull myself together. When I emerged, they had moved to a banquette in the dining room. The lad, Johan, was laughing; his face was radiant, though hidden a bit behind the menu. I wasn't remotely hungry but decided then and there to have dinner, and I tipped the Maitre'd to seat me at a banquette directly across from the gloriously sexy Johan and his companion.

Whenever I dine alone, I read, but tonight I only pretended to be absorbed by the Playbill I had brought from the theatre—actually, the only reading matter I had with me. It was impossible to concentrate on the program book when Johan was seated so close by. I couldn't help but dart quick glances at the beautiful boy.

At one point, Johan's companion, who was an attractive, gray-haired man wearing an elegant suit —in his sixties I guessed—left to visit the bathroom. I threw caution to the winds, stepped over to the table, and asked the boy for his signature on my Playbill.

"Good to meet you," he said, very formally, in heavily accented English.

"Good to meet *you*," I echoed. "I hope you are enjoying your visit to Manhattan."

"I am," he said, and took a sip of wine. Just then, his companion came back to the table and I nodded at him. He smiled in recognition, perhaps used to this by now, and I returned to my table.

There I saw that instead of autographing my Playbill, Johan had put down the name of his hotel and his room number. Stunned, I decided then and there to leave. There was no way I could sit across from him knowing that this internationally desired Adonis was even the slightest bit interested in me.

I kept a lonely vigil in the lobby of Johan's hotel. I had used the house phone to call his room and there had been no answer, so I decided to simply wait. I presumed that they would be coming through the door any minute, or perhaps they would go to the older man's place and Johan would not show up at all.

I fell asleep in one of the overstuffed chairs in the lobby and when I awoke, it was nearly two o'clock. As I pulled myself up, the clerk at the front desk gave me a few questioning glances but went about his business. Defeated, I slowly moved toward the hotel's main entrance. I passed the bank of house phones, so I decided to try the room again. I no sooner picked up the receiver when there he was! Johan entered through the revolving door looking wilted by the heat. Still, he smiled when he spotted me, and walked toward me as I hung up the phone and went to meet him. His eyes twinkled as his smile broadened and he said, "You waited."

"Of course," I said. As if there had been any other choice!

He said nothing more, just led me to the elevator, where he leaned against the mirrored wall and sighed as the door closed. "I am so hot," he said. "I've never been so hot in my life! This city must be what hell is like."

He was hot, all right, but I was looking at him as a male sex symbol, not a sweating, somewhat disheveled youth whose feet, and maybe much else, hurt like hell.

"I'm sorry."

"You're sorry?"

"Yes, that you're hurting."

"You can help."

"I can?"

He nodded just as the elevator stopped at the tenth floor and he stepped out, then led the way down the corridor.

In his small room, I stood beside the bed, dumb, as he collapsed onto it. Finally I summoned up the courage to ask, "So ... how can I help?"

He lifted up and put his hand on the fold of my fly. I still questioned him with my eyes. He clasped the contours of my penis with his fingers, stroking it to assess its length, thickness, and hardness, fingers on the prowl for any positive feedback. Soon the positive feedback he inspired was threatening to burst the seam of my crotch. He smiled slyly. "I must check this out,"

Kneeling, he spanned the broadness of my erection with his eager mouth, shooting warm puffs of breath through half-opened lips along the length of my covered cock, as if practicing scales on a mouth-organ. I abandoned all resistance. I would have preferred to seduce him, to be the aggressor, but this was *his* party after all.

I lolled back on the bed and watched him unbuckle my belt, pulling down the zipper of my fly.

Johan took his time freeing my cock from its white cotton prison, extricating it with obvious pleasure. He kissed my cockhead as he charitably dipped his fingers into the tight fit of my underwear, seeking to comfort my balls after their prolonged isolation. I began breathing heavily as he stroked me.

"Yes, it's so big and so hard, as I knew it would be," he panted. "Oh, I want it in me. I haven't had anyone in me all week," he admitted, wetting his greedy lips with his tongue, eyes widened by lust. He propped me up facing the mirrors, presenting the reflection of his provocative ass to my view by leaning forward as he pulled my pants and shorts down to my knees and pursued his thorough investigation of my crotch. I relished having one of the most beautiful boys on the planet fascinated by my prick.

"My god," I groaned, savoring Johan's subordination, his enticing vulnerability, and the sight of his magnificent ass.

"You want me in you?"

"Oh, yes ... yes I do! I want you to give it to me," he begged.

I was deeply aroused by his hoarse voice and incredible sexiness. Then he proceeded to suck me, propelling his tongue orbit-like around my prick as though licking his chops. He gluttonously lapped up the drops of pre-cum oozing from the furrow of my glans. Narrowing his lips, he suckled at the crown of my cock, tonguing the ridge etched down its length.

"Oh yes, that's right, suck me hard," I gasped, spurring him on, lurching into his mouth, my hands now flat on his head, sustaining and prolonging the suck-job of my life.

Guiding my generous length down his gullet, he squeezed me between sucked-in cheeks, licking the tip of my prick wedged against his palate. Then he drew back, let the cock almost all the way out while he hefted my balls, assessing their weight, rolling them in his hand as if testing them. I began to be embarrassed by his masterful technique, the expertise of his fingers upon my cock. He was a thorough professional.

"Oh, that's so good. Go on!"

"No, I stop now ... I want it in me."

As he quickly removed all his clothes and got on all fours on the bed, I stood and stripped as well. Under ordinary circumstances, I would have spent an hour kissing and licking and making love to that delicious body, but he could not wait. I knelt behind him, and was at last able to observe his magnificent ass up close. I began lapping at him, forcing my tongue in. Johan braced himself, let out a cry. He said he was going to come too soon, and he wanted to come with my cock in him.

He turned his head to watch me enter him. As I got into position, his eyes became feverish, his lips shining and wet. As I brought my prick to the hole, its tip pulsating with impatience, I applied the condom, then some lube.

Ready now and breathless, my forehead began to bead with sweat as I slowly slid my hard-on into him.

I held back my orgasm, watching in the mirror as Johan's hand stroked his cock. Firmly grasping his hips, I raised his rump and shoved my cock all the way into him.

Unbearable, indestructible, my desire for him bordered on insanity. I sank into him as though falling into an abyss. I slammed into him furiously, seized by the spasmodic throbbing of his ass as he orgasmed.

I knew I was hurting him; I had to be hurting him, pounding away at him as though moved by rage, but my unexpressed desire was so overwhelming I thought nothing about his pain, only my joy and lust. I suddenly came to my senses. His suddenly inert, resigned body offered no resistance as, in a moment, I filled the condom inside his ass. I slowed my pace, but continued to slide gently in and out of him in the afterglow of the most enjoyable fuck I had ever given anyone.

Now I was exhausted, sated, filled with quiet admiration and appreciation for this boy I had so often made love with in my fantasies. I laid Johan down, kissed the back of his neck. He remained docile, immobile. I stroked his cheek, and he fell asleep.

He continued to sleep as I carefully withdrew my cock from him, freed myself from the tangled sheets, and proceeded to make my way in the direction of the bathroom whose door, swollen by humidity, was hard to keep shut. Once there, I let a thin stream of water run into the tub so as not to wake Johan up.

After bathing quietly, I left the bathroom and started to get my pants. I planned to get dressed and leave, but when I took another look at the sleeping figure on the bed, I tossed my pants aside and climbed on next to him. There was no way I could leave just then. I watched Johan sleep, looking like God's most beautiful angel, until I too fell asleep.

When I awoke the next morning, I could hear that Johan was taking a shower. I lay quietly waiting for him to return. My patience was rewarded: the sight of a naked Johan, towel-drying his hair as he walked toward the bed, was breathtaking. Besides, he already had an erection and I simply could not resist it. I scooted over to where he stood and took it in my mouth. He chuckled as he finished drying his hair and I began sucking him. After tossing the towel aside, he took my head in his hands and guided me back and forth on his cock.

But he had had enough of men sucking his cock. No sooner had I developed my rhythm than he was pushing me back to make room for him on the bed. Next thing I knew, he had spread his thighs, and crude words soon mixed with those of affection. He moaned under the touch of my unfamiliar hands. Before long, my caresses had aroused him even further.

Fascinated, I was motionless as I watched Johan suck his middle finger with delectation, as though it had been dipped in a pot of honey, then slip it into his ass and fuck himself for a few moments before he withdrew it and offered it to me, as if it was an exotic sweet. I pulled it into my mouth, licked it, savored it, and returned it to him glistening with my saliva. He was breathing hard as, over and over, he plunged his finger back inside himself, adding another finger, then a third. Suddenly he raised his hips, to bring his perfect ass close to my flushed face.

"I want it in me again," Johan begged, lifting himself to me. He jerked his cock and panted, writhing on the mattress.

His expectation made me rock-hard. He was the most irresistible lad I had ever encountered. I made a necklace of his long legs and rammed myself into him, supporting myself on my hands. I didn't want to lie down on him. I needed to see his face contorted with pleasure, the rush of excitement spread over him as I fucked him as hard as I could. And it seemed as if the boy was suffocating with pleasure, tilting his hips to meet each powerful assault until finally he uttered a long, modulated shriek, wrenched from the pit of his gut, as his prick erupted and his discharge covered his belly. He emerged from the orgasm with a pained expression on his adorable face.

"Do you want me to stop?"

"No, go on. It hurts, but I like it. I want you to come."

Johan moaned as my dick rubbed the walls of his ass, stifling a gasp at each of my assaults, his breathing cut short by the violence of my thrusts until, finally I came.

Now it was my turn to shower. Remembering our lovemaking, I wondered if I would ever be able to voice my emotions accurately or completely; no one had ever been such a receptive bottom, no boy had ever looked more completely desirable. I decided to get dressed, feeling that it was better not to overstay my welcome. But when he saw me slip into my pants, he called me back to bed, and I lay down with him again. I brushed his skin lightly, caressing him with the back of my wrist. Johan rolled over on his stomach and propped his head up on one arm. "Is it late?" he inquired.

"Twelve-fifteen. Are you hungry?"

"Oh, yes."

"What should we do? Order breakfast, or go out to lunch?"

"Let's go out. I really haven't seen anything of this city."

The air was dry, the sun shone gently on the front steps of the hotel. I was famished by the time we reached the Brasserie, a block from the hotel.

He alternated telling fascinating stories about his life and his experiences with periods of silence, during which he ate heartily and listened vacantly to my own stories. The coffee pot was large and the brew good and we drank till the bill came.

Back at the hotel, we undressed in silence. The room, through some miracle of unexpected efficiency, had been cleared of the evidence of our previous passionate struggles.

"Do we have time?" I asked as he parted his thighs and went back to fingering himself.

"Yes, yes." He looked at his watch, adding: "My next appointment is at four."

I looked at my watch then; it was just after three. We had less than an hour, hardly all the time in the world, but enough.

THE WELL

This is the John Patrick story honored by PEN American Center as one of the best of 1987—a time when the AIDS epidemic was reaching its apogee. A grim and touching account of Johnny's visit to a hospital to visit his friend, Jack Dodge, who is afflicted with the terrible disease, and in its final stages. This story hasn't been seen in print since it was originally published in 1987. —JB

"To lust," he said, saluting me. His fingers trembled as he lifted the paper cups to his lips. Some of the water trickled down his chin.

"Ah, lust," I said, taking a sip of the water from my own cup.

The two of us, Jack Dodge and I, were sitting in Room 302 at Broward General in Fort Lauderdale. Jack was in his bed, propped up, an extra pillow behind his back, a lint blue smock hiding his now fragile frame. I sprawled across the visitor's chair, my long legs stretching under the bed.

"Yeah, lust," Jack went on, a twinkle of amusement in his brown eyes. "You're dead with it or without it, so you might as well enjoy it." That was Jack. Full steam ahead. Damn the consequences.

Although his face was now ravaged and gaunt, there was still strength and obstinacy in his jaw, a hard determination in his eyes, and about his manner, the same unsettled, untamed quality that had been so apparent when I first met him four years ago, in '81. He had just turned 35 and, while he was short of stature and undistinguished in appearance, his pugnaciousness, enhanced by his strong neck and shoulders, was appealing. He was clean-shaven except for a tiny mustache which he kept as fastidiously trimmed as his close-cropped brown hair.

I got up and walked over to the window. As I took another sip of water, the street lights below began to flicker on. A summer storm was brewing. Gusts of wind blew trash across Andrews Avenue and into the entrances of the graceless, characterless shops and offices that lined the street. In the vague twilight, the city seemed suddenly still, a certain stupor of downfall in the air. The long hand on the big clock on the facade of the bank at the corner edged toward the top of the hour. Seven o'clock. Time was running short.

I turned away from the window and leaned against the ledge, facing Jack. He was looking at me intently.

"Are you going to write about me, Johnny?" he asked expectantly.

I thought for a moment, then, reluctantly, "I've thought about it," I told him truthfully.

180

With a tissue he gently wiped away some of the saliva that seemed to flow continuously from a corner of his mouth. Then he said, incredulously, "Really now! So, tell me, what the hell are you going to say?"

I didn't answer. I stepped over to the tray table and picked up his yellow legal pad. He had been jotting notes all over it with his trusty BIC ballpoint. He bought the same cheap pen, dozens at a time. He liked things disposable. "Business as usual, I see," I said, lifting the first page and glancing at the second.

"Well, you know how it is. Gotta keep my hand in." Even now, even here, he needed to feel a part of things, arranging dates for his "stable," as he was fond of calling them. "Yes, life goes on," he added, sorrowfully. He knew I knew the truth.

There was little arranging he needed to do these days. The customers had all been frightened off. His boys were relying on their regulars to sustain them. There was no new business. And the gravy—the tourists—began dying a couple of years before and now, in the heat of August, was non-existent.

"Yeah," he went on, "even James is taking precautions. He's insisting his customers use rubbers. He carries 'em with him."

"Smart boy," I said dryly.

"I just hope it isn't too damn late for him," he said.

James' regulars were all ancient men. To them, sex was secondary. They found great delight in taking their 'nephew,' as they liked to call him, to fancy restaurants and watch him tear into a steak. James was a cute little strawberry blond with a swimmer's body, a wide, easy grin, and a playful manner. He had recently turned twenty and Jack sent him a bouquet of flowers. It was part of Jack's remembrance ritual: a white poinsettia at Christmas and a bouquet of flowers on birthdays. The bouquet of a half-dozen miniature red roses I had sent him were in a vase on the nightstand next to a giant get-well greeting James had sent.

James was the last of the *crème de la crème* of Jack's stable, a breed that began with Willy ten years before.

Jack met Willy when he had his fishing boat and was living in St. Petersburg. He hired Willy as a deckhand and they became close. Before long, Jack discovered Willy was willing, and they began living together. They worked side-by-side during the day and went home to each other's embrace at night. But such togetherness eventually took its toll. They started to argue frequently, and often Willy didn't make the boat as it slipped out of port just before dawn.

Then, in the early 70's, when the crunch hit, Jack lost all of his highly leveraged property, including his boat. Destitute, he and Willy went to live with Willy's father, a recent widower who worked for the Post Office.

Jack considered various things to support himself. What he came up with, at first as a stop-gap measure, was an escort service. He knew several boys who partied frequently at the bars and who were anxious to supplement their incomes. Working out of a shed at the far end of Willy's father's two acres in northern Pinellas County, he had a phone installed to arrange dates for the boys. He told them to put his share of the proceeds, usually $25, under a rock a couple of blocks from the house. That way he avoided having to have the boys come directly to the house and he managed to keep Willy's father in the dark as to what he did.

Eventually, when Jack got a call and had no boy from his stable to send out, Willy was recruited. At first, Willy enjoyed the change of routine. Most of the johns were considerate, and lavished considerable praise upon him. Jack often talked about Willy's innocence and how the boy had artfully mastered his technique of passively spreading his legs for the old men. He laughed that Willy could please a trick without ever touching him with his hands. In Jack's opinion, it kept Willy chaste for his trips to "The Well," a place Jack took his lovers, sometimes for days on end.

After a few months, Willy grew bored and restless. When he turned 18, he helped a girlfriend move to California and never came back. Despondent, Jack decided to, in his words, "shove St. Pete." He moved to Fort Lauderdale. Within a short time, he had made some lucrative connections and built a formidable stable.

By the time I met him, between the boys and the dope he peddled along with them, Jack was clearing a grand a week, enough for him to rent a small house on an acre of ground to the west of the city. He built a greenhouse on the property and raised tropical plants. He made a few dollars selling the plants through ads in neighborhood shopping papers, but, mostly, Jack tended the plants as a break from the sixteen-hour days he put in on the phone. His dream, he often said, was to eventually save enough so he could get out of the escort business and grow plants he could sell wholesale to florist shops.

Over the years, he developed intimate relationships with many of his clients. He never actually met any of these men face-to-face, but between what the boys told him and what he was able to elicit from them over the phone, especially when they had had a few drinks, he developed an impressive mental dossier of their kinks and foibles. He reveled in tawdry secrets. Having the inside scoop on these men gave him keen pleasure.

I dropped the legal pad to the tray table and resumed my seat in the visitor's chair.

"So what are you going to say about me?" he pestered.

"Oh," I answered reluctantly, "I'll definitely write something about you and Michael."

"Yeah," he said excitedly. "Mike and me. Me and Mike. Oh, what stories I could tell you!"

"Oh, what stories you have told me," I corrected him.

"Yeah, but it's about The Well you want to know. But I can't tell you. You just have to go there. God, I miss it. You know, Johnny, it all ended in January—January, when the sweats started. And then the business just dried up. And then Michael having to die. All in January!" he said torturously.

"I remember. It was horrible."

"Yeah, nothing is like before. Everything has been contaminated. This fuckin' disease …. it's turned everything to shit."

"Yeah, I could never make 'Biscayne Boulevard' now."

"No, and if you hadn't made it when you did, you never would have met Michael. And that would have been something to regret." He stopped and thought a minute. Then, happily, "You? Now, he had this way about him, that look of innocence. That shy manner. You knew he knew all the right moves, yet he let you think you were the first person he'd ever been with. It was such a beautiful, unconscious, effortless thing on his part."

"Yeah, and that magic came across on the screen," I said, picturing Michael on that first day of filming, and then later, when I saw the completed film. His face was unusual, handsome rather than pretty. Photographically, his mouth was his best feature. It was large and sensual. He had a seductive way of baring his teeth when he smiled. His body had been molded, with careful diet and considerable effort, into a beautifully defined torso. But his eyes. His eyes always bothered me. They were bleak and dark, with a bitter enmity. "Yes," I said, smiling, "but he was your baby. You had him at his best."

"Oh, god, how I miss those days. You remember how I'd take a break from him and call you up and breathe into the phone …"

"'I've taken Michael to the well!'" I said, mimicking him.

"You do remember!" he said in mock surprise.

"Of course."

"Oh, but you have no idea really," he continued, tauntingly now, his eyes flashing. "The Well is a place where only us true degenerates go. A place where some don't ever come back…alive. Where anything goes."

"Especially after some coke," I interjected.

"Yeah. and Chivas. Love that Chivas! God, I can remember Michael lying there, just like a little puppy, this six-foot fuckin' Adonis, just begging me. Me!" he said wonderingly. "And when you'd be on the phone and he'd call from the bedroom …"

"I'm red-eee," I said, mimicking Michael. "You know, I told Carole about that and she started whispering that in my ear at the oddest times. What a laugh?"

"Carole! What do you hear from her, anyway?"

"Oh, she's still in New York."

"Still the hostess with the mostest, I suppose. God what big tits! Too much woman for me. But she was great for you."

"Only to look at."

183

"Shit, you loved every minute of it," he said fervently.

"Well, if I could have just looked at her and fucked her ..."

"But what else are they good for?"

"But now I appreciate quality over quantity...brains over boobs," I lied.

"Now you see the light and it's too late! You wouldn't go gay, so now you've gone crazy!" he said delightedly.

"Gone celibate, dear friend. There's a difference."

"Bullshit! Celibacy is crazy. Doing it alone in the dark, with one of your lousy movies flickering away. Oh, and don't forget to turn off the sound."

"That way you create your own soundtrack."

"No, that way you can just look at the pretty bodies and you don't have to hear what's coming out of their mouths, showing you how ignorant they are."

"It's not their fault. It's the scriptwriter who puts those words into their mouths," I said didactically.

"Scriptwriter my ass! Those kids could appear in 'Hamlet' and make it sound like drivel."

"But you did like 'Young and Foolish,' " I said, admonishing,

"Only because Michael was in it."

"Well, then, you liked them all because Michael's been in every one, except the first, of course."

"Every one? How many of those things have you done? Three!" he said, with glee. "Three in four years. What the hell do you do with your time?"

"Well, right now I'm looking for some sweet thing to appear in yet another epic." I lied.

He sighed with puzzled awe, then blurted, with halting appreciation, "So all you do is look for sweet young things, is that it?"

"Yeah, everything I do is geared to it! No, truthfully, I've no stomach for it any more. All the fun has gone out of it."

"Yeah, it's all turned to shit," he said with vengeful passion. "It's that Meese character. And all the others. They're greedy—greedy for power and greedy for money. That's all they think about. The people can go screw themselves as they're concerned."

"Oh, maybe they mean well, trying to save the people from themselves."

He lapsed into a brooding silence, and then blurted, "Have you heard anything more about the investigation?"

"No. I operate under the delusion of reprieve, clinging to the last shreds of hope. Now's the time I should get out of Florida—go to California."

"Naw, they'd hunt you down wherever you went, like a mad dog," he said scornfully.

"I hope not."

"Oh, God, Johnny, they'll get you," he said portentously. "They won't rest till they do. They've got the phone records, we know that, and God knows what else. If it isn't this, it's that. It's tiring me out," he said, his expression now resentful and defensive. "Tiring me out thinking about all the trouble. And all the arrangements I have to make."

"But you've taken care of everything. No need to worry," I said in a quiet tone.

"But James'll screw it up. He's been acting flaky lately."

"Has he been to see you?"

"No, not this time around. He's terrified. He hates this hair, all orangey. And this body, nothing but skin and bone. Hell, the only meat I got left is between my legs."

"That's good. That's the only meat he ever cared about anyway."

"Got that right! These fuckin' kids! Ingrates, all of them!" he said with lofty scorn. "Why, I shoulda taken that little fucker to The Well. But he'd never go. He's not Michael. No, he's just trash, street trash. But, Jesus, he'll do. Damn him!" He fell back into the pillows, a grimace of sour exasperation on his face. "Oh, God, I still want it. My spirit isn't dead yet. My balls ache for it. I'm alive!" he cried rebelliously.

"Of course you are," I said. The sense of disaster in which we were both involved had robbed us of our inner freedom. I lied to him.

"Oh, where is Michael when we really need him?"

I didn't tell him about the last time I saw Michael. How shocked I was that he had yielded to drugs and had gotten so disheveled no one would hire him. He was reduced to running ads in local gay newspapers in Los Angeles:

Michael Compeli
Film Star/ Hairless Italian Stud/Super hung/
$100/24 Hours/Credit Cards Accepted

"I hope you don't blame me for Michael" I said.

"Blame you? Hell, no. You made him a star. He deserved to be a star—a star at something. No, he's the one that went Hollywood and started shooting that shit into his veins." A solitary tear rolled down his cheek. "Now look at me. I promised I'd never cry again."

"Cry if you want. If anybody's got a right, you do."

"No, no. I'm not giving in to self-pity any more. But, God, how I wish we could walk out of here, get into your Mercedes, put the top down...ah... and go to town and order those tenderloins," He closed his eyes.

"Yeah, it sounds great, doesn't it? And we will, soon," I lied.

"Yeah, and I almost forgot. We'll let James make us feel good. You know, he really can. Best damn blow job in the world."

"You've told me," I said with indifferent finality.

I stood up again and walked back to the window. It had started raining—a typical summer shower. It would be even hotter when it was over. Raindrops pelted the windowpane, and then trickled down the glass monotonously. "Well," I said, noticing the clock again, "they'll be throwing me out soon."

"I know. But before you go, take my hand," he said, proffering one toward me. I turned and stepped close to the bed. His grip was feeble, but resolute. We held hands for a brief moment. His eyes were closed. I might be wrong, but it could be he was saying a prayer. Then he opened his eyes and lifted his head from the pillow. "Why'?" he asked, plaintively.

"I don't know. Just one of those things." At that moment I could think of nothing profound to say to him.

"Well, they can't fuck friendship, can they? You've been a real friend, putting up with me, coming to see me," he said, his eyes becoming moist again.

"It's nothing," I said, smiling at him.

"*No!* It's everything," he said with hungry appreciation. He let his arms drop to his sides.   "I tire so easily now. It's the business. It's all these headaches with the business."

"Oh, of course it is. And having to rely on James."

"He's a good kid," he breathed. "I want him to make you feel good. For me. Promise you'll go see him while you're in town."

"I promise," I lied.

"I'll call him tomorrow. And I'll tell him to come to your hotel and see you. One on the house, okay?"

"Maybe. Yeah, okay," I said laconically.

"But now, I gotta get some sleep. My beauty rest. Who knows, maybe Michael will be waiting for me when I get there. I wanna look my best!" He laughed.

I stepped to the door and opened it. Shafts of light from the corridor streamed into the room, bathing it in a strange, milky radiance.

"Well, goodnight, Jackson," I said. He didn't answer. I closed the door and as I walked down the corridor I tried to picture them, Jack and Michael, going to The Well again, together.

THE DIVINEST BOY

The boy Alberto and his lover picked up around the motel pool was obviously not schooled in making love to a man, much less taking a gargantuan organ like Alberto's up his ass—but he was a very rapid learner! A story from Fresh 'n' Frisky. *—JB*

"Oh, c'mon," Alberto said. "Why did we bother to come out here anyway? A little change will be good for us."

We were on vacation, traveling from Miami to Tampa, and we had stopped at the only bar listed in the gay travel guide for Naples. For some odd reason, Alberto thought that finding a partner for us to share would be easier in a little town. God knows, if the size of the town had anything to do with it, it surely would have been much easier in Miami. But no, this was about Alberto watching me have sex with a stranger, and I had managed to avoid it for a year. If this was about me having sex, I wanted it to be on my terms, not Alberto's. Now here we were at another crossroads. We arrived to find the bar closed. Not closed permanently, just CLOSED MONDAYS, as the sign on the door read.

"Is it Monday?" Alberto said, standing there with his hands on his hips. "Is it fucking Monday?"

"It is," I assured him, "Monday. Yesterday was Sunday, remember?"

"This is just fucking great." He kicked the door with an unsatisfying thump. "Now what?" Alberto folded his arms.

"I'd say we find a liquor store, then find a motel."

"Shit," Alberto said, kicking the door one final time.

We found a liquor store and a nice motel with a huge pool. We were the only ones there for a long time, enjoying dips in the pool between tumblers full of rum and Coke.

At one point, Alberto went to get ice and he came back not only with a bucket overflowing but with a youth in tow. Alberto explained they had struck up a conversation at the ice machine. It was obvious to me why Alberto had done so: the boy, who was skinny, barely legal and even younger than I, wore a Speedo that left little to the imagination. He wasn't the cutest guy perhaps, but he seemed pleasant enough. He said his name was Chris and he was a college freshman, on his way to his grandparents' place after a few days of spring break in Fort Lauderdale. To me, he looked as if he were still in high school and not of legal drinking age in Florida, but Alberto immediately poured him a drink.

I proceeded to get drunk, of course, which is everyone's excuse for the fuck they might regret or want to pretend to forget.

Chris was quite a swimmer and I leaned back and enjoyed the sight of him diving in and getting out of the water, swimming lap after lap.

At one point I realized Alberto was studying the way I was watching Chris. "What?" I barked.

He gave a little smirk. "You're so... into this. Your eyes are bugging out of your pretty head."

"Give me a break," I said.

"Oh, I intend to, darling."

I was shaky, in need of a little assistance, when I finally stood up after sitting so long and having way too much to drink. I let Chris help me, and Alberto went before us, opening the door to our room. Chris hesitated at first, but Alberto practically dragged him in and closed the door behind us.

I fell on the bed and Chris just stood there until Alberto threw him a towel. "You want to take a shower?" he asked.

"I'd really better be goin'," Chris said, fumbling with the towel. "Really."

My head had begun to clear a bit, and I knew that if I was going to do anything, I had to make my move. Alberto wanted it and now I wanted it too—and we had my ideal stranger right there in the room with us.

I rolled over and fell off the bed. On my knees, I scrambled over to Chris. "Will you let me kiss that nice dick goodnight?"

Chris backed up, and his ass hit the doorknob. "What?"

"C'mon, don't be shy. Anybody who wears a bikini like that is proud of what he has."

Chris pushed me away, but gently. I fell right back on him, tugging at his Speedos, which had appeared very well-stuffed out at the pool, and now looked as though the crotch was going to burst from within. Chris relaxed. I pulled down his Speedos to reveal a truly beautiful erection. I don't know how else to describe it. Neatly circumcised, his cock curved upward at a graceful angle and had a certain symmetry about it. The sight of it made my mouth water and my ass ache. I thought about all the dreams I'd had of some other person fucking me while Alberto watched, but I wanted a cock that was different from Alberto's, and this was it. A blond boy instead of my dark, hairy Latin lover, and now I could see Chris definitely had the tool for the job—and I wanted it, desperately.

All right, I'd had enough, I'd tortured myself long enough, and I was drunk enough. I reached a hand out to the shaft pointing toward me and gripped it gently in my fingers. It was fiercely hard, but still felt velvety, and I tugged the boy closer to me.

Chris, stunned, was staring down at me now, this total stranger wanting his penis, wanting it madly. His gaze flickered from my face to his cock sheathed in my hand. Then he turned to look at Alberto. Alberto got up. "Three's a crowd," he said, and went into the bathroom.

Chris took my hand off his cock and pushed me slowly but firmly back onto the bed. He climbed on top of me, his cock pressing hard against my butthole, and said, "Okay, you want me? I only do it one way."

"What do you mean?"

"I mean, I can only do it like this," he responded, rolling me onto my back, "as if you were a bitch."

"Okay," I said, smiling.

He started by stripping off my swimsuit. Then he lifted my knees and spread my thighs. "Oh, god, you got a nice pussy here." He ran his hands up my thighs but did not touch my cock. He spit on his fingers, then slid them down into my asshole. I thrust my hips up a little at him, wanting to feel him inside me. He ran his finger around in a circle and I moaned.

"You want my cock, don't you?" Chris asked harshly, seeming much more a man now, rather than a young boy.

I groaned, "Yes. Oh, god, yes!"

He got up on his knees but kept fingering me. I could tell that however young he might be, he had fucked a lot of ass, that he knew what he was doing—and now I wanted him doing me!

He stared fiercely into my eyes, and smiled lewdly as he said, "Look at me. Look at my pretty cock."

I smiled. God, it *was* a pretty cock! Not unusually large, but perfect. It would be so easy to worship this cock. It was redder now, flaming in fact, and I wanted to touch it, to lick it, to wet it, get it ready for shoving inside me. I lifted up and he brought it to my lips. I kissed it, then took the head in my mouth.

His finger made deeper circles inside my ass. "God, you're tight, really tight! Are you sure you can take it?"

"Yes."

"All of it?"

"Oh, yes. I'm used to big ones."

"All seven and a half inches of it?"

"God, yes," I said.

He pulled his fingers out and got off the bed for a moment. He saw the condoms Alberto had left on the nightstand and he put one on his erection. He returned to the bed, kneeling between my legs and spreading them apart. If anything, his cock looked bigger now that he'd slid the rubber into place. He pressed the head against my asshole and rubbed it back and forth there, smearing the lube around. Then he sank in about a half an inch. "Okay?"

"What?"

"It's what I say to every pussy I fuck. I don't go any farther 'til I hear it from you that you want more, that you're absolutely sure you want to go through with it."

"Oh, for Chrissake, yes," I said, and I put a hand on his chest and stroked the fine hairs there as I began to gyrate my ass around the end of his cock.

"Really?"

"Oh, god...."

"You want me to fuck it until I'm satisfied?"

"Yes! Yes!" I tried to pull him down onto me. He held off for a second, but I wrapped my legs around him and pulled another inch into me. He let his weight drop then, and as I sank back into the mattress he sank into me. True to his word, he began to grind. It was a tight fit, but I didn't mind— quite the contrary! I sucked in my breath as he doubled his speed, slicking in and out fast, slapping our bodies together on the springy bed.

"Oh, yeah, you like that don't you?"

"Oh, yeah," I gasped. The angle and the rhythm and the speed and the duration all worked together, and I began to come. I tried to hold back, but it was no use: The orgasm had been building since the moment I laid eyes on Chris's cock, and letting it all out just seemed like the natural thing to do. And somewhere in the midst of all the noise I was making, he came, too. I blanked out for a while then, blissed out, lying there in a wet, happy heap. I forgot who we were, where we were. It wasn't until he pulled away and began peeling the condom off and said, "I wonder where Alberto got to?" that I came back to reality.

I realized then that he hadn't been there to watch the drama he had orchestrated. I looked towards the bathroom door and saw it was partially opened. I figured he had been watching after all, seeing the fuck reflected in the mirror over the desk. "Come on out, Alberto!" I called.

Sheepishly, Alberto came back into the room. We eyed each other, wary now. I found myself staring into those dark, once more questioning eyes, a little apprehensive perhaps. The haughty smirk was gone; his lips pressed together in a thin, tight line. He stood facing me, his slender fingers playing nervously at the bulge in his swimsuit.

"I've been waiting for you to fuck my ass, too," I said curtly. "What have you been doing?"

"Well, you were having so much fun, I didn't want to interrupt."

"We're done now, so stick it in."

Alberto looked at Chris, who was still lying next to me on the bed, nervously playing with the cum-filled condom, which he had removed from his cock. His eyes were on Alberto as my lover slowly turned away and tugged his suit down, then kicked it off his feet. Then he turned slowly, *presenting* his dick dramatically, for Chris to admire.

"Oh, god," Chris gushed when he saw Alberto's cock. I saw a new respect creep into his eyes. Although Alberto is not a handsome man, he does have a firm, muscular body and the biggest cock I have ever seen. When it is hard, it measures a full eleven inches, and is very thick; as he produced it for Chris's admiration, it was enormous—fully hard, and standing almost straight out from his body. Chris gasped in astonishment. His lips parted, but no sound came out. I waited, tense and keyed up, scarcely daring to breathe. Alberto's giant cock swayed seductively as he made his way forward, finally to kneel between my parted legs and stopped there to look at me. I couldn't help smiling as I looked over at Chris, extending his hand toward Alberto. This self-proclaimed hetero stud was about to touch my lover's cock! Grinning, I reached down to fondle Chris's sopping cock, savoring the feel of it as it swelled and grew again when he bent his fingers around the shaft of Alberto's magnificent organ, and began to stroke it. His was beginning to respond despite himself.

Chris's eyes had become curiously vacant as I slowly rubbed his cock while he stroked Alberto's. He let out a long, shivering breath as, using both hands now, he was mauling the cock.

"You like that, don't you?" I demanded with sudden vehemence.

"Ooooohh Jesus, oh yes!" Chris hissed through clenched teeth. "Oh my god... yes, I like it. I've never seen anything like it." His voice trailed off, low and throaty. His hands were now cradling the amazing bulk of Alberto's huge ass-rammer with the kind of reverence and awe one accords an unbelievably precious object.

I released Chris's cock with a vicious twist of my hand, and his renewed erection bobbed and swayed seductively. His shoulders heaved as he leaned in toward Alberto, panting. With a great thrust, Alberto shoved his cock at Chris's face and the head bounced off his cheek.

"Go on, it's okay," I said, holding the back of Chris's head steady and urging it forward to the throbbing cock-head. "Nobody here but the three of us. Go ahead, kiss it."

"No," he complained. "I just wanted to...."

Alberto took over, holding Chris's head with one hand as he peeled the foreskin back and exposed the enormous cockhead. He steadied the cock with one hand while he guided Chris's mouth to it. Chris tried to pull away. "You want to see what it would be like, I know," Alberto said, seductively.

"No, no," Chris protested.

But Alberto was intent on humiliating this stud. "Come on, open wide. Very wide."

My eyes were soon glued to the sight of Chris's mouth wrapped around Alberto's cockhead, his lips stretched wide to receive the massive shaft. He nodded as Alberto slowly slid inch after inch into his by-now-accommodating mouth.

The face-fuck that followed was a sight to behold. Chris gagged several times but stuck in there, even taking Alberto's hairy balls in his hand and playing with them while Alberto slid his cock in and out of his mouth, driving more of that monster deeper than I would have thought an inexperienced cocksucker could possibly take. The saliva was flying all over by the time Alberto decided enough was enough. "Now I'm going to fuck my boy while you watch."

"Oh, yesssss, I want to see that!" Chris said. But his hand stayed on Alberto's cock. He was surprisingly reluctant to give up the prize.

I was ready for it now. All my inhibitions had melted away. I had never imagined I would enjoy it this much, sharing Alberto. I got into position. Chris's hand did not leave Alberto's cock; in fact, he helped him stretch a condom over it. Normally Alberto didn't use one when he fucked me but I knew there was a reason he was using one now, and that reason would soon become evident. Chris followed the upward curve of the cock as it entered my ass.

"Ooh, baby…. you've got such a perfect little ass," Alberto breathed.

"Oh, yes, he does. It's a beauty—and it's really tight," Chris affirmed.

I stiffened, lying tense and expectant as I always did when Alberto began to fuck me. I knew how much it would hurt when it was first thrust into me. Then a single exquisite thrill shot through me, and Alberto was half-way in. I felt Chris's lips on my cock-stuffed behind. I felt the cool slither of his tongue licking me, lapping the creamy smooth curves of my ass, which clenched in pure delight as Alberto drove his cock home. I couldn't help squirming excitedly, rubbing my cock as the two men were electrifying me, one with his kisses and licking, the other with repeated stabs of blinding pleasure. The velvety wet feel stopped momentarily, and suddenly Alberto pulled out of me, and Chris was in me again. I spread my legs to provide even greater access for Chris's skillful fucking. I felt suddenly, gloriously, free. My legs spread even wider in happy exultation.

Now Alberto's tongue was on me and I sighed as Chris burrowed into me. My head was thrown back, my jaws clenched against the maddening thrusts of pure pleasure. They were driving me wild, and they both knew it. It would not be long before my own raging lust would be out of all control once again.

Alberto scrambled off the bed and ran his flattened tongue into Chris's exposed asshole. Chris arched up and tight little whimpers escaped from his pressed lips. In a heated rush, Alberto entered Chris's tender butt, and Chris groaned. He opened his eyes and looked down on me with hard, cold, desperate eyes. I smiled. Then he reached for Alberto in a vain attempt to restrain him. Alberto was not about to stop humiliating this boy once more. He showed no mercy, and Chris was pushed down on top of me by the sheer force of Alberto's full entry. As Alberto tore into Chris, Chris kissed me full on the mouth. And I accepted the kiss, letting my mouth fall open. Soon our tongues were dancing in an exuberant *pas de deux*.

"Oh god, yeah," Alberto breathed, kissing Chris's back, hungry for him, moving with a mounting intensity, a terrible urgency. Chris pulled his head up as the cock slid all the way in, and cried out loudly—clearly in pain, but just as surely in rapture. Then I was being kissed again, hard, and this time I returned the kiss with even more vehemence, thrusting my tongue into Chris's mouth, reaching out to clasp his hot, writhing body to my own.

Alberto seemed totally enthralled by the searing sight of raw lust beneath him, of Chris and me squirming on the sheets, our bodies writhing in a passionate embrace as he fucked Chris, and Chris fucked me. It was as if Alberto was fucking both of us at once.

"Ohh," Alberto breathed, a long deep sigh that turned into a low plaintive moan as he continued to jam his cock in, forcing a series of tight grunts out of Chris.

"Oooooh ... yes ... yes ... yes," I mumbled, tossing my head from side to side each time my big-dicked lover jammed his stiffened cock deeper into the boy whose stiffened cock was driving so rabidly into me.

With a cry, Alberto blasted his load in Chris's ass and collapsed over his back with a huge sigh of pleasure. After a few moments, he pulled out and Chris stepped up his pistoning of my asshole.

Alberto dropped down beside us. "You love it, don't you, you slut?" he spat at me all the while Chris was fucking me. I could do no more than whimper.

"Say it ... say it ... say 'Fuck me, Chris,'" Alberto screamed at me, forcefully kneading the nape of my neck and stroking my cock at the same time.

"Eeeeh, eeeeh, ooooh, yes ... fuck meeeee!" I whispered urgently, pleadingly. And Chris, driven crazy with passion, obliged happily, thrusting into me in a frenzied blur of motion, till I was twisting and raising my hips off the mattress, arching up with every fiber, straining as I was suspended in the air for an impossibly long moment. My hips bucked furiously as Chris tore into me, a wild stud, his own excitement raging out of control. We raced together to a mutual orgasm that had both of us thrashing about uncontrollably, and reanimating Alberto's semi-hard penis which soon rose up in proud salute of our performance and after a few strokes, began gushing cum yet again.

Gasping, I let my head fall back on the pillows and closed my eyes. Chris pulled out and went to the bathroom. Then I felt my lover's lips as they paid their obsequious devotion. Satisfied at last, Alberto smiled and said, "That was divine, a divine boy. Divine! Two divine boys ...." He wrapped me in his arms and held me tight. I hated to admit it to Alberto, but it had been worth the trip after all.

AT FIRST SIGHT

While dining with George, one of his johns, the narrator of this story spots a sexy busboy named Paolo. Although the narrator normally collects money from his 'clients' when he has sex with them, it is mutual attraction, not money, that leads him and Paolo to share lovemaking. As the affair ends, and Paolo turns to his fiancé, George has apparently fallen prey to the practice described by the title of this anthology—living vicariously— envying the actual love his playmate-for-hire has felt for Paolo, instead of the commercially inspired relationship he shares with him. The story first appeared in Intimate Strangers. —JB

At first sight, I thought I knew him and I felt my blood heat, my cock stir, the breath evaporate from my lungs.

I remembered his touch, so strong, so sure. The memory of his cock shoving roughly inside me aroused a need I hadn't admitted to myself for a long time, a desire to be abused by a hot young topman.

"What is it?" asked George, my 'date' for the night.

I was looking across the table at DaVinci's restaurant at the boy with the handsome face, so much like the one I remembered that I couldn't stop staring at him.

"Someone you know?" George persisted.

"No," I said, taking a long swallow of the expensive red wine George had selected.

I was being truthful, in my fashion. This boy I was looking at across the room—a busboy, with a name tag that proclaimed he was 'Paolo'—was not the one I remembered. Certainly. He wouldn't be *that* young. The boy I remembered was my age, and the busboy across the room couldn't even be legal. If he looked at me, he'd see someone nearly thirty, still attractive, but sexually invisible to a boy like him.

I looked back at him. He turned his head, and his clear-eyed gaze fell on me with a shock like cold water, and he smiled.

"You're blushing," said George with interest. "Is he an old boyfriend?"

"No. Oh, no." Hardly *old*, I thought. *You* are old, George. "Just someone I met once—in another country. Do you want to taste my salad?"

As we ate, I remembered that I first saw the abusive stranger at the mall, drinking a milkshake by himself. He had a tumble of black curls surrounding a deeply tanned face. I admired the fit of the stranger's jeans. I got a shake for myself and took a seat. I wasn't looking for trouble. I was content, I thought, to look and not touch.

I liked the way his lips curled around the cigarette that he lit up after he finished his shake. I liked the way his eyes narrowed against the smoke. I

194

liked his slender fingers as he threw his empty cup in the trash and then stood, as if waiting for me. I liked the way he moved, shifting his weight or rolling the stiffness out of his neck and shoulders as unselfconsciously as an animal.

That was it—he was animalistic. A brutish-looking sort, unlike anything I had ever seen in one so young. He moved to the pavilion, but didn't sit down. He leaned against a bench, as if he were displaying himself. I gazed for a time at his intriguing, less-than-classical profile, then shifted my stare, let it fall in a visual caress on his shoulders, his back, down to the ass that so nicely filled his tight, faded jeans. He turned his head lazily toward me as if he'd felt, and liked, my attention. I moved my eyes back up his body to meet his, and I didn't smile. He was the first to look away. Then I did smile, but only to myself.

Someone else, a gray-haired man, approached him, cigarette in hand, and the boy gave him a light and absently responded to his conversational ventures, his attention hooked by me. I could feel his senses straining in my direction even when his back was turned, his eyes fixed elsewhere, his ears assaulted by the blandishments of the man, who eventually gave up and took his need to someone else.

He followed me to my car. I had parked far from the buildings, in a dark corner of the lot. He said nothing, and his silence held us both still. He was hungry and I had become *his* prey. I became uneasy about this, and finally told him I had to be rushing home, it was getting late. This was not what the animal expected, so he pushed me into the gully beside the parking lot. He grabbed me by the belt loops and kneed me to the wet grass, face down. It had been sprinkling earlier and it was still thundering. He fell on top of me, and humped his crotch against my ass. My pride melted into his thrusts. My cock was hard as he laced his thick, grimy fingers around my clean, skinny ones when he pushed me deeper into the wet grass. He got up on his hands and knees and whispered, "Turn over."

I did what the stranger said. I didn't care who this youth was. I just knew that he wanted me, and in his wanting I wanted him back. I rolled over, and he opened his jeans. He too was hard, or nearly so. His heavy balls hung over me like bait. I kissed them, sucked them, while he jacked himself. His moans told me I was doing what he wanted. Eventually he opened my pants and pulled them down and off, along with my underwear.

The grass was warm and wet where I lay, my legs spread in eager submission. His hands were solid and hot. He smelled like the smoky tip of a match. He had lit me: I was close to orgasm when he slicked his cock with his spit and started shoving it in as raised my legs to rest on his shoulders.

I heard nothing but the thunder overhead. We were alone. I wanted to explode as he got it in me. I reached behind him and pulled his ass harder against my body, to get it all in. God, it hurt, but it was wonderful at the same time. He covered my mouth with his hand. My bug eyes darted quickly from the edge of the piney brush that surrounded us to his writhing body over me.

As long as we were quiet, I thought, no one would find us. He didn't seem afraid. He eventually pulled back and out, to blow his cum all over my belly. My body was still while he lifted up and stuffed his filthy cock into his jeans. I closed my eyes, and when I opened them again, he was gone.

It was nearly eleven o'clock by the time we had finished eating. I watched George smoking his cigarette.

"Have you always smoked?" I asked, now making polite conversation.

George had fallen into a funk of a sort because the busboy had made quite a nuisance of himself once he realized I was watching him. In a final flourish, he had brushed against me and excused himself, but the connection had been made.

After that, George was in a hurry. George was always in a hurry, it seemed, but tonight he wanted to leave in the worst way. He wanted to fuck me and then go home. He tried not to look at his watch too obviously. George tried to give the impression that he was always in control, but he was not nearly as in control as he pretended to be.

George was one of my clients who would go running back to his wife after sex, which suited me. I could never understand his need to make a "date" out of fucking me. I really would have preferred it if he had just come over, fucked me, and left. But then, if he had done that, I wouldn't have had the distraction of the curious busboy that evening.

Back at my apartment, I yawned, stretched, and then looked at George. He opened his arms, as if he wanted to kiss me. I said in a flat voice, "Follow me." By now it all seemed so completely cold-blooded.

The narrow hallway to my bedroom seemed longer and darker now that I had swallowed several glasses of wine. I turned right into an open doorway. The room was dark. I felt his hand pulling me quite vigorously. He ran his hands up and down my body. In the darkness his fingertips found their way to my zipper. He pulled it, frantic now to get me out of my pants. I felt a surge of lust, a sensation so intense it was almost painful. I had never felt this with George before. Perhaps the memory of the stranger raping me had turned me on more than usual, or perhaps the idea that another boy had paid unusual attention to us during dinner had turned George on.

He pushed me onto the bed, pulled my clothes off, then tore off his own. He straddled me as he donned a condom and applied the lube to it and to my ass.

Tonight his going into me was ecstasy. Normally, while George's immediate, uncomplicated demands satisfied his week-long need—and paid my rent at the same time—they gave me little satisfaction. But this

196

was different. His fucking was incredible—well, for him, anyway. My mind was focused only on his cock driving in and out of me. He lunged into me, desperate for it. I held him fast. I could hear his gasping breath and then a long, drawn-out sigh. He hadn't finished yet, so I waited for him, and came when he did.

When he finally shuddered to a halt, he rolled off me. I could see he was smiling. I watched him lying languidly on the bed. He lay with his legs splayed out in front of him. I turned on the lamp. He was flushed with a post-orgasmic glow that made his blue eyes shine brightly. I could see a patch of damp on his belly: my cum was drying there. I peeled off the rubber and stroked his cock.

"Would you like to fuck me again?"

"I can't for a while," he confessed. "That took everything out of me. You always do that, but tonight... ."

"You were good tonight."

"As good as that busboy?"

"Damn, George, the kid just looked like somebody. Somebody from a long time ago."

"Oh, yeah, I remember. In another country."

I kissed him, feeling good about him for the first time since our first night together.

He pulled away. "Hey, I've got to get back. I'm sorry I can't stay, but you know how it is."

"Sure." I looked at him. My eyes were level. "I know exactly how it is."

I knew this made him feel uncomfortable, but damn him, if it weren't for him, I might well have been with the busboy, Paolo.

Yet George was good tonight. I didn't want him to go. I hung on to him.

"I really have to get back. You knew I was married. I haven't tried to hide anything from you. I've really enjoyed this evening and I'd like to come back and see you next week for your birthday. You're such a darling."

Now I wiggled out of his embrace. "Don't call me darling. I'm not your darling."

I rolled over and lay flat on the bed, my ass in the air. God, I don't know why but I wanted to provoke him again.

He got to his feet. I knew he hated this bit; he much preferred it when the lights were off and he could creep into his clothes and slip away. Now he was conscious of the unforgiving light beaming on his sagging, middle-aged body. I began undulating my hips, trying to entice him to fuck me again. I burrowed into the pillows.

"I don't care what you say. You are my darling, my darling little boy."

"I'm not you're little boy. Don't keep saying I'm your little boy."

"What the fuck's gotten into you?"

He turned out the lamp. A good sign.

"You! You got into me, and I want you in me again."

"You've never talked this way before. God, I can't believe this!"

"Believe this," I snarled, rolling over, exposing my hard-on, which was clearly visible in the light-spill from the adjacent bathroom.

"Jesus!" He leaned over me, stroked me. "Did I ever tell you how much I like this cock of yours?"

"Yes. Once, a long time ago."

"It really is a gorgeous cock."

I couldn't believe this. He was actually going to suck it. He hadn't sucked it for weeks.

Slam, bang, thank you...that's what it had come down to. But suddenly he was sucking me. He got back on the bed, on his knees, between my thighs. He started in, taking his time. He played with my asshole, still moist from his fuck. Two fingers, then three. He was splendid, sucking while finger-fucking.

"Oh, George," I moaned, over and over.

After a while he was panting, "You want me back in there, don't you?"

"Oh, yes," I pleaded.

Finally, it was over. Really over. I don't think he came again, but I did. He was pleased that he could arouse me so. He kissed me gently on the forehead, told me he'd see me on my birthday. "Thanks," I said, not really wanting to be reminded I would be turning thirty. Of course, I told him I was turning twenty-five. He probably believed me.

I waited for him to leave by the front door and then switched out the lights. I lay back on my pillow and my eyes filled with tears. I hurt, a dull ache, deep inside, where his prick had been. Then I thought about the busboy, about how good he would have felt, wondered where he was now, and fell fast asleep.

Over the phone, the busboy promised to meet me after the restaurant closed. I waited in the car, but he never came out. The next night, I honked as I saw him leave the building.

"You promised," I said, rolling the window down.

He leaned toward me. He was smiling. "I know I did, but I break all my promises." His eyes were sparkling with mischief.

"I'll keep that in mind."

He got in the car, saying he would leave his car at the restaurant. I sped off but got only a block before I had to stop for a light. He raised a hand to my face. I turned to look at him and he kissed me.

"I've been waiting to kiss you ever since I first saw you."

"Love at first sight?"

"Yeah, I guess. You've got the cutest little ass!"

The light changed. I hit the accelerator. "You wanted it that much, and yet you broke your promise?"

"Oh, I was sick last night. I knew you wouldn't want me when I was sick."

198

He didn't look remotely sick, or recovering from being sick, but I let it pass.

He insisted we go to his place. But it wasn't his place exactly, it was his parents' house. I didn't want to go in, preferring to take him to my little apartment.

"Where are they?" I asked, growing impatient.

"On vacation. See, they had a delay, that's why I didn't work last night."

"So you weren't sick?"

"No."

"So you tell lies too?"

He took me in his arms. "Just little ones."

What am I doing here? I kept asking myself.

I followed him through a large square living room, furnished lavishly. The sofas were covered in a soft-pink floral material. There was a big fur rug in front of the fireplace, and the lamps were mostly art deco. The floor was of polished wood, and small Persian and Indian rugs lay pleasingly about on the floor. "God, what a neat house." I gazed about the room with delight.

"Yeah," Paolo said. "I'm gonna miss it."

"Oh?"

"Yeah, when I go to college in the fall."

Soon his tie was gone and a lock of his black hair fell over his face. I felt my heart thump. He was so devastatingly handsome, even more handsome than my stranger at the mall.

He took my hand and pulled me gently to him. "I won't do anything you don't want me to do," I said. "Just let me kiss you a little. You need kissing. I can always tell when a boy has not been kissed enough."

He gently pecked at my mouth. I felt a quite extraordinary feeling invade my body. In his gentleness he was more appealing than any boy I could remember. George's kisses were often so demanding, but Paolo kissed me as if we had all the time in the world. And we were in his parents' house! I found myself moving deeper into his arms. I felt his hardness, and he felt mine.

He led me to the bedroom, his bedroom—a jock's bedroom, or so it appeared. My mind was full of questions, but at that moment nothing mattered but getting his clothes off him.

He had broad shoulders, and a very long back. He kicked off his shoes and pulled off his socks, shirt and undershirt He climbed out of his trousers and hung them neatly over the back of a chair by the bed. Then he slipped off his underpants and let them drop to the floor. He had not turned on a light, but the light from the open bathroom door fell across his shoulders. I stared between his legs and Paolo saw where my eyes had settled. He gazed at me quizzically. "You don't mind if I'm uncut, do you?"

"Oh, no," I sighed. Of course not. Indeed, I had expected my young Italian stallion to be uncut; if he had *not*, I probably would have been disappointed. What I had not anticipated was the size of Paolo's penis: it was one of the biggest I had ever seen, at least ten inches, and thick. I wanted to suck it immediately, but he wanted more kissing. His kisses became deeper and more passionate.

He slid his hands under my buttocks and squeezed. "Oh, yes," I murmured. I felt like I might come right in my pants with the pleasure of it all. My back arched and my body fell into rhythm with his. He was on top of me, dry-humping me, while he continued kissing me. He was a fantastic kisser!

Then I heard the sound of my own voice gasping and moaning as he removed my clothes, piece by piece, taking his time.

When he had me nude, he started stroking me. In no time, I felt the tidal wave of my orgasm taking me out of my body and into space. Somewhere so far away. When I came back to earth, he was still stroking me. "I hope you haven't finished," he said.

"Finished? We haven't even started!" I moved against his fingers, which were now lodged up my ass.

I couldn't stop thinking about that kiss. Paolo literally took my breath away. Nobody had ever kissed me like that. Most clients' kisses were either quick pecks, or a total plundering of my mouth. I didn't know that men could kiss the way Paolo did.

I sank my fingers deep into the silky waves of his hair as his tongue slid into my mouth. Paolo caressed my back and shoulders, then moved down to the rounds of my ass.

He rolled me over and raised my ass so that I was kneeling on all fours. He cupped his hands around my cheeks and eased them apart. He teased the sparse blond hairs, touching them with the tip of his tongue, driving me wild with excitement. Then I felt the warm tongue washing the sides of my crevice. My hole expanded, begging for something to fill the emptiness. I gasped when I felt the thickness of Paolo's tongue pushing deep inside. Involuntarily, my cheeks tightened, and his stubble rasped against the inner walls of my cleft. His tongue plunged into me over and over again while I moaned and writhed, the pleasure almost beyond bearing. None of my clients would have dreamed of doing such a thing. It was so intensely intimate; I felt decadent, but I had never felt anything so wonderful in my life. If Paolo didn't stop, I was going to shoot again all over the sheets. "Please," I begged, "you have to stop or I'll come again." But I couldn't move one inch away from the incredible pleasure.

My words only seemed to drive Paolo to greater efforts. He reached between my legs and carefully drew my rigid cock back, driving it deep into his hand, then quickly pushing back, unwilling to stop the tongue-fuck that was driving me to such delicious heights of sensation.

I came again, overflowing Paolo's fist with thick streams of cum. Paolo pulled me into his arms, holding me while my breathing steadied. I could feel the heavy club of Paolo's incredibly large sex throbbing between us. In a minute, he was going to have to do something about that. It had been months since I'd touched an uncut dick, and I couldn't wait to explore its mysteries.

Paolo rolled me to my back, straddling my waist as I raised my upper body and tilted my face up for more of his kisses. I lapped the stubble on his chin and kissed a wet trail down his throat. I nuzzled my face in the thick mat of chest hair and made a short excursion to his armpits. This got him going—moaning, groaning.

At last my fingers wrapped around his thick cock as he leaned back, propping himself up on his hands to give me full access to his monstrous organ—the skin a rich mahogany against the bronze of his thigh. The flaring head stretched the foreskin tightly, exposing the small circle of a spongy head. He shivered as I circled the shiny red button with my fingertip. I tightened my hold and pushed my hand down. I watched in amazement as the skin slid smoothly behind the crown. I darted my tongue inside the glistening slit and made Paolo groan. Gently, I stretched the skin forward beneath the silky overhang and swirled my tongue over the sensitive rim. Paolo had a hard time staying still, but he let me play as long as I wanted. I held the plump head in my mouth, sucking gently, while I weighed his furry balls in my hand. Hungrily, I drew in more of the veiny shaft. He cupped the back of my head, but he let me set the pace. I wanted more, suctioning in more each time my head bobbed. At last, he shoved his hips forward and plunged his prick all the way down, packing my throat, and my lips were soon pressed tightly against Paolo's wiry groin.

But sucking it wasn't enough. I pleaded, "I want you inside me."

Paolo took a condom from the nightstand and rolled it over his cock. He pushed my knees back and knelt over me. "You sure?" he asked, his rod nudging the portal.

I looked up into his eyes and smiled. "Oh, yes! I want every inch of you inside me."

Holding Paolo's hips, I pulled my body upward to meet the descending cock. I gasped as the broad head entered, stretching me to the limit, slowly filling me until I felt Paolo's balls swing against my spine. "Oh, yeah," I sighed.

He rode me slowly. My cock stood straight up, rubbing through the silky hair on his chest at every stroke and leaving a glistening trail of precum. My arms tightened, urging him on. Paolo started pumping harder, his balls slamming against me with every thrust. Sweat dripped off his forehead. My tongue caught the salty trails and lapped them eagerly. Paolo groaned and kissed me, licking the salt off my lips. I started jacking my own cock. I didn't know if I could come again, but I wanted to. I rubbed my hand through Paolo's chest hair and used his sweat as lube. My hips rose off the bed to meet every lunge, and Paolo's hips went into overdrive, pistoning wildly. It was heavenly for several minutes. Then he froze, arm and neck muscles straining as he filled the condom with his load. My own balls tightened and I shot a small volley of jizz onto Paolo's chest. He collapsed, groaning, crushing me to the bed as the final spasms racked both our bodies.

Paolo held me for a long time afterwards, kissing me passionately.

"This can't be a sin," I gasped. Nothing this wonderful could be wrong." I was holding on to him as if my life depended upon him. Then I realized that I was crying, really crying, and Paolo held me gently in his arms. "What's wrong?"

"I have to go." I raised my tear-stained face to his.

His eyes were pleading with me to stay.

"I can't stay, Paolo. I have to get back."

"Is that guy waiting for you?"

"That guy?"

"The one at the restaurant."

"Oh, no. I live alone. It's just that …."

Paolo suddenly frowned. "So he was just a john?"

"A john?"

"You are a…." He looked away, finding it hard to spit out the word.

"Professional?" I volunteered.

"Yeah, that."

I rolled away from him. What was going on here?

He rubbed my shoulder. "Look, it's what I wanted. I wanted somebody who did it for a living. That was the only way I was going to do it. I knew that's what your story was."

"*Is*. That's what my story *is*. I'm a professional. Right now, that's what I am."

"Well, then, how much do I owe you?"

I didn't answer. All I wanted to do was leave, but I couldn't move. Finally I said, "First time's free."

"Oh," he said, smiling, forcing my thighs apart. He slid a fresh condom on his renewed erection. "Why's that?"

"'Cause you're so cute, that's why."

"And this, how much will this cost?" he asked, shoving his cock into me again.

"Oh, just shut up and fuck me."

And fuck me he did. Every night, after he finished work, he'd come to my apartment. During those late-night sessions, I got to know him a bit better. His father had insisted he work to help pay for college and his getting a job at the restaurant was easy because his family owned it. He had always been interested in gay sex but had never acted on his impulses.

He was engaged to his high-school sweetheart, a nice Italian girl who wanted to remain a virgin until she wed. "Her loss," I said.

For my birthday dinner, I insisted George take me back to DaVinci's. It was even more fun this time because I had been to bed with the person I was gazing at across the room—many, many wonderful times. None of this was lost on George, of course, and it made his fucking that night even more heated when we finally got back to my place.

After George had gone, I soaked in the tub for twenty minutes before Paolo arrived. He was stunned by the grand display of gifts from George: flowers, candy, and even a new suitcase. The suitcase, George said, was 'for the convention.' Every year I went with him to a convention held in Las Vegas for owners of shopping centers. His wife hated the place, but I loved it. George owned several malls and strip centers, and DaVinci's was located in one of them. That made him Paolo's family's landlord, making my nightly trysts even more dangerous—and delightful, because Paolo had no idea who George was.

Paolo nibbled on a chocolate and pouted, "But I have nothing for you."

"Oh, I wouldn't say that," I countered, my hand squeezing the bulge in his jeans, which immediately began to grow alarmingly.

But Paolo did have a surprise: after he had joined me in my nakedness and led me to my bed, he pushed me down on my back—and sucked my cock! Well, not really. He licked it, nibbled a bit on the head. Then he dropped my shaft from his lips and sucked in my balls, rolling them around with his tongue and sucking on the skin of my scrotum. He shifted his position so that he knelt over me in sixty-nine, and fucked my face while he traced a line on my skin on the underside of my crotch with the sharp point of his tongue; from my balls, it followed the bridge of flesh that led to my asshole and I tensed to the pinprick sensations as it circled my quivering asslips. His tongue darted into me and I groaned, my throat clogged with his huge cock. He rolled me up onto my shoulders and I felt his face against my buttocks as his tongue lathered and stroked my hole. He spat into it, then got some lube. I could feel the blunt tip of his finger, smearing the lube around, probing. He dribbled more spit into my hole, then worked in two fingers, opening it wider with his driving knuckles.

I took his cock out of my mouth and began licking up and down the hard shaft. I wanted it in me so bad. "Fuck me," I begged.

In response, he withdrew his fingers and positioned himself between my legs. While he slid on a condom, I put my hands on my knees and pulled them back, offering myself to him. He leaned forward and kissed me, then straightened up and pressed the sheathed, swollen head of his cock against my asshole. He entered me, slowly, lovingly—so unlike George who, just this evening, had rushed it.

I've always liked the entry even better than the orgasm. When you're having an orgasm, you're not as aware of yourself and your lover as you are at that exquisite moment of entry. Paolo grunted with pleasure when he was all the way in. Then he leaned forward until my own erection was rubbing against the muscled, hairy surface of his stomach. He cradled my head in his hands and put his face close to mine. "Let's come together," he whispered.

But I had come with George and I was in no hurry to come now. It was so seldom I really *enjoyed* sex anymore, rather than practiced it professionally, that I was going to prolong this as much as possible. I had yearned for some affection, some excitement in my life again, and this was it. I was not about to rush it. I groaned in response.

"Am I hurting you?" he asked.

I met his eyes. "No," I managed to croak, and I cleared my throat. "No, I'm okay. I just... I'm fine." Then I smiled and added, "I mean, *really* fine!" Thus assured, he returned my smile, and started in.

It was a glorious fuck. Now and then, he paused in his exertions to rain kisses on my face. It seemed that his desire was increasing in proportion to the loss of my need. Only with the most ardent kisses and caresses was he able to weaken my resolve to hold off my orgasm to still another victory. But we did, indeed, come together. I envied his future bride as I have never envied anyone.

We stayed in that position for a while, and, as his long, thick cock slowly softened inside me, we kissed each other's faces, eyes and lips. Then his cock slipped out with a smacking sound, and we fell asleep in each other's arms.

George sat across the table from me at DaVinci's, sipping his wine, looking very sad. He appeared to have forgotten how to smile. I asked him what was wrong.

"You're missing him, aren't you?" I asked.

"I guess. Yes."

We had come here "just for old times' sake," and George noticed the cute busboy was no longer here. George seemed to miss him almost as much as I did.

George knew more than he let on; he always did. He went on talking, eventually getting around to the subject of death. I had no idea what he was talking about, until he said: "You know, when you have been feeling so intensely for so long, and then it stops, it's like death. An orgasm is a little death in itself, and you've had quite a lot of them lately."

I looked away from his concerned gaze. He had not spoken of the end of my affair until now, but he had begun to ask questions about "that boy." He wanted to know what we did, when we did it, where. He was living vicariously, I thought, and loving it.

I looked at George in a new light, seeing Paolo thirty years from now, living a double life, with a wife and a boy kept on the side. A sad life, really, but one to which George had adjusted. Tuned into my thoughts as never before, he asked, "Will you see him again?"

"I don't know."

And George, as vague as ever, said, "Well, time will tell. It always does."

THE TOUCH OF THE STRANGER

The 1995 anthology In the Boy Zone *is the source of this story—the tale of a meeting at the beach between a beautiful boy and an older man who has for some time relied on paid sexual companionship. Many people find treasured souvenirs of trips to the beach—shells, suntans, and memories*
of good times--but the almost mythic lovemaking that Terry freely offers Wilbur proves to be at once the most exciting and the most tender souvenir of all   —JB

Wilbur sat by the azure sea and it seemed the air shimmered, a kind of blurred, fractional movement, like a heat haze, making the boy in the dunes appear to be only a vision. "Or is it my eyes?" he thought.

Wilbur had been coming to this beach three times a year for longer than he cared to admit. He always brought books with him, from the spring, autumn, and summer best-seller lists, and always he brought a companion. He would just pick up the phone; there were always boys ready to flee Boston for Florida, if the price were right. But he discovered that the latest companion, Johnnie, was so deeply into drugs that he became uncontrollable; he disappeared the day after they arrived and Wilbur hadn't seen him seen since. So, this time he decided he would sample the local offerings.

Wilbur got up from his chair and walked towards the boy in the dunes, who was adjusting the crotch of his sky-blue Speedos. Wilbur had been here for a week, and no one had paid him any attention. For that matter, he hadn't even seen anyone who truly excited him. Now a godlike young stud was walking directly toward him. No, his eyes had not been deceiving him: this was no apparition.

Wilbur didn't mind being obvious about what he wanted—he was fully confident in his sexuality. However, the boy merely nodded at Wilbur as he passed and broke into a sprint for the water.

Wilbur watched the boy dive into the warm water of the Gulf and began swimming; he was a powerful swimmer. Wilbur shrugged and returned to his place on the beach. The boy swam for several minutes and then, just as Wilbur became absorbed again in his book, a figure was blocking the sun.

"Got an extra towel?"

"Why, yes," Wilbur said, reaching into his beach bag. "I was saving it for you."

"Thanks," the boy said.

The towel covered the boy's face and permitted Wilbur's eyes to feast on his nearly hairless swimmer's body, and the abundantly bulging crotch almost in his face.

"Wow," Wilbur said to himself. Through the tightly stretched material of the Speedos he could make out the head of the penis, and some of the shaft, as if the cock was semi-hard. Maybe it was, Wilbur thought, perhaps the idea of driving an older man wild somehow appealed to this kid.

"There, that's better," the boy said, dropping the towel to the sand and spreading it.

Wilbur was immobile in his lounge chair, staring, a benign smile on his face.

"My name's Terry," the boy said, extending his hand.

Wilbur introduced himself, using his now-preferred nickname of "Wil."

As Terry sat on the towel, Wilbur gulped. He was dumbfounded. No boy had ever ingratiated himself this openly, and he wasn't sure what was expected. He picked up the book he had been reading. Terry noticed it, asked what it was.

"*Sexual Outlaw*, by John Rechy," Wilbur responded. "This trip I'm catching up on a lot of the old ones."

As Terry nodded and Wilbur handed him the paperback, the long plumes of the sea oats lined up behind them bobbed drowsily.

Soon Terry was scowling prettily into the sun, pretending to read the book Wilbur had handed him, waggling his toes in the sand. Wilbur, elegant and jaunty in his straw sun hat, stared down at him, and sighed. But they were getting so young, he thought, admiring Terry's sculpted face even though he was wearing a petulant frown.

Wilbur looked away momentarily and told himself that the beauty didn't have to be here, on the beach, in Florida. At any time he could be back in the city, in his regular world, with friends, and everywhere he would be admired. Oh, how greatly admired! He thought, "Yes, he would probably hate me if he knew" as he gazed at Terry with thirsty eyes.

Tourists swarmed and splashed and smiled around them and sometimes they stared, as if pointing at them—the slim man with his much younger companion, the beautiful boy with the soft, angelic face. Wilbur smiled at them as if he knew them and he found they smiled back at him. Terry paid no attention, engrossed in the book. Wilbur pushed his hat over his eyes and lost Terry's face, but when he lifted it again, there it was again, like a sun over the horizon, glowing. Wilbur bit his lip, and looked away, then quickly back again.

Terry stretched his fine legs, elongated his spine, cattishly, for the world to see. It was as if he paraded his beauty.

Another group of tourists walked quickly past, self-conscious and stiff-necked.

"They are probably thinking he's young enough to be my son," thought Wilbur, "if I weren't so well-preserved." And he was. Wilbur had taken care of himself.

The smooth-limbed youth pushed himself up onto one elbow and lifted his head from the book with learned insouciance. Said Terry: "Gives me a hard-on reading about guys getting off." The bulge in his trunks lengthened and thickened, the plump, uncut head now peeping over the waistband. Wilbur's eyes widened.

A sudden salty gust stung Terry's legs with sand as he shoved his cockhead back inside the fabric. "My best feature," Terry snickered, seeing Wilbur had noticed. "At least that's what everyone says."

"Yes," Wilbur said, blushing and averting his eyes.

Now Terry rolled away from him, as if teasing him.

The smell of the sea, the chatter and fresh breeze faded, giving way to a heavy, tropical silence.

Finally, Terry rolled back towards Wilbur, asked the time. Wilbur checked his watch. It was nearly five.

"I've got to be going," Terry said.

"Me, too," Wilbur said.

Wilbur folded his chair and put his things in his beach bag.

They followed a path into the dunes, overhung by sharp, shiny fronds, almost concealed from the sky. The air was dank, and under their feet the ground was creepily soft. Strong, wet leaves brushed against their faces and arms; there was the noise of water dripping. The undergrowth rustled as they passed. Finally they came to a clearing and some cars parked there. Much to Wilbur's disappointment, Terry had not stopped along the way, had made no move to leave the path and find a thicket where Wilbur could suck him.

They arrived at a new white LeBaron convertible, where the boy removed an elastic bracelet that had the car key attached. He looked at Wilbur and hesitated. "Well …" he began, allowing Wilbur an opening.

"Well …" Wilbur stammered, "uh … will you have dinner with me?"

Terry smiled as he opened the door of the convertible. "Of course."

Wilbur stood beside the car, his breath caught sharply in his throat. He held back his head and smiled up to the sun, in case tears rolled out.

As Wilbur climbed into the passenger seat, he picked up the rental contract lying there. Terry turned the ignition and "I'm So Excited" by the Pointer Sisters blasted from the speakers. Terry turned down the volume as he grinned at Wilbur. Wilbur chuckled, and his heart beat a little faster.

At his condo in the tall building overlooking the beach where they had just met, Wilbur offered Terry the guest bathroom to shower and change into the clothes he had brought up from the car. Wilbur went to the master suite and began undressing. When he heard the water running in the guest bath, his cock grew hard. It had been months, perhaps years, since he had been this excited. He started humming "I'm So Excited."

They walked to the French Hearth, a fairly elegant cafe a block from Wilbur's condo. The same waiter Wilbur had taken a liking to on previous visits here, showed them to their table; his name was Paul, and he was extremely attractive. When Paul saw Terry, he seemed to show new interest in Wilbur, even calling him by his name for the first time.

Once they were seated, Wilbur ordered a martini. Terry had a Perrier. As the waiter moved away, Wilbur said, "It's so strange ..."

"What?" Terry asked, reaching for the bread basket.

"My vacation is almost over and I hadn't really met anyone, and now..."

"Now what?" Terry teased.

"Well, I'd given up, I guess. I suppose it's an ethereal thing. When you seek it out, you get nowhere, get nothing." He nodded. "Yeah, it's an ethereal thing."

"Little do you know just how ethereal," Terry chuckled. As Wilbur sipped his martini, the boy added, "You look so sad sometimes."

"I haven't been well."

"Oh?"

"Yes, depressed. My entire department was laid off. I was moved into another position. I'm secure, but the ..."

"You mean you were in charge of a whole department?" Terry interrupted.

"Yes, in computer programming. All forty people were out of work in a day. Corporate downsizing they called it."

"I've heard of that. Where I come from they call it greed."

"And where is it that you do come from?"

"Oh, here, there, everywhere."

"Very mysterious."

"Yeah, guys like that."

"I imagine. I mean, I know."

Terry buttered his bread. "So you *are* sad."

"Well, I've been sad. I should have taken the whole department and set up my own company."

"Why didn't you?"

"Oh, I'm too old to do that now."

"You're never too old—for anything."

Wilbur shook his head. "If you say so."

Terry smiled. "If I promise to go to bed with you tonight, will you start your own company and take those forty people with you?"

"What?" Wilbur couldn't believe his ears.

"That's all I ask."

"You're kidding, of course, but I just don't know. If you think I could do it ..."

"I *know* you can do it. Trust me." Terry reached his hand across the table, touched Wilbur's. The hand lingered, toyed, teased.

Wilbur smiled. "Somehow I do trust you. I can't figure it out, but somehow I do."

Over the next hour, here with Terry, Wilbur found that his anger and his frustration had departed, and he felt instead a kind of longing, an exquisite, gentle longing for sex with this beautiful boy. His cock stirred in spite of himself.

At the end of the dinner, Wilbur ordered French champagne. Paul brought it, grinning. As Terry filled and refilled Wilbur's flute (he took nothing for himself) his hand toyed with his own empty glass, encircling it and sliding his hand suggestively up and down as he fixed his startling, greenish-blue eyes on the older man. It seemed to Wilbur that the boy was suggesting he desired him as much as he desired the boy, and the thought stripped years away from him more surely than his hair dye had ever done. Finally, Wilbur took the bottle from Terry and let their hands touch when he filled Terry's empty glass.

As the waiter brought the check and hovered at their elbows, Wilbur noticed Terry showed no interest in Paul. His eyes were only for him.

When they left the restaurant, the streets teemed with people, young, ardent, untouched, all of them, and the men and women alike were sleek-haired and shining with youth. With Terry at his arm, Wilbur was in splendid isolation, as if in a dream.

At the condo, Wilbur sat on the balcony with his robe half open. The wind had abated, and the moon was swelling in the indigo sky. The air was sticky, balmy, with a heat that almost seemed to pulsate. For the first time in months, Wilbur had an erection that would not go down. It seemed he was drugged. The touch of the stranger had made him high. His bare feet danced on the warm rose-colored tiles. The lazy slapping of the waves, the murmuring in the trees, the sound of Terry taking another shower lulled Wilbur into a euphoric state.

Terry had a towel wrapped around his waist when he came out on the balcony. Saying nothing, he guided Wilbur into the master suite, sat him down on the bed. Wilbur stared up at him as if he'd never seen him before, biting back his full lower lip. Terry, looking at him intensely, reached out for his hand and gently placed it on his sex; Wilbur's fingers trembled as they touched the incredible hardness. Terry lifted Wilbur's chin, commanding him to look at his face. Then he bent and gave Wilbur a kiss, the tenderest kiss the older man had ever known.

Wilbur smiled, then gasped as he stroked the sizable cock through the terrycloth towel. Terry loosened the towel and let it drop to the floor. Wilbur moaned in appreciation and buried his head in Terry's crotch, enfolding his body with his arms and losing himself in the heat and clean smell of the boy.

Tears ran freely down Wilbur's cheeks, his mouth gaping, choking on, and drinking in, Terry's eight inches of uncut cock.

"Oh," Terry cried softly.

In the noise of the night—the sound of the waves and the far-off, fading music and the murmuring of the trees—Terry kept saying "Oh," with occasional gasps of inhalation invariably followed by Wilbur's gasps and muted exclamations of "Oh, God" around the mouthful of dick driving into his throat.

After a lengthy period of sucking, Wilbur begged Terry to put it in him from behind, and he got on his stomach on the bed when Terry eagerly promised to give it to him. The boy thrust himself into the older man, arching over him, quite lost in lust, as Wilbur gasped beneath him—his hungry ass welcoming the violent, deep probes. No matter how much he wanted it, Wilbur could not help gasp: Terry's plunges hurt him, making him feel almost like he was a rag being shaken out by an overly zealous housekeeper—but making him feel absolutely ecstatic at the same time.

After a while, Terry's breathing changed, became regular, quieter, listening. Then, panting a little, he tensed briefly as he lifted Wilbur up and reached beneath him to clutch the older man's erection. Wilbur's eyes widened in acquiescence. Both of Terry's hands were coursing and roving, and masturbating frantically as he resumed the ferocity of his profound fucking, and his movements became even faster and more frantic; with his head thrown back while he muttered excited groans of animal lust, his big cock plunged feverishly in and out of Wilbur.

Wilbur's body tensed and he cried out loudly a few minutes later when his orgasm approached. Terry's head was still thrown back and his eyes squeezed shut, as if possessed, until he came also, groaning in joy as his copious emission erupted inside Wilbur at the same moment Wilbur's cum shot out onto the sheets.

Terry's hand continued to play with Wilbur's now-spent cock, and Wilbur's hand covered it until the boy was calm enough to dispose of the condom and lie down beside Wilbur, facing him. Their sweat had begun to cool and they got under the covers.

"I don't think I've ever come together with somebody the first time," Wilbur said. He burrowed his face into the curve of Terry's collarbone.

"You were good. So good, I want some more."

Wilbur shook off his fatigue and leaned over to examine Terry's prick, which was hard again. He was soon sucking again, continuously licking and savoring the sweetness. Drunk from the taste, he desperately took the entire shaft into his mouth and buried his face deeper and deeper into the reddish pubic hair.

As Wilbur ravenously devoured him, Terry began fingering his own asshole, then fucked himself with one digit, then two.

Suddenly, Terry let out a loud moan. He grabbed Wilbur's hair. Bucking wildly in deep pleasure, his entire body shuddered as he began another orgasm, moaning, "Yes, baby! Oh yes, baby!"

Wilbur continued to suck madly on Terry's throbbing prick. Barely able to breathe, he sank his entire face in Terry's crotch, hardly conscious of anything else but the delicious tangy taste, the musky inviting scent. This was it as far as Wilbur was concerned—this was heaven!

It had been an unbelievable night. But it was not over.

Now Terry wanted to get fucked. Soon he was on his back on the bed, his legs spread, jacking his cock. "Come on," he whispered.

"Oh, I can't. I haven't done that to anybody in years."

"Oh, come on," Terry begged. "Give me that big dick."

Wilbur did have an erection, as hard as any he could remember, so he knelt between the outstretched thighs, and began applying grease to Terry's anal lips.

"That's right," Terry was moaning.

As Wilbur entered him, Terry said, "Oh, that's just what I want."

Wilbur could not believe how hot Terry's throbbing anus felt as paused, with only the head of his cock inside it.

"Go ahead, go ahead!" Terry pleaded, and Wilbur sank his fat, hardened prick all the way in.

Now Wilbur was crying, "Yes," half breathing and half whispering in Terry's ear, as Terry echoed him. Wilbur's heart was pounding, almost into his throat, it seemed. He finally remembered to breathe deeply. He inhaled and drew every bit of energy he could muster into his shoulders and down the length of body. But he would not hold this energy in his body; he would use it to fulfill his own pent-up desires at last.

He held the boy's firm, freshly showered ass in his hands and fucked it. If there is a Creator, he thought, He's probably enjoying a good laugh over his awkward gyrations—or perhaps the chance meeting on the beach had really been a Blessing He bestowed.

"Is it okay?" Wilbur was foolish enough to ask. He was beyond surprised to find Terry so ready to be fucked, to use his knowledge and skill as a top and a bottom for the purpose of Wilbur's pleasure. As Wilbur thrust into the boy, the distinction between top and bottom disappeared, and neither of them cared that it had. Wilbur knew only that Terry's palms and manicured nails were playing all over his skin. It felt surreal.

Wilbur raised up to look at Terry again, the strong shoulders, the tight pecs, down his muscular stomach to his again-burgeoning cock. Suddenly Wilbur's equilibrium faltered and his cock slipped from Terry's hole. He held Terry's body still while he shoved it in again, then resumed his long, hard strokes. He was no longer hesitant: If this boy wanted to get fucked, Wilbur was ready to go all the way for him.

"God, it's so big," Terry moaned.

Wilbur seldom thought about just how big his cock was. He remembered the days, years ago, when the guys at the baths begged to suck it, but few of them wanted it inside them all the way, the way Terry seemed to. Wilbur could now feel the muscles of Terry's ass twitching and gripping to keep the cock inside.

Terry grabbed Wilbur's asscheeks to force his cock all the way in. Wilbur was thrusting madly and surprised at his own strength. Terry's lips were inches from Wilbur's, his eyes searching with a fierceness.

"So you want me, huh?" Wilbur cried, then kissed Terry, so hard it almost seemed as if he was trying to absorb Terry's beautiful face into him, as if he felt beyond any hope of relief.

Suddenly, Terry's body tensed, and he gripped Wilbur by throwing his legs around him, locking him in.

Terry began grinding his face into Wilbur's, kissing him, inspiring fierce, demanding thrusts of release. To Wilbur's delight, as his orgasm began to burst, Terry was making him come harder and harder.

"I can't stop," Wilbur cried at last, rocking and coming and lifting Terry with all his might. Terry bucked against him, and that made Wilbur's orgasm surge yet one more time. Terry was completely locked around him, and he rolled them both over. Now on top, with Wilbur's cock still inside him, Terry easily pinned Wilbur, and kissed him violently on the mouth.

Wilbur was completely exhausted. He thought he must now be almost dead: He felt he was merely a ghost of himself, weightless. His mouth was open and wet against Terry's smooth chest.

Terry kissed Wilbur gently, and raised up, disengaging their bodies. He stepped off the bed, and began to walk away. Wilbur watched as Terry's buttocks undulated in the moonlight—two cool scoops of vanilla ice cream.

As he walked toward the bathroom, his image in the mirror stopped Terry for a moment. Wilbur could see Terry reflected there—rosy, perfect, more beautiful than ever before. Although he was not a religious man, Wilbur was stunned to find himself whispering a prayer of deep thanks for the short time he had shared with the young Adonis.

He looked over at the real Terry, not his reflection, and saw him gazing intently in his direction behind a radiant almost-grin, and then he vanished behind the bathroom door. Presently Wilbur fell asleep. He dreamed vaguely of music that, in the dream, had a very important and perfectly obvious meaning but faded away and could not be recalled when he later tried to translate it into words.

Dawn light, rose-hued and clear, filled the bedroom of the spacious master suite. Wilbur frowned at the empty space beside him and eased out of bed. He threw a robe around himself and went through the condo, looking for the boy. The air was cool and silent, the rooms empty.

He returned to the bedroom, stared at the bed as if Terry might have reappeared during his search. Then he noticed the two hundred-dollar bills were still on the bureau where he had left them for Terry.

Wilbur went out to the balcony and looked down at the parking lot. The convertible was gone. Wilbur blinked. No, he thought, it did happen—the boy had been here, it wasn't a dream. In seeming desperation, Wilbur called the boy's name, and a soft, cool breeze from the direction of the dunes touched his sunburned face.

THE PICK-UP

Another excerpt from Intimate Strangers, *the story of Joey, a young hustler, whose john takes him to the Royal Palms—where one sexual adventure follows another, and yet another, and even two more!* —JB

Joey is getting ready to leave Shorty's bar, to rest. It's been a long day. He's taken three out-calls today and just stopped in to pay his pot supplier. Then, when he turns around, he sees Roy watching him across the bar—about forty, trim, dark hair. Joey gets up, walks over. "Hi," he says.

"Hi," Roy says, lifting one eyebrow.

During the space of fifteen minutes of keen observation, Roy has become infatuated with the young hustler, with his high, delicate cheekbones and his aristocratic nose combined with a strong jawline and cleft chin. Roy is also attracted to the shiny blond hair that tumbles down nearly to his shoulders. Best of all, Joey's tight jeans leave little to the imagination.

Two beers are ordered, and Roy tells Joey he always comes to Fort Lauderdale in March, when it's sunny and 77 degrees. This is the last night of his week in the sun, Roy tells the boy, and he has spent the whole time looking for someone like Joey. "Now here you are," Roy says. Joey smiles; he says he is also from Ohio, Roy's home. Joey says he left the Buckeye State in October and he's been here ever since. He has a job at the Marriott, he says, but he's behind on his rent. Roy would like to help him out. Joey nods, lets Roy buy him another beer.

Joey's ascent up the stairs to the door of Roy's room at the Royal Palms Bed 'n' Breakfast is blessed, his ass inciting Roy to open the door urgently. Roy leads the youth through the door, and, street-smart as he is, Joey is checking for intruders lurking in the shadows.

Roy clicks on the desk lamp and Joey collapses on the bed, sinking back into the welcoming mattress, legs loosely apart, exhausted.

While Roy starts undressing, Joey closes his eyes and reclines seductively on the double bed, waiting. Roy goes to the bathroom, pees. When he returns, Joey has taken off all his clothes, except for his red nylon briefs, and has rolled over onto his belly.

Roy stands over the bed, clad only in his trousers. He smiles down at the lascivious display, and his bittersweet blackberry eyes savor the sight of the youth's ass. Throbs of intense lust power through him. Impishly, he pushes the nylon deep into the hidden valley and watches the cheeks clench instinctively.

Now he lays a flattened hand across Joey's bottom, relishing the silky smoothness of those taut mounds and, spanning his asscheeks with his splayed fingers, he clasps them together, squeezing while Joey turns and twists in heated passion.

The incredible sight and feel of the excited youth squirming hotly on the bed while he plays with his ass brings Roy to an immediate state of full arousal. He is barely able to restrain himself as he snatches at the waistband of the boy's briefs, eager now for the final unveiling and the act they both now know will inevitably follow.

And so he draws the briefs down, Joey lifting his hips to help. Roy yanks the briefs away and for the longest time he lets himself contemplate the lovely sight of Joey's upturned bare bottom: two smooth hemispheres, perfectly rounded. Joey closes his eyes and waits expectantly.

Gazing at that trim, appealing bottom, Roy finds himself enchanted anew by the hustler. He can't help caressing him. Slowly, almost reverently, he cups the pleasing curvature of the buttocks. He strokes them, and murmurs, "Such a perfect little ass."

Roy brings a hand up along the back of Joey's leg, idly stroking his extended form, lightly moving his hand up and down, feeling the curve of the back of a thigh, the contoured rise of the splendid ass. Joey rolls over and reaches up to get at Roy's belt buckle, which Roy left hanging open when he peed. Joey manages to pull the belt completely free, then undoes the front of the pants and pulls down the zipper. Through the fabric, Joey grips Roy with surprising urgency considering how tired he was before, fondling him with a determined hand. He squeezes tentatively, as if testing his hardness. Roy opens his mouth but no words come out; Roy is putty in the hustler's hands. As Joey struggles to work the loosened pants down over Roy's hips, the increasingly impatient man reaches back to help, twisting out of his pants and pushing them farther down in a fevered rush of excitement. Once the pants have been removed and Roy is standing completely naked before Joey, the hustler is stunned to see the size of Roy's equipment.

"Ummmm...I want this," he says, his voice soft and husky, as he squeezes Roy's penis.

Roy looks down at the kneeling boy and nods, dropping his hands to Joey's naked shoulders so he can hold on as he surrenders to the waves of pleasure and the tender ministrations of this determined youth. He groans as the knowing fingers explore his incredibly large cock. Through half-closed eyes he watches as one hand lightly cradles his balls, while the other wraps around the thick shaft. He feels those hands pass lightly over his cock, examining every inch, playing in his pubic curls, easing along his inner thighs, clasping his hips and then sliding around so that he can hold him by his butt. Joey extends his tongue and draws it wetly all the way up the entire nine-inch length of the underside of Roy's erection, sending wild tingles pulsing through the older man. Roy tightens his butt as Joey leans forward and covers the throbbing crown with his lips, letting Roy push so that Joey has the full knob in his mouth. Then he takes it all, deep down his throat.

"Oh, god!" Roy groans, squirming uncontrollably, helplessly tossing his head from side to side, arching his back and struggling to hold on.

The boy continues to demonstrate an incomparable talent for fellatio, hollowing his cheeks rhythmically. Roy tightens his grip on Joey's shoulders while the taut ring of lips slide up and down on his shaft, up and down, up and down in a smooth, piston-like motion. After a few minutes of this, Roy is feebly trying to stop the boy before he comes. He steps back, causing his lust-swollen prick to pop from Joey's mouth. It stands proud, glistening with Joey's saliva.

But Joey won't stop; he reaches out for the cock, demands more of it, and Roy is soon moaning again. Joey is not bothered by the moaning much because the moans are so regular, and they come so predictably. Normally, Joey likes it when a trick is quick about it, but if it takes longer, he is patient, waiting for him to get off. Sometimes he wants to count, to count down. "Okay, now," he says. Then there are the guys who never come at all. Those are the hardest. It takes so much time; if only he could charge by the minute. If they are nice, he'll work at getting them off. They say they just can't, but they've never had Joey.

"It doesn't matter," they say. Sometimes they act irritated, disappointed.

"We can always try," Joey tells them. He likes nothing more than a big, thick, hard, cut prick.

Roy sighs, trying to overcome the overwhelming urge to shoot. Joey realizes Roy is close and he pulls the prick from his mouth. Joey looks up at him while Roy clamps his head rigidly in place and bucks his hips furiously, fucking his face in a frenzy that soon has him teetering on the brink of orgasm. At the last possible moment, he wrenches himself free, extracting his cock.

"Okay, that's enough. I'll give you what you want."

"Thank you," Joey moans.

Roy slides on a rubber and covers it with lube.

Joey remains on his back, which surprises Roy. Roy is unsure if the youth might change his mind. Relinquishing sexual power must be hard for a boy like Joey; boys like him are such schemers. Yet here he is, on his back, legs wide.

Roy decides he will be the boy's benefactor and give him the fuck he craves—on his own terms. He climbs on top of him like he has watched people do a thousand times before in porn videos. Joey, seeing how huge the cock looks now, shows fear for the first time. Roy can read the boy's apprehension in the tension of his mouth, the way he bites his lip, holding back the demand as Roy guides his cock between Joey's splayed legs. Rubbing the head against Joey's sweet asslips, he slowly taunts him. Then, in one movement, Roy pushes his way in until he is buried deep inside Joey. Grasping Joey's hips, he begins to stroke in and out, building tempo until he is pounding, slamming into Joey, and Joey's body is rising and pushing into each stroke.

"Oh, good boy," Roy says. Roy shows no mercy; he drives savagely into him. He stares at Joey, watching him sink into another place, probably with another man than him. Roy's sweat drops on Joey's face as he lunges heavily into the boy. It is a voracious hole he's fucking, Roy thinks, as Joey's legs wrap around him, clasping for deeper penetration. Gasps and grunts greet Roy's astonished ears. He leans on one arm, biceps pumped up with the strain, and grabs at Joey's luscious prick. Now with his body quivering in orgasm, with barely suppressed sobs, Joey is done. Roy is concentrating on keeping his cock inside Joey. He lowers himself onto the boy and holds him tightly. "Oh fuck it, fuck it hard!" Joey whispers in Roy's ear.

Roy's excitement continues to build. He gives Joey another stroke, his cock burning into Joey's ass, and then another and another, until he can't hold back anymore. Finally, he is moaning and crying out, delirious with orgasm. Joey is rocking his tight little ass against Roy's cock and spreading his own fresh cum all over Roy's face and into his mouth.

As Roy lets his post-orgasmic body slide down Joey's sweat-drenched torso, Joey looks at Roy with a bit of real embarrassment, perhaps because he enjoyed it so much.

Roy disappears into the bathroom again. When he emerges, freshly scrubbed, Joey is on his belly, still naked, undulating his hips.

"You want me to fuck it again?" Roy asks, bewildered.

"Oh, please. Be good to me, and I'll be good to you," he says, almost pleading. He begins grinding his hips, his buttocks pushing into the air, his fingers preparing the way for another assault by Roy.

Pressing on, Roy reaches below Joey's writhing body to touch his cock, which he finds, reassuringly, is rock-hard once more, slick with pre-cum. Roy plucks at Joey's still-sopping asshole, prying the buttocks apart. Joey waits tensely, and Roy's wet tongue begins to lap at the puckered hole, sending Joey into a spasm of delight. The boy tightens his buttocks and wags his hips as if to shake off the flood of lewd sensations, but Roy offers him no respite. His tongue is flicking deep within the boy, and Joey is bucking his hips furiously. Next, Roy's finger slickly penetrates Joey, to be immediately joined by a second, then a third. Roy begins fingerfucking the hustler, who is flinging his head from side to side, moaning, begging for Roy to stick his cock in him once more.

After a few minutes, Joey is being driven crazy with passion. Roy pulls back and the mattress sways as he gets into position behind Joey, applying a new rubber to his hard prick

"Yes, yes," Joey says as Roy holds his hips in his hands and teases the opening with the head of his cock. Roy gazes down at the magnificent ass as his now fully-erect cock slides slowly into it. Roy is methodical, the cock moving in a smoothly mechanical stroke that keeps Joey begging for more. Roy raises Joey's excitement to fever pitch, holding him there teetering on the edge, then withdrawing the glistening shaft till only the tip remains buried in the boy's ass. In and out he goes, with a fucking that is slower, deeper, and more satisfying than Joey has ever known.

But by now Roy's own restraint is breaking down. He pulls back, forcing himself to hold off a little longer. He eases back on his heels, only to have Joey push back and bury Roy's cock to the hilt in one powerful thrust. Roy seizes Joey's hips and keeps the boy impaled on his cock as he lies on his back on the mattress, Joey over him, holding his ass all the way down on Roy's prick. Joey doesn't move at first, just holds the big cock in him; then he begins riding up and down with growing speed and excitement

At first Joey's self-fucking is wildly erratic, but somehow he manages to slow down and it becomes more rhythmic, even smooth. Soon Roy is meeting each plunge with his own pelvic thrust. In this way they scale new heights, and quickly Roy can feel the tension rising in Joey's sweating body. Soon Joey is jerking furiously, at last coming, with a violent tremor, crushing Roy's groin against his ass, burying Roy's penis to the hilt. Roy reaches around to feel the cum spurting from Joey's cock. He lets it ooze all over his fingers.

Joey lifts himself away and drops to the mattress, exhausted.

Roy knows he should get up and shower again, but Joey's smell is too good to wash away. As he drifts into a deep sleep, he thinks about the times when his friends have accused him of never living life for the moment, like it was gonna run out and leave him stranded, suspended between visions of possibilities. But, boy, if those friends could see him now!

In the morning, Roy dresses and packs quietly, not wanting to awaken the sleeping hustler. As he leaves the room to catch his flight, Roy plants a final parting kiss on the back of Joey's head.

Later, when Joey wakes up, he finds he is alone in the bed. He realizes immediately that Roy has vacated the room. He also realizes he didn't get his fee upfront and that no money has been left for him.

Joey hadn't been kidding, his rent is due, and an overnighter would have cinched it for him. This is not the first time he's been fucked over, but this one doesn't hurt as much as the other ones. What hurts more than anything is Joey's asshole. He decides to partake of the amenities of the Royal Palms. He grabs a towel, wraps it around his waist and heads downstairs to the hot tub.

Jerry, a thirtysomething vacationer from California, is sprawled out languidly on a chaise, working on his already formidable tan. Joey lowers himself into the steaming, whirling waters, then looks over at Jerry, smiles. They are alone in the courtyard, so Jerry decides to play with Joey.

219

He spreads his hairy thighs and is soon displaying a proud erection that rivets Joey's attention. Almost reverently, the man's long elegant hands explore the swollen shaft, caressing the prick. Joey sighs in silent admiration. With loving care Jerry works his cock, one hand easing down to cradle the wrinkled sack of his balls while the other clutches his erection in a loose fist. Jerry's grip tightens and he begins to pump his fist up and down in slow, steady strokes. He arches and mutters something, and smiles up at Joey with a lewd, sexy grin. Joey slides out of the hot tub and kneels down over Jerry, bringing his mouth close, to plant a single kiss on the sensitive flesh just below the ridge of the tumescent crown. Wrapping his fingers around the base of the shaft, Jerry tilts it toward Joey. Joey excites the throbbing sex with delicate, fluttery kisses.

Quickly changing tactics, Jerry asks Joey to show him his asscheeks. Like most men, Jerry delights in the sensual feeling of Joey's hairless leg as Joey stands up, and in the boy's low moans as Jerrry's eager fingertips travel a few inches higher, and explore the asslips. He presses his finger in, testing him, getting a soft shuddering moan of pleasure from the blond.

Jerry spends a few leisurely moments delighting in the warm, satiny feel of Joey's splendid ass, affectionately fondling those heavenly mounds, then moves his hand in a slow caress up the boy's back. Joey says he would love to stay here playing, but, with a reluctant sigh, he says he is eager to get to the main event. He wraps his towel around himself as he leans down and brings his lips close to Jerry's ear. "Let's go up to your room," he mutters.

Jerry nods, slips on his swim trunks, and they make their way quickly upstairs. Jerry stops at the door to his room, just two doors down from Roy's, and opens it. Joey enters, and, tossing off his towel, flings himself immediately on the bed. Jerry dumbly nods acquiescence. Joey begs Jerry to begin, his body tense with anticipation, breathing audibly in the quiet room. Without having to be told, Joey parts his legs in invitation.

Joey watches with widening eyes as Jerry tugs off his swim trunks and climbs between Joey's legs. Joey blinks, reaches out to stroke Jerry's renewed cock. He is pleased with the cock; it is not too small yet no way near as large as Roy's monster. Jerry takes a lubed condom from the nightstand and applies it to his cock, then he reaches down to insert it into Joey's well-fucked ass.

Joey throws back his head and groans at the breathtaking swiftness of the penetration. Jerry soon has Joey writhing in frantic urgency as he drives the shaft up into the boy. Joey is flinging his head about, mumbling incoherently as Jerry presses all the way home. Now Jerry starts fucking, using short, choppy strokes, while Joey utters a series of tiny grunts through clenched teeth, his pretty features distorted with the throbbing hurt. Lines of distress etch his brow as he steels himself to endure the fuck.

Wildly excited by Joey's sensual squirming and the soft moans of pleasure he is making, Jerry pumps even more furiously, driving the frenzied hustler to even greater heights of ecstasy.

Soon Joey is whimpering as he senses the imminent approach of Jerry's orgasm. Joey begins gyrating wildly, totally out of control, thrashing about on the bed, snapping his head from side to side while his legs flail in the air. Joey raises his hips high off the bed, bucking up to meet Jerry's pounding strokes, and he moans long and desperately. Soon Joey's eyes are clenched tight, his breathing heavy through parted lips, as Jerry labors over him until his body stiffens and he is caught in the throes of an all-consuming orgasm.

On the way back to his room after a late breakfast, Lance, a thin, 24-year-old vacationer from Virginia, stops when he hears the hiss of a desperate whisper coming from one of the rooms just down the way from his own. He can't quite make out what is being said. He moves down the hall, listening closely, his head cocked to one side. There comes an unmistakable groan, an animal growl of helpless passion, and he knows without a doubt: two guys are fucking and they have not closed the door!

Instinctively, Lance turns in the direction of the sounds. As he peers into the shadowy interior, he distinctly hears a second groan, longer and deeper. For a brief second he struggles with inner doubts; then, on impulse, he reaches down to rub his crotch. Fired with an intense curiosity he simply cannot contain, he moves stealthily towards the sex-sounds. This is sick, he thinks, yet he can't help himself as he is drawn inexorably to the hidden possibilities behind that partially opened door. Hardly daring to breathe, he creeps closer to the doorway, being careful to keep well back from the opening, leaning in just enough to peer around the door frame.

Just then, Jerry explodes inside Joey, letting out a long, satisfied sigh. A little sigh also escapes Joey's lips.

So stunned at the sight of Jerry apparently blowing a load deep inside Joey, Lance falls against the door and it swings open. He stands there, just inside the room, taking in the riveting action.

Joey turns toward the doorway, his body motionless, submissively accepting the last thrusts of Jerry's cock.

Seeing Joey's eyes on him, Lance is petrified, caught in his voyeurism, his hand frozen in place over his hard-on. After what seems like an eternity, Joey smiles at Lance. His heart racing, Lance takes the smile as an invitation to step deeper into the room.

Lance approaches the bed and Joey extends his arm toward the man. Lance stands with his legs pressed against the mattress. Joey squeezes the bulge in Lance's swim trunks. The newcomer looks over at Jerry, who is still slowly sliding his cock in and out of Joey, unwilling to give the ass up even though he has come. Jerry smiles at Lance, and Joey tugs at

Lance's trunks. Lance backs up and slips out of his suit, freeing a cute, cut erection. Joey grabs the cock and stuffs it in his mouth. Joey's cheeks become hollowed as he sucks Lance, looking up at him from beneath his long lashes, watching his face for each subtle reaction, playing him like the professional cocksucker he is. He soon has Lance groaning weakly and tossing his head from side to side.

Jerry finally pulls out of Joey, his spent prick gradually reviving while he watches Lance's succulent member enveloped by Joey's mouth.

Lance's hands fumble to hold Joey by the head, his fingers digging in the thick mass of blond hair. Sensing Lance's need, Joey freezes, letting him hold his head steady while he fucks his face, his hips bucking up and down in frantic rhythm.

Jerry studies the hairy-chested stud standing before him having his cock serviced by Joey. He climbs off the bed and steps behind Lance so he can catch a whiff of the manly smell of the stud. He feels Lance's body surging with lustful urgency. He runs his fingers up the inner walls of Lance's thighs, and bends over. His lips force open the asscheeks and he buries his tongue inside Lance.

Jerry is aware that Lance is so desperately hard that it is almost painful for him, and to continue rimming him would send him off like a shot.

Joey is totally immersed in the task at hand, licking and lapping at the glistening cock. Jerry rises, peering around Lance to watch as Lance resumes stabbing Joey's mouth repeatedly. Finally, Lance lets out a long, shivering moan and reaches down to clutch a fistful of Joey's hair as he comes in his mouth.

Joey lies exhausted on the bed, his labored breathing gradually subsiding. Lance grabs his swim trunks, bends down and kisses Joey on the forehead, then turns to Jerry. "Thanks," he says.

"See you later," Jerry says, slapping Lance's ass as he passes him.

Jerry goes into the bathroom and turns on the shower. Joey is still for a few minutes, catching his breath. Then he rushes from the room. Joey hears Jerry call out as the door slams shut behind him, but he doesn't look back.

In Roy's empty room, Joey hurriedly showers, dresses. Suddenly, a key is being turned in the lock. Joey stands still.

"Oh," Gino, the youthful janitor, says. "I thought you'd checked out."

"I did," Joey says, "I just had to pee."

Gino sets the vacuum cleaner he has in his hand on the floor and says, "I'll come back."

"No, that's okay. I'm done."

Gino smiles at Joey. "You sure?" His eyes are riveted at the bulge in Joey's jeans.

Joey shakes his head. "God, I don't fuckin' believe this."

"What?"

<hr />

222

"Is there something in the water here or what?"

Gino's smile becomes broader. "I don't understand."

"Everybody is on the make here."

Gino closes the door to the room. "Well, we are pretty free here."

"Well, I'm not. Free, that is. I have my rent to pay today."

"Didn't make enough last night?"

"No. He ran out on me while I was sleeping."

Gino steps closer to Joey. "How much do you need?"

Joey brightens. He steps up to Gino, grabs his crotch. "How much you got?"

"Eight inches."

"That's enough."

Joey drops to his knees before Gino, bringing his hands to the well-built janitor's crotch. Joey slowly unzips the shorts, and his hand is moving fast, snaking up between Gino's legs to capture his balls, softly cradling them, then caressing and squeezing the hairy sack. With his other hand he reaches up to grab the turgid, uncut prick. He lets the dark shaft rest in his cupped palm, while he bends forward to nip at the foreskin.

Gino's eyes close and he sighs blissfully as Joey makes love to his tasty foreskin. Gino, aching for sex, runs his fingers through the silkiness of Joey's hair and, grasping him by it, he pulls the boy's head against his straining erection. Thus, Gino can now control Joey's movements, guiding his head, restraining him just out of range, forcing him to extend his tongue as far as possible to reach the now fully erect, swaying cock. Gino wiggles his hips, teasing Joey with it. He watches delightedly as Joey's talented tongue slithers lavishly over the whole crown, circling it before concentrating on the sensitive flesh along the underside, pleasuring Gino with quick, fluttery strokes.

Gino closes his eyes, and clenches his fists as Joey thrills him. Joey then switches to long wet strokes along the underside of the shaft. Gino grunts as he struggles to hold on, driven to new heights by the insatiable hustler. Joey works with the determination that is his trademark, working his tongue up and down along the sides, over the top ridge and then sliding down underneath once more, until he comes to the balls. Here he licks the ample, cum-filled sack thoroughly, soaking the dark hairs, and then opening his mouth wider to suck Gino's balls ever so gently. Groaning helplessly, Gino tightens his fists on the handfuls of Joey's hair. His prick is incredibly hard now, gleaming with the wet sheen of Joey's saliva. He looks down at the blond, a smile on his thin lips. Joey grabs the throbbing shaft, and, bending his head, he slips the crown between his parted lips, lightly scraping the shaft with his teeth, and drawing Gino's prick into his mouth. Joey works his jaw, bringing his mouth, tongue, and lips into play, using everything he has to work Gino over, while Gino groans and twists in ecstasy.

Gino holds on to Joey's locks, twining his fingers in them, his eyes closed, rolling his head from side to side. The eager hustler bobs his head up and down in a slow, even rhythm. Joey knows instinctively when Gino is near climax, and he abruptly slows down, even stops for a moment, while Gino clings to the edge. And Joey waits, perfectly still, letting Gino catch his breath. Then Joey gradually starts over, slowly building Gino up once again. The young janitor can stand it no longer—besides, he has to get about his work. In a heated rush he holds Joey's head rigidly in place and bucks his hips, pumping the shaft in and out of Joey's mouth, fucking it with incredible urgency. At last, Gino lets himself go completely, arching back, plunging his thick shaft deep into Joey's throat as his hands clamp the sides of his face. Spasms of pleasure shoot through Gino's body as his exploding cock sends his cum into Joey's hungry mouth. The orgasm seems to go on and on, and Joey pulls the janitor's cock out of his mouth, squeezing it, watching the rest of his cum drip to the floor.

Finally, Joey falls back weakly, collapsing onto the floor, as Gino's softening cock slides from his fingers. Joey looks up at Gino.

"Was that enough?" Gino asks.

"Oh, yeah," Joey sighs, lowering his head and leaning forward to snuggle against Gino's leg, his head resting against Gino's thigh. Gino takes three twenties from his wallet and drops them on Joey. Joey grabs them, smiles back at Gino, then gives the cum-coated cock a tender parting squeeze.

As he starts to leave the Royal Palms, the three twenties wadded in his hand, Joey reaches into his back pocket for his wallet. He withdraws it and opens it. He stops dead. He cannot believe it. Roy hadn't fucked him over after all. He pulls out two crisp hundred dollar bills. He laughs out loud and, putting the twenties with the hundreds, slides them into his wallet, and returns his wallet to the back pocket. He'll be able to pay his rent after all, and, in celebration, he's going to sleep the rest of the day.

As he enters his little apartment near the beach, the phone is ringing. At first he thinks he'll ignore it, just crash. But he relents and picks up the phone. It is a john; he saw Joey's ad in the gay bar guide and wants to meet him.

"Where are you stayin'?" Joey asks.

"The Royal Palms," the john says." I just checked in."

Joey puts his hand over the mouthpiece and howls.

THE GREAT MAN'S BOY

Another tale from Mad About the Boys. *When your neighbor drops in for a visit, you usually offer him refreshments, but when the beautiful blond kept boy from next door came over to visit, he was the one to offer something wonderful to eat—something long and hard and full of the kind of refreshments only a horny youngster like he can provide! —JB*

He was the perfect boy for The Great Man, a truly graceful specimen of a boy. He had long, golden hair that fell in rings and spirals around his shoulders. His eyes were lapis lazuli, and his skin so fair it was nearly transparent. To my mind, he was beautiful beyond words.

I suspected the boy was asked to stay at The Great Man's mansion because he was great in bed. The Great Man was, without doubt, great as well. Although we had exchanged little more than perfunctory nods as he drove by my house in his dark blue Rolls, I knew much about The Great Man. I knew from his appearances on television he had a marvelous vocabulary, a vivid imagination, and a body that was remarkably well preserved. I knew from magazine articles that he had once been a minor film actor who had taken a percentage on a film rather than salary and the silly comedy had made tens of millions. As his looks began to fade, he retired to sell real estate and become a multi-millionaire. I began renting his films. Yes, in his prime, I would have been terribly attracted to him.

After the boy was ensconced at the house, I began to imagine them in bed. The boy's tidy limbs would be uncharacteristically askew, his neat torso flattened by The Great Man's greatness. Being accustomed to the superior position, The Great Man would probably splay his hands on the mattress, rising above the boy, his elbows a mighty lever. I pictured The Great Man poised above his young whore, looking down upon him with the kind of serene tolerance only great men can give.

I sensed The Great Man, his amusement great, answered everything the boy asked him with, "Oh?" or "Hmmm." After all, The Great Man had been a pretty fair actor.

For weeks I had noticed only the presence or absence of cars in the driveway, lights in the windows. I hadn't seen the boy. Perhaps, I wondered, The Great Man was into S&M and kept him tied up? Whatever, I hoped the kid knew somehow he wasn't entirely alone while I was next door.

It seemed to me that something was bound to change over there. I mean, how could such happiness continue unabated for long? I awaited signals of distress, sounds of despair. But there was nothing. Spring came and the

225

remains of the garden bloomed and tangled and wilted right on schedule. The Great Man came and went, staying home no more than a day or two between trips.

And the lights would go off at three, then two, and I soothed myself with this sign that the boy was handling being with The Great Man a little better. By the time summer was fully upon us, I'd sometimes see his windows dark as early as midnight.

Nothing was really different otherwise—except now that the weather was nice, I finally saw the kid in the yard. And when he saw me he acknowledged my presence with a nod. As time passed, I managed to find excuses to engage him in conversation. Occasionally I called him "son," but mostly I managed to avoid calling him anything. Just looking at him in his little yellow Speedos as he cleaned the pool gave me a hard-on and I had to keep my moments with him brief.

When the weather got really warm, the boy spent hours outdoors, sitting in the sun beside the pool, sometimes with a magazine, a look of pure absorption on his face. The cat, Dickens, would slither under the plastic slats of his chaise and lie there in the shade, panting. Without looking up from the page, the boy would reach down and pat whatever part of the cat that was handy.

The boy almost always took the cat with him when he went out in the car The Great Man bought him shortly after they'd been together four months. It was a red Mustang convertible. On those rare occasions when the poor cat was left behind, he would collapse in the driveway to wait. No matter how long the boy was gone, his eyes wouldn't leave the direction in which he'd vanished.

Waiting for someone to come home was something I could relate to. Even now, around dusk, I still catch myself listening for the garage door to open and ex-lover Ben to drive in and turn the engine off.

Much as I missed Ben, though, the days didn't feel too big for the things I had to fill them with. There are all sorts of possibilities. And if I couldn't always account for my time, it was only because I kept too busy to worry much about it. Yet, I was never too busy *not* to think about my new neighbor. In fact, paying attention to the boy made me more mindful of time. The days of June and July seemed unbearably slow and heavy to me, and I imagined how they weighed on him, being alone so much of the time. He made me glad I was there.

I invited him over and at first he refused, but eventually he relented. We would sit on the terrace and talk. He had a beer while I drank my martini. The cat would follow him over and eventually I would serve him something to drink also: some milk in a dish.

It saddened me to see the boy get up and go home, especially when so little seemed to be calling him back to that huge, cluttered house. By then, the evenings The Great Man made it home were rare, but the boy never mentioned that, nor did I. Around four-thirty, five o'clock, he'd say, "I better start dinner." I'd detain him briefly with pointless observations, another beer, but eventually he always slipped away.

Those nights, after he'd been here, seemed longer than others. I hated to admit it but I was growing fond of him. *Terribly* fond. I longed to tell him that even though he had a lover, he could love other men. But I think too much, or so Ben always said. It made the advertising business hard on me and forced me into semi-retirement. And besides, I reasoned, if I had been remotely attractive to the boy, having a lover already wouldn't have stopped him.

Although the boy talked little about himself—in fact, talked very little, period—I had pieced together quite a life for him from the tidbits he had thrown out. I knew he'd been active since he was 13 and his last real job was stripping in a bar, which is where The Great Man met him. I never imagined that I would actually make it with him, but I did. It happened one full-moon night in early August. It was so warm that I went out to sit by the pool in the breeze for a few minutes before bedtime.

I heard footsteps, so soft I thought a thief was sneaking around my place. I tried not to sound alarmed. "Who's there?"

"John?" His voice was thin, startled.

"Hey."

He slipped from the darkness, wearing little white shorts, and sat down on the chaise beside me.

"Dickens died this morning. Or during the night, I guess."

I just looked at him.

"He was awfully old," he said.

"I know. I'm sorry."

"I just wanted you to know."

"Thank you."

"Well...it's late." He started to get up.

I thought about reaching for his hand. But I remembered if you have to think about touching someone, then it probably isn't the right thing to do. But I did manage to say, "Hold your horses."

"Yeah?" He stood.

"Look, tonight you shouldn't be alone." I stood.

"Well …."

I couldn't help myself, I wrapped my arms around his tiny waist. He didn't pull away, and I crushed his body to mine as we shared a long, slow, sloppy kiss.

Then he recoiled from my embrace. Concern that it would be over in a matter of minutes threatened to drown my desire. I didn't want our sex to be a series of fumbling grunts and embarrassed apologies after I sucked his cock in the moonlight.

"Uhh, I don't know about this," he pleaded.

"I'm sorry," I said.

Then he chuckled and began kissing me with a kind of passion I would never have guessed he possessed. His tongue surged deeply into my mouth. His teeth gently bit into my lower lip. With a wild and urgent need his hands gripped my body, molding me to him. My breath became harsh and rasping in my throat as he clutched my hips to his.

I led him up the stairs to the bedroom. Silently, he eased me to the edge of the bed, lightly forcing my shoulders down with just the merest touch of his fingertips, till I sat facing him.

Posing in front of me, he slowly removed his shorts. I tried to reach for his cock when it was revealed, but he spun away from my grasp. His eyes met mine with a silent message. But I was too intent on his body to continue looking into his eyes.

Moving towards me, he reached for my hand. I gave it to him, trance-like, totally mesmerized by his movements. Taking my hand, he put it on the shaft of his erection. I groaned with the excruciating excitement that raced through my body. I thought it was the most beautiful penis I had ever seen, absolutely perfect in every way. He was more than worthy of The Great Man's love—of any man's.

Suddenly he pulled away. I was dumbstruck and pained. He moved behind me and his hands glided over my shoulders and unbuttoned my shirt. He pressed his naked body against my back in a catlike motion, and his hot, probing tongue licked my neck and earlobes.

"Please," I said in a strangled voice, "I can't hold off much longer."

"Sssh," he whispered, "we have all night."

Finally he removed my shirt and reached down to my shorts and opened them. While exposing my erection, he kissed me with promises of ecstasy. His tongue rolled in and out of my mouth, while his teeth gently chewed and bit as he sucked my lower lip into his mouth. Again, I groaned and reached for him, again he resisted my grasp.

Sliding down along my legs he tugged my shorts off, purposely grazing my legs with his incredible pecs. He lightly stroked my cock.

"Please … I want you," I begged.

"Oh, it's so big and thick," he said in awe as he gripped the shaft tightly in his hand. "I'm going to love having you fuck me." He blew a stream of hot breath on the throbbing head.

Instead of feeling shy and insecure about my nudity, I felt bold and brazen. Thank goodness I had begun going to the gym when Ben moved out.

I gritted my teeth, but a small droplet of semen leaked out of my cock. It glistened in the light. The boy bent over and gently rubbed it off.

A deep low growl forced itself out of my mouth. "Fuck, I want you," I said in an agonized voice. "I've never wanted anyone the way I want you."

He delicately placed both his hands on my chest and pushed till I was lying on my back. Slithering, he crawled up the length of my body. My eyes were fastened on him as he positioned himself over me. I pointed to the nightstand.

He reached behind me and took a lubricated condom from the drawer.

"Please, hurry," I begged.

He quietly tore the package and carefully took the condom between his fingers. Then he slowly rolled it over my erection, his palm and fingers caressing the shaft. I groaned. The warmth of his hand and his skilled fingers sent a jolt of pleasure through my genitals.

Very gradually and deliberately, he straddled me. My cock slid into him. I was enveloped in heat and softness. He sat atop my hips, melding himself into me.

He straightened his back and locked his legs around me. Then he forced his inner muscles to tighten and contract on my throbbing erection.

"Yes!" I screamed loudly. My hands shot out and clutched his hips to mine. The tremors of my ejaculation jerked my body in a spasm of sublime release. My own buttocks tightened as I thrust deeply inside the boy, filling him. Within seconds I was completely spent. He lay next to me.

Coming down, I realized he hadn't climaxed, and I felt guilty. "I'm sorry," I said quietly. "I tried to make it last, but you had me so excited I couldn't control myself."

Gently stroking my cock, he removed the wrinkled condom. His lips caressed my shaft lovingly. I raised my head so I could watch as he slid the shaft in and out of his mouth, enjoying the sight and the sensation equally.

He got on all fours over me. Holding his lips around the base of my stiffening member, he began to stroke me. He synchronized the rhythm of his mouth and hands with the semi bump-and-grind dance he began performing with his ass, which I saw reflected in the mirrored closet. I could almost hear the music.

He cupped my balls, kneading them between his long, graceful fingers. My penis immediately responded and I yearned to enter him again, but he wouldn't remove his mouth, nipping, sucking, and tongue-whipping the head of my cock till I was once again in a frenzy of excitement.

"Please! I can't take it...!" I warned him. It seemed as if he was on fire, blazing, out of control. His hands cupped my ass, coaxing me deeper, slapping my gut against his face. I felt saliva dripping on my balls. I tried to slow him down; I brought my hands around his pretty neck. I felt his muscles flex and shift as he started to suck the very life out my prick. The intense pressure and release took me by surprise. I groaned and buckled as I erupted, spurting my juices in exuberance and sublime satisfaction.

He lay quietly next to me, then began running his hand along the curly black hairs on my chest, which were beaded with sweat droplets, catching the light like tiny prisms.

He jumped up and began to dance for me, his erection bobbing wildly. My eyes were riveted on the lovely cock as he caressed it, knowing that with each movement he was inviting my touch, my kisses.

Seductively, he ran his finger over one nipple and then the other, until they practically begged for suckling. Then he licked his own finger slowly, sucking it in his mouth as if it were my cock.

Watching me, smiling devilishly, he moved closer. I sank to my knees in front of him, buried my face in his crotch. As I sucked and kissed, he put his arms around my neck. He drew my face up and kissed me with a passion that almost singed my lips. He kept drawing me up, into his arms. Soon his prick connected with mine; our bellies crushed our cocks, trapping them. Then we started humping and I sank down, my tongue lapping his sweat. I backed off for a moment to look at it again, that magnificent boycock, jutting, bouncing, leaking precum. I began licking, greedy, knowing his proclivity for moving away. But he seemed to want it now, and simply thrust his hips forward, driving into me with an urgency that excited me further.

My tongue traced the pulsing veins of his cock, coaxing precum from the slit. It was as if I had never tasted a cock before—sweet and salty at the same time. His fine hairs caught in my teeth as I drove my lips all the way down to the pubic hairs. As I nipped at his throbbing tool, his breathing became ragged and it became even harder. Sweat dripped off of him as his cock swelled and the flood began. His body stiffened. He whimpered, soft, low. I jerked the erection from my mouth and squeezed it, watching the cum spurt from the head, coating my chest, my shoulders.

He stepped back slightly and smiled, his fingers rubbing the jism into my skin. Now I went briefly mad, lunging for him, taking the throbbing cock into my mouth once again, sucking it. In no time his cock head, swollen, was battering at my throat, his smooth thighs squeezing the breath out of me. His soft hands crushed my shoulders as I traced the contours of his cock with my tongue. His fingers curled urgently against my neck and he began another orgasm. My mouth filled and overflowed, yet he still kept on, until at last he was finished, telling me with a final thrust of his hips. I rose up and began to kiss his belly. I worked my way up his torso to his mouth and, slow and easy, we kissed.

I went to the bathroom and got a damp cloth and a towel. He was tugging on his shorts when I returned to the bedroom and I knelt down to wipe him clean, then tucked his cock and balls away, but not before giving them a farewell kiss. He ruffed my graying hair and chuckled.

I followed him down the stairs and out the back door. As he made his way across the yard, he called out something to me. I couldn't tell whether it was goodnight or goodbye.

The lights were on over there until two-thirty. Not just in the master bedroom but all through the house. By three I was feeling kind of panicky. I got up, went to the window in front and peered out. He had pulled his car out of the garage and turned on the floodlights. I stood at the window for a long time, watching him bring out suitcases, boxes, a pile of pictures in frames. Finally, he came out carrying nothing but a pair of sneakers. He tossed them in the passenger seat. Then he disappeared. The outdoor lights flicked off, then all the lights downstairs.

I got back into bed, propping my pillows so I could see the bedroom windows. When the last light was extinguished—the one in his bedroom—I scooted down into the bed, pulled up the sheet, and finally fell asleep.

It was still early yet when I woke up in the morning, but his car was already gone.

The Great Man came home tonight. I saw him pull into the driveway around supper time.

Now it's after one o'clock in the morning, and the bedroom light's still on over there. I can't go to sleep for thinking, thinking about the boy, wondering where he might have gone. I hope wherever he's headed, it's to a place where things belong to him.

And I'm thinking about Dickens, too, silly as it sounds. In some way the cat's death had something to do with everything that finally changed over there. Like all such relationships, eventually, it just snaps. Maybe I had a hand in that. I suddenly feel guilty about fucking the boy.

I wish I could get to sleep. But with that light burning over there, I can't help wondering what The Great Man is thinking. If he's got any idea what he's lost.

I'd have guessed it would make me glad, seeing him the one left high and dry. But no, now I almost wish I knew the poor man so I could stop by in the morning and make sure he's all right. Maybe put an arm around him. Or something.

LOVING UNCLE

Sometimes the familial love of a close relative can become a welcomed sexual relationship. Such was the case with Freddy's admiration for his gay Uncle Jasper—who also became his expert instructor in the ways of gay boys and men. Together they went places Auntie Mame and Patrick never thought about exploring. From the anthology In the Boy Zone. *—JB*

I'll always be grateful to Uncle Jasper for teaching me all the things he thought I needed to know about life, love and sex.

Especially sex.

After my grandmother's demise, Mother took a quasi-maternal stance insofar as her brother Jasper was concerned. His gentleness of nature and persistence of sunny common sense moderated some of her inordinate apprehensiveness. He charged her often with the sin of soppiness and he told me that while he was not soppy, he was nonetheless a romantic. Mother and he formed a curious contrast, so much, yet so little alike. Both were quick, bright, intensely loyal. They laughed at the same things. But while Mother placed a heavy emphasis on what she considered the real values—family and religion—Uncle Jasper seemed more concerned with what he called the "standards of the world."

When Father died, Jasper took over the running of the bank and he urged Mother to become more of a lady of the world. He saw to it that her small fortune was invested well so that she could afford to travel. Then the war came and she plunged into the cause, often leaving me alone with Jasper.

I was to discover Jasper had a fondness for fashionable clubs and parties, cultivating the beautiful people of his generation and, later, of younger generations, but his life was never touched by scandal. It seemed he picked his romantic opportunities carefully; only when he was absolutely sure of himself would he make a move. Near the end of his life he told me he had envisioned seducing me as something that might take months, perhaps years. Indeed, he thought he would never consummate it. It didn't seem to matter: "I enjoyed the fantasy for so long, it seemed almost a sacrilege when it finally happened."

My sexual education really began in the fall of 1944, when I was 15 and staying with Uncle Jasper. He had no live-in servants and over the years I had enjoyed tidying up the mansion for him, making meals and serving them to us. He took to calling me "Jeeves" and I loved it, not understanding why, just knowing that I was giving pleasure to an older man I adored. Little did I realize I was actually deeply involved in a

232

master/slave relationship that could, with the slightest push, have become kinky.

One night, as he indulged in a nightcap in the cool, comfortable, leathery library, with its reassuring rows of books, a bar table of glittering bottles and a crackling fire in the fireplace, I was perfectly at ease, but he had noticed I had been suffering from anxiety recently.

When he asked me about it, I explained it as 'girl trouble.' "Strange feelings about sex in general," I elaborated. "I really can't explain it."

"I've been troubled with those strange feelings for thirty years, Freddy!" And then, in a monotone, pausing from time to time to stare at me with what seemed to be almost defiance, he poured out his story. I assumed the role of a judge, listening to his pleading, his self-justification. He told me that his lifestyle was not a matter of choice; he had simply been unable to establish a satisfactory relationship with a woman. He did not accept his fate passively; rather, he went into psychoanalysis and eventually found a doctor who reassured rather than condemned him.

"I found sex with women boring. They wanted me to do all the work and they seemed as disinterested as I was. I began to realize I could enjoy things other people might not understand, that I could let myself enjoy my feelings toward all kinds of people without feeling guilty or out-of-step with society. I stopped going to the doctor because I knew I could make peace with myself and my condition. What did it matter, after all, whether I *ever* loved? Or didn't love, for that matter. I ceased comparing myself to other men. They didn't care what I was; they were perfectly willing to accept me for what I appeared to be. I could be a frustrated homosexual but they didn't care. I made a life of order, routine, work, theater, books, music." He paused, letting it sink in. "Does that shock you?"

"No. You explained to me what homosexuals were a long time ago. And I've studied the subject. You know how curious I am about life."

He smiled and clenched his fists, as if to stop his hands from touching what I somehow knew he desired. He had dropped so many clues over such a long time that I didn't need any explanations.

"But I do not consider myself a homosexual," I told him. "I guess you could say I'm pansexual, in that I enjoy all kinds of sex."

I crossed the room and sat on the arm of his chair—the big wingback where he always sat in the library. I told him I was sad that he had struggled with his moral dilemma for so long.

He thanked me and began stroking my thigh, then pinching my knee. There was no question of deception. He knew at all times I was aware of what he was up to; by then we had developed a kind of symbiosis. He hugged me, drawing me close. My hand fell to his groin and found a firmness there, a firmness that matched my own. He pulled himself up and allowed me to slide into the chair as he slid out. He began by removing my shoes and socks and fondling my bare feet, kissing them, sucking the toes. I unbuckled my trousers and started unbuttoning the fly, but his hand

233

moved to stop me. He wanted me to surrender to him completely. I smiled at him, gently and invitingly, and watched spellbound as he pulled my trousers from me, then kissed my feet again and ran his hands over the smoothness of the hairless skin of my legs and thighs. My feet pressed against his chest; his hands finally came to rest on my crotch. He reached into the opening of my boxers and brought my hard cock into view, followed by my balls. He played with my cock, sliding the foreskin back and forth over the head, driving me to heights of ecstasy I had not known before.

"You will be a great success in life," he said, admiring my erection as he removed my shorts. "Many times you will be judged by the size of this, and it will never fail you."

Then he pulled my legs up so that they rested on his shoulders, and he brought his lips to my cock, then his open mouth. He didn't cease sucking until I exploded as never before. He swallowed most of it and continued kissing me all over.

I wanted to go to bed with him, to lie with him and feel his whole body against mine, so he let me stay in his bedroom. As I watched him undress, it seemed that he was well aware of his power over me.

His body was thin. but strong, and as he got into bed with me I caressed it, caressed it everywhere. His cock grew when it met my hand and I stroked it. He knelt on the bed and I squirmed over to kiss it. It was smaller than mine but still quite sufficient. In my fervent desire to do what he had done, I began to suck it. I fear I scraped it with my teeth because he quickly took it in his hand and held it back from me. "I must teach you," he said softly.

"Yes," I murmured adoringly, "I want you to teach me everything."

"The first thing you must learn is how to tell when someone is ready, like now …." And he proceeded to stroke his cock several times, and came into his hand.

Later, I made myself small and childlike in his arms and fell asleep with him holding me.

Jasper had aroused a sexual fever in me so potent that I could never resist his touch. I was sure I could never control myself again. Often, as we sat on the couch together, reading my assignments, our hands wandered over each other's bodies. I responded madly to his teachings and wanted to practice my new techniques on him daily. He taught me to hold back my orgasm until both of us were ready, using slow, rhythmic motions, then quicker, then still quicker, as the temperature of the blood began to boil and the pleasure mounted. Often we would stay in the sixty-nine position, sucking competitively to see who could get the other hard again the quickest. Away from him, I would re-enact the scene in my mind, see his cock quivering as it erupted, and I began to learn the meaning of unfulfilled desire.

Mother became concerned over my protracted absences and confronted me with the reality of Jasper. She was quite unaware of the issue at hand. "I think it's time you knew about your Uncle Jasper," she said, in hushed tones. "He's odd. Not like other men." She explained that his wit and easy adaptability with people made up in good measure for any 'deficiency in moral character'—which is apparently what it was called in her day. "And I'm afraid you shouldn't be seeing so much of him," she concluded. "It's not healthy."

But I did not heed her warnings, and when I was not present at times she thought I should be, she forced me to endure long grillings; and while I would never compromise Jasper, she somehow knew exactly where I had been.

After the war ended, she told me she had decided to move to Florida. Ostensibly, she wanted to devote her energies to doing something with the thousands of acres of Florida land Father had left her, and she said it was the best thing for her health. But I knew it was *my* health, my mental health, that really concerned her.

My last two years of high school were wretched. I missed Uncle Jasper. All the teachers were women and the closest I got to male companionship was when I went to the beach.

In those days, there was a pavilion where people could change clothes for bathing, and I happened upon "Pass-a-Grille" quite by accident. There I saw men lurking about, making tentative eye contact. I soon came to look upon it as a place where I could relieve myself in more ways than one.

At first, I was shocked to see what went on there. It seemed sordid, dangerous and pathetic, and I felt an overwhelming sadness that I lived in a place and a time where men were forced to seek their pleasure in this clandestine way, skirting the authorities, courting danger and perhaps even death. I felt that the furtiveness of their sexual play was probably necessary because those men couldn't stand closeness; they didn't look into each other's eyes, preferring to bury themselves in each other's crotches, hiding their shame. Yet I felt compelled to return, intrigued by the strange, erotic darkness of these men.

Being just a teen, I was seldom approached directly—which was fine with me because I wanted to do the picking. Often the pickings were slim, but on some days the cubicles were filled with adventurers, and there was plenty to pick from. I learned shortly before sundown was the best time; most of the bathers would be gone and a few of us would linger.

Late one afternoon, there were seven of us in the place—all completely naked. Two were in cubicles and all you could see was their feet. Four of us stood at the urinals, and one acted as a lookout. A man moved next to me. He was old, very old. I put my hand down and felt his cock and he immediately started to play with mine. Another man, a younger one with glasses, moved closer and got behind me, running his hands over my ass.

When the old man dropped to his knees and began sucking me, the younger man began sliding his cock up and down the crack of my ass. I pushed him away and backed up against the urinal. With that, the older man shifted his body so he could continue sucking me, and the younger one dropped down and joined him.

A fourth man walked up to me with his hard cock resting in the palm of his hand, offering it to me. I grasped it eagerly and began playing with it. The man who was acting as a lookout kept puffing on a cigarette, turning back occasionally to watch the action in the dim light. The two men at my cock began sucking like maniacs, almost fighting over it. I came for them, shooting my cum on their faces and into their open mouths. I knew I could come again soon for some other man, or men, whose attentions I might desire.

The two men kneeling in front of me licked my cum off each other and focused their lust on the fourth man, whose cock I had been stroking. He put one hand on each man's head as one sucked his cock and the other licked his balls. I stepped away and the lookout came over to me, stroking his enormous hard cock. I knelt down and began sucking this challenging monster until he came very forcefully down my throat. As his cum was feeding my hunger, I felt at home among these men, at once hopeful and desperate.

I stood and pressed on the shoulders of the man I had just sucked off, until he knelt before me. I filled his mouth with cock and fucked it until I filled it with another orgasm.

A few weeks later, I met a young man there who was standing near the entrance. We nodded at each other and I asked him if he worked at the pavilion, in one of the shops.

"I don't work," he snarled.

"You don't? What do you do then?"

His face brightened. His teeth were irregular and one was chipped. "I have a good time."

"That's what I want to do. "

"Then come with me."

He was perhaps a couple of years older than I, had curly black hair, and his skin was sunburned. I followed him eagerly.

"I'm fed up with girls," I told him as we walked across the boulevard heading I knew not where. "I take 'em to dances and we go to the parking lot and they let me get my hand inside their panties but they won't let me take them off. They won't touch my cock, they just stare at like it was some kind of strange creature."

"And I'll bet it's a nice one."

I smiled. "You'll see."

He took me back to his tacky furnished room near the beach and began by peeling off my shirt. "Yeah, you're kinda cute," he told me, running his hands all over my hairless chest. "And you got a great tan. "

"I come here a lot."

"Me, I just moved here from Jersey." (He pronounced the word almost as if it were spelled 'Joisey.') He kissed my nipples. "Hmmm! Yeah, I guess I've found where to go." He dropped to his knees, undid my pants and shorts and pulled them down. "Oh, yeah," he smiled, "it's a nice one, all right."

As he slid back the foreskin and began sucking, I cringed; his ugly teeth were scraping painfully against the sensitive skin. "Hey, easy," I cried. He began licking rather than sucking and my cock grew to what seemed, even to me, an enormous degree. "God, I want that in me," he said finally, stroking my erection, now slick with his spit. He took some Vaseline from a jar on the bureau and coated my cock, then turned around and dropped his trunks, revealing a slim, hairy ass.

"Oh, no," I said emphatically. "I couldn't."

I tried to pull away but he held fast. "Yes, yes you can," he said, guiding my cock to his crack. He leaned over and brought his hands to his cheeks, spreading them, and shoved backward, forcing my hard cock deep into him.

"Oh God," he cried. "Oh, oh you're hurting me." But it was obvious that it was what he wanted. I began to fuck him in earnest. It was tight, incredibly tight and it felt incredibly *right*. For some reason, I wanted to hurt him, perhaps in retribution for the way his sucking had pained me, but there was more to it than that. The longer I fucked him, and the more violent I got, the more he loved it. He kept begging me to stop, that the pain was killing him, but he kept right on shoving his ass back to meet every violent thrust of my cock.

When he came, he told me not to stop and I kept on hurting him until, at last, I came also, gripping his shoulders tightly and jamming it into him as far as I possibly could. I left my prick in after I came, then started again. He shot another load while I continued my assault on his hole, and tears were streaming down his face when I finally came again.

"Where'd a little kid like you learn to screw like that?" he asked as we were dressing.

"Oh, along the way, I guess. Along the way." I was not about to tell him it had been my first time.

The summer I graduated, Mother let me return to Chicago, ostensibly to see Aunt Edna, my father's sister. By this time, I had dated girls and brought a few of them home to meet Mother, convincing her she had nothing to fear if I saw Jasper while I was there.

The day I arrived, I went to Aunt Edna's, but I didn't stay. I never warmed to her. She, as a former debutante, was restrained by the stifling inhibitions of her generation and by her own attraction to just the sort least likely to respond to sexual impulses. She had been briefly, unhappily engaged, and thereafter her favorite expression seemed to be, "All the evil in the world comes from man!" She could not imagine how Uncle Jasper could've happened to my mother's family and, beyond that, how I could have been so corrupted by him.

But there was no stopping me. I couldn't wait to tell my uncle about my adventures. He planned a little welcoming dinner at his house. His housekeeper had left the meal for us and we were alone. I regaled him with my indulgences at the beach and after dinner when we settled in the library with snifters of cognac, I confessed I'd fucked a man. "He was a beach bum," I told him. "He was coarse, just in from New Jersey, and talked like it."

"Did he do it to you, too?"

"Oh, no! I wanted to try it but I didn't want it to be him." I stood up and moved next to his chair, laying my hand on top of his. "Uncle, I wanted that to be with you. "

He turned away, sighing, "Oh, I couldn't do that."

But before the evening was over, my dear uncle came to realize that I had become an inveterate tease, each new man a challenge—and in sex, as in everything else, I was used to getting my own way.

I told him I thought I had to rush it or I'd never get through it. But my problem of receiving it was minor to Jasper's problem of giving it. It was the first time I realized the limitations of a man's erection. As much as he wanted to please me, he couldn't bring himself to it. We'd get it hard, aim it and it would wither.

It was then that I conceived the notion that there was safety in numbers. I calculated that if Jasper saw me about to lose my cherry to someone else, perhaps he would respond.

I went to the beach north of downtown where Jasper had told me boys hung out. There were several possibilities that bright, clear day, but none approaching the appeal of one slim fellow in his early twenties, with dark, greasy hair. He appeared to be one of those hustlers who had once been extraordinarily good-looking, and the tarnished glamour attracted me. I responded to the challenge of his seeming disinterest in me. He kept riding his bicycle back and forth on the walkway separating the parking lot from the beach until I finally stepped in front of his bike and made him stop. "Hey, I'm looking for work," he said, shaking his head, as if to explain himself to me.

"I'm looking to put you to work."

"Oh yeah? How much does it pay?"

"How much do you need?" In those days, two dollars bought a lot. Five bought the entire evening. I hailed a cab, stuffed his bike in the trunk, and took off for Jasper's house. The young man, who introduced himself as Jerry, was immediately taken with the place: big, dark, very old-fashioned and stuffy. Upon meeting my uncle, he quickly decided he had hit upon a lode beyond his wildest dreams. Jasper was less taken with him, even going so far as to berate me privately for bringing such riffraff to his house: "These boys will pick your pockets, beat you and leave you for dead in the gutter."

Although I was bluffing, I told him I knew what to do with such desperate characters. Jasper calmed down considerably when Jerry, sweaty from all that bicycling, wanted to take a bath. Even more of Jasper's reserve melted when he saw the young man, his weary face flushed from the bath and dressed only in a pair of tattered boxer shorts, return to the library, Jasper's sanctuary away from the eyes of the housekeeper, Mrs. Tyrell.

After appraising the sleek torso—replete with tattoos in the oddest places—Jasper reluctantly told me Jerry had to dress for dinner. I loaned him some nice clothing and we were served elegantly in the dining room, chatting as if we were old friends. The hustler ate as if he hadn't eaten in weeks; his appetite pleased Mrs. Tyrell, although his table manners left a great deal to be desired.

After dinner, we returned to the library. Jasper poured cognac, but I didn't want to waste any more time. Surprisingly, neither did Jerry. He slipped from his clothes almost immediately, sat on the divan and started to stroke his cock. During the long cab ride, I had managed to rub the hustler's crotch, bulging in tight, dirty white pants, to preview the quantity that awaited us. What was not revealed was the quality of it. On close inspection, I marveled that his circumcised cock was the most perfect one I had seen up to that time. The head was of average size and shape but the shaft thickened magnificently as it approached the base. To me, it appeared to be the perfect cock to be fucked by. In my mind, I had created a scenario with Jasper becoming so aroused he would go first, followed by Jerry. But Jasper was still reluctant. He sat stiffly in his chair and watched as I blew Jerry. So captivated was I by my find, I ignored my uncle for several minutes. But Jerry brought him into the action, exhorting him in a deep macho voice to join in, having me suck both at once.

When I had both of their cocks in my mouth, Jasper held the hustler around the waist and said: "Young Freddy's still a virgin. He has brought you here to help cure this condition."

Jerry laughed, saying I wouldn't be his first.

Jasper had explained it to me years before: "Your asshole has a sphincter muscle. It's like a fist, it clamps tight against all invaders but it is weak, it gets tired and relaxes. I'm told that's when you begin to enjoy the sensations."

"You've never done it?" I asked.

"No," he answered, "it's something an older man does to a young protégé. I've never allowed myself the luxury of a protégé."

When I got on my knees and Jerry mounted me from behind, a great, but soundless and invisible collapse of barriers began in my mind. As his cock slid in, it was as if he was massaging the muscles. He never pulled all the way out, just kept slowly fucking me, pushing all of his marvelous cock into my body. Soon he began in earnest, like a piston in an engine, harder, stronger, and urgently, as if roaring toward a destination. Jasper moved, positioning himself in front of me so that I could suck him while Jerry blasted his flesh into me.

After I came, I could take no more. Jerry was horny and wouldn't rest until he got off. He told Jasper to lie on the bed in my place. Jasper protested but he was not about to admit he, too, was a virgin. It seemed Jerry sensed that perhaps the old man had not enjoyed a plugging in some years so he took him gently. I watched in awe as my dear uncle began to feel the same sublime sensations I had felt. But he was to enjoy one I hadn't because, after several minutes of gentle probing, Jerry stepped up his assault and came inside my uncle. Jasper moaned so contentedly that I vowed I would feel that ecstasy myself before I took Jerry back to the shore.

Jasper permitted Jerry to stay with me in my room, and it was the first time I had slept with another man other than my uncle. It was a sleepless night. I kept waking and watching the stud, listening to his muffled snoring across from me in the huge bed in the guest room.

The next morning, after breakfast, we returned to the room and I told Jerry what I wanted. With an exchange of more cash, he was ready to fulfill my demands. Because my ass was still hurting from its initiation the night before, Jerry gently insinuated himself, bringing me to orgasm almost immediately. But I gripped the mattress and begged him to continue because I wanted to feel the warmth of his ejaculation inside of me. It didn't take long; he lunged into me with a ferocity that shocked me, finally gasping and pressing his body tight against me as he experienced an almost seismic orgasm. As the wetness filled me, he assumed a potent, thoroughly masculine dominance over me that fulfilled my most persistent fantasy.

I was able to see Jasper often during my two-month visit that summer, and it was as if the hustler had freed each of us to practice sex in every position we could think of. I felt I had finally emerged from the shadows. I considered myself a butterfly that had escaped its drab cocoon to become a more compact version of my adored uncle.

Truth be known, I would have sacrificed anything to be just like Uncle Jasper in every way. Following his lead, I went on to college and law school and then went into banking as he had. He wanted me to stay in Chicago and work for him. "Only a city has places where someone can hide," he said prophetically. "You'll not be able to lead a double life in St. Petersburg. "

While I had to admit I'd always been attracted to the ambiguity of the city (The Loop, for example, not being the heart of the city, simply a dead center, and surrounding it areas that were dissimilar yet still so very close to each other). I felt my place was with Mother, taking over the reins of the land development company Jasper had helped her found.

Over the years, I would visit Jasper, or he would visit us, but sex never occurred again between us. I reasoned that I had gotten too old for him. "What was, was," he was fond of saying.

"What it was, was simply wonderful," I countered.

And he would nod, and across his face would spread a smile, a knowing, kindly, loving-uncle kind of smile.

THE HOUSEBOY

One of the Lover Boys *in the anthology of the same name is Billy, who plays the title role in this story. Billy's services to Roger extend far beyond the traditional job description for his position—and Roger makes sure they extend to Jack as well.* —JB

"Roger says you have a big dick - "

There I was trying to catch some rays and Roger's new little houseboy was blocking my sun. "Yeah?" I grumbled, coming out of my lazy doze.

"Yeah. He said it's the biggest one he's ever had."

"Well, I don't know …."

"It doesn't look very big to me," he grinned, staring at the slight bulge in my Speedos.

"That's 'cause it's resting."

"Resting from what?"

"From the workout Roger didn't give it last night."

"I know. He wanted to, but I wouldn't let him bother you. Besides, I was horny."

"Thanks."

"But I'm always horny. You'd better get used to it."

As the head of my cock slid between Billy's lips, I reminded myself to talk to Roger about this.

I was fresh out of rehab. I was lucky I hadn't been sent to jail by the judge. At least no one in the other car was hurt. I had lost everything—my savings, my condo, my car, my job—and most of all, my pride. But Roger had come to my rescue. Now I was looking at Roger's houseboy and wondering how I was going to handle this. Was I to fuck the kid? Is that the way to pay back Roger's kindness for letting me crash there for a while?

But I realized, as Billy removed my Speedos and returned his lips to my cock, I was not going to have too much to say about it.

"Hmmm, yeah! This is the biggest one I've ever seen," Billy said, coming up for air.

"Thanks."

"No wonder Roger likes it so much."

"I didn't know he did."

I didn't know Roger well, really. He met me in a bar one night and I'd gone back to his place and fucked him. He called me up occasionally and we'd get together, but he was not someone I would call a real friend. Until now.

"God, this is fuckin' unbelievable!"

"No, you're the one that's unbelievable. I've been fucking you for an hour now and you still want more."

Billy was on top, bouncing up and down on my cock. "Yeah, this is awesome, man!"

It was true. An hour of steady in and out and around. He started by climbing over me and lowering himself over my dick. Then he was on his knees, then he was on his back, then he was standing up. Then he was over me again, impaling himself with it. He came twice, gobs of cum. God help me, but I was smitten with him.

That night, Roger came home around seven. I was sitting by the pool reading the latest issue of *The New Yorker* which had come in the mail.

Billy had smoked another joint and was fast asleep in his room.

"Well," Roger said, joining me poolside, a martini in his hand, "I guess we go out to dinner this evening."

"I can whip something up," I said, not raising my eyes from the magazine.

Roger chuckled. "I bet you've done your share of whipping it up today. Poor Billy's sound asleep."

I ignored him and turned the page.

"Well, was it good?" Roger said after a few moments of silence while he drank some of his martini.

"What?" I asked, still refusing to look at him.

"His blowjob?"

"I suppose."

"You *suppose*?" he chortled. "God, if there's one thing that kid can do it's give head!"

"If you say so."

"But I *wanted* you to like it. I wanted you to have fun. God knows you've been cooped up for too long. Did you get any while you were in that hospital?"

"Handjobs. No blowjobs."

"The nurses gave you handjobs?"

"Only one young guy. But he was gone the next day. Maybe they saw him. They never left you alone for long."

Now I looked at Roger. He was gazing out across the pool to the bay beyond. A sailboat was gliding along as the sun was setting. It was a beautiful moment. But Roger had to spoil it.

"Did you fuck him too?"

"Christ, Rog ..."

"You did, didn't you? I thought it might have taken a day or two but I should have known better. I bet he jumped up and down on it, didn't he? He couldn't leave it alone, could he?"

There was a sadness to his tone, bordering on anger, and it irked me. "Shit, Rog, what did you expect?"

"I don't know. I guess I was just wanted to be there when you did it. You didn't know that, did you?"

"What?"

"That I'd really rather watch."

"No."

"It's true. I love it." He shrugged.

"I'm sorry."

"So am I," he said with finality, rising from his chair and escaping into the house.

I sat dumbfounded, my eyes focused on the sailboat as it slowly, inexorably disappeared.

"This is Hawaii Gold," Billy said, his words shrouded in sudden mystery.

We were alone again, the room filled with an exotic fragrance of freshly mowed fields and plush tropical forests. He crumbled a bud of green-gold leaves between his fingers and packed the small pile into a silver pipe.

"I don't know . . ." I mumbled. "I'm just out of rehab, you know."

"C'mon, just one little puff." His voice was satin.

He lit the pipe and inhaled deeply. The smoke circled me as he exhaled, as though coaxing me to try. And why not, I mused.

I reached for the pipe. The silver bowl was heated, the scent rich. I took a deep breath, sucking in the harsh sweet taste. It burned as I sucked it into my lungs as if forcing each cell to expand into a dream.

"This shit's awesome." His words were thick honey. "I don't very often smoke shit that's this good, but this is a special occasion, wouldn't you say?"

I nodded. My head felt light, yet heavy all at once. A sudden heat sifted through my body and I leaned into the plushness of the couch. I felt hazy, warm and very, very good.

"What do you think?" He brushed his lips on my cheek.

"I think," I said, wondering if my words sounded as cumbersome to him as they did to me, "that I like very much that you're a houseboy."

We both broke into giggles. I couldn't remember feeling this relaxed in a long time.

"Yeah, I'm a houseboy all right." His voice was suddenly cocky.

"I like houseboys." Words were coming from grayness as I spoke.

He looked me straight in the eye. His mouth had curled into a devious smile. "You like cocksuckers, that's what you like. Little boys who like to suck big dicks."

"No, actually." I paused. The heaviness had seeped into my tongue, "I like houseboys." I smiled back with a look more devious than his. Mine was a slick smile, a sly smile, a come-on-and-suck-me smile.

I liked the way I felt all right. I was cheating on Roger. We were both cheating on Roger, but we had his permission.

Billy grabbed my hand and led me to their bedroom.

I watched dreamily as he slipped out of his Speedos. A subtle breeze of music drifted provocatively from the stereo. Stripping out of my own Speedos, I lay back on the bed.

The curtains were drawn and he joined me on the bed, lit the pipe. The hypnotic scent swirled like a genie's magic.

"Have another taste." He leaned toward me, his dark eyes glittering as though he was bewitched.

As I drew in the hot smoke, the genie pulled me through a thick fog. "Come on," he chanted like a captivating siren. "Let go, out-of-town. Let go."

He began sucking my cock, gushing over its size and heft, and over the beauty of my cock, my face, and my ass.

I felt his words, like soft caresses. Sweet words weaken me like bouquets of flowers and gift-wrapped perfume. I wondered if I *was* more than he had ever had?

He moved to the music. A slow beat, a steady beat, Depeche Mode sang desperate words about danger. And caught in the genie's steamy spell, I gave myself to him again.

His breathing was heavy as he stared intently at me; the air was thick with desire.

"I like your big dick," he purred. He stroked its length. He seemed surprised at how smooth it was.

He spread his legs as I rubbed the head of my cock against his throbbing wet butthole. It was nasty and I was hot. To the music, I swirled the lubed tip, to the music I rolled it.

"Jesus," he moaned as I entered him.

I leaned over farther, spread my legs wider. I wanted him to have everything I had to give. I wanted him never to forget the way my cock felt as it went into him.

As I pushed the tip farther in, I had visions of the countless men who had been here before me, including my pal, Roger.

"Yes, oh yes," he moaned.

I squatted, sliding my cock even deeper inside.

The high from the weed had intensified. I was dizzy, lost in a maze of shadows and dim lights. The music blended with his moans and groans of pleasure, which slurred into tiny heat waves on the pillows.

I was barely hard but he lunged against it, hungry to take in as much as he could.

I plucked his nipples, pinched them, then plunged my cock deeper.

He gasped. "Easy."

I backed off, let him recover, then plunged in again.

Suddenly, the door opened. Roger stood there, spellbound, the knob in his hand.

"I can explain," I muttered stupidly.

"Billy and I had made promises, had a certain trust..." Roger said, speaking in short, sporadic bursts.

I didn't know what to do. Billy was no help—he just lay there, his eyes closed. I started to pull out as I said, "Sometimes things happen—unforeseeable things—that no one can understand."

"I understand," Roger said, finally letting go of the door knob, entering the room. "Don't let me disturb you. Finish. Please, let me watch as you finish."

That totally unnerved me. I faked an orgasm for the first time in my life. But Billy made up for it—his orgasm was not only genuine, it was huge. I got the idea he liked having Roger watch while other guys made him happy.

Roger took us to Cafe Suzanne. Billy looked adorable in a nice pair of white linen trousers and a pink Polo shirt. He had just had his dirty blond hair cut short and was on his best behavior, idly toying with his shrimp cocktail while Roger discussed his heavy travel schedule for the next two weeks. He had inherited the family's electronics business when his father passed away, and for two weeks every month he made the rounds of all the company stores.

"I hate to leave you two alone for so long, but I'm sure you'll find plenty to do." He turned to Billy. "You haven't made much headway on cleaning the garage. Do you think you could have it done by the time I get back?"

Billy grinned and looked at me. "If Jack'll help me."

Roger looked at me. I nodded and smiled at Billy. Roger shook his head and called the waitress over. He ordered another martini. It was going to be a long night.

All things considered, Billy was a pretty decent housekeeper. He knew how to make simple meals, he kept the bathrooms clean, made the beds, dusted, and watered the plants.

But he was best at sex. His blowjobs were astonishing. As he performed, I would watch Billy's head bobbing between my legs and admired the sleek sheen of his newly-cut hair, the play of muscles in his arms at his every movement. During the two weeks Roger was away I studied every part of Billy so completely that I could create him in my imagination whenever I chose, and lately I chose to do so often. I had to fight not to laugh when Roger came home and Billy sat so compact and attentive at dinner, playing footsie with me. I made a game of observing his eyes until just the split second before they turned to me, and instantaneously shifting mine so that he could not catch me watching him.

That night, after he had taken care of Roger, I waited for the sound of his soft voice as he crawled into the bed next to me.

Now that Roger had returned, there were moments when I found approval of Billy in his gaze, times when some word of his sounded almost like a joke. The trip had apparently been successful; he was at peace. He was warmer, more solicitous of Billy's needs, more delighted by the food he brought. He was still full of advice for Billy, full of ideas of how Billy could please me, full of reminders that he was in complete agreement with whatever went on between us. But the peace was short-lived. Soon Roger became impossible again; no matter what Billy did, Roger would not look at him or give him any sign of approval or encouragement.

Nobody could have blamed Billy if he didn't please Roger—so many others had failed to in the past, and Roger was even harder to live with now that he ran the family business. I noticed that Billy began to keep his suitcase in plain view. He seemed to be expecting Roger to find fault with the strange frozen food he served, with the housekeeping he despised, with the positions Roger warned him were now off-limits in bed. He apparently wanted Roger to know he was prepared to leave at a moment's notice.

But no matter what the boy did or didn't do, Roger hung on as tightly to the fantasy of this one working out as he hung on to the money he wouldn't spend.

The thing was, the boy recognized the bossiness for what it was: the instruction booklet that up to then his life had been lacking. It was as if it were a relief to have so many decisions already made for him.

Even though the sex between Billy and me remained the high point of my days, I still had no clue as to his feelings toward me. Even when I was actually inside him, he seemed totally beyond my reach, a focus of mystery and impossible desire.

He seemed to act as if servicing me was part of what he was supposed to do around the house. When I would protest that he had already blown me twice on some given day, he would want to do it again, saying he was just doing his job. "I hate to do anything for free. Getting paid is another story. Besides, what else do I know how to do? Can you see me in a store? Selling suits?"

I tried to imagine him behind a counter, with an inviting smile on his face, but the image scrambled in my mind, like interference on the TV.

One night, Roger took me to Tampa. Billy didn't accompany us; he had apparently done something the night before which caused Roger to "ground" him, but I didn't dare ask what had happened. Sometimes Roger acted more like Billy's father than his lover. I thought it all terribly strange, but, of course, that's what I expected from Roger—the

247

unexpected. He was not quite a handsome man, very tightly wrapped unless he drank, very decisive but impersonal.

Tampa, too, was strange when we went there that night. It had changed so much in just a few months: there were no whores on the street. Sitting in a gay strip bar, waiting for the show to begin, I told Roger I was shocked to see there weren't even any whores in the bars.

"That's why I went to Fort Lauderdale," Roger said. "That's where I found Billy."

"Was he on the street?"

"In a manner of speaking. He was just walking along ...."

Just then, the dancers came on. They didn't dance so much as they mingled with the men sitting at the bar. An hour later, Roger announced he had made a little deal with two of the boys.

"Two?"

"One for you, one for me."

The more Roger drank, the more open he became—and the less he thought about Billy waiting at home.

When we got home, Billy wasn't there. He had left a note saying he had gone to see some "friends," and would return tomorrow.

Roger was visibly shaken. Apparently this had happened frequently before I joined the household. "Why does he do this?" Roger cried. As a way of dealing with this, and with every problem, Roger did what he always did: he fixed a drink.

There was a knock on the door and Roger admitted two young men, whom I recognized as dancers from the bar. He formally introduced me to Jeff and Brad. Roger fixed them drinks while I went to the bathroom, and toyed with the idea of locking myself in there.

Although Jeff was rather cute, in a blond, effeminate sort of way, Brad was hairy and dark, too tradey for my taste. I decided to try simply picking the one I wanted, and let Roger make do with the other.

One drink led to another, and before I knew it we were all very relaxed and talking as if we had known each other for some time. For some reason I was feeling uneasy about the situation and was worried about Billy's absence.

Roger began to talk about their performances at the club, how delighted he was with them and how he had often wanted to ask them home. He even told them that Billy was "dying to meet them" after Roger had told him about them. "Damn little shit!" Roger blurted.

Jeff stood up and said, "Well, Billy or no Billy, we'll perform for you right now." Brad tuned the radio to a different station and began to dance around. Jeff pulled me up to him, and we danced together while Brad danced all around us.

Roger sat on the couch, bemused as always, sipping his Drambuie. When Jeff was naked, his cute little cock wiggling, getting harder and harder, I lost it. I grabbed him, pulled his body close to me and kissed him. As I was kissing him, I felt Brad's hands on my body. He began working on my shirt buttons. Jeff dropped to his knees and opened my pants. "God," he moaned. In moments, he was sucking me to hardness while Brad was slipping off my shirt and kissing my shoulders.

I pushed Jeff onto the couch next to Roger, who had by now removed his clothes. Jeff spread his legs wide and I plunged my cock into him. I never thought I would enjoy having an audience, but Roger had changed all that. He began caressing my skin as I fucked Jeff. Brad stepped over and Roger reached for his cock and pulled it to his mouth. As he sucked Brad's cock, Roger reached down and started stroking himself.

The squishy sounds of sex filled the living room. Jeff played with my nipples as I slammed into him. Suddenly Roger rolled over and positioned himself on his hands and knees. After he had taken Brad's more-than-adequate erection inside him, he began to kiss me. I stopped moving for a moment, then began to move in rhythm with Brad's steady fucking of Roger. Soon Roger bucked, and Brad panted as he went over the edge.

After Brad pulled out, Roger wanted me to leave Jeff and fuck him. I refused, for the moment. "Not until this boy comes." Jeff's hands went to his cock and his explosion quickly followed. Satisfied, I lifted myself away and slid into Roger. Brad and Jeff disappeared for a moment but returned just in time to see Roger helpless in his orgasm. The two of them, mindful as to who would be tipping them, sat on either side of us and brought towels to Roger's belly. I gasped in pleasure as the two began caressing me, urging me on. As I continued to thrust into Roger, the two dancers got on their knees and dangled their pricks in his face. He went from one to the other, kissing, licking, sucking, until I finally came.

After the dancers left, richer by $200, we sat in the den and Roger had a nightcap—not that he needed one. Seeing Roger drinking so heavily had begun to get to me. I was not allowed to have a drop, and it seemed Roger was drinking my share. I nursed a Coke while he ranted on about how irresponsible Billy was.

"But he's just a kid," I argued.

"Exactly, and I think I've outgrown kids." He came over to me on the couch and dropped between my thighs. I knew what was coming.

"What do you want, Rog?"

"You. I really want you."

"You have me."

"No, I mean, forever. Right here, as my houseboy."

"I'm an art director, Rog, not a houseboy."

He ignored me and went about unzipping my trousers, pulling out my cock. I quickly became hard again while he sucked and nibbled on my balls. One thing I noticed about being clean and sober was I never had any trouble getting hard.

Because I didn't answer him one way or the other, Roger must have assumed I had agreed to become his new houseboy. When Billy finally arrived late the next afternoon, Roger was home. It was a Saturday and he only went to the office for half a day. Billy was stoned out of his mind and Roger was livid; he packed all of the boy's things in a suitcase and told him to get into the car. Roger was taking him wherever it was he had just come from.

Billy became hysterical and ran to me for comfort. I stood in the hall holding him against my chest, saying nothing. Roger pulled him away from me and shoved him down the hall, out to the garage. I followed them and stood in the garage as they backed down the drive. I surmised that Roger had played this scene perhaps a dozen times. I had seen some of the houseboys over the years and never thought much of them. But Billy had been different.

"You know, Jack," Roger said as he lay by my side that night after sex, "I think you'll make the best houseboy I've ever had."

I shifted my position and propped on an elbow. In the moonlight Roger's face was seamless and young. I thought I might be able to handle this, at least for awhile. I had a grudging respect for Roger: he was onto everybody, especially himself.

He ran his fingers along my cheek. "You're a good-looking man, Jack," he said.

I caught his hand and brought it to my mouth, let it feel my smile.

"Enough talk," I said, forcing his head down between my legs.

As he began sucking my cock, I realized just how much I missed Billy's incredible talent. I decided then and there that once I got my own place again, I'd have to look for Billy. I'd be so busy art-directing, I'd need a houseboy, myself. I mean, it was worth a try.

PROLOGUE TO "THE SEX TRADE"

A brief recounting of an episode in the sex life of a world-famous escort/hustler/pornstar, which serves as the introduction to a series of stories about his exploits in the anthology Heat Wave, *and provides one clue as to what might drive a highly sexed young man to become a professional. "The Sex Trade" is not specified by John Patrick as a* roman à clef, *but it almost surely is. —JB*

The apartment is dark, but there is enough moonlight coming through the windows that the lights don't need to be on. I like fucking in the dark. As a kid, I discovered that illusion is more exciting than reality, more compelling. I feel stronger when I am in darkness, sensing my surroundings rather than seeing them. One of the reasons I love sex so much is that senses more imaginative than sight—touch, smell, taste—are the most important.

At an early age it became second nature to me to exercise my sexual power; why was I given it if not to use it? But no matter how calculating I can be, some amount of pleasure is always there for me to enjoy, some touch, some taste, some smell. People ask me how I can go to bed with certain men they might find repulsive. I always respond that I believe what my father always said: "You can find some good in everyone"—one of many stupid platitudes my father lived by. Granted, my father was a jerk and a total drunken loser, still, he was right about that—but only when it came to sex. I also learned very early in life that when it came to the rest, it was bullshit—there are plenty of people you can't find anything good about. The majority of people, in fact.

Besides, I love being wanted, being desired. I love the buzz of the unknown, of potential, of possibility. Being wanted so badly that the john can taste me before he's tasted me. I love the feeling of new hands on me, not knowing how they'll move, where they'll go. The smell of a new client, familiar but unique. The slick slide of sweaty flesh. And the sounds a john makes when he's about to come, sounds that come from so deep down they seem to be coming from his very depths. I want him to talk to me.

When I first meet a man, I don't care what he has to say. I just want to see his mouth move. I want to see how he punctuates his conversation with his hands. I want to see his hands moving. I want him to have to lean in close to share some confidence with me. Then, when we are comfortable with each other, which might take a moment or a couple of hours, I want to hear what matters to him, what he wants to tell to me before we fuck.

But tonight I skip all the preliminaries with my late-night caller, Gardner. He is not even a paying client; he is my "mentor," my acting coach. He strides into the little apartment I share with another "mentor," a businessman named Jackson. He kisses me hello, and soon he's sitting on the worn leather couch; his shoes are comfortably off, and I am wearing only my skimpiest briefs. I start to go down on him. When he is fully hard, I take him by the hand, pull him up from the couch. "C'mon, stud, I'm horny."

He smiles at the erection tenting my briefs. "You're always horny," he says. In moments, he has stripped and is sitting on the bed, taking off his socks—the last remaining article of clothing.

I strip off my briefs, dab a bit of K-Y on my hole and bend over, shoving my ass in his face. I am ready for him, but I don't really want to rush him; I let him go at his own slow, agonizing pace.

His finger rubs ever so lightly around my butthole, lubing itself as it does, causing my ass lips to pucker and then open up. Slowly he inserts his finger into my hungry hole, which I know is by now pouting eagerly, although it is so dark Gardner can't see it. He moans when two fingers pop in easily. "You've been fucked today?" he asks, knowing the answer full well.

"At noon. That guy from Japan."

"Can't get enough?"

"No...." I moan, because he shoves in three fingers, then four.

He groans a low animal growl, and I know he is enjoying my talk about my earlier sex as much as I am. He finger-fucks me, slowly at first, then faster. I go on about how the Japanese visitor does it, doggie at first, then ending up missionary, so he can watch me come. Gardner loves it when I describe how my clients come inside my ass. He begins twisting his finger inside me and I can't hold back any longer; the heat is too much.

My skin is now copper-colored from my days in the sun at Fire Island so I present a stark contrast to the pasty white of Gardner's skin as I move onto the bed. The dark and the light. The top and the bottom. The young and the older. I love contrasts.

"Put it in!" I cry out. I get on all fours with my ass in the air, and he gets behind me. I can feel his heavy breath on my asshole as his tongue darts in for a moment or two. He squeezes my cheeks, rubs my crack. Finally his big cock is poised at the entrance. I push back, and he thrusts into me. He goes in all the way to the base without effort; I have been well-prepared.

I don't tell him that the Japanese client paid to do it twice today. After the first fuck, he took me to lunch, and then he took me back to his hotel room for another round. I earned an extra hundred. Hearing that might be too much for even Gardner. I only tell my men what I want them to know, what I think they need to know, whatever I know will turn them on.

252

Sometimes, after I have been fucked out, Gardner will just face-fuck me with his thick, smooth cock, his hands holding firmly to my head as he thrusts deeper and deeper into my throat. But this is what I prefer, having him bang away for at least half an hour, and coming deep inside me. This is my idea of heaven.

Now he climaxes, and I am groaning loudly as the power of his punishment of my aching asshole pushes me over the edge. I jerk myself to orgasm, my piddling load barely marking the sheet beneath me. It feels so good, to be consumed with pleasure and pain in equal measure—too good, really.

"When's your lover due?" I ask after I return from washing myself off. He's sitting up in bed, smoking a cigarette. He never showers after sex. He says he likes having the smell of me on him as long as possible.

"Tomorrow night, I think."

"I'm jealous of him, you know."

"Why?"

"How can I not be?"

"Don't," he says, cutting me off. "Don't get started...."

"I'm not starting...."

"I love Chad, you know, it's just that...." he hesitates.

"Just that what?"

"Well, he's ... well, he's cold."

"Cold?"

"Look, that's all I can say. Cold."

"But...."

"I love him very much. I wish I didn't."

"I hope he never finds out about us, then."

"Oh, he won't."

The apartment is hot and still. We sleep naked on top of the sheets and I fall asleep in the strong arms of someone else's lover.

JUST A FARMBOY AT HEART

Paul came to the club fresh from the farm, just to see his sex god Sonny perform. He would never have guessed that the friendship Peter extended while he was waiting would lead to the kind of performance he wound up personally enjoying with Sonny—and with a few others as well! *This story originally appeared in* Huge 2. *—JB*

It was a weeknight, and Club-X was busy, but not packed. A new show was starting, and while the regulars anticipated a good time, they were not particularly excited about seeing Sonny Masters exposing himself yet one more time. But Paul was a true fan, and he had taken a couple of days' vacation and driven four hours just to see the star of the video *Big Shooters* for the first time in person.

Truly a farmboy at heart, young Paul seemed ill at ease amid all the black vinyl bar stools, mirrored walls, and colored lights. Whether a man simply glanced at him or took a good long look he felt he was being appraised for his sexual value and, somehow, coming up short.

Paul settled down near the stage—and it was a real stage, though quite small. Two rum 'n' Cokes later, the lights on the stage came up, and the audience yawned imperceptibly as the first dancer, Tony Tanner, was announced, but once they saw him strip off his bib overalls, revealing a black G-string, they clapped wildly. The stage lights went out, and only shadowy movement could be seen. Music drifted through the room—atonal and electronic. Gradually, bit by bit, the lights came back up, soft rose lighting flattering to Tony, whose body Paul thought was incredibly voluptuous.

Tony moved with graceful slowness, and then he turned, pulling the back of his Speedos down to reveal the ass that Paul had loved in the video *Frat House Brats*. The crowd collectively gasped as Tony reached behind to spread his cheeks. His beautiful ass seemed to shimmer in the rosy light.

Then Tony began wiggling his bottom, and Paul was astonished. It wasn't like anything he had ever seen, wasn't like what he had imagined a strip show might be—it was far more. Seeing this incredibly hot man naked and writhing so erotically wasn't an experience Paul could readily catalog; it exceeded all expectations and left breathless anticipation in their place. He wanted to poke his fingers into that narrow place between the cheeks of Tony's glorious ass, wanted to wiggle them in there and hear the stud gasp in pleasure.

Tony moved lazily, rotating in place until the front of his skimpy shorts revealed the obvious bulge of a major hard-on. He delighted in occasionally pulling down the front of his Speedos to flash his cock to the audience for a quick glimpse, and even inviting one man to come on stage and play with it. The man declined, even though his tablemates pushed him toward the stage.

Paul caught his breath, his eyes tracing the upward thrust of Tony's penis when it was exposed, and he felt himself grow faint. His hands clamped the edge of the table, holding himself back as he poised on the edge of his chair, wanting to leap onto the stage and consummate the promise of the tease. The act became even more lewd as Tony stepped up the tempo and pulled the waistband of his Speedos down to nestle below his balls, exposing his throbbing cock for all to admire at length. Then he pranced through the audience, allowing men to grope him freely.

One man knelt between Tony's legs, bowing before the stud puppy's body and jutting cock as though he were a shrine, and commenced to lick his bobbing shaft. Shudders ran through Paul's body. He pressed his hands to his crotch, longing to join the amorous worship, but he didn't dare. Suddenly, Tony folded his legs around the head of his worshiper, squeezing fiercely, almost suffocating the man. Tony held him there until the man's body twitched spasmodically, then went slack. Tony opened his legs then, and the limp body fell to the floor. Everybody laughed, and Tony scurried back up on the stage.

Tony did a few more minutes of prancing, not really dancing, and walked off stage. The lights dimmed. In the moment of stunned silence the man at the table next to Paul looked at him and said, "Yeah, I'd love to plug that ass! What he needs is a *real* man!"

Paul looked at the stranger as if he were an alien from outer space, then looked back toward the stage. He remained sitting there, dazed by what he had just seen. The man at the next table introduced himself as Peter Prescott, and playfully let his hand rest on Paul's inner thigh. Leaning close to Paul to be heard over the noise, Peter shouted in his ear, "So tell me, pretty boy, didn't that turn you on even a little bit?"

Paul nodded silently. He rather enjoyed the attention but really wished Peter would just leave him alone so he could enjoy the show. Paul had driven all this way to see Sonny, not be picked up by just *somebody....* *nobody, anybody.*

Peter moved his hand upward and groped Paul's erection. He whistled slowly, and said, "Hmmm, you should be dancing."

"Hardly...."

"You're really cute."

Paul ignored him, or at least tried to. "I'm just waiting to see Sonny."

"Ha! You wanna *meet* Sonny?" Peter asked.

"Yeah, that's what I'm hoping for."

"Okay," Peter said, removing his hand and grabbing Paul's arm. Peter led a reluctant Paul backstage and shoved him down a dark corridor. A bouncer met them, taller than Paul by a head, and heavier by about fifty pounds of solid muscle. He blocked the way, smiling unpleasantly. "Nobody backstage."

Peter moved from behind Paul and opened his wallet. "How much for a private show for my friend here?"

The bouncer looked contemptuously down on Paul. "Well, I dunno. I'll see if Tony's taking any clients tonight."

"No, no, not Tony, *Sonny*," Peter insisted, but he was saying it to the bouncer's back.

In moments, the bouncer had returned, and he led the pair deeper into the dark labyrinth, to a green door. He knocked, and the door opened. Tony looked less impressive up close. Peter grudgingly removed a hundred dollar bill from his wallet, and tendered it to Tony. "My pal here and I enjoyed your performance. We'd like a private show," he said. "He really wants Sonny.""

Tony took the hundred, looked the twosome up and down. Paul waited, then it occurred to him that the stud was not accepting the initial offer. Reluctantly Paul pulled two fifties from his wallet, all he had left, to add to the money Peter had given Tony.

Tony frowned and glared at Peter, who looked anxiously back at him. Then Peter withdrew another hundred. "That's our last offer."

Tony turned to consider Paul. "So, what are you into, cutie? Sonny'll want to know."

Paul felt faint. "Oh, anything," he stuttered, "anything at all."

Tony chuckled and turned back to Peter. "Okay, but...."

"But what?"

"But when Sonny fucks this cutie's ass, I get to watch."

Peter grinned broadly. "Hey, no problem! We'll both watch."

Suddenly, as if on cue, a toilet flushed, a door opened, and Sonny appeared.

"This kid wants to meet you," Tony said, pointing to Paul.

"Yeah, okay," Sonny said, "but I gotta go on first. You guys wait here."

Paul's jaw had dropped. Sonny was his dream stud and in person, this close, he was even more masculine, more brawny than he appeared in his videos.

Smirking, Sonny brushed past them and headed for the stage. Tony made the bills disappear—a neat trick considering he was clad only in a G-string. He led Peter and Paul into the room, which was narrow but very deep, with exposed rafters, and mirrors along one wall. Two other dancers were preparing to go on after Sonny. Tony told Paul they were the regulars who put on a sex show on stage as the "closer" for the night. Under any other circumstances, Paul would have gone with either one of them, but the deal had been made for him to be with his sex god tonight. Tony led them through the dressing room to another, darker area, which had been made more private by hanging sheets on a clothesline to mask it off. The entire area reeked of sweat and cum.

Paul was told to sit on the edge of a filthy, narrow bed at the far end of the dark alcove. Tony stood before him, drawing Paul's head into his abundant crotch. "Why don't you start on this, kid," Tony said.

Paul kissed Tony's cock through the fabric of his g-string for a few moments until Tony finally began to lower it. Paul sighed when he at last had the bare cock right in his face. It was long and thin, nicely cut. Paul kissed it, and fondled the hairy balls hanging below it as it began to harden and grow in size.

Peter sat down next to Paul. He was grinning, occasionally taking a lick at various parts of Tony as they came within reach of his mouth.

Before he would allow Paul to begin sucking the cock, Tony ordered him to get naked. Paul obeyed, shedding his T-shirt, jeans, and shoes more rapidly than he ever had in the past.

"Lie down on your back," Tony demanded, slapping Paul's ass and gesturing toward the rumpled bed.

Paul did as he was told. Tony climbed over his chest, and the stripper's cock, which had gone soft again, dangled in Paul's face. Paul's hands found the edges of the bed and clutched them as Tony slid his penis into his gaping mouth.

"So, you like my cock?" the voluptuous dancer asked.

"Oh, yes," Paul sighed, kissing the head of it.

"Suck it. Get it hard again."

Paul obeyed, and the cock quickly became hard once more.

"Oh!" Paul cried as he suddenly felt a warm tongue lapping at his own cock.

"So, you like that?" Tony asked as Peter lapped at Paul's cock, each flick of the tongue sending little jolts of electricity up Paul's spine.

"Yes! Oh, ye-sss...." Paul moaned.

Tony spit on his fingers and slid one into Paul's ass while Peter sucked on Paul's cock. "And that?"

"Oh, yes," Paul sighed.

"Here, I want you to see yourself havin' a good time."

Paul was woozy as Tony helped him to sit up and confront his image in the long mirror next to the bed. His skin gleamed with sweat as he sucked Tony, while Tony went back to finger-fucking him and Peter licked his erection.

Plaintive whimpers escaped Paul's lips as he gripped the warm, swollen flesh of Tony's prick with them. His squirming fired Tony's lust, and his cock slammed into Paul's throat, deeply, viciously.

The sight of this incredible face-fucking energized Peter, who began jacking off wildly.

Tony emitted a long, desperate groan, quivering while his fingers worked deep into Paul's ass, giving him a sweet promise of things to come. He told Paul he was preparing him for Sonny's cock, and a fucking he would never forget. "I can still remember every big load Sonny's has blown up my ass," he leered.

Then Paul heard a door opening, followed by heavy footsteps. Tony and Peter stood, leaving Paul vulnerable, alone on the bed. "I warmed him up for you, Sonny," Tony said, as the brawny porn star brushed aside the makeshift curtain and stepped into view, wearing only a tiny g-string, which did more to reveal, than conceal, what it was intended to hide.

Sonny approached, saying nothing. He wiped the sweat off his magnificent body with a dingy towel, which he then tossed into a corner. He yanked off the useless G-string and brought his enormous prick to full erection with only a few strokes. He fell eagerly to his knees between Paul's thighs. He shoved Paul's loose, unresisting legs apart, then dropped over his body, squirming his hips as Paul wriggled under him. They moved together in sensual delight, each luxuriating in the sheer pleasure of their first body-to-body contact, Sonny's enormous prick pressed tightly against Paul's undulating belly. Paul's arms rose in a welcoming embrace, while Sonny slipped his feverish hands up under his behind to grip his sweaty bottom. Paul felt Sonny's fingers following his rounded asscheeks, digging into the soft, malleable flesh. A barely suppressed groan escaped Paul's lips as Sonny leaned back, pulled the foreskin tight down his cock and motioned to Tony to apply a condom to it. Tony fetched a rubber from his gym bag and slowly slid it onto Sonny's gargantuan boner, obviously loving the feel of the swollen, steely shaft, and leering at it as hungrily as Paul and Peter were doing.

Then Sonny leaned over Paul and, for a moment, the huge head of his immense cock fought a fierce struggle with Paul's sphincter muscle, which at last suddenly gave way under the determined assault, and the bulbous head began to inch into the tight hole. Sonny smiled at the feeling of the tight ass ring gripping his hard, fat cock. He gave Paul a few seconds to adjust to the sensation, then he lunged his hips and shoved his prick up Paul's ass with one powerful thrust, which elicited a long, lingering groan from the impaled Paul—in which ecstasy clearly overrode pain.

Paul clung to the stud as Sonny lifted his loins and began fucking his intensely hot, slick ass savagely. Except for Paul's occasional, appreciative grunts and whimpers, and the heavy breathing of the two witnesses to Sonny's brutal fucking, the scene was played in eerie silence.

Then, for the first time, Sonny began to speak to Paul, softly, soothingly, crooning to him as though to a child. In velvet tones he assured him that he had a most admirable ass, an altogether perfect ass, one just made for fucking. He whispered that he loved Paul's warmth and tightness, the satiny feel of his body, smooth against his surging prick as he drew back, then plunged into him again and again with growing passion, flexing his hips, sending Paul into spasms of pleasure that had him whimpering uncontrollably and gibbering in mindless lust. Paul hung on to Sonny, clutching him tighter, wrapping his slim legs around the famous stud's thrusting hips, seeking to draw him in even deeper, and pounding his back with his flailing heels.

With one fantastic stab of pleasure, Paul's eyes snapped open and he became aware of Peter and Tony watching intently. Tony's hand was slowly massaging his thin prick, which was only half-hard. He was pleasuring himself as, through half-lidded eyes, he watched Sonny fucking the farmboy on the bed before him. The look on his face made it clear he wished he were in Paul's place at that moment—he had often known at first hand the incomparable joy Paul was experiencing just then.

Peter was also jacking off, and his prick was rock-hard. He was moaning and quivering as excited tingles coursed through his body, but he held off, delaying his orgasm so he could continue to enjoy, to the maximum, the best sex-show he had ever seen.

Tony watched enthralled as Sonny and Paul moved together in a strong, easy rhythm that rolled along till they were thrashing about in erotic frenzy and Paul felt the powerful surge of an onrushing orgasm. Paul held that ecstatic moment for an incredibly long time, all things considered, but the thrill finally climaxed with a long, delicious sigh of satisfaction as cum shot from his cock to coat Sonny's chest and his own hard belly. He had been fucked by the man of his dreams.

Sonny pulled out of Paul and told Tony he wanted to fuck him now. He sat on the edge of the bed as Tony backed up to him and eased his asshole down onto Sonny's cock. Straining upward Sonny plunged into Tony savagely. Then Tony took over, bouncing up and down on the massive prick, completely burying it in his clenching ass, wriggling and bouncing until he could stand it no more. Then a pounding, surging climax sent ropes of hot, white cum shooting from his prick, erupting in spasms of pure rapture. The bed shook so hard that the reverberations could be felt on the floor. Paul, stuck in the corner, was transfixed by the fucking, knowing full well the thrill that Tony had just experienced.

Sonny had prolonged his pleasure all day and now he felt the urgency of his own climax. He knew it had to be soon. He held Tony's ass pressed to the base of his cock and started to hump upward into it, luxuriating in its satisfying, familiar warmth. Tony clamped Sonny's cock, desperately clinging to it as the stud drew it back, ready for the final thrusts. Tony tightened his buttocks against the upsurge from Sonny's loins, determined to hold on to the cock as long as possible. Sonny continued, and Tony's moans punctuated each driving stab of the monster cock invading him.

Soon Tony felt Sonny tense under him. His ass gripped the cock with an incredible tightness, like a small fist. His head rose up and arched back farther and farther. Sonny grabbed Tony by the hair and held his head up as a low moan escaped from his mouth and his taut body was wracked with massive convulsions.

Peter had held on, teetering on the edge for some time, but now he, too, felt the inexorable pressure, and knew his time had come. His cock exploded, sending jets of cum onto the floor at Paul and Peter's feet.

"Talk about big shooters," Paul said in awe.

"Good night," Paul said, as he and Peter were led back to the green door only a few minutes later. Tony smiled, but did not respond, then closed the door behind them with a resounding thud.

Paul stood there in the gloomy corridor, Peter at his side, his eyes adjusting to the dark.

"Boy, you must be hungry," Peter said.

"'Yeah, I'm famished."

"Let me buy you something."

They took Paul's car, and, as they drove into the night, Peter reached for Paul's crotch.

Paul pushed his hand away. "Hey, I'm sore. Sore all over."

"I can imagine."

"I hope you didn't mind."

"Mind?"

"I mean, you paid more than I did and I got...well, everything, it seemed."

"No, no. It was a fabulous show, really."

Paul couldn't stop thinking about what had just happened. He was happy to have shared it with Peter. "It was wonderful, and the biggest surprise of my life. I'd always dreamed of being with Sonny. But I would probably never have paid for it, you know?"

"It was wonderful for me too."

"Really?"

"Yes. I love to watch."

Paul looked at Peter for the first time, really looked at him. He wasn't an ugly man; in fact, he was rather pleasant-looking, and he had pushed Paul to new heights of sexual awareness. Paul reached over and took Peter's hand, placed it back on his crotch. "I'm gettin' hard again just thinking about it."

"Turn here," Peter said.

"Here?"

"Yeah, we'll eat here. Is that all right?"

"Sure."

After steakburgers and Cokes at the Wayside Inn, Peter invited Paul back to his house. Paul accepted; he had planned on renting a room for the night, but he had spent all his money. He could have just driven home, but he feared falling asleep at the wheel. Besides, it had begun to snow, a spring snow of large, wet flakes.

Peter brewed Paul some chamomile tea with a touch of comfrey in it. Paul could smell it steeping from where the cup sat on the white Formica counter of Peter's spotless kitchen. The sensation of having had Sonny Masters fuck him continued to strobe through him. He felt sexy because of it, and his cock throbbed and grew hard again with just the thought.

Peter came around the counter and sat next to Paul. He noticed Paul's crotch. He stroked the bulge. "What'll you let me do?"

"Anything." Paul said, then sipped his tea.

"But you must be really sore. I mean, Sonny Master's ....?"

"Oh, I feel better now."

Peter smiled and knelt between Paul's thighs. Instinctively, Paul pushed himself back a few inches.

There was power in the way Peter yanked down Paul's pants and shorts and attacked his crotch, a fierceness, a hunger that stunned the farmboy. Paul held still, caught his breath, and spread his legs wide for Peter. Peter had Paul's cock in his hand, nibbling at the balls while he stroked it to full hardness. Paul felt the sensations building, moment by moment.

Paul had never in his life known such sensations as he had already known on this night, and he felt a flutter in his stomach. But as Peter pressed him to his back on the bed and began sucking, a sense of shame overcame Paul. He was not yet fully accepting of his sexuality, usually just deferring consideration of what he was. And now he was, in a sense, giving Peter what he wanted in return for the money and the experience Peter had provided for him that night, which had made the thrill-of-a-lifetime fuck with Sonny possible. He felt that he was basically being bought and paid for. Still, Peter was an expert cocksucker, and Paul decided his goal should be to enjoy it and make it through to the end.

Peter just kept sucking and sucking. Paul was amazed at the older man's delight in fellatio—he was simply insatiable. Paul's cock was on fire, Peter's hands were grabbing at his ass, and Paul let himself go, his whole body rigid, but resisting nothing, his fingers clutching at Peter's head. He thought about Sonny, over him, assaulting his ass, and in his mind he was observing what had happened with him when Sonny fucked him, as if it were happening to someone else, like he was watching some Sonny Masters fuck movie in slow motion—but this time he *knew,* rather than imagined (as he usually did) how the fortunate bottom felt when Sonny's monster cock drove in and out of him. He knew that from then on, every time he saw Sonny's cock in a movie, his ass would tingle with the sense-memory of it filling him.

As Peter's hands found their way to Paul's nipples, Paul held them there while his hips bucked hard, pulling Peter forward and rubbing his cock against Peter's belly. Paul rolled them both over, so that Peter now lay on his back and Paul moved his body up so that his cock slid into Peter's welcoming mouth. He fucked the hungry orifice, while Peter sucked hard, until his cum filled Peter's mouth. After a few minutes of savoring what Paul had given him, Peter swallowed it.

As the orgasm subsided and his fingers could move again, Paul shifted his weight to let Peter get up, but Peter stayed, flicking Paul's softening cock with his tongue while he jacked himself off. They sat there a moment, taking deep breaths, until Paul sat up slowly, his face impassive, and drew a shaky breath. Peter shifted, composed himself, and even began to smile. He wiped cum from his lips and grinned at Paul. "Thank you," he said.

Paul wasn't sure if "You're welcome" was the right thing to say at that juncture, not when it was he who should be thanking Peter—for everything. Instead, he looked down at Peter and smiled. "I didn't expect all this to happen."

"Of course not," Peter said, a wistful sound in his voice.

"You have a power, you know."

Peter shook his head. "No. That is, I don't know. I love to suck dick …."

"No, it's not just that. You're really good at it, sure, but there's more to it than that. It's your way of …uh …*arranging* things."

Peter smiled; the kid appreciated him. So few boys did.

"God," Paul sighed, "tonight you've taken me to places I've only thought about going to."

Peter nodded, and returned to Paul's prick, sucking it with even greater pleasure now after Paul had acknowledged his ability.

Paul gasped when Peter deep-throated his prick. "I never knew I needed it this much," he said—and he realized it was true. Peter's fingers began to play inside Paul's asshole, teasing him.

As his prick began to harden once again, Paul knew it was going to be a long night.

By morning, five inches of snow covered everything and Paul was glad he hadn't tried to drive home. He stretched, remembering that Peter had told him he was going to fix breakfast. He could smell bacon frying. He pulled a blanket around himself and stepped over to the window to look at the new snowfall. It hurt to walk, probably from Sonny's fuck and then— once Peter got him into bed—from Peter's fuck. Paul could hardly have refused Peter. Besides, it had proven to be an excellent fuck—passionate, yet surprisingly tender. Peter's cock, being beer-can thick, had truly filled him and thrilled him..

Outside Peter's bedroom window, icicles hung from the eaves, and, all things considered, Paul was glad he had stayed the night. In the golden light of morning, the icicles sparkled like the finest, most delicate, most fragile crystal. A cold wind gusted. The crystal broke, fell, and was lost in the whiteness.

IN THE ARMS OF A STRANGER

He loves Jeff, and he relishes his lovemaking, but he cannot avoid an occasional lapse from fidelity to him—perhaps because he enjoys the special fucking he gets from Jeff afterward, the stern way his lover has of reproving him for yielding to temptation. From Fresh 'n' Frisky.*—JB*

I am quiet and still on the bed. Naked now, I luxuriate in the smell of my body, in the smell in my skin and my freshly washed hair, and the heat that remains from our fucking. I turn my head to the pillow and smell Jeff, his musk cologne, his sweat. I bring the pillow close, hold it as I held him a few minutes ago, before he said he had to go.

Now I'm alone in our bed and I think that every small sound is his key in the lock, and my body readies itself for him. I roll over and shift my hips slightly. My heart beats faster and faster, and if he were to walk in he'd see my ass in the air, waiting for him again. But he's gone. And I have no idea when he's coming back.

I reach down and find the beer bottle he left. I sip from it, my hand sliding around the cool neck of it, and think how it reminds me of his cock. God, what a cock! I love Jeff's cock. His big, thick, uncut cock. I drop the bottle on the floor and stroke myself remembering how good he felt deep inside me. I fall asleep before I come.

When the night is finally over, I make my way through the empty apartment to brew some coffee, then I take another shower.

I dress myself carefully, keeping in mind what he would like to see me in if we were to run into each other. Keeping in mind that he likes me in jeans—the tighter the better—and a white, long-sleeve shirt. The mirror suggests that I've become hollow, gaunt, unsteady. Because of him. Of his promises, all unfulfilled. I know now he will never divorce his wife. Bastard.

I move quickly to the door, before the fear can work on me to hold me home. My keys are in my pocket, my sunglasses shielding me from the light. A few steps to the red convertible, the one he bought me on our first anniversary, and I am safe again, ready to cruise, blocking out his last words. Maybe finding a moment's peace in the arms of a stranger.

I'm late for work, but Stanley doesn't seem to notice; he's involved with Mrs. Fitch (I call her Mrs. Bitch, and Stanley grimaces). I sit at my desk and begin trying to make sense of the accounts. Stanley has been writing checks again without me, I realize, and the business may well be overdrawn. Bastard will blame me.

Stanley finishes with Mrs. Fitch, promising he'll find her just the right *objets d'art* for her beach house, and turns his attention to me. "I'm glad to see you finally showed up. I've got a luncheon date." Just like that. That's Stanley. No "Good morning," no nothing. After a quick visit to the john to make sure his toupee is on straight, he's out the door. I take a deep breath and grab the phone. If I can keep a few of those checks from bouncing, I may keep my job.

I take my lunch at my desk. No customers have come in since Mrs. Fitch, and I've had a chance to keep the wolf from Stanley's door once more. Then the doorbell buzzes. I consider just letting whoever it is go away, but we need the money so I go to the door.

What greets me is the closest thing to Jeff I've seen in months: Tall, dark, handsome, and dressed impeccably. He asks about our recently acquired sculptures by the New York artist Lynda Benglis, who caused a sensation in the early seventies with an advertisement in *ArtForum* magazine depicting herself naked, straddling an enormous dildo.

The man, who introduces himself as Spence, says he now finds the sculptures extremely ugly and wonders whatever happened to the dildo. He is obviously a connoisseur, either of art or of dildoes, but it doesn't matter much because I think he's going to leave. But then he decides to look around a bit; I say, "Take your time," and go back to my desk.

After fifteen minutes he finds me, wonders if I've had lunch. I say I have, and he says that's too bad because he'd like to treat me since I have been so very helpful. I chuckle because I haven't done anything but ignore him, but maybe that's what he's into. I look up into his brown eyes. Sometimes you can see it in the eyes of a stranger: You can see a need, a longing. Spence's eyes are sad and lonely. I know that I—only I—could fulfill his wants. All too often a man will enter the gallery, look around, and leave with his urges unspent, his longings unfulfilled, never knowing that I held the key, that I was the answer to all his wildest fantasies. I vow not to let that happen this time. I bat my long eyelashes at him and tell him I am free for dinner. He smiles. "Okay. I'm staying at the Radisson. Room 1030. Ring me when you get to the lobby and I'll come down."

I show him to the door. "Till six then?"

"Yes," I say, shaking his hand. I have trouble concentrating on the accounts. Stanley never returns, which I half expected. I lock up and aim my little red car in the direction of the Radisson.

"Oh," Spence says. I have surprised him by coming directly to his room. A mistake—maybe. But he lets me into the room. He seems flustered. I fear I may have erred, been far too bold for him, but such thoughts are quickly dispelled when he offers me a drink.

We chat about art, the store, Stanley. "You and Stanley ...?" he asks, pouring himself another drink.

"Oh, no," I answer. "If you could see Stanley...."

He sits on the arm of my chair, offers to freshen my drink. I tell him I'm fine for now and set my drink down on the table next to me. I lean back in the chair. "Yes, I'm just fine," I say, wanting him to kiss me, waiting for him to kiss me. Bizarre. Dangerous to have those feelings for a total stranger. But we aren't to remain strangers for long.

"I have the strangest desire," he says, looking me up and down.

"Oh?"

"I think I want to kiss you."

"Then do," I say, reaching up and putting my hands around his neck.

It is a long, passionate kiss. When he finally pulls away, I say, "You're very good." This, of course, leads to his wanting to show me just *how* good he is.

As he explores my body I remember how it can be with a stranger: so new, so exciting. Still, the image of the one time Jeff caught me with someone else, and the price I had to pay, fills my mind. I remember I said nothing. Not "I'm sorry," since he would have detected the lie in my voice and be ready with his classic answer: "You're not sorry now. But you will be." Not "I love you," since he already knew that. And, anyway, Jeff and I don't love each other like that, not in the classic sense. Yet, his jealousy is more intense than any husband's, so intense I cannot stand it sometimes.

That night, after he caught me, I bowed my head, waiting. He pushed me back onto the bed with the simple, brute force of his power. "Little sex machine," he said, a whisper-hiss, prodding me. "Just out for a trick? A good ride? A game?" His words were switchblade sharp and they cut me; he made me tremble. "Why do you do it? Why do you cheat on me, you … sex machine?" Again and again he screamed at me, and I could hear the taunting in his voice. He accused me of being a bottomless pit, a fuck-toy for some stranger. He yelled that I had been searching the streets for love, using impersonal sex when I could not find it. I didn't bother telling him that it served just as well—at least for a moment or two.

Now, here I am again, with a stranger sucking on my cock. He has made it hard, so hard I fear I will explode before he even gets his clothes off. Two strangers alone in a hotel room with no ties to each other, no claims on each other. Just want. Just need.

I watch as he undoes the buttons of his shirt and reveals his hairy chest. In a second, he has his fly unbuttoned, his trousers down and off, and kicked into a heap on the floor. All I want in the world is to erase the hurt that seems to linger in his eyes. Someone else left that look there, and I feel it is my job to nullify it. His cock is not as big as Jeff's, and it is cut. It is a nice cock, and he is gentle as he uses it.

The sheets on the hotel bed are powder-blue and they crinkle like tissue paper when he lowers me to them. The pillows are thin, so he uses two under my fine-boned hips to raise them high enough. I meet his cock as he pushes forward. He plunges it inside me. He begins a heated thrusting that reminds me of Jeff. He loves fucking me; I can taste it in his kisses, can smell it in the perfumed air that surrounds us both. "My sex machine," Jeff always says while he's fucking me, but he's the sex machine, not me. I just lie back and take it. Yes, there's no fuck like one from a real sex machine, and Spence is one too. I must attract them.

Suddenly, Spence pulls his cock out, teases my asslips, and just the feel of it as he gently presses it forward makes me moan and sigh, my eyelashes fluttering against my flushed cheeks. He works me hard then, suddenly rises up to watch me, needing to see the change in my face as he thrusts inside me, deep inside me. He raises himself to his knees, giving me the full length of his cock all at once. Oh, Spence is good. I love the pounding motions, the deeper thrusts. I bring my fingers into the action, to feel his cock sliding back and forth.

Now Spence is banging away. He wants to hear me moan, wants to hear me beg for mercy, but I will not give in. I grip the mattress tighter, drawing the muscles of my back into a taut line, offering myself to him. And he comes. I feel the trembling vibrations work through his body and into mine. He moans, his actions slow, ever slower, then they cease. I move away for only a second; he rolls onto his back and I take my spot above him. As I do, I see that the look in his eyes, that haunted look, has changed to one of relief. His lips open and close, wordlessly, begging me to come. But he is not like Jeff, he does not get hard again, still I move over the cock as I jerk myself until I come, come all over his hairy chest. He watches me coming, but he doesn't say anything.

Now, I can't help it; I remember what Jeff said after he found me with the other stranger, the kid I picked up. In a voice that betrayed both his displeasure and his disappointment, he had asked, "You need this, don't you?" even though he knew the answer. He knew it all by that time—the tiresome routine, the boring answers. He made love to me and made me come, but he teased me, tested me, made me wait for my orgasm. "You need me to make you come. That's what I do best, make you come."

"Yes, yes," I cry—and I realize it is Spence inside me, not Jeff. He is stroking my cock, squeezing out the last drops of cum. "Oh, yes," I cry. It was a great orgasm, leaving me breathless, but still hungry. If this were Jeff he would be hard again, fucking me again....

I lie atop Spence. In his eyes there is enough heat to burn me forever, yet in his heart I sense there is enough darkness to make me afraid of him.

My earlier transgression ended a bit differently. I had cruised the kid I spotted walking along the boulevard, and it hadn't taken long before we were back at his place. His parents were out of town, and we went directly to his room.

Oh, how the boy liked to touch my cock, to stroke it, to pull on it while I kissed him! And then, while I fucked him, how he sighed and moaned and gave me what I needed from him. In our lovemaking he conceded all of the power to me. Jeff couldn't possibly have had any idea how lovingly I kissed that boy I had picked up, how I cradled his sweet face in my

266

hands while I made him come, how I licked and lapped at his mouth until it was bruised from my kisses.

Spence's fuck was hardly loving. The pain was wondrous, all-consuming, much like Jeff's fucking. At this point in my life I have given up denying how much I love it that way, given up wishing that I did not need it the way I do. Because I do need it. In fact, I think, I deserve it. I deserved this moment with Spence, this moment in the arms of a stranger. Spence has made my fantasies real again in the twisting and turning of a night no longer lonely.

At home, hours later, I listen for the sound of Jeff's key in the lock while I undress. I keep one ear always ready to hear it, hoping against hope. There have been no messages and he, obviously, has not been here looking for me.

Naked in bed, I imagine him sliding his cock into me, driving his body hard against mine. A low moan escapes my lips, then a sigh, a silent mouthing of his name with my head thrown back as I imagine him coming inside me. I jack off to this vision. My finger explores my ass, but another man's cum covers it.

I fall asleep, but soon I am disturbed by the ringing of the phone. Jeff's normally lazy drawl is dangerously menacing. It's got an edge to it that lets me know just how pissed he is: "I'll be over in twenty minutes. You be ready for me, you slut. You be ready. I want you to show me what a good boy you can be."

"Yes...." I start to say more, but he's severed the connection, cut me off. With my hand still holding the phone, I replay the conversation in my mind. A bad boy first, then a good boy. His words echo hollowly as I hang up the receiver. I turn to stare at my reflection in the mirror over the antique hallway table, stare at the image of an unfaithful lover. But we are both sinners. Jeff should be home with his wife, not fucking me, but he can't help it. And I can't help wanting him.

Twenty minutes. Twenty minutes to transform myself into a good boy. An impossible goal, so why even try? In the bedroom, I lose myself for a long moment in the late afternoon sunlight that filters through my ricepaper blinds. The light makes shifting designs on the walls, hazy shadows that are somehow comforting. I pull the cord to raise the blinds an inch or two. I squint, staring harder, working to break through the fog that clouds my vision, trying to picture myself through Jeff's eyes—confessing my transgressions to a lover who is my Master, who owns my heart, who holds my soul. Who fills the hole inside me—both figuratively and literally.

I step back and look at myself in the mirror. I keep my hair straight and golden brown, cut short, the way Jeff likes it. My eyes are green—bottle green when I'm serious, darker emerald when I'm afraid. Now they look as dark as I've ever seen them. Am I afraid of Jeff? Yes. He'll want to know where I was last night. Of course he will assume I was unfaithful. He knows everything.

I hear the key in the lock, hear him walking towards the bedroom. No greeting, except, "Little whore." He uses both hands on my shoulders to push me down on my knees in front of him. I look up and gaze into his big brown eyes. I have noticed many times how dark his eyes are when he's angry, but this afternoon they seem darker still, coal-black, hollow, deep—glossy, like marbles. I bow my head to my chest, waiting. He pushes his crotch against my forehead. "Just slumming, was that it?"

"No," I murmur. "I was just flirting."

He takes my head in both hands and pushes my mouth toward the bulge. A shudder, a twinge, then I'm fine again. I peel back his pants to reveal his erection bulging in his briefs. I suck it through the fabric but I need to have more. I need to feel his skin growing flushed beneath the steady strokes, the silky caress of my hands.

In a rush, it comes, that yearning, that uncontrollable desire to have him in my mouth again. He is digging his hands into my hair, and his cock is soon excited by the force of my desire.

"Flirting, my ass," he says, scornfully.

"Oh, please, I couldn't help it," I whisper. "Couldn't have stopped if I'd tried."

"Did you fuck him like you did that boy before?"

"No."

He is silent at this. I can almost hear the images being processed. But as I deep throat him, he sighs, "Ohhhhh." Half-moan, half-breath, and I can feel his heart start to race. He lifts me to a standing position and then up into his arms, then carries me to the bed. "You like to watch," he says, a statement, not a question.

"Oh, yes," I sigh. If I don't watch, then it's not real. I gaze into the mirror and see him preparing my ass. He sticks his fingers in, as though he is trying to see if the stranger left his calling card. He swallows hard. He's having a difficult time with this. No matter how many times we have been here, it doesn't seem to get any easier for him. But this is especially hard because I have admitted—sort of—that this time I bottomed for the stranger.

Another swallow before he is able to speak. "You really need the pain this morning, kid," he says to me, not without compassion.

"I didn't mean for it to happen...."

He's not listening to me, though; he's consumed by the task before him: getting his big cock all the way inside me. But I will not be still; I have to tell him. I have to confess my sins. He knows that I will continue tormenting him, torturing him. "I didn't mean for it to happen," I continue. "He was from out of town. He came into the gallery and...." My voice finally becomes a choked sob.

"Did he hurt you?"

"No," I say, swallowing hard. "He was smaller than you. Ordinary. An ordinary stranger."

"It was my fault. I shouldn't have argued with you."

We go back and forth like this, taking the blame, sharing it. This isn't a game. This isn't about power or control. This is about giving someone what they need and taking what you need, and together, somehow, making it all right. Because somehow it's possible, despite everything that's wrong and dirty, somehow you can make it all right. And, thinking this, I see my face in the mirror across the room. My eyes are sad, but the need is almost erased.

Breathing heavily now, he turns to look into the mirror himself and sees me watching him while he fucks me. I begin moving sensually beneath him now, well caught up in my own rising passion. My lithe, supple body squirms excitedly, ass tingling with delight, as I urge him on in husky whispers. I arch my body, push my ass up to meet his thrusts when he drives into me, seeking even more of the magnificent shaft that fills me so completely. I feel him fucking with renewed fury, sending me over the edge. My orgasm is overwhelming, unstoppable. A spasm of pure pleasure tears through me and, a few seconds later, his own powerful orgasm shakes him in a sudden violent tremor. "Oh shit," he gasps, "I love you so much."

I lie sprawled out in front of him as he slams his erection into me one last time. Then his cock slips from my ass. He goes to the bathroom. Before long, the throbbing in my ass begins to subside. He comes back into the room, toweling off his prick. He pulls me up and rolls me over. Then he kisses me. He is laying claim to me. If it weren't morning, he would have me suck his cock until it hardened again and he would stick it in again. But he must go.

I want to keep him here forever, but I cannot. It is enough to know that's what Jeff really wants as well, But it cannot be. I close my eyes and listen to his footfalls disappearing down the hall, out the door. Once more I am reminded, "Things happen for a reason."

SEX ON A SUMMER'S NIGHT

The affair with the young hustler he picked up at the bar was always too one-sided to become a full-blown love affair. Just as it 'takes two to tango,' both participants in a relationship need to have similar goals as well as similar appetites for the dance of love to flourish. A bittersweet tale from the anthology Boys of the Night. *—JB*

Florida is not at its best in the summer. With each day a carbon copy of the last, temperatures hovering in the 90s, it's too uncomfortable to leave the house during the day and claustrophobia sets in. One lives for the nights.

On a steamy night in '84, I was at the Carousel Club where, amid chaos and ugliness, there always seemed to be a modicum of beauty. I was following my usual practice of taking in the entirety of it and, within that, disregarding the things that disgusted me, concentrating on the things that seemed to grow more lovely with each drink.

Suddenly, at the opposite end of the bar, I saw a new face, a fine face, one that inspired me to approach and take a closer look. I stood behind him and drank in the sight of the young, lean, beautifully tanned torso and, when he turned to see who was staring at him, the sly smile. He wore no shirt and I admired the highly developed pectorals. The jeans were filthy and showed no basket, but his face was divine, his dishwater-blond hair falling over it because of an unflattering cut. Considering the total look of him, I knew that with a bit of scrubbing, a bit of polish, this could be a diamond.

He was paying unusual attention to the balding, 50-ish man sitting at the bar to his left. I observed the interplay for a while until finally the man got up to go to the john. My desire for the boy was so great that I threw caution completely to the winds and approached him. "Whatever he's paying, I'll double it."

The boy blinked, shook his head incredulously, then smiled. "Okay." Saying nothing more, he reached up and yanked his T-shirt from a rafter above the bar and began moving towards the exit.

As we approached my Mercedes roadster, he chuckled, "Oh, yeah."

"I like it," I said, unlocking my door and hitting the button to open his. As he slid into the leather bucket seat, he asked, "Where do you live?"

"At the beach," I replied.

"All right!" he said emphatically, then introduced himself as Tracy.

During the 45-minute ride to the beach, he laid his history on me: he was from Texas, had only been in town a short time, had a job at Intertel fixing phone lines, and his car had broken down so he had no way to get to work. I vowed if I had anything to do with it, he wouldn't have to return to that job.

After a drink at my bar, we retreated to the bedroom and I went to relieve myself. When I returned to the bedroom, he was sitting on the edge of the bed, nude. He wrapped his arms around my torso and hugged me, then proceeded to devour my cock. In my heightened state of sexual hunger, I came very quickly, but not without appreciating the quality of his efforts. He seemed to have no desire for me to reciprocate so I joined him under the covers and he fell asleep in my arms.

The next morning, Tracy repeated the process, this time jacking off to climax as he sucked. At the height of our passion, I asked him to stay a few days. This involved picking up his things, which were—to use his phrase—"stored" at a man's apartment in Tampa, where he had been living. He told me he'd lied about the car—he didn't own one—and had lost his job at Intertel. He reminded me of Jean Genet's line, "For a time I lived by theft, but prostitution was better suited to my indolence."

Later that day, we went to the man's apartment in Tampa and I witnessed my new lover's ability to open a door by sliding a credit card between the lock and the jamb. I knew then my property would never be safe with him around. Still, he was quite methodical about taking only those things that he said were his, and leaving a note for the man. On the way home, we stopped at a department store and I bought him a few new items of wardrobe, then got his hair cut and highlighted. That night, dressed for dinner, he was absolutely stunning. We celebrated our mutual good fortune with a bottle of champagne.

When we returned home, he hurriedly undressed me and began blowing me. When I was hard, he undressed himself, lay face down on the bed and moved his hips seductively, offering up the prize he had not shared with me to that point. I kissed the ass cheeks, then invaded the space between them, first with my tongue, then with fingers coated with lube. Before long, I was charging my swollen flesh deep into his anus and he was bucking to meet every stroke. I wanted it to continue long into the evening but I came quickly, so excited at finding such a perfect sexual match. He rolled over and I crushed him with my spent body. He kissed me lasciviously on the face and lips, and before we drifted off to sleep, he thanked me for "everything."

The next night, after a late supper, we lay beside each other on the chaise on the deck, a salty Gulf breeze blowing. I entered him gently and soon his cum was gleaming in the moonlight, splattered against his thigh. Palm-tree shadows skittering across my tanned skin, he let me finish inside of him and I went crazy as I did so. Later, he said he wanted to watch a movie on TV so I went to bed. I switched off the light and the moon was like a lamp outside, illuminating the ripples of the Gulf. I closed my eyes and fell asleep at once, like the falling of a shutter in a camera as it ends a time exposure. I slept peacefully and, if I dreamt, I didn't remember it the next morning.

Around noon, Tracy got up and, as he was coming down the stairs, still nude, I sat at the table eating a Swiss cheese sandwich on pale crusty bread, slathered with mayo. I felt like Isak Dinesen, who was said to have eaten only white food.

The beautiful blond boy dropped to the cushion of one of the bar stools, just staring at me, a look in his eyes that was at once hopeful and desperate. I smiled, almost as if saying to myself: *Take it easy. This too shall pass.* But I knew it wouldn't pass quickly, not this time. It had been two days of bliss. The monotony, the ennui of the summer, had been erased in a single, decisive stroke. I knew what I was doing.

As he approached me, I held out my arms. He kissed me as he lowered himself into my lap. In a matter of moments, he was on his knees between my legs, fellating me with an eagerness that shocked me. I closed my eyes, sighed deeply and prayed that this one would not pass quickly from my life.

In order to keep Tracy, I knew I had to invent something for him to do. He was enamored of my computer so I had him take over the fulfillment operations of the real estate magazine I published. Like everything else he took up, he became immediately proficient at coding the subscriptions and processing the labels.

A routine developed. In the morning, he would work at the computer, then take my second car, a Corvette, to the bank and post office. Our lunch consisted of wine, sandwiches and sex, usually only him blowing me. But sometimes he would treat me to a full-blown fuck, depending on his whim. Then he would run on the beach and go swimming in the Gulf while I worked.

Dinner was usually a fancy affair at a fine restaurant. I loved to watch him eat: his appetite was enormous. Afterward, we'd bar-hop, see a movie, go shopping, or just go home to make love.

The affection seemed to flow naturally from him. He could never ride with me without holding my hand.

And I could never stop spending money on him. Evening always ended with his repayment of my favors and expenditures on his account, in the form of sex, usually with him on his stomach, moaning in ecstasy with my every thrust as I fucked him to orgasm. After I drifted off in a satisfied slumber, he would lie on the floor at the foot of our bed and jack off to pictures in *Penthouse*. At first I was shocked when he told me about that, but then I decided if that was what made him happy, so be it.

As summer turned into fall, we flew off to Key West for Fantasy Fest, to California for Thanksgiving, and New York for Christmas shopping. It seemed I had found the tonic for my boredom in the person of a loving 20-year-old.

One day in early March I was on my way to a meeting when the car phone rang. "Please come," Tracy cried. He had been to the bank and on the way home he had run a light and had an accident.

When I arrived at the intersection where the accident occurred, I found the Corvette was totaled but he was not harmed. "It's a miracle," I said when we were in my car following the tow-truck.

He was numb. His pride was hurt, he felt he had hurt me. "I'm so sorry," he kept saying over and over.

"But you're all right, that's what matters."

"But the car ...."

"Really, you've done me a favor. I couldn't afford it anyway. Now the lease is paid off."

But our routine was broken. Tracy lost his driver's license for six months, and he was deeply depressed. He moped around the condo for days. And our regular, wonderfully satisfying sex life suffered a serious slump.

One day, I returned from the bank to find him gone. Minutes dragged into hours. Finally he showed up, stoned out of his mind. He sat at the bar while I fixed drinks. Before I had a chance to vent my frustration with him, he fell backward, his head narrowly missing a glass-topped table. I put him to bed.

The next morning, he was still passed out when there was a knock on the door. It was Brett, a former prostitute with whom I had maintained a monthly assignation.

Brett was always short of money and I was always eager to help him out. But I had begged off every call he had made to me since Tracy moved in. Now, however, my anger with Tracy was such that I wanted to attack someone, something, and the short, dark-haired bottom boy Brett provided the perfect outlet. But before I let things go too far, I wanted to show off my prize. We went quietly to the bedroom and I opened the door. Seeing Tracy was still out cold, I let Brett have a peek. When we returned to the living room, he said, "God, he's gorgeous. You'll have to have me over some time for a three-way."

"Tracy's not that kind. Strange as it may sound, he's very jealous of me."

Brett groped me. "Yeah, I know why."

We went into the garage and I locked the door behind us. As I leaned back on the hood of the Mercedes and began massaging my hard-on, Brett dropped his shorts and backed over me. His hand steadying my erection, he lowered himself onto it, then pushed.

"God," he sighed, "I'd love to watch this big fuckin' dick going into Tracy."

"Maybe someday, but I doubt it."

"Oh, god, I love it," he moaned as he jacked off while he bounced up and down in my lap. We came simultaneously, but I was still in the mood to vent my frustration. I turned him around and made him lie across the hood while I resumed my assault on his ass. I fucked him until he was fully hard again, and I continued to hammer him while I reached beneath and masturbated him. After he blew his cum on the hood of my car, I showed no mercy in my final thrusts, filling his ass with another load. For the first time this experienced prostitute admitted he would come over for this even if I never paid him.

Later that afternoon, Tracy finally awakened. Part of me wanted to listen to him, the other part couldn't welcome the hassle. He had become expendable, and he sensed that immediately.

Eager to make amends, he wanted sex. As I sat on the edge of the bed he caressed my arm, my thigh. As always, I bloomed under his magic touch and, as he eagerly took my cock in his mouth, I knew I was beginning to think too much.

He lay face down across my knees and I played for a time with his incredible bubble butt. I stroked it, pinched it all over, rubbed my hands up and down the division, then pulled the cheeks apart. I put my lips there and slathered the area with my saliva. He was always clean; I never feared touching, kissing, or licking any part of him. I reached under him and played with his erection as I worked my tongue into him. When he was close to coming, I worked two of my fingers in. After he came, I rolled him over. Kneeling in his cum on the bedsheet, I mounted him and slid into his ass. Holding his cum-covered cock tightly, I made love to him in earnest; heaving his bottom up to meet my plunges, he came again, this time more intensely than I had ever remembered, completely covering my fist with his hot, white offering. I followed suit, coming inside his hungry ass—amazingly enough, since I had blown two loads inside Brett only a short while before. After giving a final wriggle of my cock inside him, we lay in each other's arms, breathing heavily. I decided I wanted to try to work things out with Tracy—sex with him was too good to abandon.

But, as the days went by, his afternoon disappearances grew more frequent and prolonged. Occasionally he would return home after running on the beach and mention he'd met a girl and they had talked, but I reacted so negatively to such information that he stopped providing it. When he didn't show up until after dinner, I would be furious with him and we would fight, only to make up and have sex.

But I realized he had begun to feel trapped. I could sense he was psyching himself up to enjoy our sex, pretending that it mattered. Early on in our relationship he had maintained he was basically straight. Although he clearly loved to suck dick and take one up his ass, he showed a peculiar lack of interest in passive sucking or active fucking. Those things, he led me to believe, he did with girls.

I began to sense he was beginning to think that just having a place to stay was a sorry excuse for his sticking around. It had become a difficult, complex relationship of dependence and attachment, such as often arises between victim and victimizer, abuser and abused. We each had our own idiosyncratic moral vision and our affair became a thing of knots and complications, often sending me into despair—but somehow it never seemed to be truly hopeless.

Each argument seemed to be a revisiting of the pleasant past upon the often appalling present. Finally, I suggested we both seek psychiatric help. Tracy agreed but went only the first time, to take the test and to have a short chat with the doctor. He told me that he would not go back. To him, it was so much "idiosyncratic bullshit." *("Bullshit" was a word I had frequently heard him utter, but his use of "idiosyncratic" took me completely by surprise.)*

A week later, after I had visited alone with the doctor twice more, he confronted me with his opinion:. "If you stay in this relationship, eventually one of you will be harmed. Terribly harmed, perhaps physically, almost certainly mentally." After only a week's consultation, he was able to tell me everything I had come to know about my lover over a long period. I was amazed that a test and a simple chat could reveal so much about someone. "Oh, there's no mystery to it," the doctor said. "We study sociopaths like him all the time."

I wanted an answer to the question that might give focus to my dilemma: Why? But this was the very answer the experts couldn't provide.

"We have few definitive answers," he said. "These people have had troubles from their earliest days. We have studied heredity, looking for a genetic explanation, and there has been some evidence that it plays a role."

"Yet Tracy's parents aren't criminals. His father works for the phone company in Texas."

The doctor shrugged, as if the answer was beyond reason. "He may be lying to you. These people learn to become good liars, effective manipulators, as you've seen by his taking you on sexually, thereby learning, in effect, to assert control over his world. But no matter how much in control these people think they are, they are completely unable to sustain meaningful relationships with anyone. If you know what's good for you, you'll end this."

Tracy was uncharacteristically silent when I returned from my visit to the doctor. He seemed to sense from my quiet demeanor that I was deeply troubled. He did what he always did in those moments, cajoled me into sex, knowing that at the height of orgasm, all would be forgiven.

We went to Tampa, to dinner. I had too much wine, and, having done coke earlier, I became unreasonable. Tracy and I argued about the psychiatrist. I wanted Tracy to see him again, but he refused. He left the table and called a cab. I followed him. I knew he would go to the Carousel, to return to the place where we had met, to remind me of what a treasure I had found there amid the sleaze. As he was paying the cab driver, I parked the Mercedes and ran to him. Under the influence of drugs or booze or both, my wayward intelligence guttered like a candle. I grabbed at him, tearing his shirt. He swung at me and connected with my eye. I saw bright lights, then black, and fell to the ground on the street in front of the bar, blood seeping from my eye.

The bouncer witnessed the scene and came to my rescue, whisking me to the hospital where an eye surgeon happened to be on duty. After stitching my eye, the doctor wanted me to stay overnight. When I refused, they ordered me a cab. I had the driver take me to where I had parked the Mercedes. The bar had closed, and the lot was empty. I paid the driver $40 to lead the way while I slowly drove my car to the beach.

On the way home, I recalled the trauma connected with my father's beatings: Fear. Pain. Hurt. Embarrassment. Degradation. Humiliation. Anger. Resentment. Helplessness. Revenge. When he'd been drinking, I knew to keep my distance. The worst time was Friday night, when he would watch boxing. The slugfests would put him in such a state that once they were over, he would seek me out, berate me for being such a sissy and throttle me as I lay helpless in my bed. If Mother had not intervened, I'm sure I would have been killed. One of the consequences of corporal punishment is that it sets the stage for the child to try out the behavior he has experienced.

In my case, I nearly killed several of my pets. When I tried this, I was scolded and often spanked. Very confusing. So I learned that I needed to grow bigger before I had the right to be violent. I learned that Dad's rules don't have to be consistent. I learned to mistrust him. Dad's love was painful, yet I looked forward to growing up so I could be just like him: Mean. Tough. Big. And, maybe, just maybe, I would be big enough to kill him.

As I grew older, I sought out people I could dominate so if they disobeyed, I could discipline them. Power coursed through my body as I would lash out at the girl I dated in college, and who eventually became my wife. My violence was effective when I worked it on her, but she couldn't take it. Most of the time she spent locked in our bedroom—until at last she left me.

I had earned my privilege of power. The cycle of violence was complete except for one thing, I didn't need to kill my father. I saw he was slowly killing himself with drink. But Tracy was not so easily disposed of. My violence did not work on him. He fought back and his rage was greater than mine.

When I arrived at the beach, Tracy had packed his things and his two suitcases were sitting by the front door. He sat on one of the bar stools.

"I'm sorry," he said.

"So am I." It could have been much worse, I realized. It was as much my fault as his. More, really. If I hadn't been drinking, hadn't been doing coke...but, still, it had been simmering for weeks.

"I'll call a cab," he said, reaching for the phone.

I let him make the call. He could always tell the cab he'd called in error.

"I wish you wouldn't go," I muttered as I lay down on the couch in the living room.

"Does it hurt?" he asked, standing over me nervously.

"No, it's numb. But I'm sure it'll hurt tomorrow and again when they take the stitches out in a week or so. But what hurts more than anything is what I've done. What I've done to you—to us."

"It was my fault. All my fault. I haven't been right since the accident. I thought you'd take me back to Tampa and dump me right then, but you didn't."

"No, I couldn't. I love you. I love you, but we can't live together."

"I know. I've been all messed up. I really want to date girls."

"Perhaps this was just something you had to try out. Now you have to put it behind you. And it may not worry you anymore."

I rented a car for him for two weeks and gave him enough money to rent a room and keep himself together until he found work. He called every day and finally I agreed to see him. For lunch.

He didn't bother to knock, just walked in. I was opening a bottle of wine and when I looked up my anger with him, with myself, returned. He was so beautiful I wanted to smother him with kisses but I stood where I was, waiting for him.

"Hi," he said sheepishly, sliding onto one of the bar stools.

"Hi." As I poured the wine, a chill descended upon me. I handed him his glass and he sipped it.

"Tastes good," he said, half-smiling.

I came around the bar and sat next to him. He took my hand and squeezed it. I shook my hand free, like a young boy confronted with an over-ardent admirer.

He shrugged his shoulders and brought both hands to his glass of wine. He said he'd gotten a job at a gas station in Tampa and he was dating the owner's daughter, who was only 17.

"Nice pussy?"

"Shit, I haven't got that far yet."

"That's right. Take it easy. When they're that young they need to be broken in slowly."

My denial of his power was coming at a high cost. I remembered what my psychiatrist said, that such repression is unhealthy. Sooner or later the hate turns up. In my case, it was a fine line between love and hate. I could only hate something that much if I had loved it a great deal. I wanted to cry, but instead I smiled and kept listening as he chattered on.

We sat at the bar and ate chicken salad sandwiches and then I cleared the dishes away. When I returned to the dining room, he was still sitting on the bar stool, but now he was nude. "I've missed you," he said, stretching his arms wide, "soooo much!" I stepped close to him, letting his arms envelop me, press me tightly against his smooth, hard body. We kissed. It was a harder, more urgent kiss than any I had remembered with him.

His hand groped me. Feeling the bulge in my shorts, he whispered, "Yeah, you missed me, too."

The removal of my shirt and shorts was swift and he was on his knees, sliding my prick between his lips, down his throat. Before long, he was on his back on the carpet, his legs spread wide, and I was between them, entering him. As I lowered myself on top of him fully, his arms held me again and we kissed. My cock buried in him, I began fucking madly, and it was as if nothing had changed. Yet everything had changed. As I climaxed, I thought about offering him a hundred a week just to visit me on Fridays for lunch, but by the time I had withdrawn my dripping prick and was lifting myself from the floor, I came to my senses. He seemed to feel I was remorseful. As he pulled on his shorts, he said, "It's just not right, is it?"

"No, I'm sorry. This will have to be the end. I can't go through this. Neither can you. I love you more than you'll ever know, but it's just no good."

"No, it's me. I'm no good," he muttered and raced out the door.

I slipped into my shorts and ran after him but by the time I reached the driveway, he had driven away.

Three days later, I found the little rental car in the driveway, the keys in an envelope on the front seat. There was no note of explanation.

LOVE, LANCE

A New Roman à Clef

The lengthy odyssey of porn star Lance Larkin from his beginnings as Artie Anderson, a callow boy in Michigan, living with his grandfather, to a world-renowned stud desired by millions of men all over the world, as well as by the hundreds—perhaps thousands—of gay men all over the United States, who realized their dreams of lovemaking with him in person. First published in the book Lover Boys   *—JB*

Author's Note: The *roman à clef* you are about to read had its origins in a short tale I wrote for *Heartthrobs*, "At a Party in Miami Beach." After the book was published, a fan wrote saying that he wanted to know more about the hustler. He was right; the story was basically about the john, a fascinating character I met once in Miami Beach. As I set about to tell the full story of the porn star in the story, it became obvious the name I had given him, Todd (based on Todd Fuller), was not right. This megahung stud was definitely a "Lance," and he was, rather than the conflicted tops we have these days, a true homosexual and an extraordinary lover. This is his love story.

It is also the love story of Kirk, the older man who becomes obsessed with Lance. Having once loved a boy who worked as a prostitute, I have always been intrigued by other "respectable" men who have also lost their hearts to hookers.

A host of other writers have also addressed the matter, probing in powerful novels and short stories the love of reputable males for reprobate females. Something about such relationships tantalizes the imagination. No doubt this is because they speak to a secret part of ourselves, a place where reason disappears and fantasy takes over.

ONE

Postcard of the Hollywood sign, postmarked December 5 from West Hollywood: *Hi, Big Daddy! I'm on my way to Miami Beach. Wish I could call you. Why don't you call me? Love, Lance*

"He'll pick you up at the airport," Manny told Lance over the phone.
"How will I know him?" Lance asked.
"He'll know you. He's seen all your videos."

"But does he tip?"

"Hey, for you, my number one boy, more than a tip. Look, he's loaded and he's got nobody to leave it all to. His sister was killed in a car accident. He just needs somebody to make him feel good."

"He's come to the right place."

"Like I said, my *numero uno*. But be careful, he's liable to try to sell you one of his condos."

Lance chuckled. "No, he'll give it to me."

"*Numero uno!*" Chortling, Manny hung up the phone.

Lance was waiting for his luggage at Miami International when a skinny man in a pink sport coat, yellow shirt, green trousers and white shoes with gilt buckles approached him.

Lance snickered, thinking "Piece of cake."

What hair remained around the man's bald pate was the color of silver. The round face reminded Lance of a red apple. A long cigar was thrust out of the tiny mouth. The man held out a small, damp palm, pressed Lance's hand once, twice, three times, then said, "This is a pleasure. I am Max."

The smiling brown eyes that were studying him were, Lance felt, too big for Max's size. They were, he decided, a woman's eyes.

At the curb, the trunk of a huge white Cadillac was gaping open. Lance tossed his suitcase into it and slammed it shut. Max opened the passenger door for his young visitor and Lance got in. As Lance sank down into the seat, upholstered in red plush and soft as a pillow, Max slid in behind the wheel. He pressed a button and his window rolled down. He spat out his cigar, pressed the button again, and the window closed. "I'm allowed to smoke about as much as I'm allowed to eat pork on Yom Kippur, but habit is a powerful force. It says somewhere that a habit is second nature. I don't remember where it says that. I'll have to remember to look it up. Trouble is, I can never find the book I'm looking for. I have three homes—one here, one in New York, one in Tel Aviv—and it seems like I can never find anything."

"Well, you found me," Lance said, stretching his legs.

"On the phone. I love the phone. Yeah, I had no trouble finding you. You know it's easier to call Hollywood or Tel Aviv than a number right here in Miami Beach? Goes through a ...." he paused, as if struggling to find the right word.

"Satellite?" Lance ventured, sinking further into the seat, his crotch now bulging obscenely.

"Yeah, a satellite. I forget words. I put things down and don't remember where."

"I hope you don't do that to me," Lance said, a grin spreading across his sun-kissed face as he brought his left arm across the back of the seat.

Unable to contain himself any longer, Max groped the boy's bulging crotch. "I don't think I'll be able to put this down. Hmmmm."

"Yeah, we'll have fun, I can tell."

"Fun, that's what it's all about. Yeah, each day I live is like a miracle from heaven. The doctor allows me a nip of whiskey now and then, and just that, but he didn't say anything about sex. And I didn't ask him!" He chuckled, "Maybe with an *alte* like me, he didn't think he needed to bring it up!"

Max's hand eventually left Lance's crotch and soon he was pulling the Cadillac up to a huge condominium building on the beach, glistening in the sun. A parking attendant took over.

The lobby reminded Lance of a colossal movie set, with ornate rugs, mirrors, lamps, and paintings, and Max's condo was just like the lobby— with rugs as red and plush as the Cadillac's upholstery.

Once inside the apartment, Max hugged the porn star. "Oh, I'm glad to have your company. I'm in such a state I can't be alone for a moment. This fine apartment turns into a funeral parlor."

Lance dropped his suitcase in the hall. "Do you have a bathroom in this place?"

"Hey, more than one, more than two, maybe three," Max answered, leading Lance to the guest bedroom. They passed a giant picture of a little boy urinating in an arc while a little girl looked on approvingly. In the bathroom, the toilet seat's lid was transparent, with a two-dollar bill implanted in the center. Lance lifted the seat and "Over the Rainbow" began playing.

Max stood at the door, his eyes studying the stud as he unzipped his pants and pulled out one of the biggest and surely one of the most photographed dicks in the world. Lance was used to people staring at it; he reveled in the pleasure it gave them just to look at it. Lance closed his eyes and began pissing.

Max continued to stare. "Excuse me," he said, "you don't mind if I stay?"

"No," Lance smiled. The mighty stream had dwindled to a trickle. Lance shook the last drops from the head of his monstrous organ. "I enjoy it."

"You are quite a performer. I have every video, you know, every one."

Lance turned and the long, fleshy cylinder dangled provocatively between his legs. He slid his hand along the full measure of it, reputed to be eight inches—soft!

"Is it really ten and a half inches?" Max asked. "That's what they called one of your videos, '10 ½ .'"

"When it's hard. Really hard. It takes me a while to get it hard all the way."

"Well, we have a while," Max said, kneeling down on the white bathroom rug.

Lance unbuttoned his trousers and spread open the crotch. He was wearing no underwear. Max touched the glistening pale-pink knob of the famous cock and gently ran his nimble fingers up the thick shaft until they reached the dense patch of light-brown pubic hair at its base. Max reached into Lance's trousers and pulled out his balls. They were lightly furred and full.

The cock was as white as alabaster, and richly veined—and it was beginning to grow in size and rigidity. It began to throb in Max's face, as if it were beckoning him. He leaned forward, rubbing the shaft against his cheek. Lance stripped off his shirt and tossed it on the floor. Max slowly lowered the boy's trousers down his legs and, as Lance kicked off his shoes and stepped from his pants, his cock careened across Max's lips. Max opened his mouth and tried to catch it but Lance stepped back, tantalizing him with it. He tweaked it and it began to harden even more.

Max took a deep breath and slowly began taking the cock into his mouth. Before long, he had five inches of it in, but it had grown so that about half of it still remained showing past Max's lips. Lance began bucking his slender hips. Max braced his hands on Lance's smooth asscheeks as the stud took over, lunging in and out of Max's mouth as if he really meant to come. Harder and harder Lance pressed into the older man's tiny mouth, his manhood swelling to truly epic proportions. Max clenched the boy's hips and hung on as Lance slowly pushed him back until he was lying flat on his back on the carpet, the cock never leaving his mouth.

Lance straddled Max's chest and held his head while he continued to plunge into his throat. When the orgasm began, he jerked the cock from Max's mouth. The cock pulsated and jets of cum covered Max's face. As he stood, Lance saw Max wiping his face with his fingers, then licking and sucking the thick, white cum from them.

"Hey!" Lance said. "Don't do that."

"I wanted you to come in my mouth. I wanted to taste it."

"But you don't do that these days."

"Why not?"

"It could be dangerous. You never know."

"I have lived a long time. Dangerous? Hmph, I can afford dangerous."

Later, they stepped out onto the balcony, which overlooked the Atlantic Ocean. Far off in the distance, a ship could be seen riding the horizon. From sixteen floors up, the people Lance spotted on the beach looked small as insects.

Max brought glasses of wine out to the balcony, and they toasted each other. "It is good to have you here." Max said. "I feel so very alone now with my dear Goldie gone. My sister was my only living relative, and she was crazy. She had every complex you can find in Freud, Jung, and Adler. She married a Gentile, a truck driver, drank like a fish. They were visiting me, right here in Miami, then decided to go to Disney World." His eyes misted over. "He was driving, he had been drinking …." He shrugged.

"Nobody should drink and drive," Lance said.

Max pulled himself from his reverie. "Tonight we walk."

"Walk?"

"To the party," he said as he re-entered the apartment.

In a few minutes, Max reappeared on the balcony wearing a white tie with gold flecks on it. "We're going to my old friend Reuben's. He bought one of my condos when he moved here from New York."

"Am I dressed okay?"

"No, you shouldn't wear anything. It's a shame to cover all that up." He slid his hand across Lance's ass. "But nudity isn't allowed in Miami Beach so, yeah, you're fine."

The door to the living room opened and Reuben greeted them as if he hadn't seen Max in weeks, but in fact, they had played golf the day before and couldn't stop kidding each other about their lost balls.

The apartment was smaller than Max's but still seemed huge to Lance. Spotlights illuminated every painting. A piano concerto was blasting from the stereo. Two other men stood at the small bar in the living room, deep in conversation. They ignored Lance and he stepped over to the windows, comparing the view to Max's. In all the commotion, Lance could scarcely hear what Reuben was saying to him when he brought him a glass of wine. "I'm glad Max invited you. Isn't Max a nice guy?"

"Nice and rich," Lance said with a sly smile.

"Yes, he has a way of making money. He's dealt in everything: buildings, lots, stocks, diamonds. He took care of his little sister like she was the daughter he never had. Pampered her. She was a brat. He wanted her to marry a rabbi but she ended up with a truck driver with a big dick." His eyes fell to Lance's crotch. "There's just something about a big dick, isn't there?"

"Yup," Lance grinned.

Before long, the compliments started, the handshakes, the pressing of the flesh. A stout man seized him and held him around the waist. "I'm Jerry. I loved you in *Long Haul*. I'm in the freight business. I wish stuff like that went on in my trucks!"

Another man, white-haired, short, with an enormous belly and a square head that sat directly on his broad shoulders, brought Lance a fresh glass of wine. He smelled of alcohol and hair tonic. Running the fabric of Lance's shirt through his fingers, he said, "Nice goods. Calvin Klein?"

"Yeah, I guess. It was a gift."

"I'm in the garment business." Then he chuckled as he patted Lance's ass, "I know good goods!" He held out a heavy, sweaty hand. "Sam."

Lance shook the extended hand as he brought the glass to his lips. "Hi, Sam."

"Dinner!" Max cried, pulling Lance away. "Everybody follow us."

They trooped across the street to a hotel resplendent with multi-colored lights and a gushing fountain in front. Two uniformed attendants bowed as the men moved through the huge glass doors, which *whooshed* open for them. The lobby of the hotel was even more lavish than Max's condominium, with tropical plants, vases, sculptures, and a parrot in a cage. They went down a long hallway and entered the dimly lit restaurant. The head waiter greeted them effusively, bowing and scraping to Max as if he was overcome with joy that the man had made it there safely.

"Yeah, that walk across Collins can be a killer," Max joked.

Two waiters attended to the table. Max knew both of them by name. They appeared to be twins, Jack and Jim. Max whispered to Lance, "It's really Jack and Jill but we humor them." Both wore tuxedos, patent-leather shoes, bow ties, and ruffled shirts. Jack took the orders, Jim wrote them down. They both affected French accents. Max said they were French Canadians.

When Lance said he was a vegetarian, Jack assured him he would be served the best dish a vegetarian ever tasted. This got a guffaw from Max. Max gave Jack precise instructions on how his fish was to be roasted and specified the spices and seasonings for his vegetables.

"There are times if you would have told me I'd be sitting in such a place eating such food with Lance Larkin, I would have considered it a joke. I had one fantasy in my life: one time before I died, to get enough bread to fill my stomach. Now look at me," Max said, rubbing his belly.

A man with a camera materialized. "Let's have pictures taken," Max said.

"Smile!" the photographer ordered. The men leaned into Lance, Max on one side, Reuben on the other. They smiled. The camera clicked.

Max told Lance to go around the table, lean over and have his picture taken with the others. Sam held Lance's cheek against his, and Jerry stroked Lance's leg as the camera flashed.

The photographer said he'd have them developed and be back in half an hour.

"Ah, what fun. So many here, they are rich but they just sit. They have no one to dress for. Outside of the financial page in the newspaper, they read nothing. After breakfast, they start playing cards. Can you play cards forever?"

Reuben said, "They have to, or die of boredom. But there is one consolation for them: the mail. An hour before the postman arrives, the lobby is filled. They stand with their keys, like they were waiting for the Messiah. Pity the postman if he's late! And the poor bastard who opens his box and it's empty, he starts to grope and burrow inside, still hoping."

Max laughed. "And if the Social Security check doesn't arrive, they worry about it more than the people who have no bread. In my way, I'm every bit as silly as they are, but at least I follow my doctor's orders. He wants me to walk, I walk. He wants me to eat right, I eat right. He wants me to stop drinking, I only have a nip. He wants me to give up smoking, so I only suck my cigars."

"What about sucking dick?" Jerry asked.

"He never said, so I guess I can do that as much as I want to! Why is it taking so long for my fish?"

"It's probably still swimming in the ocean," Jerry said.

"And the fruit in Lance's salad has yet to be planted," Reuben said, patting the stud's knee.

"Here they come with our food," Max said. The door opened and the headwaiter entered leading three men pushing carts.

As they ate, Max talked about the changes in Miami Beach. "It used to be that seeing the plaque they put up on the oldest tree was the highlight of your trip. Now, there's South Beach and all those gay clubs. The gay boys know how to have a good time, I tell you. They make the place fabulous. They should give them a medal. Instead they want to put them in jail. When I was a boy and studying about Sodom, I couldn't understand how a whole country could become corrupt, but now I know. Like here, Sodom had a constitution and all their lawyers reworked it so that right became wrong and wrong got to be right."

"Yeah," Jerry said, "that area below Fourteenth was dangerous in the old days. Now it's all the swish and fish crowd."

"Too much attitude for me. More attitude than there is in L.A. for sure."

"Yes, in New York and L.A., people are all business. No time for attitude, eh, Lance?"

"Just business as usual."

"Is business good?"

"Are you kidding?" Max said. "For a kid like this, business is always booming."

"Here you just have people sitting by the phone waiting for someone to call." Jerry said.

"Yeah," Max said, "with so little time, you want to snatch pleasure where you can."

"To Lance!" Jerry said, raising his glass in a toast.

Each clinked glasses with the other and Lance, as if he knew something no one else did, had the biggest grin of anyone at the table.

"Ah," Max cried, "here's the photographer! A fast worker! Let's have a look!"

The photographer handed all the prints to Max, who gave him a fifty-dollar bill. Max passed the photos out after glancing at each one admiringly. He held up the one he was in with Lance and Reuben.

"Ah, Lance is so young. So handsome. He has his whole life before him."

"He's had a pretty full life for one so young," Reuben said.

"Yes, he's full of life. So full!" Max said, smacking his lips.

"And now they say you shouldn't swallow all that life," Reuben said.

"Oh, but just a taste can't hurt," Jerry chimed in.

As they left the hotel, Lance stopped at the gift shop and bought postcards. Max waited patiently for him outside the shop while the others walked on through the lobby.

Max beamed when he saw the postcards Lance held in his hand. "I like a boy who writes," he said. "Nobody writes these days."

"I like a postcard because I don't have to write very much."

Max chuckled. "I'll bet whoever they are for will enjoy hearing from you."

"That's what I'm hoping."

On the way back across the street, Max drew his arm around Lance's slim waist. "If we go back up to Reuben's, will you entertain my friends a bit?"

"I don't know. That could get expensive."

"I'll take care of it."

Lance smiled. "In that case, the more the merrier."

When they were in Reuben's apartment, Max said, "Reuben, why don't you show Lance your new Jacuzzi?"

Reuben nodded. "Love to."

Max turned to Lance. "Reuben took out a bedroom just to make room for it. Some people think it's a swimming pool."

"Big enough for five?" Lance asked, grinning.

"Well, no, you might have to stand!" Max chortled.

While Reuben led Lance away, Jerry and Sam joined Max in the kitchen where he was pouring brandies.

As Lance went into the separate room that housed the Jacuzzi, Reuben turned off the lights. The remodeled bedroom had a panoramic view of the wall of neighboring condos up the beach and the light from the building next door gave the room a warm, seductive glow. At Reuben's suggestion, Lance went to use the toilet before getting into the hot water.

When Lance emerged from the bathroom he was naked. Reuben was also naked and already seated in the swirling waters. As Lance stepped over to the pool, his cock swung enticingly from side to side. A sigh came from deep down in Reuben's throat. Lance climbed into the water and stood before the older man, whose hand reached up and gently stroked the semi-flaccid cock. As many times as Lance had played this scene, he still found it fascinating: how men could spend hours worshipping his cock. It was a gift, he thought, he had nothing to do with it; it was nature having fun, creating something unusual. Still, he felt it was only right to take advantage of it.

Before long, slurping and smacking sounds filled the room. One by one the others had entered, stripped, and climbed into the pool. Every few moments, Lance felt new hands stroke his skin. Strong, aggressive fingers glided over his body, pinching, kneading, rubbing. Lips touched his skin, his buttocks, his thighs, his cock, his balls, his nipples. He just stood in the center of the Jacuzzi, his head back, his eyes closed, and allowed himself to be adored. At times, there were three on his cock at once, then there were only two, then just one, all the while someone sucking his ass. When the last one had orgasmed, there remained only the one at his ass. As Lance began to turn, the sucking stopped. Lance saw it was Max. Now Max made love to Lance's cock even more ardently than he had in the afternoon. At one point, Lance opened his eyes and noticed they were alone. "Let's go back to your place," Lance whispered.

"Okay," Max said, before taking one last lick.

"It's late," Max told Lance after they returned to his apartment. "If you don't mind, I will retire to my room. You have a TV in your room, there is food in the kitchen. Be comfortable. I will see you in the morning." He kissed Lance lightly on the cheek.

"Goodnight," Lance said, heading for the kitchen.

Lance slept late and, after a shower, he wrote a postcard, then joined Max in the kitchen for breakfast.

"You pleased my friends. I thank you."

Lance nodded, his mouth stuffed with a bagel topped with cream cheese and strawberry jam.

"Today you will please me before I take you to the airport, okay?"

"Sure."

In a few minutes, Max was naked, lying on his stomach in the middle of the king-size bed in his bedroom. After watching some videos, while Max sucked him, Lance had gotten almost completely hard. He excused himself and went to the guest bedroom. When he returned, he had sheathed his cock in latex.

"Why are you wearing that?" Max asked.

"I always do."

"Not today. I hate those things."

"But …."

"I have so little time, let me enjoy it."

"So little time, bullshit. You've got another twenty years."

"No, I don't need another twenty years. I'm sixty—it's plenty."

Lance sat on the bed, stroking his cock. "You don't want to risk that. I've seen guys die that way. It is a lousy way to die."

"You take care of me, I take care of you."

"No, I couldn't."

"You are okay, I am okay. There is no harm."

Lance pulled the rubber off his dick and plunged his throbbing erection into Max's butthole. The old man cried out with the pain but Lance did not slow down. He knew if he did, he would go limp and he would not be giving the trick what he was paying for. And Lance wasn't Manny's number one boy for nothing.

As Max was taking him to the airport, Lance remembered only too well the last time he was in Florida and he grew sad. He had gone to Miami Beach to dance at the Boardwalk on a three-night gig over the Memorial Day weekend.

On the second night, he had no pre-arranged "date," so instead of letting the other dancers roam the crowd and collect all the tips, he decided to join in the fun. When he finished his first number, still wearing his jockstrap, he bounded from the stage and started making his way through the crowd. He did not linger the way the other dancers did, just took his dollars for allowing a quick feel. Some men were bold and could not resist the huge bulge, but Lance would adroitly squeeze their hands and push them away. They had seen the cock—that was allowed in Miami—and that was enough; if they wanted more, they could pay for a private show later. He had three more sets to do, and by the last he would have picked out a likely prospect.

A fat man was very aggressive and wrapped his bear arms around Lance. Lance tried to pull away but the man, sitting on a stool at the bar, held him fast. It was then that Lance noticed the most handsome young man he had ever laid eyes on. The object of his desire was sitting next to the fat man who wouldn't let go. The object turned, opening his thighs to Lance. Lance reached out to the object and shoved his elbow into the fat man's gut. In a moment, he was between the object's thighs and the object's arms were around him.

"Well, hello," the object said.

"Hi." Lance looked into the azure blue eyes and couldn't help himself. He kissed the man on the mouth. The man returned his affection.

When their lips finally parted, the man said, "What are you doing later?"

"Nothing," Lance teased, and danced away.

In the bathroom that passed as a dressing room, Lance asked Jeff, one of the regular dancers, who the man at end of the bar was.

"Cute isn't he?"

"Yeah."

"He's here a lot. His name is Hart. He's Senator Taylor's son, just slumming."

"Does he take anybody home?"

"No. He's just a looker."

"He's a looker all right."

"I mean, if you looked like that would you have to hire somebody?"

The Senator's son soon became the most unusual "date" Lance ever had. Lance went back on stage to dance his final set and when it was over, went directly over to Hart, who was still sitting at the end of the bar. As soon as Lance approached him, Hart's arms went around the stud's waist.

"I want to make love to you," the Senator's son whispered in Lance's ear as he held him. He introduced himself, and said he was in town to attend a conference.

"Will you give me a ride back to my place?" Lance asked, running his hand up Hart's thigh.

"No, I'll give you a ride to my place."

When they arrived at the hotel, Lance went to the bathroom, and when he emerged, he found that Hart had lit a vanilla candle. Except for the narrow flicker of light from the candle, the room was dark. A shadow danced erratically across the hotel room wall.

Lance was taken aback by the romanticism of it all. Soon Hart's lips were pressed against his ear. "Tell me what you want. Tell me." He kissed Lance's cheek, his forehead, his eyes. "Please."

But Lance would not, *could* not tell Hart what he really wanted to know—what he was really looking for—because he had not fully articulated it, even to himself. But he knew he'd recognize it when he found it. But he knew that if he revealed too much, there'd be nothing left for him to hide, to keep to himself as something that was his alone--and even the weak light from the candle was far too bright.

Hart dropped to his knees and began sucking Lance's limp cock. He worked it up to near-hardness and then stood. He took Lance's hand and led him to the bed. They hardly knew each other and it made Lance feel vulnerable and apprehensive. but he knew that in this case he couldn't say no. With a single kiss Hart had weakened Lance's reservation.

Hart was all over Lance. "You!" he muttered, his voice deep. "You! You! You!" His desire poured from him and swamped the stud. He covered Lance with kisses, licking, and small nibbles. His lips, fast and desperate on the stud's body, sent currents of intense pleasure through Lance, who closed his eyes and reveled in the feel of Hart's tongue working his nipples. He was pulling him, dragging him deep down into a place he had never been.

Hart's mouth found Lance's navel. Then he spread Lance's legs and raised them before his finger flicked the opening of Lance's ass for a minute before he plunged his tongue into the hole. Again and again, he fucked the ass with his tongue. A trail of hot saliva criss-crossed the cheeks of Lance's ass, and he slid further into the abyss. Lance, willing prey to Hart's lovemaking, succumbed completely, spreading his legs farther apart and arching his body even higher to offer it to his new lover.

While Hart's predatory fingers plunged in and out of Lance's ass, he took the stud's cock in his mouth and began sucking profoundly. Soon Lance's monstrous sex was hard—as hard as he could ever remember it being. It was slippery with spit, and Hart's saliva was soaking the pubic hair at its base, where his lips nestled when he took in every inch of the enormous dick. Watching his cock completely disappearing inside the beautiful man's mouth, Lance was struck with what a great feat of cocksucking he was witnessing—and enjoying to the fullest! It inspired him to start fucking Hart's ravenous mouth savagely as Hart's head and lips drove as fiercely downward to meet each thrust.

"I can make you come. Just tell me how you like it," Hart whispered around the enormous shaft inside his mouth.

"Oh, god," Lance groaned.

Hart's breath was hot. And soon Lance was aroused to an unbearable degree, in a dangerous place—a place he thought he'd never come to. A constant throbbing radiated from between Lance's legs, and in a near scream, he cried, "Fuck me!" He could not believe he was begging this handsome, sex-crazed stranger to do to him what he had done to so many men—many hundreds, surely—but which he had never permitted one of them to do to him before. But he had never been quite so excited or so hungry for a sex partner before.

Fortunately, Hart had lubricated Lance's ass well while he had been finger-fucking him, so that when he quickly abandoned Lance's cock and sheathed his own with unbelievable swiftness, rose to his knees and with one fierce lunge plunged his entire cock inside Lance's ass, the stud was able to accept it—although his loud cries continued for several minutes. Lance gasped in pain, but even more in the discovery of a level of ecstasy he had never even suspected could exist.

As Hart fucked him, Lance wanted to shout in ultimate pleasure, to try to express his thrill to the man who was fucking him so magnificently, but he didn't want to let Hart know that he was the first, that no matter how hard the ache, how insistent the pressure *it* was finally happening, and that he was in heaven. He couldn't express the degree of enjoyment he was experiencing without betraying his inexperience as a bottom.

But Hart had been here before, had fucked many a virgin ass, and he somehow knew that Lance had just come home at last.

Lance's fingers gripped Hart's ass while he was battering him, pulling the cock even farther into his ass—harder, faster, more thrillingly.

It seemed to Lance that Hart had been fucking him for over an hour. Or had it been two? Three? He opened his eyes the tiniest bit. The room was darker. The candle flame was guttering as Hart's orgasm exploded, and continued to erupt inside Lance. It was a monumental orgasm—*epic!* Hart shook and held Lance tightly to him while his cum spurted and finally slowed to a stream, kissing him full on the mouth and receiving in return the grateful, passionate kisses of a man who has just been given the most wonderful gift he had ever received.

They lay in each other's arms for a long time, kissing tenderly, with Hart's semi-flaccid cock still inside Lance. Slowly, Hart's prick slipped out, but as they continued to kiss, it began to return to it former glory, and he panted, "God, I can't stop...."

Lance moaned, then watched in anticipation as Hart lifted himself up and parted Lance's legs again. Hart looked down as he held the root of his cock and slid it back into Lance's ass. Lance groaned now. He had never ached like this before, but his body was still afire with desire.

Once he was fully in him, Hart caressed Lance's face with one gentle finger and then took him in his arms and kissed him with the same gentleness and sweetness, but their kiss quickly became passionate as Hart's cock began to pound again. Amazingly, Lance had not yet blown his load, and just before Hart filled his ass with cum again, he did so. His arms were around Hart at the time, and they were kissing feverishly when, without his touching it, Lance's cock began to discharge, bobbing wildly as it forcefully sprayed cum on their chins, their chests, and their bellies, and inspired Hart's prick to do the same, again within the confines of Lance's ass.

Although his gig in Miami was over, Lance stayed on to be with Hart and dance for him alone.

Hart had turned the radio on and the music snaked into the bathroom like a thin spiral of smoke. Lance's reflection stared from the mirror. He had never felt so sexy. Alone, he danced to please himself, luxuriating in the swing of his cock as he moved. His hand slowly followed the thin line of hair that went from navel to pubic patch. He imagined Hart passing by, seeing him, desiring him like he now desired himself.

As if he could hear Lance's thoughts from the other room, Hart came to the doorway of the bathroom, wearing only his briefs. He simply stood there and watched as Lance danced. Lance felt lost in the music, lost in his incredible sensuality, and then he noticed Hart watching him. It seemed to Lance that Hart had a way of looking through him that sent a vivid sexual impulse careening through his body. Hart smiled and followed him with his eyes and a throbbing began in his cock.

Seeing Hart standing there—an Adonis, the first man who had ever fucked him, and who had then miraculously fucked him again—Lance's cock began to heat up also, and the graceful swinging of his cock as he danced began to turn to a heavy lumbering as his huge organ began to grow and stiffen.

Lance had always hungered for a man like Hart. One look at him in the bar, and he had known he was his. When Hart fucked him, he fucked as if he knew how desperately Lance enjoyed his fierce lovemaking—ramming him, blasting into him, doing whatever he pleased. Hart could get as rough as he wanted, knowing Lance would never break, never ask him to stop.

Lance's clear hunger for Hart's violent fucking was one of the things that most attracted Hart to the big-dicked stud. But he was already with someone, lived with someone who was fragile, someone he treated like a little doll: his wife.

When Lance heard that Hart was married he was shocked and worried about Hart's continued interest in him, yet it was a fine line that he found stimulating. He craved, for once, walking the edge between being out of control and being controlled. And Hart was an exquisite lover.

Hart turned from the doorway and Lance knew exactly where he was headed. He heard him switch off the radio and put in a cassette—*that* song, Whitney Houston's "All the Man I Need." It was the song that had been playing as they left the club, just after they met.

Lance entered the bedroom and resumed his teasing, tempting dance. He danced to please them both. He wanted Hart to watch, to become so aroused that he could barely breathe. Hart made no physical effort to come to Lance, but Lance could almost feel him soar across the room and grab him, shake him, devour him. Their eyes locked as Hart dropped his briefs to the floor and stepped out of them, then backed up to the bed and lay on it.

Hart's eyes drifted down to gaze appreciatively at Lance's bobbing monster cock—only semi-hard, but still jutting out alarmingly as he danced. Hart's own cock lay back, the head pointing to his chin and standing a few inches above his stomach,   obviously fully erect. He took it in one hand and began to stroke it slowly and suggestively for Lance's enjoyment.

Continuing his dance and alternating his gaze between Hart's eyes and Hart's cock, Lance brought his own dick to full rigidity with only a few strokes. As he rotated his body, his erection swayed from side to side, and slapped against his right and left thighs. Then he spread his legs and began humping his ass forward and back, and the unusual size and heft of his cock as it jumped up and down, caused it to dip all the way down in between his legs and then swing upward to slap his belly.

From opposite sides of the room, they made love. Even though Hart didn't move from the bed, yet he was at Lance's side, all the same. With a pleased nod of the head he caressed Lance with his appreciative eyes. Lance danced, danced, danced, working up a sweat as his body undulated wildly, and his mammoth prick jumped around alarmingly. Hart's fist traveled up and down the shaft of his cock in time to Lance's frantic dance, and soon two thick ropes of white cum shot upward, and fell back to coat his chest, followed by a flow of cum over his fist.

The scent of sex filled the room as Lance approached the bed slowly. He was tweaking his nipples, which stood out like hard cranberries, and he pinched them and fondled the flesh around them as Hart raised up so that Lance could bend over him and offer his aching nubs to be sucked. Hart tried to grasp Lance's cock while he sucked the stud's tits, but Lance would not allow it.

Lance pulled back and resumed his dance in a steamy circle around the bed. He felt exhilarated. The more he moved, the deeper he descended into another dimension. They were separate yet intertwined, all at once. Soon, Lance was on the bed—soaked in perspiration, and rabid for Hart's cock.

Hart harshly rolled Lance to his stomach and quickly lubricated his ass with the thick cum that still coated his chest. Lance reached behind himself to spread the cheeks of his ass wide, and without a word or the least bit of hesitation, Hart rammed his amazingly still-hard prick all the way inside Lance's hungry hole.

Pulsating, churning, Hart hammered into Lance as hard as he could. He had blown a load only minutes earlier, so he was able to fuck endlessly without coming. After he had fucked for twenty minutes, he still wanted more.

They both wanted more. "Oh yes!" Hart cried as he plunged and withdrew, plunged and withdrew unceasingly into the welcoming, hot tightness of Lance's busy ass.

"Oh god, yes!" Lance screamed as he frantically writhed and humped his ass backward, reveling in the profound, savage thrusts of Hart's insatiable cock

Their lovemaking became poetry—even art.

Hart's fiery words added to the intensity of Lance's enjoyment of his fuck. Lance's appreciation of Hart's performance combined with Hart's admiration for Lance's body and his stupendous prick to inspire Hart to take from Lance what he was giving him so lustfully. After he blew another load inside Lance's ass, Hart mounted the stud's cock and rode it wildly until Lance exploded his own load deep inside Hart's ass—as deeply as only a titanic cock like Lance's can probe.

After their ecstatic lovemaking was finished, Hart stood at the window, deep in thought. Something was off. Something desperately guarded. "I have to tell you, we need to keep things safe. No involvement beyond right here in bed. Agreed?"

"No involvement," Lance replied. "Yeah, exactly what I want, really."

"Believe me, it's best."

Lance went to him. Hart wrapped his arms around Lance, pulled back slightly and peered at him. "I have to go home tomorrow."

"So do I."

"Will you be back this way soon?"

Lance looked away. He didn't want to think about it. "What's the use?"

Hart understood, but chose not to reply. He wanted to have his cake and eat it too. He had his wife, but he desperately needed to possess men like Lance from time to time—and even be possessed by some of them, as the remembered pain, the *wonderful* pain still tingling in his ass attested

Hart cupped Lance's face in his hands. His voice was soft and soothing, but the azure-blue eyes now held a sliver of dishonesty. Although Lance knew Hart was the son of a senator, he never let on he knew. Hart merely told him his family was in banking and he was attending the conference without his wife because that was his one chance to indulge his "other side." Lance did not press his lover for more; indeed it was as if he didn't want to know more. But the hopelessness of the situation was evident now.

Still, Lance would not let it spoil their last night of sex. He knew now that Hart wasn't looking for love, but only wanted to feel a transitory touch, enjoy homosexual intimacy for a moment in time, with the sexiest boy his inherited money could buy. He was not looking for anything more, surely not looking for a relationship.

Lance was the one who had walked that tightrope—and fallen. For three days, he had been caught up in his own moment in time, his own love story, a kaleidoscope of all that a great love with a wealthy, handsome young man could be.

For days after his fling with Hart, Lance could imagine making love with no one else. After having been with Hart, he wanted nothing but the feel of his touch, the scent of him, his dirty, lewd whispers as he fucked.

From Miami, Lance went on to Washington, to dance, to give private 'shows.'

The first night there, his john, a pleasant-enough salesman from Iowa, spent several minutes sucking on Lance's nipples—back and forth, so very lightly. His nipples taunted, his nipples teased, but what the man was doing was too much—and yet, not enough. Suddenly the man grabbed Lance's nearly limp cock and began sucking it roughly—as if they'd run out of time, as if he would go crazy if he didn't get the cock that very second.

Lance knew what the man sucking his dick wanted—what they *always* wanted. And who could blame them? But for Lance, it seemed as if he was falling backward, stumbling. His cock was rising, but his spirits were sinking. The john was going down on him, but he was himself going down spiritually.

Soon he was ready to give the man what he was paying for. He let the john take his cock deep into his throat, choking on it while he masturbated at the same time. As Lance thrust his cock in and out of the man's throat, strong hands clasped his thighs, nails pressed hard into his sweaty flesh. All he could think of at that moment was the thickness of Hart's cock, and the tightness of his own ass as Hart had fucked it so gloriously, and at such length.

Submerged in a potpourri of passion, he shoved the man's head into his crotch as his cum began to fill the john's throat. The bulk of Lance's monster prick, and the cum spurting from it, left no room for the man to breathe. He gasped for air, panted for it—but he never stopped sucking, nor did he let a drop of Lance's hot discharge escape his hungry mouth.

To Lance, it was as if the cocksucker wasn't even there. He had imploded into himself, engulfed in the most pleasurable memories, rather than the reality of the present.

After a few moments, he returned to the present and realized he was in once again in a strange, darkened hotel room, and the middle-aged man licking cum from his lips and murmuring his satisfaction was not Hart.

TWO

Postcard of the Detroit skyline, postmarked January 12: *Hi Big Daddy! I know this one is a surprise! Detroit? Well, my Grandpa died and I came for the funeral. He would have liked that. But it's so damn cold. I wish I was with you so you could warm me up, as only you can! Love, Lance*

The stud known to gay video fans as Lance Larkin was born Arthur Anderson in East Tawas, Michigan, on the shores of Saginaw Bay. When his parents were killed in a boating accident, he went to live with his grandfather, who owned a bait and tackle shop. It was assumed Artie would grow up to take over his grandfather's business, but the boy had other ideas.

Artie lay on one of the benches outside the shop, the sun warm on his back, reading.

"Do you know where the old man is?" the boyishly handsome man asked as Artie looked up.

"My grandpa?" The boy closed his book and stood up, gazing silently for some moments at the man's bulging crotch. "He's not feeling well," he said, "but I can take you out. It's slow today."

The man had been there all that week, and each day Artie's grandfather had taken him out into the Bay to fish. The man had smiled at Artie, was pleasant but diffident. The man said he needed a "guide," wouldn't know where to go to fish for the perch, salmon, trout and walleye the area was known for, and besides, he didn't like to fish alone, he was in need of company. He was visiting the area, his mother was in the hospital, and it was a trying time. A couple of hours on the Bay had a calming effect.

Every day the man's outfits got skimpier. Now, wearing only a tank top and short white shorts, there was little left to the boy's imagination and he was so compelled by the man's powerful masculinity that he could not take his eyes off him or the ever-more-prominent crotch of his shrinking below-the-belt attire.

Sideways, out of the corner of his eye, the man watched the boy who, without waiting for a reply, deftly prepared the battered boat for their trip.

"Are you a fisherman too?" It was not that the man was curious; he spoke only to break the silence.

Artie started the motor. "Yes, I am," he replied.

After a little while Artie dared to study the man again, who was now trailing his fingers through the waters of the Bay. His thighs were spread wide apart and Artie could see he wore no underwear.

"What's the matter with your grandfather?" the man asked.

"He has rheumatism."

The man nodded, gravely. Then he smiled. "I doubt that you're a fisherman, even if you do fish sometimes."

"Isn't it all the same to you?"

"Oh, sure," answered the man, coolly, "but I bet there are things you *are* very good at."

This confused Artie. As far as he was concerned, he was good at nothing. "Good for nothing," his grandpa always said, and Artie believed him.

There was a flash of lightning, followed moments later by a peal of thunder. The thunder reverberated for a long time, as though huge empty tin barrels were being kicked with amazing force from one hill to another. The surface of the Bay became pitted with rain. They had to make a run for the shop as the rain came down suddenly in torrents.

The boy unlocked the door, politely ushered the man into the tiny shop, and then stood on the threshold watching the storm. As Artie delightedly watched the spectacle outside, the man saw that the boy's features changed: his thin, bony face grew more beautiful, his stubborn mouth sensitive as a girl's, his expression calm and bright.

The man peered over his shoulder to look at the view and deeply breathed in the rain-washed air.

Artie blinked rapidly and sighed. "Your name is Tom, isn't it?"

The man placed his arm around Artie's shoulder. "And you are Artie."

"Yes." Artie sighed again, then turned to look at Tom. "When you said there were things I was good at, what did you mean?"

"There are things you can be good at without any practice. You know, instinctive things."

"Instinctive?"

"Yes. As if you were just born with the ability to do it."

"Like what?"

"Like making love perhaps. Things like that."

"There's nothing like making love."

Tom chuckled. "Yes, that's true. See, you do know. You just know. No experience necessary."

"But I have had experience."

"Oh?"

"Yes."

"I see," Tom said, and looked very solemnly into the boy's eyes.

The rain was falling gently Now; the turmoil was over, nature was once more at peace. To the south there was a brightness in the sky as summer clouds formed and dissolved.

The boy shifted his weight from one foot to the other.

"I'm going now," said Tom, holding out his hand. "Goodbye."

Artie took the outstretched hand and shook it firmly, looking into the man's eyes. He breathed out slowly, increasing the level of the pent-up emotions inside him. "How long are you staying here?"

"Not long. They don't expect mother to make it."

The boy looked gravely down at the ground. "I'm sorry." Then he looked up. "I'm also sorry I lied."

"You lied?"

"Yes. I'm not much of a fisherman. And I'm not very experienced at making love either."

"You are very young."

"Not so young. Guys I know at school have had lots of experience."

"They just say that."

"No, I've seen them. I know."

"And you didn't get in on it?"

"I didn't want to. I don't know why, I just didn't. They all think I'm some kind of freak anyway."

"Oh? You don't look like a freak to me."

"I am. I'm deformed."

"Deformed? Where?"

"In the worst place of all."

Tom was really interested now. He could hardly contain himself. "You've got to be joking."

"I wish," Artie said, looking back out to the Bay.

Tom was disarmed by the boy.

Artie was silent, swallowing hard and sighing deeply.

Tom rubbed the boy's shoulders.

Artie waited meekly while Tom struggled with himself. After a long pause, Tom asked, "Do you find me attractive?"

"You're a nice man," replied Artie.

Tom rubbed his temple. He was amazed that he was so stirred by this adolescent, almost uncontrollably aroused. But somehow it seemed quite natural that they should be there, talking to each other about their problems.

Artie felt Tom's crotch rub against his ass and he shifted his weight, but did not move an inch.

Artie was quiet for some moments.

Tom felt encouraged by what the boy had said, but he was irritated by his silences, his reticence. Still, his hands drifted down the boy's body and came to rest on his tiny waist. "It's time I was going," he said.

Artie could think of no appropriate reply, though Tom waited expectantly. He found himself becoming unaccountably uneasy. In the silence he heard the buzzing of a mosquito. When it had settled down, Tom squeezed his shoulders.

Tom's tongue flicked at the skin and kissed and sucked, and it soon was becoming too much to bear for Artie. Tom shifted his position so he could lie between Artie's legs and bury his face in his crotch, cupping and lifting the boy's slender ass in his hands while he sucked.

Artie was running his fingers through Tom's hair, stroking him, as Tom burrowed his way down to the very root of his cock. He stuffed a finger in Artie's ass and it was incredibly tight, unyielding.

Tom continued to circle his tongue around the glorious young erection. He was drunk with pleasure, delicately running his tongue up and down the shaft. Artie's cock was at last fully erect in anticipation of each delicious stroke as Tom traveled back down to the base, only to return to the huge pink head. Up and across in a flicking rhythm, always returning home to the head.

The boy writhed in pleasure, pushing his hips upward to drive his cock deep down Tom's throat. He let go of Tom's hair and fondled his own aching nipples, squeezing them sharply while Tom continued that remarkable tempo on his cock. Tom felt a hungry impulse to take in more and more. With his face submerged between Artie's legs, his gentle licking from moments before evolved into a ravenous sucking. In a moment, it was over and Tom again took all Artie had to give. He held the sperm in his mouth a moment before spitting it over the side.

Artie lay sprawled in the sun, his cock exposed, while Tom went back to fishing.

After awhile, Tom said, "The biggest cock in the world, that's what you have, isn't it? Do you like to show it off? Do you like knowing that I'm sitting here watching you?"

Artie looked up, smiled, and took his sex in his hand. "I'd like it better if you would come back over here and do it again."

And, of course, Tom did just that.

Before Tom began sucking, he held the hefty cock in his hand and said, "You are not deformed. No way. You are a small person and you have an extraordinarily large cock. Any boy that says you are deformed is just jealous."

Artie was pleased to hear this and he was also pleased he had finally met someone who could provide him even more pleasure than he could give himself. Surely his friend Timmy, the only one he had ever been intimate with, was not experienced enough to give him the pleasure he sought.

The school had an annual ski trip to the Upper Peninsula, and Timmy pleaded with Artie to accompany him. Artie hated skiing but he went along, only to find to his delight that they would be alone together in a room with only one bed. They wore their briefs to bed and it was so cold in the room, the boys cuddled when they first got under the covers. This aroused Artie uncontrollably and Timmy could feel the bulge of Artie's enormous cock pressing against him. His hand went to it, and before long, Timmy had pushed back the covers and slid the cock from Artie's briefs. He began playing with it while he played with his own, and Timmy did not insult Artie by saying his giant organ was deformed. Artie didn't pressure the boy to suck him, although he was eager for him to do so. It was enough that another boy wanted to adore his cock rather than defame it.

If Timmy did not seem to want to suck Artie's dick, he certainly was fascinated by it, and, over the weekend, couldn't keep his hands off it. Timmy spent every spare moment they were alone together touching Artie's prick, examining it, even kissing it. He did not yet suck it, however.

After they returned to East Tawas, Timmy spent the night with Artie, and finally tried to take Artie's prick in his mouth to suck it. He was unable to take more than a couple of inches of it, and when Artie's cum blasted forcefully into the boy's throat, Timmy coughed and gagged— immediately spitting out the substance that Tom would later savor so greatly.

But Tom was something else. He knew just how to get Artie going. In fact, the lad came twice in the three hours they were fishing on the Bay.

The next day, after Tom had started their day together by sucking Artie off, and they sat fishing, Tom told the boy it would be his last day there. He had to get back to work. His mother lingered on, and now doctors were saying that she might last for weeks.

"Where do you work?" Artie asked.

"At Ford. I'm in the advertising department. We're very busy with the new model introductions."

"Do you get a free car?"

Tom chuckled. "No, but I do get a discount."

"Can you get me a discount?"

"You want a car?"

"I want to get out of here, that's what I want. If I had a car, I could just drive away." He swept his arm toward the sun.

"Aren't you happy with your Grandpa?"

Artie turned sad. "He drinks. Worse now than ever. He blames himself for the death of my parents. But he had warned them not to go out, that there was a storm coming, but they ignored him." He shrugged, "I guess everyone has always ignored him."

"Does he beat you?"

Artie stared at his sneakers. "Yeah, sometimes. I hate him. I really do."

"I wish I could help."

"Take me with you."

Tom shook his head. "It's no good running away. But maybe I can come up with a plan. There must be somebody at your school you could talk to."

"No. Never mind, it was just another one of my foolish ideas."

Artie grew silent, pouting, but Tom understood. As much as he wanted to, he didn't ask to suck the boy one last time.

"Artie!" Tom cried, excited to see the boy, but angered at the same time.

Artie was silent. He stood at the door of Tom's house in Grosse Pointe, a battered suitcase in his hand. He was trembling.

"How did you find me?"

"I called the hospital. They gave me your address. I told them you had left something in one of our boats."

"I did …. you," Tom said, shaking his head and opening the door wide so the boy could enter the house.

Their reunion was the most blissful night of Tom's life.

After a day or two, Artie opened up to his new friend. They sat in the living room, Tom with his bourbon and Artie with a Dr. Pepper, talking long into the night.

"Grandpa is always talking about dying," Artie said. I guess he wants to. Anyhow, he said to me, 'I'm sorry. You're going to have to grow up faster than you should have had to, which I guess is why I push at you sometimes. To help you get ready. But I won't be going for awhile. Whenever I go, I'm sure you'll be all right.'

"I was where I had to face up to things. You said I should try to see it his way, and I did. After all, he had a hard life, too. So I tried, and it did make me feel a little bit better, but it was difficult, and just as often I hated him. Maybe he had a secret thing in him, too, and none of it was his fault. As for loving him like I was supposed to, I couldn't manage it. Mom was the one I loved, maybe the same way you'd love somebody that died.

"I remember a time when I was six. It was spring, near the end of first grade, and there was this kid named Eddie who'd been beating me up all year. He even beat up Harry Fisher who was a year ahead of him. He hit my friend Timmy across the face with a long piece of wire, like a whip, and laid his cheek wide open. You can still see the scar. Anyway it got to where I was so scared of Eddie I'd be shaking whenever he was around. I had tummy aches all the time, and when I didn't, I pretended I did, so I wouldn't have to go to school. Teachers never help, of course. When you're actually in class, it's the law of the jungle, and if the teachers are on anybody's side, it's Eddie's because he's a real man and you're a crybaby.

"Everybody must have known something was real wrong, but even then I knew you weren't supposed to tell, so it took Mom a hell of a long time to get it out of me. But she worked at it and worked at it, and finally I broke down and told her about Eddie. The next day she let me stay home and went to school herself, and from what I heard later she raised all kinds of hell. She told the principal to tell Eddie's mother to pick him up right after school let out for the day and drive him home, and if that didn't work she personally was going to put a leash on him and walk him home herself. She said if she didn't get full cooperation she was going to not only take it up with the School Board but have Dad write a friend of his at the paper about how the school authorities refused to protect their pupils from brutality. That took care of Eddie for the rest of the year.

"When she came back from school that day and told me I didn't have to be afraid any more—and why—we had a long talk about it. Finally she said, 'Now let's take a piece of paper and write down all the bad things you feel about Eddie.' So we did. I told her and she wrote, or printed rather, so I could read it: *I'm afraid of Eddie. I hate Eddie. I'm a crybaby. I shouldn't have told. I hate myself for telling.* 'Now,' she said, 'take the piece of paper with all the writing on it and tear it up.' I did. 'Crumple it up.' I did. 'Now let's go outside,' she said. She got a bowl and a box of matches from the kitchen, and we put the crumpled paper in the bowl. 'Now burn it,' she said. Up to then I was never allowed to fool with matches, so I had a little trouble. But when I finally got it going ....oh, God, how my heart leaped up with the smoke!

"So if you've been wondering why I still love her, even though she can't help me anymore and I can't help her, now you know."

"Yes," Tom said, "I do know."

Getting it off his chest improved Artie's disposition immensely. He even decided he wanted to suck Tom's cock while Tom was blowing him. Tom fought against it, saying it wasn't right, but he gave in—he had fallen in love with Artie.

As the school year began, Tom convinced Artie he had to go home. "If your Grandpa gives you any trouble, call me immediately," he told the boy. Tom agreed to drive to East Tawas once a month and bring Artie back to Detroit for a long weekend. By calling his grandfather earlier and telling the old man about all the "neat stuff" he and Tom did in Detroit, Artie was able to convince him that Tom was "cool" and wanted to adopt him. The old man, naturally, drew the line about adoption but he seemed pleased someone took an interest in the "the kid."

The following summer, Artie agreed to stay on and help at the shop if he could continue his monthly visits to Detroit.

By the time he graduated high school, Artie was a fixture in Tom's home. Of all the things they did together, watching porn videos was the most fascinating for Artie. He kept telling Tom, "I can do that" when they watched some porn stud performing a feat of sexual athletics.

Tom tried his best to discourage the boy from considering work in porn, but when Artie found that porn stars were dancing at the theater on Woodward and Six-Mile Road, he was determined to work with them. Once the management saw the lad was indeed eighteen and blessed with a tremendous gift between his legs, he was hired.

And then one night Tiny Treadwell, a video director whose real name was Ray Stubbs, came to the theater. One of his favorite performers told him the next time he made a trip East, he had to stop in Detroit to see this extraordinary youth.

The rest, as they say, was history: Tiny wanted Artie to come to Hollywood immediately. Tom was upset but he knew it was what Artie wanted. Tom told him if he went to California he would come out and see him, although in his heart he knew he wouldn't. In all probability, he thought, he would never see Artie again—except on the screen.

Once Tiny had Artie under contract and living ion he West Coast, he thought Artie should pay a few visits to his own personal trainer at Westside Health & Fitness.

"*You* have a trainer?" Artie asked the 300-pound man who often dressed in drag.

"Don't be smart, kid. Yeah, you need to buff up a bit. Just a bit," he said, pinching some flesh.

"Anything you say."

Douglas stood six-three, with light brown hair that hung to his shoulder blades. His body was so sculpted that no matter which way he moved, his muscles would flex all over it. His skin was so shiny that Artie assumed it was covered with baby oil. He looked like an Indian warrior cast in bronze.

After thirty minutes of lifting weights on the high-tech machines for biceps, triceps, upper back, lower stomach, waist, and torso, Artie begged for a water break.

Douglas conceded that he deserved a break, and as they headed for the spring-water cooler, Artie watched the older man's thighs and buttocks flex while he walked across the gray carpet. During the rigorous workout he had been cracking jokes and trying his best to charm a smile from the muscle-stud. To no avail.

"Next we'll do twenty repetitions on the inner-thigh machine," Douglas said, leading him to a chrome mesh of metal that looked like something out of a medieval torture chamber.

Once on the machine Artie couldn't believe how easy it was to lift ten pounds.

"You have strong inner thighs, Artie."

"Don't I though." Artie grinned.

"Let's put another ten pounds on the machine and see how that feels."

Douglas adjusted the weights, then stood in front of Artie. Artie felt a flush of heat when he spread his legs wide, under Douglas's scrutiny. His legs rested in the metal-padded splints he had to press against to bring his knees together.

"Try it," Douglas said.

Artie pressed his legs together and moaned. "Shit, are you sure that was ten pounds, and not fifty?" he laughed.

"Only ten." He dropped to his knees, studying Artie's legs.

"I want you to concentrate very hard on isolating the little muscle right here." He pinched the small bit of flesh at the top of Artie's inner thigh. Artie grinned.

"Breathing is very important. Follow me. Breathe in, then squeeze your legs as you breathe out. That's it. Very good."

Artie could feel beads of sweat running down his back. His legs were beginning to ache. That little bit of flesh was quivering. He began to shake.

"Is it hurting?"

"Yeah, I think I'm getting a muscle spasm."

"That's not good. Get off."

Artie sat on the floor, spread his legs, and Douglas began to massage his inner thighs. The boy thought he was going to pass out—the sight of those massive arm muscles flexing were driving him wild with desire.

Douglas looked up at him, eyes half-open.

Artie noticed the stud's erection bulging beneath his nylon Nike shorts. He said, "Maybe if you kissed it, it might feel better." And he relaxed his legs.

Douglas leaned over Artie and pulled his workout shorts down to his ankles. The trainer began kissing the sore spot and worked his way up to the pouch of Artie's jockstrap, which was by then swelling alarmingly. Douglas peeled the elastic back, and Artie's hard prick sprang out. "God," the older man gasped when he saw the full extent of Artie's equipment. "Tiny wasn't kiddin'."

Douglas leaned over farther, and his lips sank to the base of Artie's huge cock in one swoop. The intense suction he exerted and the way his head drove down repeatedly, feverishly, to meet each of Artie's upward thrusts soon brought the younger man to the point of orgasm in less than ten minutes. As Artie's cock exploded, Douglas pulled his lips off barely in time, so that most of the huge load was deposited on his face. When Artie had finished, Douglas wiped the cum from his face and had Artie lick it from his fingers.

Grinning up at Douglas, with some of his own cum still on his face, where it had dripped from Douglas's, Artie begged: "Teach me."

"Teach you?"

"Teach me to suck a cock like that."

"Nothing to it. It's all in the tongue action."

And Artie's prick was still hard enough—and certainly big enough—that Douglas could demonstrate the finer points of his technique. Artie was a quick learner, as he demonstrated only a few minutes later, much to the satisfaction of his teacher—whose cock was only the least bit smaller than Artie's, but whose load was bigger when his new student sucked it from him.

Artie stayed at Tiny's spacious home in the Hollywood Hills, and he was surprised that once he had let Tiny blow him, it was all business. He expected the older man to make a nuisance of himself, but Tiny said that although he had loved sucking Artie's monster, their relationship was to be a "professional" one. Besides, when it came to what he called "love," he said he could only be satisfied by tall, studly black men. Artie was to learn there would always be at least one who met that description around the house or in the studio. They cleaned, they mowed the lawn, and some even helped with the video productions.

Tiny always seemed to have two videos in production at the same time, and he was seldom at home.

One afternoon, Artie sat by the swimming pool—nude, as was his custom—with his back to the house, gazing at the city, nearly lost in the usual haze of smog. The sun was low over the trees, and their shadows spread toward him on the water. He was alone now, since the pool boy—one of the few men whom Artie had met with a cock bigger than his own—had gone off with one of Tiny's black employee/playmates, who had been trimming hedges. Judging from the faint sounds that drifted up from the hillside below the pool, the hedge trimmer was enjoying the pool boy's special talents.

Artie basked in the gray solitude, which gave him peaceful joy. He leaned his head back, allowing the sun's warm rays better access to his already suntanned face. It felt wonderful to lie in the sun, just soaking in the heat. Closing his eyes, he dipped his finger into his lemonade and slowly applied the moisture to his parched lips.

Daydreaming, he shifted in the chair, breathing slowly and deeply. Images passed through his mind and then disappeared, leaving him refreshingly blank. He dozed for a few minutes until the heat reminded him of the tall, cool glass of lemonade in his hand. His lips once again felt desperately dry. He wet his finger and gently brushed the lemonade against them. "Mmmm..." he sighed, quietly savoring the tart liquid.

It was a sensuous combination: the unrelenting sun, the unexpected coolness of the liquid on his lips, the tingling on his tongue. Artie leaned back, allowing his legs to spread just enough for the sun's warm finger-like rays to touch his suddenly exposed cock. Aaah, that felt so nice! He dipped his finger into the lemonade again, then let a drop fall directly onto the tip of his penis. His body involuntarily jerked in response to the icy stimulus, and he let his legs fall farther apart. The cooling sensation of the first drop of lemonade quickly passed, so he let several more trickle from the glass onto his limp cock, spreading the refreshing cool liquid all around it. Slowly he moved his fingers around its base and

305

it began growing bigger and harder in his fist. He sloshed a bit of the cold lemonade on the tip of his hot, now-throbbing cock.

The sudden coolness was startling, involuntarily causing his hips to lift slightly from the lounge chair. Almost immediately he could feel more tightening, strengthening. Slowly, he began to stroke up and down, over and over. He thought about Tom, Tom's mouth on this same cock, sucking it, making love to it. He missed Tom, he really did. And Douglas, too. He wished he needed more training, but Douglas had kissed him off—as he had frequently sucked him off—saying he'd learned everything and was on his own.

The sun beat down on his cock and he continued his ritual of pleasure. He drummed his fist harder, faster, more determined, more persistent.

Clenching his eyes tightly, he arched his pelvis up from the chair and masturbated feverishly. The frenzy finally erupted into orgasm as he moaned Tom's name again and again and again. Panting, he collapsed in the chair, his body hot, flushed, exhausted from pleasure, with the thick white cum drying on his belly and on his fist, which still loosely held his spent cock.

He dozed in the sun until a sound intruded: the rhythmic splashes and lapping of a swimmer.

Artie, startled, forced his eyes open and grabbed his towel in one movement. Embarrassed, he covered his exposed cock, still sticky with his drying cum.

He looked to his right. He stared at the youth coming toward him, rising from the pool like a colossus. He was a magnificent specimen of youthful manhood. His white bathing suit contrasted sharply with the chocolate color of his skin. He stood over Artie and shook his head, sprinkling Artie's face. Laughing, he went to the deep end, dove in and swam back, then stood at the shallow end. "Coming in?" he asked.

"What are you doing here?"

"Tiny dropped me off. He had to go to the bank. He'll be back. He said you were to entertain me."

Artie laughed, tossed away his towel, and dove into the water. Soon the black was breaststroking, then bending into a surface dive, coming up from below Artie. A shoulder struck Artie's chest, an arm went around him; then the young man was behind him, the arm moved and was around his neck, tightening and pulling, and he went backward toward the bottom. With both hands he pulled at the wrist and forearm, cool and slick under his prying fingers. His jaws were clamped tight against the pressure rising from his chest. He released some, and bubbles rose toward the surface. He rolled toward the bottom, touched it for balance with his hand, swung his feet down to it, straightened out his legs, and thrust upward. The boy's arm no longer held him, and he stroked and kicked upward. He had exhaled again, and the painful emptiness in his chest made him inhale a small amount of water. As his head finally broke the surface he was choking, gasping, coughing.

He did not look behind him at the boy who had dragged him under, but swam away, head out of the water, still coughing. He climbed out of the pool and bent over, coughed and spat on the flagstones. He heard feet behind him.

"What are you, crazy?" Artie said, then straightened and turned to look into the boy's dark eyes. He had seen eyes like them before, on his school playground. Boys with those eyes rarely fought at all; they didn't need to. They threw your books in the mud, pushed you against walls, pulled your hair, punched your arm or stomach, shamed and goaded you, while the boys and girls who watched urged you to fight. But no one would dare fight those aggressive boys.

Six years ago, when he was twelve, long after his run-in with Eddie, Artie had been attacked by one of those boys and for the first time he fought back; he leaped at the boy, and they rolled around, grappling in the dust. Artie was quickly on his back, shoulders pinned by knees, fists striking his face before someone pulled the boy away. But for the rest of the school year he was free; he had fought back.

But the eyes of this dark boy at the pool seemed to change, becoming amused, playful, even suggesting a trace of affection. "I didn't know you were scared," the boy said.

"I couldn't breathe."

The boy folded his arms. "I could." Then he turned and dove. He swam to the other side. Artie walked around the pool and greeted him as he came up, playfully swinging a foot in his face. The boy grabbed it and pulled Artie into the water. They fought for a few moments, until the black held Artie tight and kissed him on the lips. Artie kissed him back, surprising himself; he had never considered a black man as a love object. This one ground himself against Artie while they continued to kiss, and his cock was hard. Artie reached down and began to massage the bulging crotch as their kiss grew ever more passionate.

Their lips parted and the black lifted himself up to sit on the edge of the pool, his crotch in Artie's face. Artie knew what was to come next and he wasn't sure he was prepared for it. He had sucked only Tom and Douglas. He didn't know what to make of this strange black boy. Still he was turned-on by the novelty of it and brought his mouth to the humongous bulge. The boy held his head with rough and callused hands while Artie sniffed and kissed and kneaded the basket.

Slowly Artie peeled back the swim suit. He was fascinated by the long, thin uncut organ which emerged. He had never seen an uncut cock hard before. A few boys in school had them but they were always limp. Artie sucked the foreskin, nursed it, and opened it with his tongue, which he brought down the length of its tight corridor.

He dropped his jaw and, using both hands, pulled the dick into his mouth. He then sucked it, blowing his spit inside the foreskin, irrigating it.

He raised his hands and palmed the boy's smooth chest. He twisted his nipples. Now the black slowly undulated his hips, grinding his dick down Artie's throat.

At last he would get the chance to utilize all of the techniques Douglas had taught him over the past two weeks, Artie thought. He ran his tongue around the rim of the dick and sucked furiously. He slid it farther into mouth, making spirals around the shaft with his tongue, feeling a pressure at the back of his throat that brought him to the edge of gagging but did not drive him over. He moved his tongue back up the impressive length, nipping gently with his teeth as he went. He moved again to gently caress the head. Artie breathed in the meaty smells of the boy's cock. He gasped for air. By now the black's horsecock was fully hard, and he pulled back. The hands pushing down on Artie's head forced the dick against his throat, and made his eyes water.

The boy obviously approved of Artie's cocksucking prowess, but he clearly wanted something else as well. They got out of the pool and the black pulled off his swimsuit. Artie lay back down on the chaise, his partner over him. Slowly, the black fed Artie his cock and was soon face-fucking him ferociously. Artie hung on to the slim hips driving the long cock into him, and let him do his thing. He fucked Artie's face until blood ran from Artie's nose. Artie could feel the black's dick beginning to spasm, and one final, especially deep plunge set him off.

The black yanked his cock from Artie's mouth and pinched off the mouth of his foreskin. His cock jerked; his body twitched. His foreskin ballooned with his own cum, some of which leaked out and dripped down his fingers. His hips and butt were still fuck-pumping, and he was still coming. His whole body was flexing. His eyes were closed. It was a glorious orgasm.

The black climbed off and knelt next to the chaise. He released his hold on the tip of his foreskin, and drizzled his cum over Artie's semi-hard cock. He knelt again, and was about to take Artie's cum-covered cock into his mouth when Tiny walked through the double doors onto the terrace.

"Reggie!" he screamed. Tiny was dressed in drag.

Reggie shot up, and stood grinning at Tiny. The big black's cock was still hard, and a thread of his cum still trickled from the angry red-purple head.

Tiny smacked his lips. "Your job here does *not* include giving blowjobs to the guests."

"Yes, ma'm, I mean, *sir*."

Tiny gestured for Reggie to follow him into the bedroom, and after winking at Artie, Reggie obeyed—his long black cock swinging and lumbering as he walked.

Although Tiny kept telling Artie he had "great plans" for him, there was no evidence the kid was going to be doing anything but hanging out at the house, honing his fellatio skills and getting face-fucked by Reggie whenever Tiny wasn't around.

The truth was, Tiny wanted to keep Artie for himself, and was plotting what he termed, "a major breakout." In fact, *Breakout* was the title of the video in which Artie would make his porn debut.

After a month of idleness, Artie found himself finally working on his debut film—in a jail cell, although only a make-believe one.

Artie had only one scene, near the end of the feature film. Tiny had decided to whet his audience's appetite for his new superstar by giving them only a short appearance by Artie in his first video.

Because Artie was nervous about his initiation before the cameras, Tiny decided to break a cardinal rule.

For some reason, probably because Tiny thought he was reading his fans' appetites correctly, he had never used a black man or boy in one of his videos before. For some strange reason, it apparently had never occurred to Tiny that many of his fans might be as enthusiastic about sex with black boys as he was—or that indeed many of them were undoubtedly black themselves. But he had observed the chemistry between Artie and Reggie the time he caught them having sex, and after that he had frequently hidden in the shrubbery near his pool and watched them go at it while he masturbated.

Tiny paid Reggie $500 to give Artie a blowjob on film. The boys laughed about it later, imagining the really hot scene that could have developed had Tiny just let them do what they had been doing at his house almost every day—secretly, they thought.

As the actual filming began, Artie was moaning in pleasure while Reggie stroked his prick and stimulated it until it was throbbing in full erection. Reggie continued to slide his finger across the slick shaft as Artie wriggled and humped, trying to position his bobbing cock so that Reggie's wandering fingertip was challenged to follow it.

"Hold yourself apart, Artie. Now I want to watch Reggie lick that sweet dick of yours." Tiny continued to monitor the steamy sex scene under his direction. "Reggie, force the tip of your tongue into a point like this. Can you point your tongue like this?" he said, pushing his own tongue out of his mouth. "Yeah, that's perfect. Run it up and down the side of his big dick like you did before with your finger. Good. Now wait till you see how hard this gets him, right, Artie?"

Artie was barely able to respond, he was so totally immersed in sexual tension. He wanted more. Eyes closed, he listened to Tiny instructing Reggie on how to rub him, to tongue him, to suck him, as if he needed any instruction.

"Now, this is important. I want you to let your tongue lap. Pretend you're a little kitty and we coated Artie's dick with milk…. Right, right, lap like that...." Reggie, with his long tongue exploring that throbbing length of flesh, was overwhelmed.

An exotic fragrance emanated from Artie's crotch as Reggie's lips opened wide to admit the head of Artie's incredible cock. They gradually sank all the way to the base of the fat shaft as Artie's hips began to thrust forward and pull back, fucking the boy's mouth as they had so often done before in private. The lovemaking was slower, more measured than the hungry rush that typified their frantic lust when they were only satisfying each other's frantic needs, not *demonstrating* them—as they now seemed to be doing for the camera.

Artie's body was rigid in pleasure, arching up and frozen as Reggie sucked profoundly, eager to suck every possible bit of cum out of his cock. His own penis aching with desire, Reggie fondled and cupped the firm, round cheeks of Artie's ass, holding his body at the perfect angle. The longer Reggie sucked, the more frantic each boy became until Artie cried out repeatedly as his orgasm approached, and Reggie began stroking his own shaft wildly.

Tiny yelled his encouragement when both boys began to come at the same time. Reggie's cum shot out and splashed on Artie's legs, dripping down toward his ankles as Artie quickly pulled his cock from Reggie's mouth and covered the boy's face with his thick, white cum. The two cameramen had successfully scrambled to record the two impressive 'money shots.'

Artie couldn't help it; he started to laugh. He was finally in show business.

"Lance," Tiny said. "That's it: Lance. It has to be. That cock is a lance, a fucking *lance!* Long, thin, pointed," he paused, for effect, "aimed at the heart of every guy watching." But what to go with it? "Lincoln, Lansing, Luft." All those got guffaws from the crew, especially Luft. "How about Larkin? That's it—Larkin!" Tiny finally said. "Lance Larkin."

And so it was. It was now "Lance," not Artie, whose legs Johnny reached between, whose penis he grabbed by its length, and whose bulbous cock-head he used to rub himself with, up and down.

As Johnny ran the head of Lance's cock along his asscrack, Lance held back, letting the other boy take his cock in just as far as he liked. Lance stiffened each time his cock-head brushed the moist hole; he *had* to be in him—he had to feel his hipbones pushing against the toned muscles of Johnny's perfect buttocks. Lance entered Johnny, who welcomed his fucker by squeezing the huge cock inside of him. They gasped together.

Tiny was ecstatic. He had coaxed the still-very-young Johnny Jones out of retirement to be Lance's first on-screen bottom. Johnny had been fucked by all of the big dicks in porn and Tiny knew he would relish being the first to be speared by perhaps the biggest cock of them all— Lance's. The foreplay went well; Johnny sucked Lance until his monster cock was about as hard as it would get, given the lights and other distractions. Then Johnny knelt on the edge of the bed and started manipulating Lance's cock, holding the head and positioning it at its target while Lance stood on the floor behind him.

Now Lance thrust his cock into Johnny, urging himself to be as hard as he'd ever been. This was where they had been leading for two hours, coaxed on now, as before, by Tiny's filthy mouth: "Fuck him, Lance, honey. Fuck the shit out of him."

As they found their cadence, Johnny's knuckles whitened and his breath grew raspy. He hadn't had one this big in a long time. Lance folded his arms around Johnny's waist, drawing the boy's arched back into his stomach.

Johnny flexed all at once and then began to change the tempo, slamming his body backwards to meet Lance's thrusts with such determined force that Lance had to step back to brace myself. Johnny wanted this cock. He *really* wanted it. He couldn't hold back much longer.

"Right now," Lance cried to Tiny. Johnny moaned and pounded back into him. His throaty, sure, growling joy as Lance came was captured by the microphone. Tiny would use that. Lance convulsed, his belly slapping on Johnny's pimply, sweaty back.

The bottom had taken more than Lance knew he had, and for days afterward Lance felt he could still smell Johnny on his cock.

Lance sat in awe. He had never seen such fucking! The part of him that only a few minutes before had considered leaving, thinking his work on the video "10 ½" was over, was totally engrossed in the scene he was witnessing. Looking at the sex going on before him, Lance could scarcely believe the set of circumstances he found himself in—first the intoxicating experiences with Reggie, then fucking Johnny, and now watching, one of the more intriguing arenas of sex. It was only a week after he had completed the shoot with Johnny, and here he was making his *second* video. It was a most amazing business.

The bottom boy, whose name was York, was silent. His only reaction to the feverish caresses he was receiving from the scheduled top man, as far as Lance could observe, was his ass arching and humping in pleasure.

"That's right, honey," Tiny shouted, "Let him slip one finger in—just enough. Just enough so we can let 'em know what you've really got there."

Lance was stunned, unable to move, spellbound with feelings of sexual heat and desire. His entire body was tensed up, on edge.

"Jack," Tiny murmured, turning to the top, a huge, musclebound wonder. "I want you to stick your tongue out. I want you to taste perhaps the finest piece of ass you'll ever, *ever* taste."

Still entranced, Lance stiffened in the chair and leaned forward—having to remember to stay in his chair, so he would not suddenly become part of the scene being filmed.

"That's right, Jack," Tiny said hypnotically. "Enjoy yourself."

Jack was directly in front of Lance, sucking York's bunghole. Lance put his tongue out, mimicking the stud, and he felt the saliva in his mouth welling up in anticipation.

After a few minutes of that, Tiny said "Cut" and the boys got into another position. Now, carefully, Jack slid his cock into York's waiting mouth; York enveloped it, blanketed it, then slowly closed his lips and began sucking, greedily trying to arouse Jack to full erection. This action left York's ass exposed, vulnerable. Lance stared at it.

Just at that moment, Tiny noticed where Lance's interest was focused. "Yeah," he teased, in an aside to his new star. "You'll get your chance at it."

Lance began to feel the pressure of his stiffening cock against the large towel he had wrapped around his waist. not believing how excited he had become. He squirmed slightly, accidentally letting out a small moan. He found himself perched on the edge of his chair, leaning forward, trying to absorb the thick air of sweat and sex coming from the two boys who were making love directly before him.

Tiny finally turned to him. "Do you want him, Lance?" he asked.

At last Lance was invited into the web of their sexual passion. He groaned a hungry "My god, yes!" as he stood, dropping his towel to the floor, revealing his formidable hard-on.

"Lift up, York," Tiny said coolly. "Lift up that perfect ass of yours and spread your legs so Lance can make up his mind if he wants you!"

York immediately arched his ass up even higher, spreading his legs as he did so, exposing his asshole, still wet with Jack's saliva.

"Is that what you want, Lance?" Tiny asked as he walked back to where he watched the action on a monitor. "Stick your fingers in him first," Tiny urged.

Lance was overwhelmed. He stood next to the bed stroking his cock, watching as Jack continued to fuck York's mouth. The air was thick with the smell of sex.

Slowly Lance inserted two fingers inside York, and began turning them inside the slippery, yielding sex pocket, with his eyes glued to Jack's ass, the buttocks opening and closing to disclose Jack's pink asshole while he slammed his cock in and out of York's mouth.

"Now fuck him!" Tiny said hotly.

Lance grabbed York's hips and began to slowly insert the large head of his cock into the boy's hungry hole. York was tight, small, and Lance wasn't sure if his enormous dick could go in—York was moaning and squirming quite a bit. "Go ahead, give it to him," Tiny panted into Lance's ear from behind.

Abruptly, Lance shoved his hips forward forcefully, and he watched as his titanic prick slipped inside the boy, who began to moan around the fat cock filling his mouth at the same time an even bigger one filled his ass.

"You've got it now!" Tiny said. "You fuck him. Fuck him good."

Lance leaned forward. Had he imagined the sucking sound he heard when as he pulled his penis out of York, just before he shoved it back inside and pulled it out again? No, York was so tight the cock actually popped when it came out.

"Faster!" Tiny insisted.

Lance crammed his huge shaft back inside and began to fuck in earnest, now leaving his cock-head inside each time he pulled back. He increased the speed of his fuck, and York began to move his hips, rotating them around and around the incredible dick driving in and out of him so forcefully.

As the cameramen swirled around him, Lance slammed into York greedily, holding the boy's hips securely, sinking into him ever harder, as deeply as his monster prick could go. The sound of his belly slapping against York's ass each time he thrust into him, and York's ecstatic moans each time he did so, combined with the sight and feel of the boy's beautiful ass gyrating as it hungrily sucked in his tool, excited Lance uncontrollably. Then, at Tiny's coaxing, and although it would have seemed unlikely he could do so, he increased the tempo of his masterful, savage fuck.

Suddenly Tiny was screaming, "Get on the floor! Get on the floor now!" Tiny re-positioned Lance and York cock to cock, with Lance lying over York. Jack knelt at the side of York's head while the boy turned his head so he could resume the blowjob he had been giving Jack. Jack was again fucking York's mouth as he put his arms around Lance, and the two shared a long and very passionate kiss.

"Spread your legs," Tiny insisted to York, who did as he was told, wrapping his legs around Lance's neck as Lance slid into him again. As Lance once more began to fuck York in earnest, Jack pulled his cock out of York's face and stood.

Jack took Lance's head in his hands, raising it so that the tip of his throbbing, saliva-covered cock rested on Lance's lips. The muscle-stud began slapping Lance's face with it, and Lance tried to capture it with his mouth, but failed. Tiny went in for a close-up. Jack continued to slap Lance's cheeks with his cock while Lance pulled his cock quickly out of York, and blasted his load on the boy's stomach. The slaps were recorded by one camera while Lance's money shot was caught by the other.

While his orgasm, had lessened his sexual arousal considerably, Lance happily sucked Jack's cock when Jack crammed it in his mouth, and he continued to suck for several minutes, until Jack blasted a load on his face and chest.

While Lance was cleaning Jack's cum off his face and body, Tiny praised Jack's performance and promised to use him on his next project. Jack smiled, but all he wanted to do at that moment was to go home with Lance and get that kid's huge cock up his ass ....which is exactly what he did.

That evening turned out to be confusing for Lance. Jack was an incredible top in his eyes, with a cock that had not gone limp even after two hours of steady screwing. But in the privacy of Lance's little bedroom at Tiny's house, Jack wanted only to be fucked, and showed no interest in doing the same to Lance's ass. It was a dichotomy of sexual behavior that Lance was to discover frequently in studly sex partners he worked with on camera, where they were strictly top men, but who only wanted to be fucked later.

One sunny afternoon, Tiny had gone to the bank and to run other errands, leaving Lance alone again by the pool. Bored, he slipped his left hand out from under his head and began touching himself, trailing his fingers down the center of his body, from his throat to his pubic patch. His pecs and the hard ridges of his belly shifted slightly as he began rubbing his hand over them. He went at it gently at first, then harder, flexing the muscles till they bulged. He raised his head off the chaise, then his legs, holding them just an inch or two above the warm towel and admiring the definition in his thighs and calves.

As he looked down over the now carefully sculpted curves, his prick began to respond. His balls were hanging loose, resting on the warmth of the towel, tingling with a familiar pleasure as he began playing with his tits. Every nerve in his body seemed directly linked to the two pinkish-brown nubs of flesh that jutted out from the curves of his chest. He grazed them with the balls of his thumbs, then began pinching them, tugging on them till his shoulders rose off the chaise.

Soon the blood began flowing to his prick. It began to stretch out, rubbing against the inside of his thigh, then slowly rising and twitching until it hit the top of its arc and flopped back heavily against his belly. He pinched his nipples harder and watched his cock continue to grow. The head swelled, inching up well beyond his navel. The shaft got fatter, the veins that twined like vines around it swelling beneath the tender skin. A drop of pre-cum dribbled out slowly. He raised his legs higher in the air, spreading them wide. The sun warmed the tight pucker of his asshole, and he shuddered. His dick twitched and rose even more. He rolled back onto his shoulders till his toes brushed the wall behind the chaise. He put his hands on the globes of his ass and pressed. The head of his cock loomed closer and closer till the sticky tip brushed his lips. He exhaled, applied a fraction more pressure against his hips, and his lips parted, allowing the tip of his cock to slip into his own mouth.

He was surprising himself. He had tried this many times as a youngster but could never quite achieve it. Now all the stretching routines with Douglas had made him remarkably limber. His prick flexed and he slurped the pre-cum oozing out of it, letting it trickle down his throat.

After a time, he slipped his fingers into his crack and began stroking the warm, moist pucker. He popped the middle finger of his right hand into his mouth, got it wet, then pressed it against the ring of muscle in his ass. It slid in just as his cock flexed and slid back into his mouth.

His finger pistoned in and out of his asshole while he tightened his lips around his swollen cock and sucked frantically.

Soon he was adding a second finger, then a third, and felt his toes curl. He moaned as he started to shoot. He took it all in his mouth before he swallowed, then lay back on the chaise, eyes closed, panting hard, his fingers still jammed tight up his throbbing hole.

"Oh, honey," Tiny gushed, "will you do that for my cameraman sometime?"

Lance's eyes flew open, and he stared up at his landlord, who was in the frightening stage of half-woman/half-man that Lance had become accustomed to lately.

After Lance slowly pulled his fingers from his ass, Tiny grabbed his arm. He brought Lance's hand to his face and began licking the skin. As he proceeded to suck Lance's fingers one by one, Lance closed his eyes. He gritted his teeth because he knew what was coming. Tiny would finish with his hand and move to the asshole, then work his mouth to the balls and, eventually, be working over the cock. This was what he loved to do and, mercifully, had only asked for it that first night. As Tiny lowered his bulk to the end of the chaise, it creaked. He took off his blond, bouffant wig and tossed to the ground, then took Lance's buttcheeks in his sweaty hands and began licking, kissing, sucking. As his tongue invaded the space, Lance resolved, once and for all, to move.

The opportunity to move came from an unexpected source. Tiny had hired Joe Crandall to shoot stills of Lance for the gay skin magazines. They went one day to a spot in the mountains that Joe favored for his shoots.

At forty, Crandall was the oldest person in the porn business that Lance had worked with since coming to California. His deeply tanned, craggy face was bearded, the salt-and-pepper whiskers cropped close. His mustache was thick and full. His lips were also full, and quite sensual. His wore his black hair long, the ends brushing his heavily muscled shoulders.

Joe had a pleasant way about him that put Lance at ease. When they stopped for lunch along the way, Lance asked, "So where will these photos appear?"

"Oh, Tiny has his favorites. When it's one of Treadwell's productions, we pretty much get to pick the magazine. I think *Inches* would be perfect for you."

Lance smiled and looked at Crandall's hands as he picked up his mug of coffee. They were huge, thick-fingered, and callused—the hands of a man who did hard manual labor, not a photographer.

"You been a photographer long?"

"It started as a hobby. I had my own grocery store at one time, but the chains did me in."

There was a sadness about Crandall that Lance found attractive. Lance liked people who could accept tragedy and keep on.

Later, as they began the session among the pines, Joe said, "No good. Shadows. Try standing away from the tree."

Lance flushed and straightened up, glancing nervously down at the front of his jeans. He thrust his hand back into his pocket, and when he raised his head, Joe clicked the shutter.

Joe told him to remove his hand from his pocket and place it on the growing bulge in his jeans. It was clear that Lance loved being photographed and the camera loved him back.

"Got a problem there, I see," Joe grinned.

Lance nodded, and smiled back.

"Everybody should have that trouble."

This put Lance at ease even more and he smiled broadly now.

"You also have a beautiful body."

"I've been seeing Tiny's trainer."

"Tiny has a trainer?"

Lance chuckled. "That was my reaction, but I don't think Tiny's ever lifted anything heavier than a hard dick."

Joe laughed.

"No, the trainer used to be in porn. He worked for Tiny but then he got a lover who didn't want him doing that shit anymore, so …."

"Stop talking," Joe interrupted. "Just smile." He clicked the shutter two or three more times, then said, his voice a little thick, "Okay, let's get down to it."

Lance nodded and slowly began lowering his jeans. Joe kept clicking. When the cock sprang into view, Joe easily got five shots of it, his eyes getting wider as he took it all in. "That's incredible," he said.

Lance smiled. "It's not hard yet."

"I know, I know."

With thumb and forefinger, Lance encircled its base and pressed his hand hard against his groin, causing further engorgement. He angled his hips so that Joe's lens could record its full grandeur.

Joe finished one roll, removed the exposed film from his camera, replaced it with fresh film and snapped the camera shut. "Stand over there," he said, "these clouds are causing shadows."

Lance moved into a shaded area and slid the shirt off his shoulders. As Lance turned, Joe pressed the shutter, capturing the ass in all its perfection.

A bead of pre-cum had appeared at the tip of Lance's cock, and Joe knelt to flick it away with the tip of his tongue. Then he went on to lick the shaft, and then the testicles, transported by the earthy smell and sharp-bitter taste of them. His hands all the while were pressed against Lance's buttocks, kneading them

Lance responded with a subtle grind of his hips. He placed a hand on each side of Joe's head and coaxed him to a standing position. "I think it's ready now."

And it was. Joe shot the cock from every angle, stopping occasionally to suck it, "just to keep it hard."

Lance smiled. He'd heard it all now. Lance reached down and stroked the bulge at Joe's crotch. "Now it's you who has the problem," he chuckled.

"Yeah, looks like I do."

"What do you think we ought to do about it?" he asked, looking into Joe's eyes.

"My problem? I don't know." Joe interpreted Lance's look as an invitation, and he reached out to touch his flank. Lance let his own hand glide to Joe's hip and then to his ass.

Fully aroused now, Joe grasped the hard flesh of Lance's cock firmly. He embraced the young stud, holding him close.

Lance put his arms lightly about Joe's waist, but Joe pushed him away so that he was free to take off his boots and socks, then peel out of his faded Levi's. Joe had worn no underwear, and had stripped off his short as they began working, so he now stood in front of Lance completely naked. His pale legs were in balance with the bulk of his upper body, the thighs beefy and strong, the calves packed with thick muscle. His ass was firm and full, and had a little triangle of dark fuzz at the tailbone that pointed to the furrow between his smooth cheeks. Even hanging loose at his sides, his arms were impressive, the biceps and triceps thick and knotted, his forearms corded with muscle and veins.

He folded his pants and turned back to face Lance. Lance saw that his cockshaft was thick, the fat knob rubbing gently against the inside of his left thigh. His balls were huge, hanging low and loose in a nicely furred leathery bag. Joe let Lance fully appraise him, then spat on his hand and reach out to coat Lance's erection before he turned around and leaned down, bracing himself against a tree trunk.

Moments later Lance was inside him, riding him easy, in a standing position, and then taking him doggie style as Joe knelt on the ground, bringing Lance down with him. Lance had been pulling at Joe's cock as he fucked him, but Joe brushed Lance's hand aside and vigorously masturbated himself. At the same moment Lance felt his partner's sphincter tighten, he pulled out and came across Joe's back. In moments, Joe stopped stroking himself and Lance reached under to touch the older man's cock, wet and slick with his semen.

They stood, embraced, and then Joe returned to the job at hand, getting close-ups of Lance bent over, spreading his asscheeks.

"Will I get to see these pictures?" Lance asked.

"I'm sure we can arrange that."

A couple of days later, at Joe's apartment in the Valley, Lance studied the photographs carefully. His smile grew ever wider, and his eyes shone. He went through the set a second time, and then looked at Joe.

"Can I have these?" he asked.

"Yes. That's your set."

"Thanks," Lance said, returning to the images.

Joe leaned toward him. "What are you doing this evening?"

"Nothing much."

"Why don't you stay for dinner?" Joe asked.

Lance did more than stay for dinner, of course. He spent the night, and the next night. After a week of 'next nights' he went to Tiny's and got his things. Tiny said, "Your bedroom will be here when you need it."

"Thanks," Lance said, bussing him on the cheek. "I love you."

Tiny smiled. Lance seemed to know just what to say and when to say it. At least Tiny knew where to find him.

Joe was, more or less, in "the industry," as Tiny was fond of calling the porn business, so Lance expected he would understand when Lance had a job.

"I don't mind the videos so much," Joe kept saying, "it's the calls. Do you really need to do them?"

"Yes, I really do. I'm sorry, but I really do."

Lance couldn't explain it, even to himself. He enjoyed meeting people generally, but he particularly enjoyed meeting those who would pay the very steep fee he charged for an hour or more of his sexual favors.

Tiny had told Lance that his escorting career would take off after the release of his first video, but the rush had begun even before that.

The moment he went to producer Max Lerner's place in Malibu he discovered there was a network of rich men, mostly closeted, who traded tips on the latest Tiny Treadwell 'find.' Lance began doing two, sometimes three calls a day, and his overnight rate went to $1,000. He was amazed that all he had to do for that was get his cock hard, which might take awhile, although it was never a problem with younger, attractive johns. The men who hired him went crazy over his cock, and mostly he merely had to lie there and let himself be worshipped.

Meanwhile, Joe was going crazy over Lance's prolonged absences. As Joe grew more difficult, Lance knew he had become something more than a roommate in Joe's eyes and that it was best that he move again, to make other living arrangements. By now he was earning enough to make it on his own and, besides, he wanted a place where clients could come and feel comfortable. Within a week he had found a little house for rent.

As a parting gesture, he let Joe take a series of photographs of him in the bathtub. The magazine that eventually ran the photographs put one of them on the cover with the headline, "The Cleanest Kid in Porn." The moment the magazine hit the newsstands, Tiny was getting calls from all over the country from men who simply *had* to meet Lance, and for whom price was no object.

THREE

Postcard from L.A.X., the Los Angeles International airport, postmarked April 1: *"Dear BD: OK, I'm back and I will not be dancing anymore (nor doing any of the other stuff you don't want me to do) but I have a contract to make videos. I hope you understand. Wish you were here. Love, Lance"*

As they lowered Artie's grandfather into the ground, in a plot containing the remains of his parents and his grandmother, Artie looked up to see a familiar face. Tom had been delayed leaving Detroit and missed the service at the East Tawas Presbyterian church, but he had followed the hearse to the cemetery and discreetly stood to the side as Artie thanked his grandfather's friends for coming.

At last alone with Artie, Tom offered him a ride back to his motel. As they sped away, Artie took Tom's hand. "Thank you for coming," he said solemnly.

"I wanted to see you."

Artie brightened and unbuttoned his overcoat. He took Tom's hand and placed it on his pecs. "So what do you see?"

Tom glanced at Artie as he steered the car around a corner. "I see someone who is no longer a kid."

"No, I'm not a kid anymore."

"No, you're Lance Larkin now. Do you think I'd like Lance?"

"We can find out." Artie pushed Tom's hand down into his crotch.

"I have a lover now," Tom said, trying to pull his hand away.

"So do I," Artie said, seizing Tom's hand and pushing it back onto the bulge.

"Really?"

"You find that crazy, don't you?"

"Yes. I don't know why."

"I know; you don't think somebody in my business could have a lover."

"I guess."

319

"Well, it is possible."

"I'm glad to hear it."

"What's he like, your lover?" Artie ground Tom's hand into his crotch.

Tom gulped. "He's my age. I met him at church. I'm going to a gay church now."

Artie moved closer. The windows inside the car began to steam up and Tom told Artie to turn the defroster on. He didn't want to pull his hand away from where Artie had placed it. He hadn't anticipated Artie being so aggressive. Memories came flooding back, of the first time, how Artie had trembled.

They stopped for a late lunch at the Black Kettle. As they ate their hamburgers, Tom smiled too much at what Artie said, fascinated by his tales of life on a film set, but repelled nonetheless. Artie didn't want dessert, he wanted to go to his motel.

The East Tawas Motel was a whitewashed shoebox on the other side of the seawall and promenade. Artie and Tom had stayed here many times before when Tom would come to the Bay to see the boy. He always asked for room 7, and that was the room Artie had rented this time. Tom asked if that was a coincidence, and Artie just smiled in reply.

"Won't you come in for a minute?" Artie asked, taking Tom's hand.

"Well …."

"For old times' sake?"

Tom smiled. His attraction to the boy was still overpowering. He was confident his lover would understand, but, of course, he would deny anything had happened. But not to go into the room with Artie was unthinkable at this point.

Tom spent a good deal of time taking off Artie's clothes. He kissed and sucked on the gleaming new muscles, the ribbed abdomen. By the time he got to the cock, it was hard. It was like returning to a beloved old friend. He had lost count of the number of times he had blown this magnificent, immense prick. Three years of weekends, holidays, trips to Chicago—the number had to be in the hundreds. But somehow this was new. Artie was far more responsive, and he quickly got in the sixty-nine position over Tom as soon as they got in the bed, and after a long session of squirming and mutual cocksucking, they finally came.

Tom was happy, and although he knew he should feel guilty, somehow, he didn't. What happened here was nobody's business; his and Artie's secrets were theirs to keep, safe from their respective lovers.

After a trip to the bathroom, Artie stood at the window, deep in thought. He was naked, and as he finally backed away he paused to admire himself in the silver-gray marbled mirror, Tom was smiling again. "You must work out every day," Tom said.

Artie chuckled. "I had a trainer when I first went out there. Tiny's trainer. I got a *lot* of training."

Artie sat on the bed and Tom stroked his thigh. "Is there no end to your conquests?"

"Conquests? Is that what they are?"

"When you have this, you're a conqueror, believe me," Tom said, affectionately fondling Artie's semi-flaccid, but still amazing cock.

"What happens if I meet someone with a bigger one?" Artie mused—asking himself as much as asking Tom.

"Never happen," Tom said, squeezing Artie's magnificent monster.

"But it has happened."

Tom blinked. "Oh?"

"Yes, it's true. And he's my lover now. I call him Big Daddy."

"Wouldn't you know."

Artie didn't want to reveal any more, so he took Tom's head in his hands and pressed it down over his crotch.

"He hasn't let me fuck him," Artie said, almost absently.

"Oh?" Tom said, kissing and nibbling, rubbing the glistening cock against his cheek.

"I don't know why. Of course, you never did, either."

"It wasn't that I didn't want to, it's just that I had a bad experience once, and sort of swore off it. Besides, just sucking this was always enough for me."

"Do you do it now? I mean, with the new guy?"

"Yes, but he's as puny as I am. I don't know that I could handle this."

"Why don't we at least find out?"

After Artie greased him thoroughly, Tom slid a condom over Artie's cock. He got on his knees and presented his ass.

Lance slid one, then two, and finally three fingers into Tom's tight ass. Roughly, he began to push his fingers deeper and then pull them rapidly out, soon alternating between his tongue and his fingers. Tom was moaning, arching up in pleasure to meet each stroke.

"Are you ready?" Artie whispered, his breath hot against Tom's hard buttock.

"I'm not sure."

Lance was soon poised at the entrance. Tom took a deep breath, trying to relax. As the prodigious cock entered him, Tom was overwhelmed with sensations. He began to see, feel colors exploding throughout his body' never had he felt so good, so aroused, so *filled*. He tried to hold off but it was no use; shortly after Artie began fucking him, he blasted his orgasm on the bed cover, his entire body shuddering as Lance continued the assault on his anus. The pleasure was excruciatingly delicious—enormously gratifying, almost unbearably thrilling. Suddenly, almost brutally, Lance withdrew from Tom. He peeled off the rubber and stood beside the bed. Tom scrambled over to take the throbbing cock in his mouth. Lance had remembered this was the way Tom liked it most, the jism splashing on his delighted face, messing his hair.

The following morning dawned bright and clear. Tom had hardly slept; he lay awake next to Tom, thinking about what might have been, of what was, and decided, all in all, he was truly blessed.

After breakfast, Tom reluctantly turned to Artie, who was putting a suitcase into his rental car, and reached out to him. Artie took his hand and gently squeezed it; Tom squeezed back. "I'll always be here for you," he said. Artie nodded and took Tom by the hand back into the motel room. There in private, he kissed him full on the mouth and held him.

"Take care of yourself," Tom murmured.

"You too."

Tom smiled at Artie and Artie grinned at him. "Thanks," Tom said. "I have all your videos, you know. Every one."

And Artie beamed with pride. Lance Larkin beamed with pride.

FOUR

A Birthday Card, postmarked from West Hollywood on May 30, addressed to B.D. signed, simply: *"Love, Lance."*

Lance was on the set of *Too Big*. The performer who had been hired to bottom for him had not shown up. "Drugs!" Tiny boomed in frustration. "That shit's going to be the death of me yet."

Tiny had just finished another scene, one that did not involve Lance, who had stood by and watched much of the filming. The bottom, Kevin Martin, was cleaning up after the lengthy, hot, and especially juicy fuck he had just experienced. Tiny pulled Lance aside, and nodded at Kevin as he quietly asked, "Would you mind?"

Lance smiled. He had wondered how long it would be before he would be partnered again with his former protégé. "No," he said. "If he can handle it, I can."

"No hard feelings?" Tiny asked.

Lance snickered at the double entendre. "You'd better hope so—there should be a lot of hards getting felt!"

Tiny knew the history, how close Kevin had come to capturing Lance's heart:

When he first met Lance, Kevin was a mischievous sprite, much given to flirting. He had a slim, sleek build. Short, streaked-blond hair, blue eyes. On the night they met, all the seats were occupied around the large circular banquet table except the one next to Lance as the gay-video awards ceremony was about to begin. Lance edged the vacant chair back slightly.

"You here alone?" The boy settled in next to him.

"Sort of." Lance knew everyone else at the table but, bottom line, he was without a date.

"Me, too." He sipped from the water glass.

Lance concentrated on the boy's eyes. They looked oddly familiar, seeming to resemble Hart's. In most instances, strangers were Lance's favorite companions; they were mirrors, reflecting that person he knew himself to be, but seemingly gift-wrapped by the way the stranger viewed his public persona. He was always Lance Larkin, the porn stud. Something about the way this stranger moved evoked memories of the self-assured, instinctively sexual Hart.

The boy looked at Lance intently. "You okay?"

"No problem." Not really, he thought. Actually, he had spent the last few months rescuing himself. "For a moment, you reminded me of someone, that's all."

"Bad, huh?"

"Just a memory, nothing more," he replied.

"Tell me about it," the stranger said, as though he felt that reminiscing could somehow be of help.

"Later," Lance said, his hand moving to the stranger's knee.

"I'd like that," the flirtatious young blond said, his hand falling over Lance's. His eyes were sharply focused on Lance's, who was made uneasy by his incessant attention and who slowly glanced at the others around the table in hopes of diverting that attention.

The boy was quiet. He was apparently going to sit there and look at Lance until he gave him the attention he wanted. Well aware of the stranger's eyes on him and his hand touching him, a familiar hunger gnawed within Lance. His cock stirred as the boy's hand began to inch toward his crotch.

They watched the ceremonies in silence. Their hands had roved so that each now had his on the other's cock. The blond could feel Lance's cock hardening and growing to an alarming dimension, while his own was already fiercely hard as Lance squeezed and stroked it.

The stranger finally said, "My name is Kevin."

"I'm ..."

Kevin smiled and put a finger to Lance's lips. "Lance Larkin. I've been wanting to meet you *forever*."

Lance chuckled. He could not escape the fact that in this small, crazy gay world he was famous. And every fey boy who loved to suck dick or get screwed apparently dreamed of being with Lance Larkin, taking that stupendous cock down his throat or up his ass.

After the ceremony ended, Lance and Kevin fled quickly, wildly eager to make love to each other. Lance took the boy to his apartment, where he lit candles and burned incense. They stripped and stood for a few minutes studying each other hungrily. Lance would have moved immediately to take the boy in his arms and begin their lovemaking, but he enjoyed basking in the worshipful adoration and hunger the boy clearly felt for him. He was pleased to see that the boy was focusing his adoration on everything he saw, not just on the breathtakingly huge prick jutting straight out from his body and throbbing in anticipation of being buried inside the beautiful boy.

Lance stepped forward and enfolded Kevin in his arms. They shared a long, passionate kiss, their bodies melting together and their cocks pressing into each other. Lance led Kevin to his bed, and they flopped down on the cool lavender sheets.

The candles flickered, and a sultry, fragrant scent hung in the air as Lance pushed Kevin onto his back and began to lick and kiss up and down the boy's splendid young body—golden, velvet, clean-smelling. He hovered over the tip of Kevin's prick—standing straight up from his body—and then rolled the boy over gently.

The breath caught in Lance's throat as Kevin's gorgeous ass was revealed. He fondled and caressed the firm globes gently for a moment before he pulled the thighs wide apart so he could get to the asshole. The fleshy folds were a fresh, bright pink, slick with moisture, little droplets of which were visible on the lips. Kevin moaned in anticipation, and undulated his perfect young ass, clearly begging to have it filled by fingers or a tongue or a cock.

Tongue first, Lance decided. This one should be tasted like a flower, with him as the honeybee. Lance firmly fastened his mouth to the wet boypussy, his tongue sinking into the sweet hole as far as it could reach. "God, what an ass," Lance groaned when he came up for air. Kevin had moaned and panted his ecstasy the whole time Lance had been eating him out.

Lance rose to his knees, between Kevin's wide-spread legs, and Kevin rolled over. Looking up at the cock of his dreams projecting over his body, Kevin lifted his knees and spread his legs wide, growing wildly excited as he watched it approaching his asshole.

Lance's hands slid down the undersides of Kevin's uplifted thighs until they cupped the firm hemispheres of the boy's ass, which he spread farther apart as he leaned forward and his cock approached them. He took his cock in one hand, and teased the lips of Kevin's boypussy with the head. The huge head wiggled the flesh gently as Lance began to press inside. Kevin started to churn his hips gently, welcoming the pliant flesh as the megahung stud gradually opened him further.

As he felt the biggest prick he had ever encountered invading his hungry ass, Kevin began to beg for Lance to fuck him. Soon Lance's cock was halfway in, and he began to fuck gently, not yet ready to drive his monster all the way inside in one fierce thrust—the customary action he took to take complete possession of his sex partner and make him ready to welcome anything the huge-dicked fucking machine wanted to give him.

Lance squeezed Kevin's ass and the boy lifted his legs high to give him freer access. The moment he did so, Lance began his final attack. Kevin's eyes were closed, his mind a jumble of delirious lust when Lance pushed his knees to his chest, and moved to make the young blond's ass *his*. Normally he would have impaled him furiously with one savage thrust, but this boy was so sweet, so …. so special, that instead he drove his long shaft all the way in with one slow, inexorable plunge, not stopping until his pubic hair was pressed firmly against the boy's asshole.

Kevin wailed in ecstasy as he felt fuller, more satisfied than he had ever been. His arms instinctively went around Lance's shoulders as the enormous prick began moving in and out of his ass in unbelievably long strokes, increasing in intensity. He looked up into Lance's eyes, and saw they were unfocused, glazed over with fuck-lust. He hugged the delirious stud's chest to his as he locked his legs behind Lance's back and completely surrendered to the fuck-lust himself.

Kevin groaned as he felt his tissues being stretched, challenged as they never had been before. Lance was in high gear now, hammering Kevin's ass fiercely, the tip of his cock almost emerging with each upstroke, and the base of it pressing against the boy's asshole as he drove in. At the same time, Lance was gyrating his hips, whipping and twisting them, his cock dancing in the tight little hole. He imagined he could feel the heat in there. His hand squeezed one of Kevin's pecs, began twisting a nipple, ramming harder as he started to come. Kevin cried out, "Oh, yes. Yes!"

Lance, sweating profusely now, kept fucking. At length he came forcefully, a long orgasm, with Kevin's hips pumping at the huge cock embedded in his spasming hole.

"Tell me about him." They had showered and Kevin was enjoying a joint.

"Who?" Lance asked.

"The guy you're missing."

"I'm not missing anybody."

Kevin wanted Lance to unravel the mystery for him, explain the deep longing that haunted him. But he was uncertain what to say, or how to ask about something indefinable. That thing, that craving that drove him, came from a place where there weren't any words, and his attempts to ask Lance to define the meaning of his life were awkward, and evoked no helpful response.

"I don't know, there aren't any words to explain," Lance finally concluded." But he wished there were.

Kevin rolled on top of Lance, kissed him on the chin, worked his way around Lance's face until he arrived at the lips.

Lance returned the kiss. It didn't matter. Nothing mattered anymore. He had learned not to hold onto expectations—not about romance, not about love.

325

This boy wanted to be fucked senseless. Lance would do that, it would be okay with him, he told Kevin that. But he also kept asking about "the guy." Kevin had no idea where Lance had been, what he was all about. How dare he ask these things?

"If you want to know what I'm all about," Lance finally said, curtly, "ask around. Ask around about how I love. "

"Oh, I know how you love. At least, how you make love—have sex. But it isn't the same. You fucked me like you fuck every one of those guys in the videos."

"That wasn't good enough?" Lance asked in mock anger.

"Oh, god, it was the best! But you know that. You know all you had to do was just stick it in me and I'd have gone wild. But you did more than that. You made me feel as if you were really enjoying it."

"I was. You love to get fucked and I loved fucking you. That's all."

If that wasn't all Kevin needed, it clearly was all he was going to get. He was hard again, crazy for it again.

That night they went out to a dance club. The place was packed. Colored lights cut through the fog of the hazy dance floor. The writhing dancers disintegrated into dreamy, shifting shadows, leaving nothing but Lance and Kevin. Kevin was an incredible dancer, which made Lance feel almost immobilized, yet he still danced to the driving beat.

What it was that Kevin really wanted, Lance did not know. Obviously he was into fucking both for fun and for profit—he was, after all, at the awards ceremony—but it didn't matter. Lance was prepared to offer him whatever it was. To have a fling with this adorable young blond would make him feel good just then.

Three nights later, Lance was lying in bed, tired but awake. Kevin slept quietly beside him. There was something about the boy, about being with him, that soothed Lance.

It was barely after midnight and the apartment was dark. Lance realized that, since Hart, he had used making love to his sex partners as a vehicle, rather than as an end in itself. They allowed him the opportunity to let go for a short while, to use them as a means of surrendering to his desire to forget.

Kevin was an ideal impromptu lover. Through him, Lance explored himself. They would be caring and passionate for a night and, the next morning when Lance walked out the door, he wouldn't leave his heart behind with the sexy blond boy. Still, in the middle of their fucking, Kevin often said how much he loved Lance, which invariably caused Lance to think: "I must be cautious."

Once Lance introduced Kevin to Tiny, things began to change between them. Kevin immediately got all the porn work he wanted. He worked two or three days a week, and within only a few months had already appeared in a half-dozen first-class videos—so well received that his name appeared as prominently on the video box and in the credits as those of the established stars. He was, Tiny conceded, on the verge of becoming the newest bottom sensation.

Regardless of his growing stature as a porn star, when he slipped into his and Lance's bed late at night, Kevin was like a sex-hungry boy. He would be all over Lance. He might have spent the day on the set, getting fucked by one, or two, or even more men, but there was still room for Lance in his life.

Lance objected to Kevin's strenuous schedule, making video after video. He told the boy that was not a good plan, that he should go slower, be more selective and make fewer videos, to cultivate an eagerness on the part of his fans to see his next movie—make them wait, to increase their appreciation when he did appear.

But Tiny overruled that plan. "That may be fine for studs like Lance," Tiny counseled, "but for a bottom, the more the merrier."

One evening Lance had dinner with one of the gay magazine columnists and then stopped for groceries. As he was returning to the building, he saw the stud known as Rex Davies leaving his apartment. He knew Kevin had filmed a scene that day with Rex. Obviously, the scene hadn't been enough. Lance ducked into a stairwell to avoid meeting Rex at the elevator.

After he had put the groceries down in the kitchen, he looked around for signs of what had gone on in his absence. Nothing appeared to have been disturbed, except in the bedroom, where the bed was a mess. He could hear the water running in the bathroom and knocked on the closed door.

Kevin opened it slowly. He was naked, wet from a shower, toweling his hair.

Lance grabbed his arms. "Your coming here was a big mistake! Did you fuck him in my bed?"

"No, honest. I swear on my mama."

Lance released his grip, and Kevin thudded against the hard tile floor. Kevin reached for a jockstrap that was on the floor, and Lance ripped it out of his hand. He sniffed the crotch.

"I thought we agreed that sex on the set is okay but ...."

Kevin snatched his jockstrap back. "You're sick. You of all people! You know what goes on."

Lance considered Kevin's complaint. The kid was right. He'd hit a nerve. Still, it was over. "Pack your bags!"

"I'm not going, and you can't make me!" he protested.

"Who the *hell* do you think you're talking to, you fuckin' queer?"

"Who's the fuckin' queer here, huh? You and your married men. You're really sick, man. Really sick!"

Lance grabbed him by the arm and threw him into the bedroom. He opened the closet and pulled out Kevin's suitcase, throwing it on the bed.

327

"Don't do this, please! I don't have anywhere to go."

"That's your problem."

After Kevin had gone, Lance tore the sheets off the bed and put new ones on it. As he slept, he luxuriated in the cleanliness. When he awoke in the morning and rolled out of bed, something unexpected had happened: the leg irons were gone. He felt freed from the memories of what was, what could have been—freed from the shackle of a lover who fucked everything in sight.

A burst of light danced on the edge of the sky and he was no longer afraid. He had a vision of Hart, a prisoner to his own darkness—married, but alone and spiritless. Lance was through with that deceit. Hart may fool himself but he no longer tricked Lance, who had nothing left for Hart. Fucking Kevin so often, and so well, had taken it all out of him. And though Kevin may have had a hundred lovers, and have hundreds more in the future, he would never again have a lover like Lance. Hart and Kevin both had their chance, and each had blown it. Lance felt like he had withdrawn into himself. Now, nothing could be taken away from him, and outside problems seemed to have evaporated like the rain in a Miami heat wave.

*   *   *

"It's been over a year," Kevin reminded Lance.

"And you've become a star. Congratulations." Lance was not smiling.

"A *star*?"

"That's what you wanted. You got it."

"But ...."

The makeup girl finished working on Lance and he got out of the chair. Kevin sat down where Lance had been; he only needed a touch-up since he had just done a scene and barely worked up a sweat, despite the lights. In fact, Lance noted, Kevin had hardly moved while the guy was doing him on camera.

"Still getting over him?" Kevin asked as they walked onto the tacky set, representing a back alley.

"No. I've got a new one now that I'm trying to get over."

Lance laughed bitterly. "We always love the ones we shouldn't."

"Kevin, over there, against the wall," Tiny barked.

"The master is speaking ...."

Kevin stood by a garbage can, waiting there as the cameras began to record the action.. Lance approached. There was no dialogue, just a close-up of Kevin sizing Lance up, his hand going to the bulge in Lance's jeans.

Kevin blushed, excited by the way Lance looked at him—with obvious lust, even though he was probably doing so just for the camera. He had longed to share this with Lance again—what was happening, and what was going to happen as they enacted the scenario for the video they were shooting together.

Lance suddenly dropped to his knees.

Stunned, Kevin moaned and, trembling with delight, gazed down and watched Lance kiss his smooth belly, each kiss warm on his skin. Lance's tongue snaked out to lick his navel, then slide along just above the waist of his jeans.

Lance unzipped the jeans and dug his face down inside them to kiss the golden fluff above Kevin's cock. The blond boy moaned in anticipation.

Lance worked the jeans down, bunching them at Kevin's thighs. He began to suck his erection expertly. Kevin was shaking with pleasure: Lance hadn't sucked him like this all the while he was with him, and he hadn't sucked him at all since the night he threw him out. Soon Kevin was seated on the garbage can, his back against a wall, his legs hanging over the edge, and his throbbing cock buried completely inside Lance's hungry mouth.

Kevin was more responsive than Lance had expected, and Lance was determined to give his former lover pleasure—to reawaken in him the same thrilled response he had enjoyed when they had been together. Of course, Kevin was still beautiful, he was still incomparably sexy, and those facts alone made lovemaking with him a treat for Lance. But when he remembered the intense, loving sex they had shared so many times in the past—in spite of his having vowed not to remember it—Lance was acting to please himself as much as he was Kevin.

Lance stopped sucking, and stood, his enormous dick jutting straight out from his flat belly. Tiny zoomed in to get a close-up of the fabulous cock. Lance lifted Kevin's legs, placed them over his shoulders, and bent to the ass. Against all apparent odds, Lance's prick managed to slip inside Kevin's hole, and the fucking began. In spite of the sincerity of the lovemaking—each remembering having done this so many times for their own personal pleasure—both Lance and Kevin remembered to play to the cameras, providing many opportunities for Tiny's trademark close-ups.

With his legs wound tightly around the back of Lance's neck, and with Lance's cock savagely driving in and out of his ass, Kevin came, bumping his cock against Lance's face, wailing with bliss. The orgasm was intense, both voluminous and explosive, and the cameras captured it from every angle, the cum splattering across Lance's face and belly, and then dripping down onto the ecstatic blond, still lost in fuck-lust.

Lance backed up to pull his cock out of Lance and show it to the camera; then he got the tip back inside the boy, then more of it, and then he shoved fiercely, burying himself in the receptive passage again in one swift plunge. He fucked Kevin for a solid twenty minutes before he pulled out again and coated the still ecstatic, still fiercely erect boy with cum.

After a lunch break, the next scene began, an orgy that was supposed to be happening on the dance floor of a deserted nightclub. It opened with

Kevin and Lance in a sixty-nine that immediately had them both hard and dripping. As the mirrored ball revolving overhead cast weird patterns on their skin, Lance rose to his knees from where he crouched over Kevin on all fours, to be joined by Chico, a well-hung Latin with an earring in each earlobe. Chico knelt next to Lance and they began to stroke each other. Soon their pricks were just inches from Kevin's cock-hungry mouth.

They teased Kevin, first one, then the other. Finally, they shoved both cocks in his mouth. Lance couldn't believe that Kevin could take both of the large cockheads but he did. Soon Kevin was on his knees, choking down Chico's fat cock and Lance was behind him, working his finger into his moist asshole. Six men slowly joined them on the set. They were all nude and there was an air of desperate sexual hunger about them as they watched Chico driving hard into Kevin's mouth—choking but not pulling away—and Lance playing with the boy's ass. Lance keenly understood the urgency of such acts, both the need to keep taking it and the urge to keep giving it. He remembered Reggie fucking his mouth back at the apartment with even greater vigor than the way Chico was fucking Kevin's.

"You like that?" Chico said while holding Kevin's head tight to his crotch. "There's more where that came from." He motioned to Steve, who had a couple of gold rings in one ear, and Steve went over to them, standing next to Chico, stroking himself to hardness as he watched Kevin sucking.

Steve took Chico's head in his hands and forced Chico's willing mouth down over his prick, while Lance continued to finger-fuck Kevin and play with himself at the same time.

Even in the flickering light, Lance could see Kevin's cock was fully hard. Another guy, Joe, older, hairy, noticed as well and came up to them. "Hey look at that! He likes it." Joe got on the floor between Kevin's thighs and began sucking him. Kevin began trembling; he looked ready to cry. "Hey," Chico cried, "the pretty boy is gonna cry. Give him something to cry about Lance."

Lance proceeded to do just that; he lifted Kevin's ass high and jammed his half-hard cock in again.

Things quickly got out of hand and tears were soon running down Kevin's face.

Two guys, one dark-haired, the other dirty blond, with big knobby-looking cocks, began stroking themselves, getting ready to replace Lance or Chico, whichever way it went. The blond, Jeff, came over first, his cock bobbing obscenely, rising nakedly from a shaved pubic patch. He took Lance's place in Kevin's ass. Then the dark-haired guy, Bill, came over to stand next to Lance, and the two groped and kissed hungrily while Kevin kept sucking on Chico. Finally, Chico came, and one of the cameramen covered the explosion all over Kevin's smiling face, then the dark-haired guy went around and jammed his prick into

Kevin's mouth. Chico licked his own cum from Kevin's face, then bent down and began kissing and sucking on Bill's balls as they swung wildly while he fucked Kevin's mouth.

Tiny barked instructions to Chico to get in position on his knees next to Kevin; Lance went over to Chico's ass and plunged his cock in.

The action continued for several minutes before it became obvious to Lance that Tiny wanted it to appear dangerous and out-of-control. And that's just what the boys gave him. At one point, Tiny handed Jeff a big dildo which he stuffed into Kevin's ass, working it in and out as Lance mercilessly fucked Chico. Lance went in deep and hard, and Chico took it, complaining that Lance was too big, and was going too deep. Lance just kept twitching his hips until he was deeper than he'd ever been in a man's ass. When he was ready, Lance pulled out and blasted a scalding load all over Chico's back. Jeff threw away the dildo and re-entered Kevin. With everyone egging him on, Jeff was able to come in short order, pulling out and jacking his cock to a shattering climax. There was still Bill to contend with, and Chico and Kevin continued to share his cock until he was ready. Again, Kevin's face got bathed in cum.

After the filming, the other performers washed up quickly, leaving Kevin and Lance alone together in the bathroom.

"I'm sorry I hurt you …." Lance confessed, wiping his cock with a damp cloth.

"I'm used to it," Kevin said, not looking up. He was engrossed in the enema he always seemed to be giving himself.

Lance stepped over to where Kevin sat on the toilet. He ran his hand through the boy's tousled hair. "Let's get something to eat."

Kevin brought his free hand to Lance's cock—he couldn't resist the temptation. Lifting it to his mouth, he said brightly, "Sounds good to me." He brought his tongue to the head of Lance's peerless dick and began to stimulate it, wielding his tongue almost like an artist's tool. As Kevin licked, Lance started running hands over the boy's smooth back. Kevin's sucking soon brought Lance to full erection again.

The short, compact Toby, a photographer Tiny had hired to take stills on the shoot, had entered the bathroom just as Kevin and Lance had begun talking, and was having a field day with his zoom lens. But Lance and Kevin were barely aware of him.

Kevin energetically slid his lips up and down Lance's massive cock. Lance was once again stunned by his former lover's technique. Kevin seemed happy and eager to be the perfect sucking machine. He relinquished Lance's cock and began to tickle his balls unmercifully with his tongue until Lance laughingly pleaded, "No, no. Please, no more!"

But Lance didn't want it to end yet. Neither did Toby. He dropped his camera and dragged Lance away from Kevin. He bent over and began licking Lance's cock, paying attention to every one of its many inches. His hands and tongue were a tormenting mixture of smoothness and roughness, and Lance closed his eyes, feeling as if he were drifting into outer space.

When he opened his eyes, he saw the full length of Kevin's rigid cock sliding in and out of Toby's ass while he clutched it and guided it back and forth on his slippery erection. Meanwhile, Toby was making lovely sucking sounds, and Lance thought he might come from the combination of Toby's superb cocksucking and the sight of the beautiful blond boy fucking him.

But Kevin wanted his turn, and begged Lance to start fucking his ass instead of Toby's mouth.

Lance pulled away from Toby and got behind Kevin. When he heard Kevin's impassioned cries, he slipped his tool inside the boy and moved it in and out provocatively. The ridges of his powerful cock filled every crevice of Kevin's well-prepared anus. He plunged in deeper. The cum gushed from Kevin's cock, still deep inside Toby, and he threw his head from side to side in ecstasy. Lance gave another thrust and then exploded inside Kevin. Hearing the cries that signaled Lance's orgasm, Toby jacked himself and cum spurted from his pulsating penis in a seemingly endless flow.

As the two ex-lovers embraced, Toby retrieved his camera, setting the shutter for fast action. Lance sat on the toilet and lifted Kevin's ass, positioning it over his half-hard cock, then pressing down until he was once again buried inside it. He held the boy there, and Kevin wrapped his legs around Lance's firm body. Soon Lance was fully erect once again and Kevin was bouncing up and down on the cock, sucking on Lance's throat. Then they rolled to the floor still entwined. Lance held on to Kevin's waist and lifted him up and down on his by-then smoking cock. Suddenly, Lance shot his juice into Kevin once more, and their bodies shook with pleasure—Kevin's tiny frame straining against Lance's enormous member. Kevin collapsed on top of Lance, who fondled his ass while they kissed passionately. Toby finally ran out of film and, just then, Tiny banged on the door. "We're shutting down, boys."

Lance smiled and whispered to Kevin, "Now can we get something to eat?"

FIVE

Scrawled on a Happy Anniversary card picturing two men kissing, postmarked from West Hollywood, dated June 15: *"Dear B.D., Do you believe it's been a year? Do I love you? Yeah! Love, Lance."*

Lance rarely went out in West Hollywood but he decided to celebrate their anniversary—alone. He sat on a stool at *Numbers* and waited to be recognized. It didn't take long.

The man who bought him a drink reminded him, in a way, of his Big Daddy. But not enough. The man walked away, saying he would be back. Lance nodded and savored the cognac. He always ordered the best when someone else was buying. It was not a night for meeting new people. No, it was a night for remembering a year ago. It didn't seem like a year had passed, but it had:

"Lance! I love it," the tall man had said when he approached the stud in the bar that night a year before, shaking his hand, clasping it firmly, not limply, or by the fingers the way some men did—like they were shaking the hand of a child's stuffed animal. The man introduced himself as Kirk and he held Lance's hand between his two palms. "I'm pleased to meet you." Lance had heard that often, but Kirk was the first person in a long time who seemed to truly mean it, to go beyond the obvious thing that everyone always seemed to be interested in: his cock.

Lance's face felt hot and tingly, his body charged with a current of excitement. Kirk hadn't taken his eyes off Lance's face. As He stepped closer to him his breath was warm, and smelled faintly of bourbon. Kirk had the deep creases around his eyes of a man who, no matter what the weather, drives fast and with the window down just to feel the rush of wind on his face. He was intense-looking, romantic, with black hair and burning dark eyes. He was possibly the sexiest thing Lance had ever seen: brooding, poetic, and passionate—very passionate. He looked sinister and dark, like a gangster.

Oooh, Lance thought. He's looks *so* rotten! Not only that, he was considerably older—and that was the most glamorous thing of all. He didn't have acne or sweaty palms. He was somewhere over thirty; how much, Lance could not be sure.

"Listen," Kirk said running his hand over his mouth, absently feeling his lips. "You have another show to do, but if I wait, maybe we could go out together afterward."

"All right," Lance said a little breathlessly, surprised and pleased at the invitation, but hoping he didn't look too much so. He turned away and was immediately chest-to-chest with another admirer, an overly tanned man with liquid blue eyes, who half-hugged him and whispered in his ear, causing Lance to laugh and shake his head, rejecting a proposal that did not interest him. Then Lance disappeared into the crowd.

It was a good gig for Lance, a weekend dancing at one of Orlando's hottest strip bars and staying at the posh Parliament House. When Kirk had said he was in Orlando for a conference, a sense of déjà vu swept over Lance. This was Hart all over again, Lance thought. Somehow he knew his new admirer was a married man but he was six-two, with broad shoulders, incredible pecs straining his T-shirt, and muscular legs encased in well-worn denims. He would do, Lance thought. He'd do for the night.

Kirk was an author, doing a book tour, and the hours he had spent autographing books at stores in the area had taken their toll. He needed to relax; he needed a drink. Also sex, of course, a way of losing the self by embracing another.

A different man might have gone home now that the tour was over, poured himself a Scotch, and, placing a needy, affectionate hand on his wife's sleeping body, awakened her to his troubles and his longing. But for Kirk, such an act was out of the question. He and Nancy, married for two decades, hadn't made love in years. Indeed, he felt he no longer loved her, at least not in the romantic way he yearned to be in love. More frequently, instead of actively sharing his life with Nancy, Kirk found himself doing more book tours, making more TV appearances, agreeing to attend more writers' conferences—and going to gay bars in pursuit of some release, something neither his wife nor any woman could give him. What difference did it make when he and his wife no longer even slept in the same room?

After the show Lance dressed and sat at the bar looking for his date. Suddenly, Lance felt Kirk's hand on his shoulder, his fingertips pressing down into his clavicle bones.

In the dim light of the bar Kirk's eyes were intensely brown—like something melted down, or maybe the leather interior of an expensive car. Something foreign, certainly. Slowly his eyes raked Lance's body, starting at his feet, pausing admiringly at his bulging crotch and his broad chest, finally smiling languorously into his eyes. "You know you are one handsome boy, don't you?" he said. "I'll bet men give you things, don't they?"

Lance smiled. "Mostly a hard time." Lance had decided to work at this a bit, be provocative and exciting, suggesting he had the power to destroy him a little bit, the power to make a mark on him.

As they walked out into the parking lot, Kirk said he was not staying at the Parliament House. He preferred the Hyatt Regency at the airport. "So tell me about Lance," he said.

Lance was silent. It had been a long time since someone had asked him such an up-front question about himself and he didn't know how to react. Finally, he said, "What do you want to know about me?"

"The Lance no one knows. The one you don't talk about."

"Well," Lance leaned back into the plush seat of the rented Lincoln, "what makes you think there's anything to tell?"

Kirk frowned slightly, then narrowed his eyes as if he was sizing Lance up. Lance wriggled in his seat, and grinned at him.

"Come on, just between you and me," Kirk said, "a kid like you must have lots of stories. The poster in the bar says you're a porn star. God, the stories you must have. Come on."

"Maybe," Lance said.

Lance didn't understand how he knew it, but somehow he sensed this man wanted to hear about something raw and personal—probably sexual—perhaps something he was ashamed of. But he was not ashamed of his "profession."

An amazing thing about Kirk was that he obviously had no idea who Lance was. This had not happened to Lance since he made his first video three years before. Since then, everyone he met knew who he was.

"Have you got a lover?" Kirk asked Lance, running the length of his index finger back and forth across the boy's lips.

"Several," Lance said quickly. That was true, after all—he did, but he didn't think that should pose any obstacle to his and Kirk getting to know each other. In fact it might turn Kirk on, Lance thought—hoped, actually.

The older man wrapped his arm around Lance's shoulder. "Come here, sit closer."

"What do you do?" Lance asked.

"What do I *do*?"

"For a living?"

"I'm a writer."

"What do you write about?"

Lance was sitting so close to him now that Kirk couldn't seem to think clearly all of a sudden. "Well," he said, "I don't know. I mostly write about relationships, I guess. How people are with each other."

"Are you famous? Are you a *famous* writer?"

Kirk nodded. "Isn't it odd? Here you are famous in your world and I really don't know who you are and here I am rather famous in my world and you don't know who I am. It seems we were fated to meet, doesn't it?" His hand squeezed Lance's shoulder for a moment.

The darkness accentuated Kirk's knobbed cheekbones, and made his mouth seem thick and lush. It made him look younger. Lance was beginning to surrender much of himself to this man.

Kirk caressed his arm. "You know you are very sexy," he murmured. "You may be the sexiest boy I've ever met."

Lance licked his lips. "I don't know if you really want me to tell you about my sex life," he said raising an eyebrow.

"I do," Kirk said, and squeezed his fingers.

Suddenly it occurred to Lance that Kirk was too much like Hart, the kind of man who wanted to do things to your body you'd never let another man do, as if it were his right. Then he'd want you to tell him how it felt, in detail, so he would own you. He regretted, for a moment, having agreed to come with the man.

At three a.m., the streets were lonely, empty, like the other half of Kirk's bed—and Lance's too, most nights. Usually, Lance would trick at a john's hotel room and then return to his own pad, but somehow he knew he was going to spend the night with this man.

When they were safely in the hotel's parking garage, Kirk reached out slowly and took Lance's face in his hands, cupping it, weighing it. Then he pressed his lips to Lance's, and they kissed, tenderly and lovingly.

His large hand tightened on the back of Lance's head. "You are gorgeous, you know that?" He smiled, "Of course you know that."

Kirk found Lance exceedingly pleasing. He was well-built of course, and the costume he wore when he danced made it very clear he was hung like a horse. But he was also good-looking in a generic, nondescript way that made him seem somehow immediately accessible and, more importantly, trustworthy. He had a mop of light-brown hair and a face that was often lit by an impish grin, as if he was in on some lewd joke.

Kirk's hand grasped Lance's and he pulled it to his mouth to kiss the knuckles, pressing his tongue between the spread fingers. His words seemed to flare and burn. "I've got you now."

Lance shuddered. This guy was even more romantic than Hart. What was he getting himself into?

Once they were in the hotel room, Kirk unzipped his pants and exposed his penis. Lance, standing before him, did the same. But it wasn't until Kirk was fully naked that Lance knew just how glorious this was to be. He had figured Kirk would be hung but he was not prepared for the fact that Kirk's cock was not only fully as long as his own monster dick, it was thicker!

Lance thought that a decade earlier, when Kirk was younger, he could have made history in porn. Now he was going to make history with Lance.

Lance aimed his cockhead straight for the folds of Kirk's pink, blind foreskin. Kirk smiled, and instead of stripping his skin back and pulling his dickhead out, guided the dry head of Lance's cock straight inside his hot, wet foreskin. Lance groaned and he guided the semi-hard cock in deeper. The generous lip of Kirk's foreskin extended a couple inches past the tip of his impressive endowment. Before the tip of Lance's penis touched the hard crown of Kirk's cock, two inches of it was enfolded within the foreskin.

Kirk wrapped his hand tightly around their connection and began a stroking motion with his hand and then a fucking motion with his muscular hips. They both watched intently what went on down below and between them. Kirk continued to massage the two enormous dicks together, head to head. He kept up his rhythmic cadence. The excitement of this new sensation caused Lance to become hard and soon he was ready to explode.

But Kirk had other ideas. His fingers found Lance's raised nipples; he pinched both of them so hard that Lance gasped, and a series of heat waves flooded his body. Excrting even more pressure, Kirk plucked and twisted, never once letting up. Lance was caught in an uncontrollable climb to glorious pleasure, a dangerous pleasure.

All Lance could say as they on the bed was, "Fuck me now."

"Now?" Kirk asked, stroking Lance's semi-hard cock.

Lance reached out, ran his hand up the exquisite shaft of Kirk's penis, pulling the skin back, revealing a bulbous head. Kirk was *so* hard. Even with the lateness of the hour, and the booze, he was ready. Yes, Lance thought, this guy should've done porn.

Lance let Kirk lie down and then he climbed atop him. Slowly he took Kirk's enormous prick into his hot ass, straddling his hips and pressing his body hard against the mattress. Over him, down on him, Lance moved his hips like he'd mounted a bounding steed.

"Go baby go. Yes, baby—go!"

Lance was riding each wild thrust. He sucked Kirk's neck, leaving marks all over him, bruising him. Lance was jerking, clinging to him for dear life. Kirk slammed into him with his hips and Lance was blasted with the heat.

After awhile, Lance was on his back, his legs slung over Kirk's shoulders and the older man was unrelenting, not coming until Lance had.

When it was over, Lance could barely stand. His legs were rubbery and weak, yet he was suspended in a cloud, a mist of pleasure. Kirk's hands found their way to the center of his desire. His tongue whipped across the head of Lance's cock in rapid, fluttery strokes.

"I like it like that. Right there. Right there. Please, please, please, please. Right there. I like that."

And Lance fell asleep as Kirk sucked on his cock.

"God, I like everything you do." Lance said. His eyes were closed. It was safer that way. It was the following morning and he could not look at his new lover; he was too happy. He hadn't been this happy since Hart. He loved Kirk's sinister looks, the scent of him, but more than anything, he loved his words: Words of love and poetry—unforgettable words, spoken by a man with limpid black eyes and, at times, a boyish countenance.

Now Kirk's entire body weight pinned Lance to the bed.

"I do. I love everything you do ...."

"Nope." He grabbed his wrists and pulled his arms above his head. "Nope, nope, nope."

Lance clenched his eyes tight. Kirk's body felt so strong, so forceful, so in control. His cock pressed against Lance's. They were covered with sweat. The slippery, hot dampness was earthy, animal—sex stripped raw. Kirk lifted Lance's ankles and with a fast push, separated his legs even farther. Pressure restrained Lance's arms, tension secured his legs; his heart pounded in delicious misery.

"Tell me, now." Kirk was uncompromising. His hands clutched Lance's wrists. "Is this what you like?"

Lance wished he had a blindfold on. If only the room were pitch-black.

"Yeah," Lance gurgled. He could feel slippery sex juice on his thighs.

337

"Just on the side. Just on the edge. Like that. Yes."

Only the head of Kirk's cock was in Lance; he toyed with the boy unmercifully.

"Good. Like that. Yes, God!" The words pushed hard in his throat.

For the longest time, Kirk's cock barely moved. His breath was hard in Lance's ear. Lance grabbed Kirk's arms and pushed his ass against his giant prick, jamming it into him.

Kirk knew what the boy wanted now. "Got you, baby. Baby, baby, baby," he muttered. "I'll really fuck you now." He rammed his cock in and out. He was soon going nonstop. The rhythm of their breathing accelerated, countering each thrust.

Oh my God, Lance thought, *Kirk is so good. So good. So good.* Lance was hot, riding the edge of pleasure like a spinning gyroscope. "Okay, yes. Jesus, yes."

Kirk crushed his mouth into Lance's shoulder. His teeth seized his flesh. Almost. Almost. Lance was so close again. "Keep ... fucking ... you ... like ... this?" His words rode a torrent of quick breaths. His fingers grasped Lance's cock even tighter.

"Oh, yes, oh yes," Lance murmured.

Kirk bit his shoulder. "More, baby? Huh, baby?"

"Don't stop. Yes, there. More. More. More." Wild and uninhibited pleas poured from him, streamed from him. He was close. Out of his body. Over his body.

"This. This is how I like it," Lance said after he had come and Kirk had slowed, taking his time, savoring the fuck.

"God, am I still in one piece after that?" Lance asked, his hand pinching his asscheek.

Suddenly, Lance felt a rush of energy pass through him, as if some sort of magic dust had been sprinkled on him, like in a Disney movie he saw as a child, changing his entire perspective, changing everything. Kirk had turned him inside out. Places not meant to be touched became electric under his caress. Lance was trembling, he was quivering. He was loose and tight, all at once. He was nothing and everything under Kirk's sure fingers.

"Fuck me," Lance pleaded later that day. To Lance, Kirk exuded strength, anger, confidence, authority. Lance tried to raise himself from the bed. He wanted to put his arms around Kirk, make contact, to delight in, to become one with this marvelous powerhouse of a stud.

Kirk smiled. "Yeah, you're gonna take it *all*." With heated breath, his reply hissed through Lance's ear, burned a red-hot trail down to his nipples, singed his cock and settled deep in his ass.

Lance's fingers pressed the mattress with the pain, then released. His cock was harder than it had ever been. "Oh God, oh God, oh God. All I want now, all I need now!"

Kirk didn't stop. He manipulated it, pumped it, drained it. There was so much Lance wanted, so much he craved—so much he received. Lance stung, he ached, and yet the very place where Kirk was driving his big cock—so roughly, so abruptly—was begging for more.

The room was quiet except for Lance's moans and the slapping sound of Kirk driving his cock into the boy.

Kirk himself was beyond excitement. With each thrust into Lance's tight ass, he became more and more aroused. He was starting to lose control, moaning loudly. Then he stopped, lifted Lance into his arms and kissed him. Lance was begging, crying, purring, moaning. Arching his pelvis up to meet the thrusts. The room smelled of their combined scents. Kirk moved back and forth, quickening his pace with every stroke.

Lance, engulfed by the older stud, was beyond control himself. Reaching down between his own legs, he quickly began to massage his cock. As Kirk increased his pace, so Lance increased the pace and force of the strokes on his own giant shaft. Faster, faster until suddenly it was too much. Feeling Kirk above him, and the now-familiar groan as Kirk reached orgasm, Lance beat his fingers back and forth rapidly and began arching in ecstasy, barely able to breathe as Kirk came inside him.

A few moments later, Kirk had removed his cock and inserted his fingers. "Twist 'em," Lance muttered as Kirk stabbed his fingers into the boy's ass. "Easy though. Easy, easy, easy. Yes. Please. Please." Almost. Almost. His cock seemed to double in size. Swollen, voluptuous. Back and forth he kneaded the flesh. Pre-cum coated his fingers.

Soon Kirk was fucking Lance again, ramming him with all he had. Almost. Almost. Lance kept pounding his own cock, ready.

"More, baby? More?" Deliriously passionate words spilled from Kirk's mouth. He began to suck Lance's neck, biting him. "Go, baby—do it!" And Lance did, with an orgasm that left him breathless.

Kirk ran his hands through Lance's wild mane, recklessly kissing him over and over. "Oh baby, my sweet, sweet baby," he murmured, continuing to kiss and hold Lance, to melt into Lance's very being.

Lance grasped Kirk tightly, wrapping his arms and legs around him. Two became one, pressed against each other, glued together by Lance's copious orgasm, the sticky cum that covered their chests and stomachs.

*   *   *

"Do you have to leave?" Lance blurted out, immediately regretting his words and their implication. He stopped at the bathroom door and turned. "I just thought maybe..." *Maybe what?*, Lance thought.

Kirk glanced at his watch and smiled. "My baby want some more?"

Lance stood there but said nothing. After all, what was there to say? The boundaries they had so clearly set during their many, many sessions of wild lovemaking now seemed too harsh.

339

"My baby need more?" He sauntered toward Lance, car keys in one hand, leather jacket in the other.

Yes. The stud's boy, his baby, wanted more. More. More. More. But Lance doubted that what he wanted more of wasn't what Kirk had in mind to give him. It was just like Hart—the same nightmare all over again. Emotionally uninvolved, no illusions about romance with these guys. Why was he even looking to see if it might be there?

"I just thought maybe..." He averted his focus from Kirk's firecracker eyes. "What I mean is ....well, what I was just wondering..."

"Yes, baby?" Kirk was inches away from him. His Armani cologne swept him into a haze of desire.

"Do you have to leave? I mean, *always?*"

He backed up slightly. "Meaning?"

"Sometimes ... maybe ... just sometimes, though... I wish you'd want more."

"Baby, I always want more," he muttered.

"I mean, more than what it is." Lance kept staring at the floor.

Kirk shifted his stance. "Baby, this is more than I've ever been able to give." And it was true. He was astonished at the quality and intensity of the hours he had spent with Lance.

When he was a guest on a talk show once, Kirk observed that the American writer in the mid-twentieth century has his hands full trying to comprehend, and then make believable, much of American reality. "The actuality," he said, "is continually outdoing our capability, and our culture almost daily throws people and situations at us that are so rich in potential as fodder for writers that we hardly know how to use them."

Little did those in the audience suspect that the people and the situations being daily thrown at Kirk involved the sleaziest, most corrupted youths he could find. But with Lance he thought he had found a true diamond in the rough, a boy who had obviously been corrupted by the sleaziest business imaginable, yet who retained and exuded an innocence, a vulnerability that turned Kirk on—beyond his wildest imagining. While he had disported himself with prostitutes before, he had never known one like Lance. The youth was not only sexually inventive, but, being a major porn star, so glamorous that he stirred in him more than just physical passion. Lance aroused in him fantasies about love that had haunted him since his adolescence. He found himself wishing he could just hold Lance's hand and go walking with him in Central Park, take him nude sunbathing on some secluded beach, find an idyllic river and spend an afternoon canoeing. He wanted to share cultural experiences with him, too, and romantic, candlelit dinners.

Before he left to catch his plane, he confessed these yearnings to Lance, who offered to make his dreams come true.

SIX

Lance was suddenly 'wired,' and sleepless. The only light in the room was a dim glow coming from the night light. He fluffed his pillows, shaking them to restore their resilience, and at the same time wishing he could shake his need for Kirk as easily.

The ringing of the phone startled him. He snatched it up immediately. "Hello?" His heart raced.

"I'm there with you. Can you feel me?" His tone was as seductive as ever.

"I can't believe you've called," Lance said quickly, as if any hesitation would cause his lover to hang up.

Kirk laughed, a long, low laugh. "I told you, just close your eyes and I'm there."

"You are, absolutely."

"Tell me about the last time I called you," Kirk interrupted. "Tell me about that." His breath was steady, hypnotic.

Lance closed his eyes. He knew what Kirk wanted. In their last phone conversation, Kirk, weaving a magnificent tapestry of words, figuratively brought Lance to New York, where he fucked him with those same magic words.

"What exactly do you want to know?"

"You know what I want."

"How it was for me? Is that what you want to know?"

Silence.

Lance took a long, slow breath and remembered the last call, the last fuck. "You found all these places in me that've never been so, well, so ....

"Exposed?"

"Yeah. Exposed."

"Never?"

"No. Not really. I mean, there was one guy ...."

"The Senator's son. Yes, you told me a little about him. Another married man."

Another disappointment, Lance started to say, but he realized that just the fact that boyfriend had been married didn't necessarily mean he would have been disappointed. Consider what was happening now. Kirk was married, but he wasn't. He was famous, yet he wasn't. They could go almost anywhere together and never be noticed.

"My fate," Lance said.

"You play with fire, you're gonna get burned."

"I guess."

"Speaking of burning, my cock's hot as a poker right now."

"Just talking to me does it, doesn't it?" Lance asked smugly.

"No, it's the sound of your voice and the memory of your body. The two together."

"My body?"

"Your ass. You have the hottest little ass I've ever seen."

"But you're one of the few who's really noticed that."

"I know, most guys are so busy with what's up front."

"That's pretty good, though, isn't it?"

"I've seen bigger."

"I know, you look in the mirror."

Kirk laughed. It was a hearty, full-out laugh. He was quick to laugh—at himself, at anything. He loved to laugh. Lance had the feeling that he himself had not laughed a lot in his life—certainly not enough.

"As a matter of fact," Kirk purred, "I'm looking in the mirror right now, stroking it, thinking about how warm it would be inside you. "

"I've taken to using my own dildo up there, just to keep in shape for you."

"That's wild: Fucking yourself with your own signature dildo."

"I don't stick it all the way in, just play around till I come."

"Did you do that tonight?"

"No. I was about to. I was restless."

"You knew I'd call."

"Yeah." But Lance hadn't. He never knew when Kirk would call, or where he might be when he did, but it was always late at night. Right now it was well after two in New York, approaching midnight here in Los Angeles. Lance didn't mind. What he minded was never knowing when Kirk could break away and meet him.

When he did call and say they could be together, he didn't extend an invitation, he issued orders, as if he were presenting a summons. Like now: "I'm going to Chicago. I'll send you a ticket."

"I don't know."

"Yeah, four days from now you'll have this huge thing that's in my hand right now planted all the way up your ass. Can't you feel it already?"

"Yeah," Lance said—resigned, knowing he would go to Chicago.

And the mantra began, the torrent of words that got Lance fully hard and kept him ever more excited as he beat off and reached orgasm. "Oh, yeah," he moaned as the cum spewed across his chest.

"That's my baby. My baby. My big-dicked baby boy." Lance could hear the receiver drop, but could still clearly hear Kirk's panting, which grew in speed and intensity as the older stud masturbated furiously. Finally Lance heard a little cry and a huge escape of breath as Kirk was caught up in his orgasm.

Kirk hardly ever came any more unless he was with Lance—either on the phone or in person. His entire sex life had become focused on his younger lover. It had freed him to write, to create, to deal-make as never before. He was still breathing heavily when he put the telephone back to his face.

"That was a big one," Lance chuckled.

"I was so fuckin' horny. It's just been so long since I've had it."

"Two weeks already. Two weeks."

"Two weeks too many," Kirk sighed, squeezing the last drops of cum from his cock while his lover, out in California, played in his own cum. While they said their goodbyes, Lance began to rub the cum on his chest over his still-hard prick, using it as a lubricant as he began whacking off again. After they hung up, he applied a second coat of white, hot cum to his chest.

*   *   *

Lance had a lover now. Kirk had quickly become all that Lance had hoped for—and yet feared getting. He had become all that Lance loved.

When Kirk came to Los Angeles or Lance went to New York, it was like Kirk had imagined it might be. In New York they went to the movies together, they attended concerts and plays, and they dropped in to gay bars, where Kirk was proud to show off the boy who was his and his alone. In L.A., Lance was the one who was the celebrity, since few ever recognized the author of *Dead Man's Eyes* and twenty other best-selling thrillers.

It bothered Kirk that wherever they went he wondered if some of the men who smiled and waved at Lance had been to bed with the stud. Kirk came to prefer it when Lance would agree to come to New York for a visit, and he began to invent reasons he had to stay there.

By permitting himself to surrender to lovers like Kevin or, especially, Kirk, Lance had come to a place so liberating, so warm, that he felt he had finally escaped the emptiness. Surely, this was the place that he was ultimately destined to find.

SEVEN:

Just a few years into their marriage, Kirk's wife was given to fits of crying which she indulged alone and in the shower. He would stand in the hallway listening to her sob, waiting for a pause. Then he'd go in and pee, flush the toilet and send a shower of cold water raining down onto her body. She'd scream and curse him, hurl soap or maybe a back scrubber at him. He'd undress, step into the shower, pull her down on the porcelain, and hold her, shove his huge cock into her from behind. He could never stand to look at her face when he was fucking her. Or even look at her at all. She was, he had decided years before, the ugliest person alive.

Then they'd sleep, and when they woke, he'd dress her. He wouldn't allow her to wear underwear. Then he'd take her out for a rare steak, and eat her French fries.

Kirk did not tell Lance this; Lance read it in "Peoria, Illinois," a book Kirk had written ten years before, but which was only recently published. It was, Kirk told Lance, a confession about the hell it was living with a rich but crazy woman. He had said, "I write the truth."

Lance has gone to the bookstore and bought all of Kirk's books. He seldom even read the newspaper, but he read these books with greedy fascination. Kirk's nature, although mean and sad, was so skillfully rendered it seemed almost poetic. And even as Lance was thinking Kirk was horrible, he felt deeply attracted to this loathsome man, who seemed to be saying, "See how you are exactly like me. You won't admit it but you are."

Perhaps in some ways he was right, but Kirk was offering his life as art. Lance's reading of the novels wasn't only a voyeuristic thrill or a vicarious pleasure, it was a way to get to know Kirk better.

At one point, Kirk wrote, "My wife is beautiful, and smart, and a better human being than I am." And no one doubted that, except maybe the bit about her being so smart. In one of the books he wrote a scene containing an interview he had his lead character giving on a talk show: "My life is full of real-life pain and drama. Why should I, if I don't need to, make anything up? After all, I own my life."

Perhaps because his wife had bought him with her money, he believed it was all right to drag her onto the page and shackle her there with clear, piercing descriptions so intimate he even described the dark hair that curled around her nipples. She was the myopic wife who couldn't see the way her husband needed her to be, and thus couldn't understand the character of a truly sensitive man. She was the wife who woke up in the middle of the night, alone, choking and unable to breathe. Her husband was gone—out of town indulging his true passions—and she would try to commit suicide. This was a rather common occurrence. She had once tried to kill herself in the brand new Mercedes Kirk had bought with the advance money for a screenplay he'd sold. She tried to asphyxiate herself in their garage, with the radio tuned to a country-western station, which he knew she despised. That's why he said he didn't believe she meant to kill herself, because she put the radio on a station that she would never listen to. The music, he said, was for cheap dramatic effect.

Kirk and Nancy lived on Long Island in a large modern house that was mostly glass. Although Kirk loved his house, he threw himself into touring and promoting each new book in order to take his mind off living with Nancy. As he traveled, he met boys who reminded him of his brother, and of the few school chums he had been intimate with.

Lance began imagining he might appear in one of Kirk's books. Kirk noticed small things about a person he never noticed about himself. He saw everything, noted every nuance. Lance wondered what Kirk noticed about him, hoping that someday he might learn through reading one of his books.

Kirk was much more handsome than his book-jacket photos, which seemed to present him either looking dark and guilty, as though he'd been caught in the act of shoplifting, or intense, gaunt, and unshaven—suggesting imprisonment in the jail of his own mind.

Lance was different from others he had known, Kirk thought. Lance could tell him something, something about a world he didn't know, something he'd never read in a book—perhaps something he'd want, something he'd like and need. He also wanted to learn Lance's secrets. He wanted to ensure that Lance imparted them to him, that he would hear them all, and that they would be for his ears alone.

But Kirk was possessive and Lance had to be careful. While stories of his days on film sets and nights in johns' bedrooms seemed to turn Kirk on, Kirk often suggested Lance leave that sort of life: "What do you need it for?"

Lance did not know the answer. Since meeting Kirk, he had refused dance gigs and the tricks, at least most of them, but giving up the films was another matter. He enjoyed the process, if not always the sex. He had even considered climaxing his career by bottoming in a video. He had gone so far as to suck cock in his latest video, something he had never done before on camera. Tiny had directed that film, "Lance's Lovers & Other Strangers," and when it was completed, he took Lance aside and showed him the finished product. "You've been practicing," Tiny kidded. "You have been hiding this great talent from me—and from your fans. You're a fabulous cocksucker, sweetie."

Tiny rewound to play the scene again from the beginning, the scene where Lance blew Jeff, his on-screen partner:

A fire was burning in the fireplace. Jeff lit a joint, and Lance took a drag, even though he didn't inhale. Drugs, he said, kept him from giving a good performance. "It's hard enough to get this up," he said, patting his cock through his pants

There was a third actor in the scene—a woman, of all things—named April. This was the first time Lance had shared a porn set with a woman, or even anticipated having sex with one. She began to laugh. "I was just thinking," she told them. "About clothes and all that image stuff. Imagine if I'd had on one of those working-girl outfits when we first met, Jeff. Or if you'd had on a suit. We'd probably never have struck up a conversation."

"Right," he agreed. "Maybe everybody should go around naked all the time. At least it would be easier." He began to laugh, rolling over on the floor.

Soon then they were all laughing, all three of them, and playfully hitting each other. As if it had been choreographed—actually, it had—the playful slaps and punches turned into caresses and hugs. Lance watched while April leaned back in Jeff's arms and he massaged her breasts, his hands roaming over her belly as he nuzzled her neck.

April reached behind her, her hand finding Jeff's crotch. She rubbed and massaged him, feeling his cock harden as she played with it through the shorts he was wearing. Soon Jeff was easing her sweater up, and Lance took it off for her, dragging it up over her head. Jeff cupped April's silicone-enhanced breasts while Lance worked the side zippers of her pants, then quickly pulled them off. At the same time, Jeff was stripping. "Maybe we should all go upstairs," Lance suggested.

"Why?" April asked, naked now, like Jeff.

"I dunno. Somebody might come in."

"Who would it be?" Jeff asked. "Jim and Carol went over to the Stardust, and Lynda is asleep. Besides, who gives a shit?"

"They could come back," Lance said.

"So what. Fuck 'em if they can't take a joke."

They began to laugh again, and Lance found himself stretched out on his back on the rug in front of the fireplace. April was straddling him and unhitching his belt, tugging off his pants, then she unzipped the sweat jacket he was wearing.

Jeff was behind April, his hand between her legs. She moved back, her body seeking his, and as Jeff slid into her, April lowered her body so that Lance's semi-hard cock probed the space between her breasts. Her tongue moved over his chest and stomach and nipples as his hands caressed her shoulders and back.

As Jeff began fucking her, April's body echoed the movements of his hips. Reaching down, Lance grabbed her breasts, squeezing them together so that there was more pressure on his dick. Buried in her cleavage, his cock began to harden. As he watched Jeff's heaving body, he became excited by the idea of fucking Jeff while Jeff fucked April.

Lance released April's breasts and pulled her to him, his mouth engulfing her purpled lips as they kissed. His tongue wrapped around hers, and as his fingertips pinched her swollen nipples, she began to rotate her hips, with Jeff's cock still buried inside her.

Jeff rolled over on his side, and they rolled with him. As Jeff fucked her from behind, April guided Lance's body upward, her tongue flicking over his stomach and darting through his pubic hair. Her fingers felt as if they were on fire as they lightly played over his loins and scrotum, and his hips began to thrust toward her. His now fully hard cock seemed to have a mind of its own, seeking the whore's mouth. She slid her tongue around the head and part of the shaft, then put the head in her mouth.

As Jeff fucked her, she took more of Lance's cock in her mouth, sucking hard. Tiny had them sustain this action for several minutes, then

346

had Jeff pull out, slip off the condom, kneel down and share Lance's cock with April. There was plenty to go around, but Jeff seemed to be restricted to licking the shaft and balls.

Tiny stopped filming briefly and told Jeff to stick his cock in Lance's face. Lance wiped the pre-cum from the head of Jeff's dick and began kissing it while he fondled his balls. He knew what Tiny was trying to get him to do and, at last, he decided this was the time. Jeff was attractive to him and his cock was hard and beautifully shaped. A woman was sucking on his cock for the first time, so it only seemed appropriate to continue breaking new ground.

Tiny zoomed in to record Lance eating another man's cock for the first time—the first time on film, anyway--and kept this action on screen for several minutes. April let Lance's prick slip from her mouth and lay down next to him so they could share Jeff's cock.

Tiny saw that Lance was still hard and he didn't want to miss the moment for Lance to fuck both of his partners. He had them get on their knees side by side, and Lance began by fucking Jeff and then going to April, alternating between a hot man's ass and a woman's voracious pussy for several minutes. Then April scrambled under Jeff, who entered her again while Lance's gigantic cock pounded away at his hungry asshole.

Before long, April could be heard panting uncontrollably as she reached her climax. Her fingers curled around her thighs and her eyes, half-closed, rolled upward. The thought aroused Lance, and he told Tiny to get ready. The money shot would not have to edited in later as was so often the case with Lance. He pulled his cock out of Jeff's ass, ripped off the condom, and shot one of the biggest loads Tiny could remember coming from his star, all over Jeff's broad back. Tiny caught every second of Lance's climax from two different angles, using both cameras that had been filming the action. In the final video, Tiny would show the orgasm several times, from both camera angles, in real time and in slow motion.

Their bodies glistening with sweat, the three lay exhausted. Tiny asked Jeff if he was ready to continue the scene. April slipped the condom from Jeff's cock, and went back to work on it with her mouth. In moments, Jeff was ready and Lance re-entered the scene to play with Jeff's balls as Jeff shot onto April's fluttering, purple-fingernailed hands, blasting his come all over the girls' smiling face.

Jeff's climactic moment was fine, but it seemed anticlimactic after Lance's sensational performance

"Wow," Tiny said, stopping the cameras. "You were great, guys, but especially you, Lance. Fucking your first woman and giving your first blowjob—we'll make a zillion on this one."

"Looks like you got a bargain," Lance snickered.

"Yeah, in any other business, you'd get a bonus."

"Yeah, in any other business," Lance echoed, with a bitterness to his tone.

EIGHT

"I'm sorry about your wife," Lance stammered. He didn't mean it, but knew he should say it.

Kirk looked solemn for an instant, then he said, "I did love her, the bitch. No one wants to believe that." He laughed, "But, now that's a closed chapter." She had attempted suicide again—and this time she had finally succeeded.

"I *am* sorry." Lance leaned into him. And he was sorry, but it was Kirk for whom he felt sorry, after so many years of despair.

Kirk held him fast. "She was fucking my brother, you know," he said. "My only brother, whom I slept in the same bed with for fifteen years, and with whom I had often …. well, never mind that. Two long years I sat there, like an idiot eating their shit while they snuck off and fucked—in the bathroom, on holidays, fucking behind my back while I slept. My brother and my wife. Now they're both dead. I think that's what sent her over the edge, you know, having him die. He had AIDS. Isn't that wild? He had AIDS."

While Kirk slept, Lance slipped into his underwear and bathrobe to go into the living room, to find the book he couldn't get out of his mind since they had talked about it.

It was in that book, called *Illusion of Love*, that Kirk came closest to the truth about his relationship with his brother Wally. Lance opened the book and re-read the passages, fascinated, now knowing what happened after the brothers grew up.

*   *   *

"Where is Kirk?" Dad asked as he entered the living room, where Wally was reading.

Wally said he didn't know. Actually, he knew, but he wouldn't say. Kirk was in the kitchen with Mother, who was allowing him to knead the dough for the bread she was baking.

Dad began spluttering, but still he bent to kiss Wally. Wally kissed him back, but really only touched his father's cheek with his lips. In spite of the warm summer evening, Dad's cheek was cold. They stood there, looking at each other.

Wally suddenly felt he was in the position of a stranger, but one who knew too much. "Kirk is in the kitchen, doing things for Mother," he said.

"As usual," Dad grunted.

Mother and Dad used to study Kirk, at least for many years. At first, it seemed, they tried to see into him, hoping to learn what made their younger son tick. But they could not could not see far enough into him, while Wally, who could, and who had grown used to what he found, might have told them.

Dad and Wally sat on the veranda. It was pleasant for them to be together there, particularly after the southerly wind had arisen. Once when a southerly had been blowing, Dad jerked his head in the direction of the wind and said, "Just about the cheapest fulfillment of anybody's expectations." It was the kind of remark that appealed to Mother—for little things like that about Dad, seemingly wise or profound, she had Married Beneath Her.

Over the years, Dad had grown disappointed in Kirk. Mother never grew disappointed to the same extent, because she persuaded herself that Kirk was some kind of genius waiting to blossom. But Dad was not deceived, Wally even less. Wally didn't believe it was possible to have more than one genius around—and he felt sure he was the one.

Kirk was certainly born with a gift for words. At times when he was free to read or write, he didn't need coaxing to help out with the household chores—but mostly just those in the kitchen. Dad was disgusted with Kirk's apparent domesticity. He said it was not the way for a boy, but Mother approved, of course.

On occasions when Wally asked whether he too might help with a task in the kitchen, kneading the bread dough or some such chore, he was usually told, "No. That's something for Kirk. He has a gift for such things."

Once Kirk, who was manually mixing the ingredients for breakfast biscuits, watched the buttermilk gush out from between his fingers, laughed and said, "It's my vocation, isn't it, Mother?"

Wally overheard, and wondered where his brother learned such complicated words; he was more jealous of the word than he was of Kirk's privilege. Kirk seemed to collect words, like stamps or coins. He made lists of them. He rolled them in his mouth like polished stones.

One evening, their parents had gone to town, leaving the boys' dinner on the stove. Kirk came to the bedroom where his brother was studying and began removing pieces of clothing, performing a slow—and, for his age, remarkably sexy—striptease.

Wally was disgusted. "You should see yourself."

"But I can see myself. I'm closest to myself."

Wally almost wanted to cry for this poor dopey brother of his. Perhaps this was Kirk's function, though: to drive him to anger, then tears.

"I don't know what you're talking about," he said.

"Love," said Kirk.

"Oh, God!" Wally cried. "You're nuts!"

"All right then," Kirk said. "I'm nuts. Nuts about you."

And Kirk pulled his pants back on and ran away.

Although he was trembling, Wally took down another book, intending to continue to work, to recover from the shock he had received. He couldn't bear to think about the many times he and his little brother had shared sex—for no reason other than the excitement and sexual gratification—and now Kirk seemed to be saying he was in love with him. Furthermore, he didn't seem to be saying only that he loved him; no, he was suggesting that he was *in love* with his brother—passionately, desperately, like a man loves a woman.

Towards evening Wally went out on the veranda. He didn't know what had become of Kirk, so he went into the yard and walked around, looking for him. He didn't find his brother, but when he returned to the house, there he was, standing in the doorway, waiting for him—barring Wally's way, in effect, apparently not to be avoided.

In the fading light of sunset, Kirk looked younger, smoother and more innocent than he ever had. But Wally knew Kirk was not all that innocent. He suspected his brother was waiting to trap him into talking about love, and then to lure him to their bedroom so that he could make love to him. Not have sex, no, *make love*. Wally frowned.

By the time he reached the porch, Wally was, for some reason he could not fathom, in tears, and Kirk opened his arms to welcome his brother in before he led him into the house. At once Wally was engulfed in the most intolerable longing, in the smell of his own after-shave which Kirk had splashed on his body. Wally could not stop crying.

Kirk led him upstairs and they lay together in the bed. Kirk held his brother tight, and soon began kissing him: wet, lewd kisses, all over his body. Wally did not return the kisses, he simply closed his eyes and let Kirk continue. But today Kirk was determined that his older brother would finally receive what he had been giving him in the past.

By then their damp faces were all but fused together. Although he remained passive, Wally was trembling with excitement, lying in Kirk's suddenly strong and assured arms. Kirk did not attempt to fully undress his brother. He tugged off the pants and underwear, throwing them on the floor. He reached for the big jar of lubricant they had used in the past, but this time it was *Kirk's* cock that got lubed, and *Wally's* ass—not the other way around, as it had always been in the past. As he greased himself, Kirk, it seemed, was unafraid of anything, while Wally regarded his brother's gargantuan cock and felt very much afraid he would not be able to take it up his ass, as Kirk obviously intended he would. Wally was also afraid of what would happen, what their relationship would be, once the deed was done.

As they lay in the vast bed they seemed to flow together like they had on other occasions, when Wally had really let himself go, those times when they had shared more than their regular perfunctory fuck and blow job. At those times, Kirk had been certain his brother was indeed *in love* with him, although Kirk had never put words to it before.

350

As Kirk gently inserted himself into his brother's ass, the pain was so great that Wally begged him to stop. But there was really no need, because it was over almost as quickly as it had begun: as soon as Kirk's prick was buried in his brother's ass, he began shooting his load deep inside. Then Kirk took charge of Wally's relief orally, which was as swift in coming as it was voluminous.

Mercifully, when their parents returned home, they did not look in on their two sons. Spent, they were lying in each other's arms, in a sticky mess.

The next morning Wally began almost at once to experience regret over their lovemaking of the night before, fearing he might once again awaken Kirk's illusion of love.

For years after Wally went on to college and lost contact with him, Kirk was not secure enough to let himself go with another man, as he had with Wally so many times—but also so many times too few. He feared he might find out something about himself that he didn't want to know. If he let go, he might be consumed by his desires. He was afraid of what he might want, what he might need, what it might do to him—who he might become. Eventually, he decided a loveless marriage was better than a life alone.

*   *   *

Finished with his reading, Lance returned to the bedroom. He threw his bathrobe on a chair and crawled in with Kirk, who woke up when he felt his lover embrace him. Kirk returned the embrace. Lying there with Lance in his arms, his heart was pounding. There was no longer any good reason to hide what he wanted, what he *was*. He was free for the first time in his life.

He began kissing Lance, first on the top of the head, then on the face, then the lips. Slowly he removed Lance's shorts and renewed his kissing, his caressing. It was ten minutes before his lips were finally around the abundant treasure of Lance's cock, which now felt harder and more monstrously hard than he could ever remember.

"God, I want you to fuck me with this," Kirk said after he had sucked Lance for a long time.

"What?"

"You want to, don't you, baby?"

"Yeah, but are you sure?" Lance couldn't believe it. Kirk had never wanted it before. He had always been so sure, so content as a top. As content as Lance had once been—before Hart.

"Yes," Kirk said, "I've never been more sure of anything in my whole life."

After the sex, Kirk lay alone on the bed, exhausted and as satisfied as he could ever remember being. He could admit now hat he loved to get fucked, and Lance was a masterful top. When he wanted a job done, Kirk had always believed, getting a pro to do it was worth whatever it took. He cursed himself for not having Lance do this to him before.

Just then, Gloria Estefan's "Coming Out of the Dark" began playing on the stereo, and Kirk smiled as his lover returned to the bedroom from the bathroom and stood by the window.

"I have great news," Kirk said finally. "I'm selling the old house and I've bought a nice apartment in Manhattan."

"That's nice," Lance said absently. He was looking at how his little garden in the backyard had turned into a kaleidoscope of blooming bougainvillea. All in all, he was delighted with the way things had worked out. He loved his little house on Spaulding, just a block from Santa Monica Boulevard, and his clients enjoyed coming there. He had invested the inheritance from his grandfather's estate and, from what he earned from interest on that and his videos—and his hustling, of course--he lived rather well. He could easily afford to take a year off if he wanted to.

"Isn't that what you've been waiting for?" Kirk asked.

"Waiting for?"

"For us to be *real* lovers, not this bi-coastal business."

"But I like it here. This is where I live."

Kirk took a deep breath. Maybe he was moving too fast, he thought. Lance needed time. Finally, trying to keep the disappointment from his voice, he said quietly, "Well, it's something to think about."

"Yeah," Lance said, still staring out the window. "Something to think about."

A year later, Lance was still thinking about it. He had been to Manhattan several times and Kirk had made a room for him in the new apartment. In fact, "Lance's room" was extraordinarily beautiful, with a glorious view of Central Park; Kirk had a famous decorator do the place, and spared no expense. But Lance sensed he could never consider it his "home."

Now Kirk was working on his annual best-seller and had come to Los Angeles to "research" the book. He rented a Lincoln at LAX; he could never understand how Lance could live in L.A. and not own a car. Lance explained that he got taken everywhere and, when he didn't, he could walk—like to the grocer and the video store. He'd never had an emergency, but there were plenty of taxis available if he did. His needs were simple, and he truly loved living alone in the little city of West Hollywood.

Kirk sat down to Lance's poached flounder, with creamed spinach on the side, happy to see Lance was no longer a strict vegetarian. By that time they'd already had sex twice.

Kirk was in an expansive mood. He couldn't contain himself any longer. They had to make plans. He asked Lance when he was coming back to Manhattan.

"You haven't been here two hours and you're starting that again," Lance berated him sternly.

"It's just that I miss you so much. I like to have something to look forward to."

Lance pushed himself away from the table, tossed his napkin down, and went to the front room. He unlocked the center drawer of his desk and withdrew his appointment book. He knew that Kirk disapproved of his hustling but he enjoyed it. He really never needed to make another video. His reputation as a porn star assured him of $1,000 a day if he wanted it. But he had only two regular clients, a famous director and a fashion designer. The director would be on location starting in June and the designer, ironically, would be going to New York. Lance took a pen and marked across the first week of June, then put the book back in the drawer and locked it.

Returning to the dining alcove, he fell into Kirk's welcoming arms. "I didn't mean to upset you," Kirk said, still chewing a piece of fish.

"I had to check my book." He began undoing the sash of Kirk's robe.

"Can you schedule me in?" Kirk asked, half-joking.

"June." Lance had parted Kirk's robe and dropped to his knees next to Kirk's chair.

"June?"

"It'll be warm in New York in June," Lance said, lifting Kirk's hardening cock to his mouth. "Now I'm ready for dessert."

Kirk shook his head, then began to laugh. "Baby, you're the horniest damn kid .... "

As Lance attacked his cock with a shocking fury, Kirk took the boy's head in his hands and tried to steady him, but he knew it was useless.

ABOUT THE AUTHOR OF THE STORIES

JOHN PATRICK was a prolific, prize-winning author of fiction and non-fiction. One of his short stories, "The Well," was honored by PEN American Center as one of the best of 1987. That story is reprinted in this anthology. His stories and novels, and the anthologies he edited, as well as his non-fiction works, including *Legends* and *The Best of the Superstars* series, continue to gain him new fans every day. One of his most famous short stories appears in the Badboy collection *Southern Comfort* and another appears in the collection *The Mammoth Book of Gay Short Stories*.

A divorced father of two, the author was a longtime member of the American Booksellers Association, the Publishing Triangle, the Florida Publishers' Association, American Civil Liberties Union, and the Adult Video Association. He lived in Florida, where he passed away on October 31, 2001.

ABOUT THE EDITOR

JOHN BUTLER retired after a thirty-six-year career in music teaching and administration, ranging from elementary and secondary school music to Dean of Liberal Arts at a major American university, where he also served as Professor and Department Head for twenty-seven years. He published his first erotic fiction in 1998, the STARbooks novel *model/escort*. Since then he has also published two other novels with the same publisher: *WanderLUST: Ships that Pass in the Night* and *Boys Hard at Work (And Playing with Fire)*. In addition to the short story contained in the present volume, his shorter fiction appears in the STARboks anthologies *Taboo!, Fever!, Virgins No More, Any Boy Can, Seduced 2* and *Wild and Willing*. He took over the editing of *Seduced 2* and *Wild and Willing* when John Patrick died.

ABOUT THE COVER

The cover art was shot by the award winning SunTown Photography.

Email: Suntown1@aol.com

WebSite: http://www.suntownphoto.co.uk

Postal Address

Suntown Photography

PO Box 151

Banbury Oxfordshire

OX16 8QN

Great Britain

355